The Devil Made Me Do It

The Devil Made Me Do It

Colette R. Harrell

URBAN
CHRISTIAN

www.urbanchristianonline.com

Urban Books, LLC
97 N18th Street
Wyandanch, NY 11798

ISBN 13: 978-1-60162-782-7
ISBN 10: 1-60162-782-3

First Trade Paperback Printing July 2014
Printed in the United States of America

10 9 8 7 6 5 4 3 2

Distributed by Kensington Corp.
Submit Wholesale Orders to:
Kensington Publishing Corp.
C/O Penguin Group (USA) Inc.
Attention: Order Processing
405 Murray Hill Parkway
East Rutherford, NJ 07073-2316
Phone: 1-800-526-0275
Fax: 1-800-227-9604

The Devil Made Me Do It

by

Colette R. Harrell

All scripture is taken from the
New International Version Bible.

Dedication

To Richard and Dorothy—who always believed.

Acknowledgments

Having a dream is like storing lightning in a bottle. You can envision it, but it can be difficult to actually achieve. If you have a Joseph moment and share your dream, like his brothers, there are those who are waiting for you to stumble into the pit. But God has always used opposition to position us. He used Pharaoh to position Moses, Peninnah to position Hannah, and King Saul to position David. There are those He used to position me. There are those who failed to dream, so mine seemed impossible. There are those who failed to follow through, so my completion was improbable. And, there are those who lacked the faith and courage to pursue, so they thought this book would remain in a desk drawer never to see the light of day. You have to love it—God positions us in spite of the opposition.

This page is for all those who positioned me for favor—who believed I could and encouraged me along the way. They are my fellow dreamers, my faith walkers, and the cheerleaders in the stands of my life. I honor you and know that yours is coming!

I give honor to God who is the head of my life and the reason I am. Thank you, Lord. My labor was not in vain. Thank you, Larry—you are my biggest cheerleader, my earthly rock, my blessing. To Langston and Melissa, who are constant reminders of God's unconditional love—I impart to you the inspiration to dream on. Your gift to me is to keep climbing. To my parents, Richard and Doro-

Acknowledgments

thy—you gave me wings and told me to fly. Rest in peace, Daddy. To my best friend, Jacquelyn—when I wanted to quit, you prayed one more prayer and stood shoulder to shoulder in the pit. Our war cry? *For Love Alone.* To my siblings: Diane (Paul), Richard (Joyce), Marcia, Angela—I did it, y'all—it's never too late to live your dreams. To Aunt Dorothy—you have always been there for us, thank you! To Cession (Khyrie, Kaiser, Koran, Kimora)—all things are possible. To Melanie (DeLon, Matthew), Taryn (Budah), Julia (Milo), Rich and Breyanna—what *can't* God do? To the Adams and Harrell family, too big to list; hearts too great to ignore. To my prayer posse, Cousin Faye, Cousin Lawrence (Cynthia), Cassandra, Kathy, Mother Joanne, Pam, Pastor Lance, Elder Kevin—thank you, many a time you shifted the atmosphere with a warrior's prayer!

To my church family—Pastors Lonnie and Tracy Keene of Kingdom Christian Center, for spiritual instruction and covering, and for all of the KCC members (you know I love you all and if I start naming people . . .) thank you. To my encouragers—Cathy, KiKi, Latonya, Jackie, Alicia, David, Denise, Vernice, Atty. Timothy, Karlos and Carolyn—you believed I could. For my work family—you are the best! To my fellow authors in eleven strong—Leslie, Claudia Mair, Mata, MaRita, Aubrey, Kristen, Olivia, Pam, Gloria, and Rodney, delayed but not denied.

And special thanks to Bestselling Author Victoria Christopher Murray who has been my mentor and guide through this process—she's truly gifted and appreciated. To my editors Joylynn Ross and Alanna Boutin, you were instrumental in this journey—thank you. To Portia O'Cannon, my agent, girl, we made it!

And to my hometown of Detroit—may you rise like Lazarus and live again.

Prologue

1975

Now the earth was formless and empty, darkness was over the surface of the deep (Genesis 1:2).

Two ominous figures sat in quiet contemplation, the larger one's head was gargantuan in nature, and foul droplets of acidic mucus fell from his protruding fangs.

The smaller one stood sixteen feet tall and his rapier tail was wrapped protectively around his middle. He sat as still as cold hard stone. His sinister eyes were yellow rimmed and telegraphed evil cunning. He was known as The Leader.

Their silhouettes cast eerie shadows against the backdrop of the smoke-filled flames that spewed from the lake of fire.

"Ummm, this is my favorite place. Listen to the melodic sound of souls screaming in agony—it is music to my ears. If you concentrate, you can hear the desperate pleas for release. Yessss . . . It allows me to know that all is right in our world," The High Master said.

The Leader shuddered as the menacing timbre of The High Master's voice snaked fear around his chest. For him, it was equal to the singe of demon skin from a thousand innocent prayers; he loathed it. His tail subconsciously tightened as he awaited his newest orders.

The High Master continued, "These human souls are pathetic with their self-serving natures. They frighten at the sound of our bumps in the dark, but create havoc in their own lives. What idiots they are and not fit for company until they have totally crossed to our side. And even then they tire me soooo . . ."

The Leader didn't stir; his thoughts were of survival. He refused to speak. He knew a wrong word could cause such suffering and pain. The High Master's punishments are prompt and fierce. One seeks death, but yet, death will not come.

The High Master continued his tirade, his grimace displaying double rows of slime-covered fangs. His was a chilling profile. "Your charges are young. Both are being raised in good homes, and, as a result, they are overconfident creatures. Leader, do not underestimate their youth; innocence is a powerful weapon. In their kingdom, the weak become strong. But we must prey on that weakness and use it to our advantage. You must destroy them before they complete their purpose. I am giving you this head start; you must not fail."

After speaking, he stood his full twenty feet in height, his shoulders reared back as his frame vibrated with his frustrated bellowing. "In the beginning, we owned their world. After the fall, we adjusted; the land we were given was dark and empty, but we were content with our lot. Then He whose name is not spoken, created man, and we were once again demoted. All we seek is our rightful power, our rightful place. Make haste, bold one, and steal, kill, and destroy all that stands in your way."

The Leader bowed his head in submission.

"And, Leader—this was a most productive conversation. You are learning."

The Leader's tail unwrapped from his torso as he swiftly rose and slithered toward his point of ascent into the Earth realm. He was determined not to fail.

Chapter One

The Detroit pollution and cold, foggy weather covered Esther Wiley's shivering body in crisp, arctic shades of blue gray, reminiscent of watercolors dancing in the jelly jar after her arts and crafts class. She shivered, but stubbornly refused to let her mother put a scarf around her small head. She was going to be Cinderella. Cinderella didn't wear an old ugly scarf. Well, maybe when she was cleaning, but she wasn't trying to be that kind of Cinderella. No ashes to ashes and dust to dust for her. She was all about glass slippers and diamond tiaras.

Esther's round cheeks were rosy from the wind, her hated freckles beet red glowing in contrast to the caramel cream of her skin. Her knobby knees were pressed together whenever she wasn't bouncing from foot to foot in the frigid air. She was on a mission. She wasn't allowing a hideous scarf to mess up her hair in exchange for a little warmth. She had endured two hours of "hold the grease jar lid on your ear pain" that produced silky pressed hair. There was torture in the quest for straight tresses. In her seven-year-old mind, her priorities were clear.

Esther's petulant voice screeched. "Mama, how much longer do we have to wait? I can't stand it. I want to try on the glass slipper—right now."

"Mind your manners. In a moment, I'm going to give you what your Grandma Vic used to call a private deliverance in a public place."

A curl of warm breath escaped when Esther sighed. She turned away, rolled her eyes, and then stared defiantly at her mother. The same hands that calmly cuddled her at night now moved restlessly after giving up trying to place a warm scarf on Esther's head. Esther didn't dare speak. She had badgered her mother to bring her and her two best friends to downtown Detroit for the Cinderella contest. When they arrived, the line to enter the historical skyscraper snaked around the building. Two hours later they still couldn't see the front entrance. As the wind bellowed, time stood still, but because of her mother's mood, she resisted the urge to tell her she was freezing.

She peeked at her friends' reaction to her mother's scolding. She could see Sheri and Deborah were indifferent to her embarrassment; their faces tense as they craned their necks to see the start of the line.

Esther puffed warm breath into her mittens. "Y'all shouldn't have come if you didn't want to wait."

Sheri's elfin face was etched in anxiety. Her shoulders sagging, she grimaced at the time on her watch. She leaned forward in a panicked whisper. "You know I had to sneak out of the house to come. If my mama finds out I'm here, I'ma get a whipping."

"You should have told her," Deborah smacked her sour grape gum, then twirled it around her finger.

Sheri's jaw tightened. "I tried." She pointed her finger in a mock role play of her mother. "'Ain't no such thing as Cinderella, and sho' ain't no Prince Charming. Get in them school books. There isn't anything worse than being ignorant.' Y'all know how my mama gets."

Laughing, Deborah slapped her hand against her thigh. "Uh, uh, uh," she stuck her gum back into her mouth and popped it. "Girl, you sounded just like your mama."

With hands on her small hips, Esther swung her head toward Deborah. "Well, what about you? You could have stayed home."

"Oh no, where you two go, I go. You can't leave me out. I can stand this girly stuff for one day." Deborah eyeballed her and popped her gum for emphasis.

Esther sighed in her trademark dramatic fashion. "Please stop playing with your gum. That's just nasty."

She wished her friends cared as much about the Cinderella contest as she did. Sheri was the smart one, but her whippings from her mama were the talk of the block. Deborah was the tomboy; she had seven brothers.

Esther's older sister, Phyllis once said, "Deborah's mama better take that chile in hand quick 'cause if she don't, she gon' end up *funny*."

Esther tried to explain that's what she liked about Deborah—that she was funny. Phyllis just stared at her with small slit eyes, sucked her teeth, and told her to get out of her room.

She didn't know why Phyllis always said that because half the drawers and closet space were hers, and she slept on the bottom bunk bed. But before she got pinched—or worse—she'd leave the room.

Esther understood her friends' mood; it was her mother she couldn't figure out. Mrs. Wiley reminded her of herself when she had to go to the doctor and get a shot; frightened.

Esther swallowed, summoned her courage, and pulled on her mother's coat sleeve. "Mama, what's wrong? Why did you say we might have to leave before I try on the slipper?"

Her mother's eyes blinked in rapid succession. "I—well—I—girl, quit asking me questions."

In a huff, Esther folded her arms, and clamped her lips tight. In a snail-like increment, thirty minutes dragged by, and finally they entered the department store.

It was so beautiful; Hudson's department store had turned the tenth-floor lobby into a lighted winter wonderland. In the center of the room, a handsome prince with dark hair and sapphire eyes kneeled before each little girl as she sat on the white, satin bench and tried on the glass slipper. To a young heart, it was breathtaking.

Esther was so excited that she peed—just a little—in her underwear. When it was her time to approach the bench and sit down, she closed her eyes, folded her hands, prayed, and waited for the miracle that her grandmother had assured her God could deliver.

"Yes. Yes . . . Yes!" she squealed. The glass slipper fit her small foot perfectly.

Her mother cried out, "Oh my goodness; you won, you won."

Her friends danced around, and they all jumped up and down together. It took them a few minutes—the silence around them incredulous—to notice that they were the only ones celebrating.

Esther hugged her mother around the waist and peeked at the crowd. Somber pale faces reflected shock, anger, and disbelief; it was plain that their small entourage's happiness lacked the crowd's support.

The distressed prince rose, his back ramrod straight. He confidently looked over at the tall, austere man who seemed to be in charge.

"I am sorry, miss," the man advanced on Esther's mother, his hawkish nose tilted in an imperious manner. "It isn't a proper fit. Please relinquish the slipper to the next person. You and your daughter are holding up the line."

Esther wailed in protest. "But, Mama—" Her mother placed a finger over her mouth and used her other hand to wipe her burgeoning tears.

Mrs. Wiley's voice was soft and gentle, her hands tender in their ministrations of comfort. "Shush, baby, let's go." Her face was strained, and her eyes inflamed with a century of unspoken words and kindled rage.

Esther discerned something unspeakable had happened, and she should not ask about it. She grabbed her mother's hand and placed her other hand in Sheri's, who then took hold of Deborah's. They were linked; one.

The friends were confused; somehow they had done something . . . wrong. The swirling abyss in their stomachs paid homage to their guilt. Shame hovered over them like the Detroit factory's smokestack stench. They huddled together, drawing comfort from each other. Stiff and silent, they exited the store into fresh falling snow. Esther felt the chill of the cold air all around her. She released Sheri's hand and with tears frozen on her face, spoke in a meek, trembling voice. "Mama, my face is cold."

Her mother reached down and slowly tied the ugly floral printed scarf around her silky pressed hair.

As the small, dejected group hurried down the street, a shadow followed along the wall; its long form slithered between the cracks of worn buildings as it hissed along the way. It was oblivious to the noise of traffic and other people rushing to and fro. It was a single-minded creature, and they were not his problem. He was only concerned with his assignment.

Today had been a good start, and he was pleased but not satisfied. He was like The High Master in that regard. Until the fruit from the vine was spoiled, his job wasn't complete. For each of his young assignments, he was just beginning. He knew from experience it was better to catch the fruit before it matured. He watched as they scrambled forward, seeking solace in each other's presence. As he followed, he wore a look of utter contempt for his charges. His yellow eyes gleamed eerily with a malignant delight against the growing darkness of the day. After all, it was a job well done.

Chapter Two

1988

The odor of musty bodies and stale beer could be smelled from anywhere in the gymnasium. The music blasted from the speakers, and the crowd of crushed college students swayed to the incessant beat. Bobby Brown was singing about things being his "Prerogative." Young athletic bodies were sweating to the song as though it was the new black anthem.

Deborah was shaking her rump like her clothes were on fire. Her acid-washed designer jeans hugged her hips and her matching shirt rode up with each bounce of her curved body.

Esther cupped her hands around her mouth and called over to Deborah, chanting, "Work that body, work that body! Make sure you don't hurt nobody!"

Deborah acknowledged Esther's call out by throwing her hand over her head and rocking from side to side as she began to prance around Jay, her date for the evening. Her footwork was so flawless, that others dancing watched Deborah on the sly.

Esther laughed out loud and continued to rock the house with her own moves.

While navigating the dance floor, Esther continued to keep her eyes on the door for Sheri and Briggs. She bit her lip and thought about Sheri and the way she always studied so hard and how she constantly worried that she would disappoint her mother. Sheri was an *A* student. How could a person be better than perfect?

Esther smiled when her thoughts shifted to Briggs, and the butterflies started spinning in the pit of her stomach. He was the stuff her dreams were made of. His nose was Roman in appearance and his low cut, waved, fade glistened like black gold. His cleft chin was a perfect fit for her index finger. He was tall, Hershey smooth milk chocolate and "smack yo' mama" handsome. Esther liked his looks, but even more, she loved who he was.

Briggs was ambitious. He had set goals for himself, and he wasn't stopping until they were met. He was a business major and knew he would have his own company one day. She wanted to help people with their problems and was majoring in social work. Many times they sat and talked and dreamed long into the night. It was those times that Esther knew they were meant for each other.

Their biggest issue was Briggs's father. He was a world-renowned televangelist and Briggs thought he walked on water. Esther was glad he loved and respected the man, but she tried to tell him that nobody was perfect and that living up to perfection was an impossible task. He and Sheri always seemed to seek others' satisfaction. Esther called it hoop jumping. And, in Briggs's father's case, the hoops had fire on them. There were times she sat and waited for Briggs, while he jumped hoops. It was a circus act with no safety net in sight.

Esther hoped this wasn't the case tonight since next to homecoming, the new semester icebreaker was the biggest dance of the year.

The song ended, and Esther thanked her dance partner. She never noticed the disappointed look on his face as she walked away to get herself a drink. Esther smiled as she glided up to Deborah who was already in line.

"Girl, you were working the fool out on that floor." She clowned on Deborah as she tried to imitate her style.

"Honey, you know you can't do me," Deborah made an intricate dance move.

Esther looked at the sweat pouring down the side of Deborah's beautiful mocha coffee face with its delicate features. This was her girl, her ace in the hole. She handed her a tissue. "No, you're one of a kind." Esther moved forward and paid her thirty-five cents for a cup of soda.

Deborah grabbed Esther from behind, "Hey, don't look now, but your Romeo just showed up."

Esther turned and watched Briggs as he strutted into the gymnasium; he was definitely looking good, and she loved his confident swagger. The brother made her molten hot.

"See ya, I hear love calling," Esther said in a singsong voice as she touched and fingered her hair and swiped lip gloss across her lips.

"Awesome, I'm going to go check on Sheri. You know she can forget it's okay to have fun and not just do schoolwork."

Esther nodded, already distracted as she sashayed to Briggs with an exaggerated sway to her hips. It was time to play.

Colgate pearly whites advertised her glowing smile. At twenty years old, she was five foot five and stacked in all the right places. Her asymmetrical haircut was a sign of the times. Her hair was fluid and with a flip of her head, its sheen shimmered in the blinking disco lights. Her luminous, amber complexion was the canvas for her cute turned up nose and wide, generous lips. Over the years, her hated freckles had faded to a memory. She carried a determined air and her dark golden cat eyes broadcasted her every thought.

Briggs watched her approach with an appreciative gaze.

Esther leaned in, placing her hand on his chest. "Hey, I almost thought you weren't going to make it."

Briggs pressed her hand over his heart. "Me, stand you up and live to tell it? Do I look crazy? I would hear about it forever." Robust laughter rumbled through his chest.

"Aw, sweetums, we gon' be together forever?" Esther whispered, inhaling his woodsy scent.

Briggs viewed her in the incandescent light, his eyes caressing her. "I'm really feeling you."

While Anita Baker sang "Good Love," both sighed contentedly.

"That's my jam. Come on, let a brother get closer." Briggs pulled Esther into his arms, and she burrowed into him, seeking her niche, her special place. He kissed her hair and took his turn to inhale her sweet fragrance. "When I think about my future, I always see you right there beside me. You're the compass that keeps me on track. You know my father—"

"The very honorable Bishop Stokes," Esther teased.

"Uh-huh. Anyway, he advises us that it is better to marry than to burn. But, baby, right now, I'm burning for you."

With Briggs pressed so close to her, Esther felt her determination to stay a virgin until marriage faltering. On the one hand, they were both adults; Briggs was a senior and had recently celebrated his twenty-first birthday. She was a nineteen-year-old sophomore. And, yes, she loved to have a good time, but she was pressing to stay in the will of God. How could someone make a person feel so good, and it be so bad?

Esther accepted Christ as her Savior when she was ten years old. Right now, with Briggs so up close and personal, she needed to stay on her toes. Her problem was she was feeling Briggs, all of him, straight through those same toes. Like her pastor always told her, a person's body could betray them if they didn't put the Holy Spirit in charge.

"Baby, you feel good to me too. Can't we just enjoy this song?" Esther kissed and blew into Briggs's ear. She loved his kisses, but was the taste of his kiss greater than her commitment to her virginity? *Lord, I'm so weak.*

Briggs guided her into the shadows of the gymnasium and slanted her head to the left before he gently sucked on her lower lip, then kissed her fully on the mouth. Both moaned, and Esther took as much as she gave. *Jesus, I'm a Rehab.* She opened her eyes and looked into Briggs's brown ones. His questioned if she would take the next step with him. Her hands sweated, and her pulse raced. *A little help, please, Lord.* She hoped Deborah would return soon with Sheri. She needed some divine intervention. Her resolve to do what she was taught, versus what she felt, was fading fast.

Deborah approached the front door to their dorm room with her key out. "Sheri better not be bent over some book when I get in here," she said in exasperation. She couldn't believe she had to leave the party to rouse her from schoolwork. Her key easily turned, but she was annoyed when the door wouldn't budge.

What the heck? Deborah banged on the door, "Sheri . . . Sheri, open up. Hey, quit playing." She continued to shove against the door as it inched open. "Finally," she maneuvered her body sideways and slipped through the sliver of space.

The room was pitch-black. She reached for the light switch, and her heart plummeted. "Nooooo . . ." The sight before her was a macabre scene from a Hitchcock movie. Sheri, a broken doll caricature, hung from the living-room light fixture.

Deborah raced forward grasping Sheri's legs fighting to untangle her from the clothesline noose. She was too short, and the noose too difficult to reach while she struggled to support Sheri's body.

Tears streamed down her face, and her eyes burned as she leaped on the desk and pulled at the once harmless all-purpose rope Sheri had made into an instrument of death. She swung her body into the rope to get momentum, pulling with everything she had, when Sheri, the light fixture, and the ceiling plaster, crashed to the floor. Plaster particles covered her hair and clung to her eyelids as she sobbed in terror.

"Please, God." she kneeled beside Sheri's pale, waxy body and shook her. Cold, dark eyes stared vacantly, while she desperately searched for a pulse. In mindless panic, she flew blindly into the hallway. "Help, help, somebody, please, please!"

Several students peered from their dorm rooms and ran into the hallway along with Ms. Renee, the dorm counselor. Her cherub face filled with concern as she intercepted a hysterical Deborah.

"Deborah, what's wrong?" she gripped Deborah's trembling shoulder to slow her down.

"It's Sheri, she's not breathing," Deborah tugged at Ms. Renee's arm wildly. "Hurry."

They ran the short distance down the hall. When they entered the room, Ms. Renee staggered at the scene. "Oh no . . . please, not this." Eyes shining with tears, she rolled Sheri over, lifted the noose from around her neck, and initiated CPR. Feeling no pulse she cried, "Call 911."

Deborah stooped beside Ms. Renee and shakily dialed the three simple numbers, twice, before she got it right. "H-h-help us. My friend isn't breathing, you . . . have . . .

to . . . come . . . now." She hiccupped the words through her sobs. "Yes, that's our location, the dorms, building 1002. Please, hurry."

While Ms. Renee continued using CPR, she stroked Sheri's cold, stiff hand and cringed at its unfamiliar texture. She opened her mouth and a seven-year-old Deborah spoke, "You've got to save her, Ms. Renee. Please don't let her die."

Ms. Renee didn't answer but continued to press on Sheri's chest and breathe into her mouth and nose. Soon, sirens could be heard in the background. Needing to feel useful, Deborah sprinted to the courtyard to rush the paramedics into the building. "Move. Dang, what's wrong with y'all?" She pushed through the drunken party crowd that rubbernecked while blocking the courtyard and hallway.

She met the paramedics and expedited their way to her room. When they reached Sheri, they spoke in hushed tones gathering data from Ms. Renee as they worked in synchronized rhythm to save her. Their expert calm and methodical movements helped Deborah's panic subside. *They'll save her.*

They lifted Sheri onto the gurney, and she followed closely with hound dog determination as they rolled the stretcher through the throng of students. At the entrance to the ambulance, Ms. Renee informed Deborah that only she could legally ride inside.

Deborah held on to the ambulance door. "What? Nah, that's not fair. Please, let me come."

"I'm sorry, you can meet us there, and, I promise, I'll be waiting for you." She pried Deborah's fingers loose, then hugged her.

Deborah backed away, running with a Flo-Jo pace, headed to the gymnasium. She had to get Esther. They both needed to be with Sheri. Her life depended on it.

***

Deborah entered the sauna like room and combed through the congested bodies swaying to a slow jam. Friends called out to her, and she ignored every salutation. Finally, she saw Esther and Briggs in the back of the gym. Esther's arms circled Briggs's waist, and they swayed in a harmonized pendulum motion like the grandfather clock in her great-grandma's living room. They were mesmerized, whispering in each other's ears.

Deborah's advance never faltered as she reared back her head and gave a Detroit, hood-piercing scream. "Esther!"

The entire room turned as the sound screeched through the air. Esther jumped away from Briggs in alarm. Her eyes glued to her grief stricken friend.

Deborah, with tears streaming down her face and plaster dust still covering her cheeks, poured out her anguish. "It's bad, real bad. Sheri tried to kill herself." She wiped at her tears, gasping for air. "Ms. Renee . . . then . . . the men came . . . in the ambulance." Deborah's hands chopped the air in an agitated manner. "Oh, help . . . me . . . come, come. We have to . . . go." Deborah pulled on Esther's arm, spun around, and ran with Esther right on her heels.

Esther, heart racing, yelled back at Briggs, "I'll call you."

Briggs's face was crestfallen as he stopped abruptly from running to accompany them. His body stooped as he watched them move away. Esther and Deborah only looked forward.

Ears that were supernaturally attuned could hear the sound of a symphony of hissing. Eyes adjusted to the spirit realm could pick up the faint shadows of several long, slithering bodies writhing together in a dance of pernicious victory. The lead one circled the group and shook his head at this emotional display. The young ones always celebrated victory much too early, he thought. As he slithered away from his minions' celebration, he began to orchestrate his next steps, knowing his mission was not half done.

Chapter Three

"Did you pack everything?" Deborah turned in an erratic circle. "Take her posters off the wall. Especially the one that says, *'This place would die without me.'*" Distress painted her face with strokes of cold blue pain and red streaks of anger. Her head hung low, she squeezed and pulled on her hair until spots laid bare.

Esther pressed to focus through her haze of heartache. It tore her down this front-row view of Deborah's metamorphosis from warrior woman to manic basket case. Her uncombed hair, last presentable at Sheri's funeral two weeks ago, had tuffs of coarse hair scattered around the carpet. Deborah's beautiful crown of glory, matted and knotted with random spots, lay bare. She cringed at her friend's self-mutilation.

"Honey, you're pulling your hair out again."

"Don't need it, stop talking. . . . Go away." Dry, ashy hands pulled her hair even harder, and mumbling, she circled the room, and then disappeared down the hall.

Esther wanted to scream and run away. She was out of answers; nothing worked. The night Sheri died only Esther came home from the hospital. Her Deborah remained in Sheri's room, clutching their friend, demanding she rise. The Deborah who walked next to her out of the hospital, got in the car, and came into their room was a stranger. She was once the tough girl, the take-no-prisoners one of the trio. But, every day, she unraveled a little more, alternating between coherent and incoherent speech. It was like watching a horror show and knowing that the boogeyman was around the corner, but nobody could hear you scream; go back. This Deborah scared her.

She wouldn't get help, wouldn't let anyone in their room, wouldn't talk to anyone on the phone. Esther called Deborah's mother, but she was in denial and only said to give her more time. She even pulled out her textbooks looking for answers, but she hadn't really paid attention in class. Her real courses were to take place her junior and senior year.

Esther turned and tripped over a milk crate. Their room was a mess. Mrs. Fields asked them to pack all of Sheri's belongings and ship them home. The strain of touching and going through her cherished items brought Esther to her knees and Deborah to her tipping point.

Esther unfolded a worn creased sheet of paper; one of the gifts Sheri left for all of them.

Dear Esther,

First of all, don't be angry. I hate it when I disappoint you. I know that you think I try too hard, and you want me to be easygoing like you. I watch you and Deborah, and everything looks effortless for both of you. I'm tired. I go to sleep and wake up scared every day of my life. Fear is my constant companion. Guilt and shame are the shadows in my life that haunt me.

I never said this, but my mom had to drop out of high school because she got pregnant with me. She loved my father, but he deserted her before I was even born. He's seen me twice. According to my auntie, he came to my hospital room, looked down on me, and said only ignorant could come from ignorant. My mother was determined to prove him wrong. The other time was when Mama took me to

*his house to tell him I was valedictorian of my class.
I didn't even know she knew where he lived. You
know what he said? Nothing. He slammed the door
in our faces. We sat in the car, and I held my mama
while she cried. I realized that all these years she
was telling me I didn't need a man, she still needed
approval from my daddy. Crazy, right? People
lie so much. They lie to themselves and to others.
And we all have secrets, dirty little secrets. So, I've
decided not to live a lie anymore. It's my way of
being free from the lies and the secrets.*

*I know that you believe me taking my own life is a
sin, and I know that for the rest of your life you will
be praying for my soul. When you do, remember
that I loved you and I wish you only the best. I never
wanted to be the best anything. I just wanted to be
me. I just didn't know how.*

*You know what? I feel at peace for the first time
in a long time. Take care of Deborah. She's not
as strong as you think. These pills are starting to
work, and I've got to go. I won't say good-bye . . .
just so long.*

Yours, Sheri

Esther folded the letter and placed it in her drawer.
Sheri's sin was now her burden. She was failing at Sheri's
request she take care of Deborah. She just didn't understand how she thought her life was easy.

Frustrated, she kicked a shoe across the room. "Are we
struggling enough now for you, Sheri?" she shouted.

Esther stood before the mirror, her reflection grim.
Who are you? Yes, she could be overbearing. But, had
she made Sheri afraid to be herself? Was her way the
only way? And, what secrets did Sheri take to the grave?
Esther's frustration mounted. There were too many
questions and too few answers.

Esther's self-examination was painful. She turned from the mirror and continued to pack Sheri's belongings. On her side of their dorm room, a poster with a picture of a big juicy burger read, "This is not Burger King. . . . You cannot have it your way." With sadness, she sighed, "Still trying to rule, still trying to be Cinderella."

One of her best friends was gone, and she didn't have a clue how to help the other one. Esther reflected back that it was Deborah who went to check on Sheri. She was busy basking in the adoration of Briggs. She was disgusted with herself. And though she knew it made no sense, somehow she also blamed Briggs.

Esther pushed the top of the clothes down and mashed them into the box. "This sista gotta change. I need to be more like Christ. Stop all this 'me' foolishness. I'm gon' pull a Vanna and buy a vowel, get me a clue."

Seven torturous days later, the early-morning sun streamed into Esther's window through the cheap regulation blinds hung in every dorm. She had not spoken to Briggs in over three weeks. She did not count the brief hug she accepted from him at the funeral. She understood she wasn't being fair, but somehow, it didn't matter. Her heart was bruised enough. The dorm room was now her alternate universe. Her energy was sapped, and she ignored the situation as alternate universes will allow you to do.

She exhaled; drained. "Goodness, maybe he'll just fade away." She couldn't feel; she was numb.

She wasn't a heathen; she tried to pray, but she became distracted by a thought or a sound. Sometimes when she prayed, her mind wouldn't stop racing so that she could hear Him. Her mother left prayers on her answering machine, but Elizabeth Wiley had no idea what was going on.

If she knew, she'd pull Esther out of school and bring her home. Esther looked toward Deborah's closed bedroom door. If that happened, what would happen to her?

Esther was soul searching. She blamed herself for Sheri's suicide. A real friend would have known something was wrong. What signs did she miss while she was hugged up with Briggs? When was the last time she had spent quality time with either of her best friends?

And, she was—get a shovel, dig the body up, and kill her again—angry at Sheri. What gave her the right to decide life was too hard? It was hard for everybody. Nobody went through life singing "Kumbaya."

Angry tears dripped down her cheeks. "Lord, I wish Sheri had used a comma instead of a period to fix her life."

The emotional day had crept into night. It was warm for October, and a breeze filtered through the cracked window. Outside Esther's dorm room, the campus was peaceful. Behind closed doors, tempers clashed.

Deborah yanked her suitcase off the floor and stormed past Esther. "You can't talk me out of it, stop trying. I can't stay here; I can't do this anymore."

Esther caught Deborah's sleeve as she passed. She gasped when Deborah pushed her back and jerked away. "Okay, you're upset. Girl, help me understand. How can you just move away?" In turmoil, Esther beat her chest with her fist. "I know Sheri's gone, but I'm here. . . . Please don't do this."

Tears rained down Esther's red, splotchy face. Deborah stood stoic, her knuckles purplish, clutched around the handle of her suitcase. She faced the door, her left hand tight around the doorknob. She shook the door in agitation. "I can't help you understand. I can't get you to feel what I feel. But, today I'm clear. The voices are quiet, and I don't know for how long." Deborah's head spun toward Esther. Her stance was rigid and determined. Her eyes drifted up and down Esther and flashed arctic heat. She then exploded and spittle flew. "I'm not going to go crazy. I've tossed and turned to the image of her death, voices tormenting me night and day. Her lifeless body swinging in every nightmare. It's been three weeks, and there's no relief. Nothing, and no one, can help. I've gotta get outta here."

The door's slam vibrated through Esther's heart; she was alone.

The next day, all of Sheri's belongings were shipped. Esther had completed something, and she felt a sense of accomplishment. Last night, she made her own plans. She only needed to tie up a few loose ends, like the insistent knock at her door.

Her eye pressed against the peephole. She counted the number of times Briggs knocked on the door as she watched him pace her hallway. He appeared determined. Esther threw open the door just as Briggs's fist was raised to knock again.

He folded his arms and gave her a granite-hard glare, "Thank you for answering the door."

Esther stepped back, her voice subdued. "You're welcome, come on in."

Briggs's stride was fidgety, foreign to his usual smooth gait. His voice strained, his hands pushed deep into his pants pockets, and he seemed to struggle for control. "Esther, I haven't seen you since the funeral, and even then you wouldn't talk to me. Will you talk to me now?"

Esther pointed, indicating Briggs should sit. She sat opposite him in her desk chair. To strengthen her resolve, she mirrored his entrance by crossing her arms and portraying a cold countenance. It was a difficult act.

His presence transmitted reminders of love-filled days. His muscular biceps attached to the arms that once held her tight. His two lips the focus of many of her prayers to God, to keep her holy. Then his eyes swollen and bloodshot berated her conscience.

Esther's resolve was melting. She chewed on her bottom lip and sat on her hands. "What would you like to talk about, Briggs?"

Briggs's voice cracked, and his cleft chin jutted out. "You're kidding, right? One minute we're in love and we're planning a future. The next thing I know, you walk out of the gymnasium and my life without a word. Esther, do you have any idea how I feel? No. Do you care?"

Esther rocked back and forth. "What do you want from me, Briggs, an apology? I'm sorry. I'm sorry you weren't first on my list when I lost my best friend. I'm sorry you weren't second on my list when my other best friend lost her friggin' mind." Her lips trembled, and her composure slipped. "You weren't on the list, Briggs. Everything is not about you."

Briggs jumped to his feet. "That's what you think? I'm selfish and don't care? Sheri was my friend too. Did you remember that when you were making decisions for our lives?" In a sudden fit of passion, Briggs swung double-fisted air punches to an imaginary foe, moving back and forth until winded; afterward he bent over with his hands on his knees breathing heavy with exertion.

"You're making me . . . look, I can't do this anymore. My mistake was thinking that if we talked we could get through this, but I can see it's already a wrap. I'm gon' step."

Esther waved her hand in the air at his antics. "What was that, Briggs? I'm sorry, but I didn't ask you here. I haven't even answered your calls." In the face of his defeat and her guilt, her voice shrieked for both their pain. "Don't you get it? I can't do this!"

Briggs moved forward and invaded her personal space. "You're going to throw us away and not even fight for us?" He paused, desperation and hope battling in his eyes. Esther remained silent; and his eyes dulled with pain. They were over. His body stretched, his chest inflated with false bravado. "This how you gon' play it? Girl, there is a line forming to get at me. You better recognize my worth."

Esther walked around Briggs. She strode across the room and flung open the door. "Here you are, still talking." She opened and closed her hand in talking gestures.

"That was real nice, Esther." Briggs's eyes clouded, and he brushed past her without another glance. His long legs carried him out of her room and halfway down the hallway in record time.

Numb, she watched him walk away. One fragile step into her room, and she collapsed on the floor. She was all cried out, so she lay prone and grieved. After a time, she crawled to her bed and pulled her packed suitcase from under it. She wrestled, gaining her composure. On shaky legs, she carried her suitcase out the door.

She had intended to make a clean getaway and avoid drama. She'd had enough of dramatic exits. Esther was going home. Her grief had recently taught her to take only those memories light enough to carry.

Chapter Four

The deep baritone voice of Esther's pastor resonated throughout the sanctuary. "I tell you, my brethren, it was not unusual that the bush burned. Many bushes burned during that time. That was the nature of things. We know about nature, don't we, children?"

Reverend Gregory, pastor of Love Zion Church, marched across the floor. His tone encouraged the congregation to lean forward. "Now hear me well, the miracle . . . was that the bush was not consumed! You ever been in a fire? Yes, you have. We all have. Some of us were consumed by what we went through. It changed you, so that you were no longer you. Ya got consumed. You quit talking to people, got hateful, stopped coming to church, you know who I'm talking to. Now, when God's fire washes over you, we as saints need ta hold on through the purifying stage. If you do, it's going to bring forth a new you. The fire didn't consume you, my beloved, it just refined you. God is awesome, church," he exclaimed as he mopped the sweat from his face.

The drummer beat his drums with fierce precision as Esther jumped to her feet and two-stepped an amen. She waved her church bulletin in the air. The usher was out of insurance agency fans or she would have used one of those instead. She didn't play with funeral home fans; she wasn't fanning death around. Esther let loose with the power of air-filled lungs, "Glory!"

She sat, crossed her feet at her ankles, and readjusted her dress around her curvy hips. Her shoulder-length hair was healthy and bounced with each sway of her head.

She was a beautiful woman who turned heads as she sashayed down the lane. In her twenties, men used to call out to her as she bounced down the street to the lyrics of the Commodores' "Brick House" playing in her head. But, at thirty-one, she was at the mercy of a society that redefined people once they gained weight. She was more than accustomed to the comments about her pretty face. She was raised well, and it showed in her acknowledgment of their compliments by her gentle smile and soft reply of, "Thank you."

Esther stood with the congregation as Reverend Gregory gave the benediction. She looked around the sanctuary and spotted Mother Reed. Well, in reality, she spotted her hat with its wide brim and long purple plumes. She was waving her hands in the air and giving praise. Esther spoke to people in general as she made her way over to her.

"How are you this fine Sunday morning?" Esther hugged Mother Reed's waif-like body.

"Chile, I'm glad to be in the land of the living. Thank you for all your help during my Anthony's heart attack and funeral. You a good girl, and God gon' bless ya. This I know," Mother Reed rubbed Esther's hands.

"You know I'd do anything for you. I'll be by to see you later on this week."

Mother Reed shook her head no. "Don't spend all your time with an old woman. Get you some nice young man and live a little."

"Now, Mother, you know I've been there and done that and all I got out of it was the heartache I brought back." Esther had a twinkle of mischief in her golden eyes.

In a solemn no-nonsense voice, Mother Reed said, "I needs to tell you something. But first, I've got to speak to Reverend Gregory. I'll meet you over in the vestibule."

"I'll be there." The twinkle faded from her eyes. As she watched her walk away she moaned, "Now what?"

Ten minutes later Mother Reed returned. Her wisdom shone from well used eyes as she made mental notes of Esther's weight of pain. She pulled Esther over, and they sat down on the worn wooden bench that the ushers used in the back of the sanctuary.

"Esther, look at me real hard. Look at this tired face. Do you see the lines? Honey, eventually black do crack. Now, I have lived long and well. You knew Mr. Anthony; he was a good man, and I was married to him for pert near forty years. I'm eighty years old. You do the math. Uh-huh, that's right, I was forty years old when we married. Chile, I was thirty-nine when we met, and I loved him for forty-one years. I plan to keep on loving him until the day I cross over; and then we gon' keep on loving each other in our mansion in heaven. Love don't stop 'cause you ain't with the person. What's sowed, nurtured, and given care will bloom continually."

She watched Esther look down at her hands and pick at her nails. "Guess you thinking you were only checking on an old woman and not looking for a lecture." Mother Reed cupped Esther's face. "I'm trying to share something important with you, honey. Life treated me hard. I was in an abusive first marriage, and did you know I have a son? He was a year old the last time I saw him. But, I pray for him every day. I call them prayers on deposit. Don't know when he'll need them, but they'll be there to bring him through. My first husband took him from me. Sweetheart, for ten years I lived in pain. I had no man, no child, and no home."

Mother Reed closed her eyes as she spoke of long ago. "The day I came into this church, I was thirty years old. I walked up to the altar, laid it, and cried my heart out. Bishop Dawkins, he's gone on to glory now, God rest his soul, took one look at me and took me up to his office. It was on a Saturday, and he was preparing for that Sunday's sermon. When he talked to me, he opened my eyes, and God opened my heart. Later, I met Anthony in the same pew I sit in today. Esther, I know you don't like to talk about your past. But Love Zion is a small church, and we all know it anyway."

Esther looked startled when she heard this.

"Now, don't get upset. People were talking in love, chile. Nobody wants to see ya in pain. Esther, he took your pride and money. But he couldn't take your soul. That you had to give to him. Let it go, baby. Be the bush that is set on fire, but not consumed. You don' let that man kill you. All that's left is the burying. I want you to stay with me in the land of the living." Mother Reed looked at the blank expression on Esther's face. "Well," she continued, "I done preached you twice today. I better get on home. Don't come by this Saturday. Go use your day off to do something fun for yourself," she admonished, rising from the wooden bench. "Bye, baby." She kissed Esther's cheek and tottered off slowly on her cane.

Esther gathered her purse, journal, and Bible and hurried out of the church.

Chapter Five

Sweat beaded across Esther's body as the sheets stuck to her plump shapely thighs. She tossed and turned into the night, but the sheets twisted, clung, and rode her wave of sleeplessness. She could not get comfortable. She hadn't come up with any answers to Mother Reed's questions. Instead of a peaceful sleep, she was caught up in a Minnie Riperton flashback and was strolling down memory lane.

Restless, she reached under her bed for her memory box. She riffled through it and dug out two pictures. They represented all that was left of her life with her ex-husband, Roger. One of the pictures portrayed two eager faces, blissful and optimistic on a day beaming with sunshine and promises. It was their beginning . . .

Esther sat on a bench hypnotized by the flow of the Detroit River. It was like life, not pretty, but it kept flowing, moving, to its rightful place. She had done it, after a three-year delay. She was getting her bachelor's in social work. Between her job, classes, and church activities she was busy but not fulfilled. She couldn't even lie; she was alone and lonely. She pushed away thoughts of the love she threw away.

"If I ever have a chance at happiness again," she spoke to the still dark water.

She loved coming to the riverfront. During the week it was peaceful, and she could think without being hassled.

A honeyed voice tinged with interest interrupted her musing. "Sis, mind if I sit down?"

Esther squinted through the sun's glare into liquid pools of pleasure. His eyes were a gray-silver that spoke of an ancestry from other lands. In contrast, his skin reminded her of her favorite Starbucks latte with a dollop of caramel on top. There was a negative; he was tall but too lean for her taste. However, he carried a carefree attitude and a teasing grin that added to the positive side on his balance sheet. Esther looked around at all the vacant benches and knew his game. She uncharacteristically decided to flirt. This had never been her skill, and if nothing else, she could practice.

Esther batted her eyelashes. "Well, I don't know. I was enjoying the solitude. Are you guaranteeing me something better?"

"Well, if I'm not better than nothing at all, I need to kill myself now." Confident, he began to sit.

"That's not even a little funny," Esther fumed.

Shocked, he sprang back up. "I beg your pardon. Let me begin again. I'm snapping a few pictures with my new camera. It was a birthday gift from a friend. I'm really a harmless guy who couldn't pass up the opportunity to meet such a lovely lady. My name is Roger."

Her eyes narrowed. "I never joke about a subject as morbid as death. If you can handle that, then I'm Esther. Please have a seat. Looking up at you is making me dizzy."

"Then we're even 'cause I got dizzy the moment I saw you." He jokingly acted out a dizzy spell resulting in a smooth move to sit down next to her.

Later, Roger bought her an Italian ice. As she enjoyed her lemonade-flavored treat, they strolled along the riverfront and he took pictures of her and passing boats. At one point, he asked a passing stranger to take their picture. At the end of their time together, he wanted her phone number but had to settle for her taking his.

Thirsty for attention, she called him the next day and over the next ten months they were inseparable.

Esther sighed heavily into her pillow. She should have read the signs: his moodiness, folded scraps of paper with numbers in his pockets, and his inability to keep a job. Her newly acquired tolerance had her making excuses for him. She felt that he just needed her steady influence and encouragement. Sheri's suicide made her second-guess her ability to distinguish fact from fiction; a valiant effort versus a waste of time. She was too naïve to understand that some drowning people will take down the one trying to save them too.

Esther flipped over onto her stomach and bunched the pillow beneath her. She flung the picture across the room. It landed facedown. Some memories were too painful and regret was a wasteful emotion. She picked up the second snapshot; she kept both pictures for different reasons. The first picture revealed how they got together. The second picture illustrated why the relationship ended; it was cliché and tawdry. Only her fingerprints gripping a photo of herself, tearful, holding her bruised shoulder was unique.

Soon the night breathed her name, and her lids drifted shut. In slumber, she rolled over on the picture burying it beneath her.

The morning tapped on her shoulder much too early. "Ugh . . ." She was tired after a nightmarish slumber. "Move it, girl." Sleep-deprived, Esther rolled out of bed. She staggered into her bathroom and plopped down on cold porcelain. The toilet made a rumbling noise through the house when Esther flushed it. She didn't mind because it was her place; therefore, her noise. When she shared a house with her ex-husband, Roger, nothing with the house ever went wrong . . . just everything in the marriage.

Esther spoke into the quiet of the morning, "Lord, I can handle a loud toilet as long as I have a quiet life. Mother Reed has stirred up some mess." She rubbed her sleep-swollen eyes in frustration. She was not about to sit back on her assets and fall back into a state of past depression. "Somebody call the king. I can't be bothered with all this foolishness. Rain down, Lord, bring back my peace. I fought for it; it was mine." Esther, more upset than ever, stomped into the shower. "Shoot, now, I'm going to be late for work."

The sun dazzled like small diamonds through the large-paned window, and the plants on the window ledge gleamed green and fertile as Esther looked over the reports on her desk. The Helping Heart Agency targeted the low-income population of Detroit; its mission to provide a hand up, not out, one person at a time. As director of Social Services, she wondered again why she ever wanted to be the "boss."

Esther sighed. "I must have been out of my mind."

She heard a throat clear and turned. One of her least favorite team members stood in her doorway. He was the manager of their home repair program. John Johnston sported a permanent scowl and a handlebar mustache. He once rode his Harley to work, wearing a bandana. As a result, to her, he resembled a pirate. Esther always thought it was an apt description since he appeared to be unscrupulous. Unfortunately, she was never able to catch him in anything.

"Hello, John, come on in." She wondered why her administrative assistant, Simone, had not announced his presence.

John stood at the door with a smirk on his face.

Esther motioned for him to enter the room, "How can I help you this morning?" *Can I slap you upside your big ol' head? Forgive me, Father. This uncircumcised Philistine gets on my last nerve. If you asked me if I had an enemy in my camp, he would be it.*

"Esther, I received your changes on the vendors' contracts. You made a really large cut in the amount of funds they'll be getting, and you want all the bids to come through you now?" He frowned. "Will you even know what you're looking at?"

Don't you curse him—stay holy—stay holy. She chanted in silence to keep calm. He had a habit of being condescending and after a restless night she wasn't up to his attitude. She had recently learned that some of the vendors who had contracts with their agency also had personal relationships with some of the staff. In a nutshell, relatives and friends were getting rich off of the government contracts, and to top it off, they were doing shoddy work. She suspected John as the number-one violator.

Esther leaned forward with her hands folded before her. "Let's see—you want to know if I know what I'm doing? Is that really your question?"

John squirmed under Esther's poised, pointed look. "Maybe I said that the wrong way. You've always let me handle the vendor contracts. It's worked well, don't you think?"

Esther's eyes hardened. "Positive change is good. I've had several complaints from customers on the unprofessional way the vendors treat them and that the work never seems to get finished."

"Oh, those people will complain about anything. They're not paying a penny so they should be happy for whatever help they get. You coddle them too much and believe everything they tell you."

Esther's neck muscles tensed. "John, may I remind you that *those people* are the reason you have a job? I suggest you learn a little compassion or you won't last at this agency. Then you might actually become one of *those people.*"

Cocky, John rolled back on his heels. "Naw. I'll never beg for help. I chase that paper. I know how to make money. . . . So when will these changes start?"

"It's effective immediately. Turn over all your case files to Simone. A letter went out this morning letting vendors know that there are new guidelines and everyone will need to rebid to keep their contracts." Esther turned to her computer screen, effectively dismissing John.

He stormed out, leaving her door wide open. Simone approached the doorway of her office with a concerned look on her face. "Everything okay, Ms. Esther? I only stepped away from my desk for a moment. I took a potty break." Simone pulled at the back of her dress.

"Yes, I'm fine, but thanks for checking. John barks a lot, but I've never known him to bite." Esther shifted through papers on her desk. She lifted folders and looked under her desk.

"Humph. My mama tol' me all dogs got teeth, and if they got teeth, they can bite. And that John? He do be a big ol' bowwow, but before you tell me to mind my business, I'll go on back to my desk. Oh, your sister called. I told her you'd call her back when you were finished. And, the report you need is on the top of the middle file rack."

Esther laughed out loud. "Girl, that is your job, security. I don't know how you do it, but if I need it, you know where it is."

Simone smiled and strutted back to her desk. "Don't forget your sister called."

Esther nodded her head. She'd have to call her sister back later. She had too much work to do.

Hours later, Esther decided to leave the office an hour early. She had been in three meetings and worked through her lunch. She was suffering from lack of sleep, and she was going home to get some.

Her cell rang. Caller ID showed it was her sister, Phyllis. "You could have called me back. What was up with you and Mother Reed? Your conversation looked intense."

"Hello to you too. You might want to tell a person hello before you start in on them," Esther said, reading through her last e-mail.

"Oh yeah, well, hello. I really called to see if you heard the news."

"What news?" Esther responded to her e-mail and begin clearing off her desk.

"Reverend Gregory is taking a year's leave of absence from church."

"What? When did this happen?" Esther stopped moving, stunned at the news. Reverend Gregory had been her rock since college.

"According to the church grapevine, he notified the deacon board today. Of course, then our first lady called Mama. You know how tight they are."

"I can't believe it. Pastor is dedicated to Love Zion." Esther's spirit sagged at the news.

"Now you know that pastor's daughter, Jeanette has those lung issues. She moved to Arizona for that job and was diagnosed after she relocated. She has pneumonia. They're concerned with all her complications; she'll no longer be able to take care of herself."

"She's worse?" Esther remembered sleepovers and church picnics with the vibrant, young Jeanette.

"Yeah, and after all that fasting and praying the church did." Phyllis had a bad habit of murmuring and complaining through every church-assigned fast. Later, she'd point out that the person or situation wasn't any better.

"Phyllis, our fasting and prayers are probably what has pulled her through so far. You have to have faith. Remember, prayer changes things, and some situations are only broken through fasting and praying." Esther resumed packing up her desk.

"Uh-huh, well, anyhow, I thought I would let you know. You being so church involved and all, and being a charter member of the 'willing to do' board. By the way, I still haven't forgotten that you never answered my question about you and Mother Reed."

"Nope, I didn't. But thanks for the info. I took a personal day off tomorrow so I may swing by to see you. I'll let you know." The phone rested between Esther's shoulder and cheek as she wrote a reminder Post-it and placed it on her calendar.

"Whatever, Miss I'm Keeping Secrets," Phyllis shot back as she hung up.

Esther picked up her purse and headed out the door. She paused at the receptionist desk. "Simone, I'm out for the rest of the day."

"Yes, ma'am," Simone replied saccharine sweet with a goofy smile.

Esther walked away, but listened as Simone used the office phone and dialed a friend. She surmised that, as usual, Simone's cell was low on minutes, and she was taking advantage of the opportunity for some juicy, uninterrupted gossip. What she didn't know was the topic: the office bad boy, John.

Esther started her Lexus and slid on her shades. She thought about her sister's phone call and burst out laughing. "My sister is a trip, Ms. 411." She pressed the praise station on her satellite radio.

Phyllis was private investigator-like nosy. She would listen in to conversations, even when she didn't know the parties involved. Her information was better than *The View's* hot topics. As a bored housewife, she needed to get out of the house and find something to do.

Esther wondered who would take Reverend Gregory's place. She hoped it wasn't Elder Shaw. He had a good heart, but he would put wood to sleep. Maybe elder was like the Apostle Paul who could write better than he spoke. The last time Elder Shaw preached, Sister Joseph's visiting grandson snored so loud that an usher had to tap him awake. When the usher hit the young man's shoulder, he jumped straight up out of his seat and moaned, "I'm getting up now, Mama."

The whole congregation laughed, even Elder Shaw, and praise the Lord, he hadn't been assigned to preach since. Esther smiled at the memory.

"Well, I do hope it's someone good." She sighed and turned up the radio's volume to counter the melancholy feeling threatening to take her over.

Gospel music blaring, her mind churning, Esther almost missed the sound of a siren riffing through her solo praise time. She glanced in her rearview mirror and saw a Detroit police squad car dead-on her bumper, its lights signaling her to pull over.

Esther grimaced and wondered her infraction. "No no no," she pleaded seeking heavenly intervention.

A tap on her window and a large hand with clean blunt nails signaled for her to roll it down. Esther touched the window's button, while reaching into her purse for her wallet.

She jumped when an authoritative voice thundered, "Take your hand out of your purse, ma'am. Place them both on your steering wheel."

Esther swallowed and complied, gripping the wheel until her hands cramped from the effort. "Sir, I was getting my driver's license. I—"

The officer bent over to peer into her window and Esther's words sat on her tongue confused. His uniform faded away, and Esther's mind registered that Prince Charming had stepped out of her imagination and was riding around the city of Detroit giving out tickets instead of glass slippers.

His eyes met hers and enlarged at the instant attraction. She watched as those eyes turned three different shades, as he methodically shook it off. "You made a rolling stop, ma'am."

Esther shook her head. "Sir, I did stop." She tilted her head through the window and reached out her hand in greeting. "Hello, I'm Esther."

The officer stepped back, looking into her eyes. She returned his stare, afraid to blink and miss something his eyes were conveying. The corner of his mouth slanted into a lopsided grin, and she breathed in relief. She hadn't had a date in more than a year. He tipped his hat. "I'm Officer Lawton Redding, Ms. Esther. In the future, make sure you actually stop at the stop sign. You drive safely."

He headed back to his car, and though disappointed, Esther still drooled in her rearview mirror. "Thank you, Lord, for me not getting a ticket. And the wonderful view. You do all things well." She hummed as she continued home, dreaming about what could have been. By the time she arrived, her daydream had them married with two children.

Amused at her daydream, Esther was unlocking her front door when her cell begin ringing. "Okay, okay." She juggled her keys, purse, and phone. "Hello?"

"Hey, did I disturb you?"

"No, Mom. I'm a little tired, so I headed home early. Everything okay?" Esther threw her purse on the couch, kicked off her shoes, and then walked out of her skirt. She talked while she unbuttoned her blouse.

"Well, now, don't get upset. I know how you hate change, but Pastor is taking a one-year leave of absence. He and the first lady are leaving at the end of the month to be with Jeanette in Arizona."

"Yes, I heard. Phyllis called me," she snapped, a ridge forming across her forehead.

"She should have waited. I didn't tell you, because I knew you were at work, and I didn't want to disturb you. Why add drama to your workday?"

"You're right, Mama. I didn't mean to snap at you. I'm sleep deprived." Esther smoothed her fingers back and forth over her forehead.

"Is anything wrong, baby?"

"Mother Reed said some things that have me thinking." Esther rubbed even harder at the hard ridges forming over her eyebrows.

"And . . .?" her mother said slowly.

"Change takes time," Esther said in a defensive tone as she moved toward her bedroom. She was carrying her skirt and shrugged out of her blouse.

"It's time to move on. I've been praying for you. You don't seem happy."

"Have I worried you?" Esther sat on the bed, in her matching bra and panty set. She picked the brush up from her nightstand and stroked her hair in a circular motion.

"Isn't that a child's job? You take chances; we worry. You hurt; we hurt for you. You pierce your finger; we bleed."

"You get cold, we put on a sweater," Esther joked knowing their love was a two-way street.

"Ha, ha, ha, that's real cute. Through it all, you and Phyllis are my greatest treasures."

"We love you too." Esther finished smoothing her hair into a perfect wrap and securing it with a scarf.

"Course you do, who doesn't?"

Esther fell back onto the bed laughing, then held her head from the jolting pain. This headache had snuck up on her. Hopefully, some sleep would cure it.

"Well, I have to go. Your daddy is looking lonely over there all by himself."

Esther overheard her father in the background sounding crabby as her mother hung up, "Woman, I'm minding my own business, so don't come over here bothering me."

She smiled, their teasing always made her feel warm inside. Tonight, she would have a peaceful sleep, with no past-life disturbances. She inhaled and exhaled deeply, willing her headache away. Her eyes half-mast, she watched the shadows of the waning day play against the skylight in her ceiling. Soon they drifted close. As night engulfed her, her mind fought against returning to a time in her life that was ruled by darkness.

Chapter Six

1995

Roger clapped his hands in her face to emphasize his message. "I said you are not going out. You at that church too much as it is."

Esther flinched. She was a grown woman standing in front of her husband being scolded like a four-year-old. This man was evil and small-minded. The caramel angular face she had once thought so attractive now held a demonic quality to it, the gray-silver eyes piercing with cruel intent.

She shivered and subconsciously crossed her heart with her right finger.

"Did your big tail just make the sign of the cross against me, girl? So now I'm the devil?" he raged.

Esther's chin quivered. "Don't call me names."

Before Esther could move, Roger snatched her backward and slapped her in the face. She backed away holding her cheek in disbelief. She knew he had been drinking, but to hit her? Was he crazy? The hallway mirror provided proof of his madness; his handprint was red against the lightness of her complexion; the wetness in her eyes testament to her pain.

Roger's chest heaved from exertion as though he was trying to control himself. "See what you did?"

Grabbing his jacket and stomping to the door, Roger spun around, heading straight for Esther's purse. He *rifled through it, found her wallet, and pulled out all of her cash; then he pushed the bills down into his pants pocket, patting it in satisfaction.*

Mission accomplished, he walked out the door, reminding her, "Girl, don't you go anywhere."

Esther felt cold hard rage, but she squashed it down and fled into the kitchen. All of a sudden she was hungry; frantically so. She grabbed containers out of her refrigerator. She placed a hefty amount of leftover fried chicken, macaroni and cheese, and collard greens on an oversized plate, as tears trickled down her face. While she heated the food in the microwave, she went to the sink and ran cold water. Afterward, she soaked a paper towel and applied it to her cheek, then slumped down onto the nearest kitchen chair.

She held her cheek and prayed. "Lord, I don't want to be here. Help me be a doer of your Word and not return evil for evil. Give me the grace to sustain this marriage or the mercy to leave it. In your precious Son, Jesus's name. Amen."

The microwave buzzed, and like a champ coming out of his corner, Esther came out of her daze. She looked down at all the food and remembered Roger's hurtful words. With purpose, she covered her plate and placed it in the refrigerator.

Marching through her living room, she picked up her purse and Bible and rushed out of the house. The cold towel pressed to her face, she was late for church.

"I can dance, dance, dance, dance, dance, dance, dance, all night," the choir sang, and when the pastor called out, "How long?" They answered, "All night." And the refrain continued.

The guest speaker had preached an anointed sermon into every heart present. The spirit was strong in the sanctuary, and the saints were dancing in the aisles. Some had caught the spirit so strong that they were running back and forth in front of the altar.

Evangelist Graham, Reverend Gregory's guest speaker, returned to the pulpit, "Do you believe, church? Well, where your heart is, so is thy treasure. Will you sow a seed today that will grow to be harvested later? If so, come now and bring your best!"

Esther jumped up with her wallet in her hand and ran to the altar. She was the first there, and the church clapped for her enthusiasm, but when she opened her wallet, it was bone dry. Esther looked around, stricken with humiliation. She was so busy making sure her face was not bruised, she had forgotten Roger had taken all her money.

When she turned to run out of the sanctuary, Evangelist Graham blocked her path.

He pulled her to him by her arm and hugged her tenderly.

He prophesied to her. "My daughter, be not ashamed for God is with you. You have sowed through your faith. Although the storm in your life rages and the weight of its rain is heavy, God loves you, and He has never left you nor forsaken you. He wants you to know that your inner light shines brightly. Hold on, sister, daybreak is coming."

As the words hit her, Esther slumped in his arms and wept for proof of God's love. She walked down the aisle and was touched and patted by those who called to her. "Keep your head up, baby," "God loves you," "Blessings to you, sister." Each word restored a little of her back to herself. God was truly awesome. Esther felt renewed.

Later, she entered the church's parking lot and inhaled the crisp night air. She was lighthearted, and her worries were miles away, probably sitting in some bar. She laughed freely with fellow church members as they strolled toward their cars. She was parked farther away, so she waved good-bye and turned down an isolated row.

Strained bursts of air filled the night as she huffed through the short hike, her stride purposeful. The earlier friendly banter was now fading background noise against an eerie silence that settled against the waning moon. Fog was moving in.

Due to a busted parking lot floodlight, she walked into an area of midnight ink. Her clicking heels resounded on the uneven cement, and she vowed to give an offering to the building fund on Sunday. The darkness and silence seemed unnatural. Hadn't people just laughed and talked along the rows? Something was off, and she couldn't put her finger on it. Now, her ears . . . or was it her imagination picked up a slight rustling? She tried to quiet her heavy breathing to hear better, but she ended up coughing. The rapid beating of her heart soon slowed when she saw her car's silhouette; it's chrome gleamed invitingly.

"Safety," she whispered and leaned forward, a sprinter at the finish line. Her hand and key extended, she clicked the door lock and her headlights illuminated the area. Her erratic heart settled, anticipating the feel of flesh touching metal, pure relief.

The first blow slammed into the back of her head. Stunned, she fell. Polyester and cotton blend slid and rode her upper thighs as she fought for balance, but settled for her hands landing on solid ground. Breathless, she was shoved from behind, her thigh scrapping the cement, leaving bits of skin mingled among the pebbles. Yanked from behind, Esther shrieked as a vicious punch was delivered to the small of her back, shooting paralyzing agony throughout her body.

Through pain-induced haze, she could smell the alcohol reeking from her assailant. Battered, she whimpered, "No money. Please . . . stop." Anticipating the next blow, her hands rose in defense mode. Her fingers spread, she sneaked a look at her assailant. Her eyes widened with discovery.

The reed-thin form hovered over her as he dragged her across the ground. "Didn't I tell you not to come here tonight? Get up and get in the car. I'm driving you home."

Roger's towering body appeared ominous against the dark sky. He gritted his teeth as he yanked open the car door and shoved her inside.

Esther trembled in dread. Roger's face was contorted in rage, veins pulsed in his neck as he snorted air. After slapping her earlier in the evening, and now this, Esther was terrified. She snuck a glimpse at him as he peeled out of the parking lot and sped down the road. Speechless and sore, her head ached, making it impossible for her to think.

She winced at the tenderness when she clenched and unclenched her hands. "Sorry . . . after . . . you . . . left, I thought—"

"Who paid you to think? That's what's wrong now. You think your degree and your manager's job make you my boss. You're not. I got tatted tonight. Should've done it a long time ago instead of listening to you saying it's ungodly. Everybody has one, but your frumpy butt. And everybody ain't going to hell."

Esther looked at Roger's right biceps, but it was covered with a bandage. He flipped on loud gangster rap, and they rode quiet for the next several minutes as Roger careened around corners and ran through red lights. "Oh, Jesus, he gon' kill me," she moaned low.

When Roger zoomed into their driveway, she breathed a sigh of relief that they arrived in one piece. Her relief, however, was short-lived. What would happen to her behind their closed door? This man was beyond her scope of knowledge, an anomaly. He was dangerous.

She sat trembling with her fingers laced and strove to focus on Evangelist Graham's message. Esther spread her feet and pressed them into the car's carpet. Roger came around to her side of the car, swung the door open, and pulled. But Esther dug her feet in and held on to the seat.

"Doggone your big butt. Shoot, you weigh a ton. Get out of the car," he panted, tugging.

Esther stared straight-ahead, looking neither right nor left, tears clouding her vision.

"I said get out," he repeatedly punched her shoulder.

Esther cowered from the blows, longing to fight back, but holding on to God, and the car seat for dear life. Eyes squeezed tight, she prayed. Minutes passed as Roger hurled insults like Mohammed Ali and his butterfly jab. Esther's thigh throbbed, and her emotions heightened at every scathing remark.

Hope dwindling, she heard tires screeching and a dark blue sedan barreled up the street.

Roger looked past her and cursed. She turned in time to see her father leaping out of the moving car. Her mother slammed on the brakes and threw the car in park.

"Fool, are you crazy putting your hands on my daughter?" he thundered, storming over to Roger, a Louis

slugger baseball bat swinging in his hand. Her mother tore out of the car clutching his arm. "Woman are you crazy? Let go of me, so I can whip this punk's butt!"

"Honey, please," her mother implored. Whirling to Esther, she asked. "You okay?"

She nodded, then collapsed. "Daddy—" He enfolded her in his arms and tenderly wiped away her tears.

Screeching tires drew their attention and a second car rolled into her driveway, lurching to a stop. Phyllis and Esther's, brother-in-law, Charles, raced out of their car, donned in pajamas, covered by robes. He ran to confront Roger, and Phyllis made a beeline for Esther. She put her arms protectively around her little sister. Overwhelmed, Esther burst out wailing in relief on Phyllis's shoulder.

Phyllis's focus narrowed to Esther's tearstained face, "Hit him, Charles . . . hit him. Beat that—"

"Phyllis!" their mother interrupted, shaking her head against her making matters worse.

"Yes, ma'am, sorry," mumbled Phyllis. In adolescent fashion, she mean mugged Roger behind her mother's back.

Esther watched Roger. His face dazed, he gulped in air. She could actually see him straining to think, but as usual, the alcohol he consumed trapped him in a fog.

Roger backed up, keeping his eyes on the men. He looked prepared to make a run for it.

Esther's father charged headfirst. "Where you going, boy? You man enough to hit my child? Well, now, you face me."

Roger pulled himself to his full lanky height and squared his rounded shoulders. "Esther is always defying me. I asked her to stay home and tend to her duties as my wife. She at that church too much."

Mr. Wiley scratched his head in disbelief. "Boy, you're trying my patience. Here you are talking about wifely duties when you have never been a husband. I've just come to the conclusion that you are beyond ignorant. Now, I'm not going to stand out here and continue to give a show to your neighbors. My daughter is going into that house, packing her bag, and coming home with me and her mama." Wound up, he continued his angry rant. "Talking about she at church too much. I told her mother, Esther should have never married a CME member."

Roger's eyes bucked in confusion. "Mr. Wiley, my people are AME, not CME."

"No, fool, you a member of the Christmas, Mother's Day, and Easter denomination. Holiday churchgoing heathen. Get out of my face." Hickman Wiley gestured to Esther. "Pumpkin, go and pack a bag. Once he put his hands on you, he stamped you 'return to sender.'"

Startled, she surreptitiously looked at Roger.

He gestured with his hands stretched out. "Please stay here with me. This is where you belong. Things got a little out of hand, but this is our business, and we need to work it out."

Esther stiffened as he hugged her, her body bruised and sore. Roger exhaled, triumphantly looking over her shoulder, he smirked. As they parted, Roger opened his mouth to speak, but Esther placed her finger over his lips. "Good-bye, I'm through."

She limped up the stairs with Phyllis close on her heels. As soon as Phyllis closed the door, she grabbed her sister in a bear hug.

"Uh-uh, that hurts, and I can't breathe," Esther muffled.

Phyllis loosened her hold and leaned away. "Yes, you can. You haven't breathed in a long time. Come on, take a great big gulp of air."

Esther did as she was instructed, holding her stomach as she inhaled deeply.

"Feel that?"

"Yes," Esther sighed.

"Know what it is?" Phyllis continued in cheerleader style.

"Freedom," Esther crowed.

"Now, my sister, be ye not entangled again," Phyllis sang in an evangelical voice. "Just give the word, and we're off to the hospital and filing a domestic violence charge. You know Daddy may force you to do it anyway."

Esther nodded, moving with renewed fervor down the hallway. Phyllis followed. "Girl, stop. I need to take a picture of any injuries you may have with my phone." Esther rolled her eyes and pulled her sleeve up to show her bruised shoulder. Phyllis snarled as she snapped pictures from several angles and continued revealing the earlier evening. "When Sister Edmonds called Mama and told her what she saw Roger do to you in the church parking lot, I thought she was going to have a heart attack." She then turned her phone for Esther to see the pictures. "It's not as bad as I thought. Drunk can't throw a punch."

Esther ignored her sister's last statement. "So, that's how y'all found out." She rubbed her shoulder as they entered her bedroom. She didn't show Phyllis her scrapped and bruised thigh or the back of her head which throbbed. She just wanted to go and leave all this behind her. But if Roger ever hit her again, she would bury him under the jail.

"Yea, while Daddy was getting dressed, Mama was calling me. As you can see, I wouldn't let Charles take the time to put clothes on. I felt this was a come as you are party." Phyllis gestured to the pajamas and robe ensemble she was wearing.

Esther opened the closet door, then pulled out several dresser drawers. "You start in the closet, and I'll pack up what I need from here."

"I'm on it." Phyllis tugged a black suit from the assortment and showed it to her sister. "Not this, you need something to say, 'I'm back.' Let me pull some new-attitude clothes for you."

"Anything that will help me move forward, I'm for." Esther secretly rubbed her sore side.

Phyllis rifled through the closet. "Umm . . . Esther?"

"Yes?" She rummaged in her dresser drawers.

Phyllis's lips trembled. "Baby, you don't have any new-attitude clothing."

"Nothing?" Esther froze, a nightgown in her hand.

"Just this old gold blouse," she held it out. "Everything else you got from the Flying Nun."

Esther was dumbfounded. She used to love clothes. She took the blouse out of her sister's hand and silent tears fell. Her energy and freedom now snatched away.

Phyllis looked alarmed at Esther's mood shift. The spirit of depression was a sneak. It made a person think it was just coming to visit and before they knew it, letters went out, telling the world that it had taken up permanent residence in a new home.

She took Esther's hands in hers and began to pray, "Merciful Father, we come humbly before you. We are in pain, Lord. We ask for your healing and your mercy. I come in your Son Jesus' name against the spirit of depression and oppression. I thank you that as we speak, you are straightening crooked roads. We have come to a fork in our journey and need your direction and guidance to travel the road that is your will. We don't want to miss a step, because we don't want to miss you. I thank you, Lord, for being in our midst. Bring us peace that surpasses all our understanding. We surrender all, everything, to you. Amen."

Esther felt a sweet spirit of peace. She hugged her sister, who could be a walking contradiction—critical controller and loving protector.

"Thanks, I do appreciate you."

Phyllis sniffed and waved away her little sister's comments. "You make a decent salary. We'll just go shopping tomorrow and buy you some more clothes. As a matter of fact, I feel a shopping spree coming on," her voice ending upbeat. She blinked away her tears.

Esther used her nightgown to wipe her eyes. Her sister didn't get sentimental often, and when she did, she usually backpedaled when she realized she was being mushy. Esther went down the hall to the bathroom to pack her toiletries.

Phyllis followed talking. "I hesitate to bring this up, but I think that the path you're on started with Sheri's death and Deborah's abandonment. You marrying Roger and trying to save him is just a symptom of a much-larger disease. Girl, I still don't believe that you ever really loved Roger. Who could but God?"

"So tell me what you really feel," Esther muttered as she shoved toiletries in her overnight bag.

Phyllis put one hand on her hip and another to point out Esther's transgressions. "Oh, I'm just warming up. What have you done about your misery? You joined church committees. Let me count them all. . . . You're on the Daughters of the Vine committee, the usher board, the Missionaries of Hope, the pastor's strategic planning committee, and you got the nerve to be the part-time church administrator. Shoot, girl, the last I heard, you even volunteered to be head of the volunteers. Just how miserable have you been? Boo, anyone that busy is running from something . . . usually themselves." She ended with a snap of her fingers.

Esther blew her hair out of her eyes and grimaced. "Thank you for your considerable opinion of my life. If you don't mind I'm a little tired and sore. I'm about ready to get out of here." Esther began moving through rooms, lifting her suitcases and handing some to Phyllis. "Dang, Sis, couldn't you, just for once have kept your mouth shut?"

Phyllis nodded and packed. There was a quiet lull in their conversation, and Esther doggedly pressed her lips closed.

"I guess I let my tongue speak before my brain was engaged. Tonight wasn't the time to say all of that. If Mama wasn't outside guarding Roger from Daddy, she'd have known the right thing to say. I'm sorry."

Esther didn't pause in her packing. "We're good. I can only muster the strength to be angry at one person a day. This is Roger's day."

Phyllis dragged the suitcase and bag to the front door. Esther was close behind. She paused at the open door; the tasteful furnishings, color coordination of drapes, wall covering and carpet attested to the time she had taken to make this house a home. She'd learned that home was about the people, not the building. This was a beautiful prison with invisible bars; it had kept love out and her pain in.

When she descended the stairs, she passed Roger. He ignored her and leaped up the steps two at a time. She looked over her shoulder and saw him enter the house and slam the door. The sound echoed in her heart, and she knew that the door to her heart would never open for him again.

Mr. and Mrs. Wiley came and placed their arms around her shoulders. "Let's have a word of prayer," he said.

The extended Wiley family held hands in the front yard.

"Well," Phyllis whispered to her husband, "I'm glad this isn't our neighborhood. I hope her neighbors don't think we're out here doing voodoo."

"Shush."

Esther adjusted the visor as the morning sun glared through the moving truck window. A caravan of cars followed the truck down Rosedale Lane. Late into the night, Esther and her family talked. It was agreed that it was best to move her out of her house today.

In the past four years, Roger had gone through her money, her friends, and finally, her patience. They tried private counseling, but Roger walked out. They scheduled Christian counseling with Reverend Gregory, and Roger never showed up.

The slap woke her up, and the punch sealed their fate. Roger was a bully, the "boo!" leftover from a child's fear of things that go bump in the night. She was cutting her losses before she woke up dead.

The caravan stopped, and everyone piled out of their vehicles. Her cousin Tony jumped out; large, menacing, and chiseled from his recent prison workouts. "Okay, cuz, you're the boss. Just tell us what needs to go and what stays." As an afterthought, he said, "I hope that fool tries to stop us." He cracked his neck and punched his fist into his hand.

Esther shook her head. Tony and his siblings were the family's holdouts for salvation. "Tony, don't start any mess up in here. We're getting my things, and then we're leaving."

Esther's parents had an important meeting and couldn't back out at such short notice. She missed their calming hand.

Phyllis marched up. "Tony, as much as I would like to see Roger's tail whipped, we are under direct orders from Mama—no fighting. And, bro, you know you on probation . . ."

The group began to get organized; unpacking boxes and labeling them by room. As they chatted and laughed, the front door opened. Roger's clothes were rumpled, as if he had slept in them. The five o'clock stubble on his face showed signs of gray. He barked, "What are all of you people doing in my front yard?"

Esther stepped out from the group. "We've come to get my things."

"Esther, let me talk to you a minute."

"No," everyone yelled.

Esther looked back at her family, serene. "It's all right." She and Roger went to the side of the house, but in plain sight of everyone.

He was fidgety and shuffled his feet. "How you gon' just leave? You know I love you."

"Really? Since when, Roger?" Her eyes remained downcast, not out of fear, but because it was hard to look at the man he had become, not the one she imagined him to be. It was a mistake to marry potential, since there was a real chance it may never fulfill its purpose.

"Okay, things got a little out of hand, but you should know how I feel. Girl, I love you so much that sometimes I get crazy with it." He leaned low attempting to catch her eye.

Esther continued to look down at the ground. Looking at Roger made her angry and sad all at the same time.

He tried tilting her chin up, but she stepped away. "Look how good you're looking this morning. All fresh and dewy."

"Oh, I don't look fat this morning?" she fired back.

*"I'm sorry, Baby. I was upset. You know I like my
meal with more than a little meat on it. I wanted you
with me last night, and I was frustrated when I came
home and you were gone." His voice was as slick as silk
and just as slippery.*

*Esther looked over Roger's left shoulder; she saw a
shadow cast against the side of the house. She shivered,
closed and opened her eyes several times, but it remained; the shadow of a serpent.*

The morning mist must be playing havoc on my senses,
*she thought. Yet, her bones were chilled. Although hazy,
it was a mild morning, and intuitively, she knew her chill
had nothing to do with the weather.*

*"So, that's why you slapped me, stole my money, and
went out on the town?" she shot back. She felt a ripple
of a chill and shivered again. In defense, she folded her
arms across her chest.*

*Roger's voice slithered out like a serpent's hiss. "See,
you got to listen. I've been feeling bad. No job or money
will jack a brother up. Sometimes a man needs to blow
off a little steam. A real woman would understand that
her man has needs, and she'd be ready to take care of
them. If you had stayed home last night, none of this
would've happened, and I wouldn't have gotten mad."
He punctuated his words by pointing his finger in her
face. "You ... hurt ... me. All of this is really your fault."*

*Esther ignored Roger's skewed logic. She was so
done with him, nothing he said mattered. But she saw it
again. Was that the shadow of a snake? She took a deep
breath and stepped toward it. When she moved, Roger
turned and the shadow disappeared. She shook her head
and silently prayed, "Whoever dwells in the shelter of
the Most High will rest in the shadow of the Almighty.*

I will say of the Lord, 'He is my refuge and my fortress, my God, in whom I trust.'"

Fear departed and warmth filled her soul. "I'm letting you keep the house, but we're done. Just let go."

She turned away, and Roger jumped up and down in a full-fledge two-year-old tantrum. "What am I supposed to do? How can I pay the mortgage on this house? You know I don't have a job. How will I eat? You ain't leaving me!" he panicked and reached for her.

Tony sprinted over, ready to intervene, but she held up her hand stopping him. "Hold up, I got this." She stretched and rolled her neck—from the I'm an Angry Black Woman Handbook—irritated that she had to go there and that this needed to be said. "Roger, the Word says in Second Thessalonians 3:10, 'The one who is unwilling to work shall not eat.' Find a job, Roger; go to work."

Roger, desperate to refute Esther's words, opened his mouth and gulped air, emitting dry croaking sounds. Esther scoffed, understanding he had no Word, and therefore, no weapon. In the realm of the shadows there was a hissing sound that slithered back into the earth.

Esther directed the crowd that had shifted closer to her and Roger into the house. As she gave directions on what to do, her cousin Tamela, Tony's youngest sister, remarked as she looked around, "Cuz, this house is hooked up. Anything you don't want, I'll be glad to take off your hands."

Tamela's home sewn weave, long scarlet fake nails, had her shuddering thinking about her nice things in her cousin's two-bedroom, Section Eight apartment. She knew Tamela's three children would destroy everything before the day was out. However, this was family, and she loved her.

Esther smiled politely. "We'll see, Tamela. Right now, I just need to get it all out of here."

Before Tamela could answer, Phyllis chimed in, "And don't none of y'all help yourself to anything you haven't been given. All right?"

Tamela swung her full head of swap meet hair in front of Phyllis's face and pointed her scarlet, rhinestone finger at her. "I came here to help out of the goodness of my heart, Phyllis Wiley. So don't ya be acting like ya better than nobody else or that me and mine steal. I coulda stayed home with my children's daddy if I wanted to be treated bad."

Phyllis huffed, "My name is Phyllis Davis. I got a husband, Tamela."

"You need to be minding him, instead of other folk's bizness," Tamela flung back.

"What did you say?"

Esther could feel a headache coming on, and the two of them were causing it. As her brow wrinkled, she placed a hand on both women's arm.

"Okay, today is about me. Now, yesterday may have been about you, tomorrow may be about you, and heck, tonight, may even be your night. But today? It's all mine, so cut the chatter and let's just get through it." Esther's voice was shrill with frustration.

Phyllis and Tamela looked at each other, and both nodded in agreement as they put their arms around Esther.

"You know how we are. . . . I got you, girl," they spoke over each other, before they broke out in a laugh.

Tony said, "Can we move away from the drama now? A brother has things to do."

Roger watched with a face of despair as they organized and packed. His mouth opened in disbelief at the amount of things being brought out of the house: beds, dressers, couches, tables, pots and pans, stereo equipment, televisions, a microwave . . . all bought by Esther.

As the day continued, he sat under the tree and watched as the last item was packed onto the truck.

"We're finished." Esther took her key off her key chain and handed it to him. "You'll hear from my attorney soon." She climbed into the truck.

Phyllis called out to Esther as she rushed past. "Hold up, sis. I forgot something."

She entered the living room and found Roger standing forlorn in the empty house. She hurried, jogging down his hallway. "Sorry, I forgot something."

Roger rolled his eyes spewing sarcasm. "What could y'all have possibly forgotten?"

He followed Phyllis and watched her go into the bathroom. The room was bare and Roger looked on in astonishment as Phyllis bent down and released the toilet paper from its holder. She stood with a triumphant look on her face as she strutted past him with the toilet paper in her hand. Standing on the porch, Phyllis raised the roll of toilet paper as a trophy of war. Car horns blew, and the small crowd hooted and barked.

Roger's face was thunderous as he nailed Esther with eyes of pure hatred. They transmitted plans for revenge and future suffering . . .

In her sleep, Esther called out in agitation. Sweat stained her nightgown, and her bedcovers twisted around her feet. She flailed her arms at unknown assailants before her body settled into rest.

"Is she still asleep?" The Leader asked.

"Yesssss . . . she's remembering her time with the loser. You were so good that night, Leader. You brought chaos so close to the church," Imp One simpered.

***

"The parking lot is a first step. I wanted to plunge right into the heart of their service and destroy all I saw. For now, at that church, the parking lot is close enough. Soon, I may get closer," The Leader said.

"You are brilliant, you are evil personified. That happened to Esther over two years ago, but still her nights are haunted by past pain. You rule, Mighty One, you rule," Imp One cheered in his best lackey voice.

"I see your point, insignificant toad. I thought enticing Roger to get a serpent's tattoo was a good move. It speaks to him even today. That chapter is not closed."

"You see, Old Bold One? You are a master strategist. Look at her. She tosses and turns, yet, she professes He who reigns in heaven is her peace. These humans are such pretenders. She is broken, she is broken, she is—"

The Leader's tail curled above their heads. "Shut up, infidel. That constant repeating is making me itch to destroy something. It could easily be you."

"I am bad, so sorry, Leader. Should I wake her now or send more visions of shame and blame?"

"No, we have played enough for tonight. Let her wake up and believe that all is well in her world. What I have planned for her, she will need her sleep."

Esther woke with tears spattered on her pillow. The past needed to stay there. Roger was history. Perspiration beaded her face, and the silk scarf she tied around her head earlier lay haphazardly on her shoulder. She shivered because she had started out dreaming about her past with Roger, but somehow she had ended up dreaming about snakes, and snakes gave her the creeps.

Chapter Seven

The alarm shrilled Esther awake. Last night had started out early to bed, and now she was facing the early-to-rise part.

After her shower and dressing in a comfortable sweat suit, Esther had her morning tea. She fingered her unruly hair in the mirror and decided against taking the time to curl it; instead, she stuffed it under a fedora. Her time was limited, and she had a lot to do. When she drove off and came to a complete stop at the stop sign, she grinned, remembering Detroit's finest.

She was still smiling when she pulled into the parking lot of Love Zion.

"Hey, Naomi," Esther addressed the church secretary who sat sentry before Reverend Gregory's office. "Is the reverend in?"

Naomi scrutinized Esther over glasses that slipped down her pinched nose. In a dry monotone, she delivered her canned message, "Reverend is busy. If it's not an emergency, you need to make an appointment."

"Naomi!" Reverend Gregory stood in his doorway, "That's not what I instructed you to say. I simply asked you to relay the sentiment that my time is short today."

Naomi smacked her lips and yanked up knee-high stockings that rolled down her chocolate reed-thin legs. "Well, honestly, how do you expect to get anything done with all of these interruptions?"

"Never mind all that, Sister Naomi," Reverend said kindly. "Come on in, Esther. It's good to see you, daughter; I take it you heard the news?" He ushered her into his office and shut the door.

Esther sat across from him at his desk. "Yes, I did. Love Zion will miss you. I'm keeping your family in my prayers."

"Well, now, I appreciate that. My little girl needs me. Listen, I'm glad you came by. I wanted to talk to you about helping the interim pastor get acclimated."

"Sure, what do you need me to do?"

"Well, the deacons will help him with his church duties, but as head of many of our committees and our administrator, I'll need you to help him with church business."

She nodded her agreement. "Who is the interim pastor?"

"Oh, a good friend's son. I wanted my friend, but he was unable to get away. I've heard his son preach, and he's a good, God-fearing young man. He'll do this church fine."

"Well, just let me know, and I'll be glad to help. In the meantime, I'll get all the paperwork together for him." Esther pulled out her tablet and made some notes.

"Good, good, let's make it quick because he's coming in later today." He stood to escort Esther to the door.

"But, Reverend, I thought you'd be here for the rest of the month." Esther was on the verge of whining.

Reverend Gregory patted her hand to calm her. "I will, Sister. I want to have a smooth transition, and with that in mind, I requested that the interim pastor come immediately. To meet this deadline, he's coming right away, and he'll send for all the comforts of home later. He'll stay with Mrs. Gregory and I. Tomorrow morning, we meet the deacons, and I'm hoping you're available around noon for a working lunch."

"Sure, I'll check with—" Esther spun around when the door flew open. Startled, she knocked a folder off the desk at Naomi's loud interruption into the room. "Goodness, Naomi!"

Naomi's glasses danced at the tip of her nose. "Reverend, he's here. Your replacement just came in," she theatrically fanned herself with her hands.

Esther stooped to gather each scattered page from the fallen folder. Large polished wing-tipped shoes strode into her line of vision. Her eyes drifted up, programming long legs encased in expensive charcoal material that draped in perfect symmetry to the cut of his step. She continued her upward exploration and cataloged the fit of the doubled breasted jacket that clung to an impressive chest. As her examination took in the pure silk tie with pink and purple overtones, she was feeling this man's style. She wanted—no, needed—to see the entire person. Mother Reed's recent reproach for her to live again floated through her mind. Yesterday's police officer, and now this. . . . Somebody better start praying for her.

She smiled, clutching the now filled folder to her chest as she stood to welcome Love Zion's newest leader. But Reverend Gregory beat her to it; he stood directly in her path, hugging his replacement. Her anticipation to see this man's full image was heightened. How rude would it be to knock Reverend Gregory out of the way?

When Reverend Gregory moved, Esther's mouth fell open. Her eyes narrowed on the cleft in his chin, and her index finger twitched to settle in its place. Standing before her in all his glory was her ex-boyfriend, Briggs, although now, it appeared that he was Pastor Stokes.

"Esther," Reverend called for what appeared to be the third or fourth time.

Shocked, Esther bumped the bottom of the desktop with her hip. As she grabbed the desk to steady herself, the folder fell again, and she hit a pile of books, knocking them off. She tried to catch them before they fell on her feet, but her fedora was knocked off her head by Briggs's elbow as he attempted to catch them at the same time.

"I see you still know how to get a man's attention," Briggs said, then laughed.

Esther smoothed her hair back as she put her fedora on once again and glared at both Briggs, who was laughing openly, and Reverend Gregory who was holding his laughter back.

"You always were a handful," Briggs chuckled.

Reverend Gregory picked up on Briggs's comment. "You two know each other?"

Esther rushed to speak first. "What a surprise. Briggs and I were classmates at the university." Esther then turned to Briggs and held out her hand. "It's so good to see you again."

Briggs took Esther's hand in his and smiled. He held her hand in his palm and turned to Reverend Gregory. "Sir, this is the one that got away." Esther's face turned red, and she tugged her hand away. "Oh, it was nothing so serious, just a college friendship," she hastened to correct.

Curious, Briggs's eyes widened as a challenging Esther stared back.

Reverend Gregory cleared his throat. "Well, let's keep matters simple and not share that with the rest of the congregation, and, Briggs, maybe you should send home for 'everything' sooner rather than later."

Briggs caught the drift of the reverend's remarks. He went over and placed his hand on his shoulder and reassured him. "Everything is fine; I consider Esther an old friend. Everyone should have friends, don't you think?"

"Yes, yes. Well, good," the reverend replied in relief.

Esther knew Reverend Gregory hated confusion of any kind. And she could tell that Briggs's reassurance allowed him to move forward, confident in his choice.

Esther backed away and gave a polite smile. "Well, Briggs . . . it was good seeing you again."

"Yes, you said that," he said with humor, his expression puzzled at her lukewarm reception.

Esther wasn't ready for this meeting. She was off balance and wished in her angst she could get away with a loud ugly curse word, but Reverend Gregory would faint, then rush her to the altar. "Anyway, welcome to Love Zion. I know you'll be happy here. I'll see you both tomorrow," she said in haste, rushing out.

Esther moved in a slow jog. The swish-swash of her thighs rubbing together echoed, and she prayed that in her rush to leave she didn't start a fire. She grumbled each step of the way. "Catches me on my day off, hair a mess, old sweat suit on, with ten years of excess weight, and here he walks in looking like Mr. GQ." Esther jerked her keys out of her purse as she kept up her monologue. "Talking about the 'one who got away.' Oh, he's smooth all right. And what's that crack about I was always a handful? That better not be a reference to my weight. Ooh, Father, help me," she whimpered.

Esther was so caught up she didn't hear her name being called.

"Esther, Esther!"

She turned and saw Briggs running behind her.

"Hey, hold up a minute. You left your day planner. Girl, you was moving," he said, catching up with her. "Now, before I give you this planner, can a brother get a proper welcome?" he asked as he opened his arms wide and smiled with the expression on his face she had seen only in the daydreams of her yesteryears.

Esther surrendered and did what she had wanted to do since she first saw him again. She slid into his waiting arms, sighed, and momentarily placed her head on his shoulder. *Perfect fit*, Esther thought as she closed her eyes and remembered that this had been her place once upon a time, this nook between his shoulder and neck.

Briggs broke away first, stepping back and putting space between them. His grin was "little boy getting his first puppy" wide. "Now, that was better," he said. "I couldn't let you leave without us making a real connection. God is so good. I knew you were from Detroit, but I never imagined running into you. Not in a city this big."

Esther pulled herself together. "I'm just as surprised to see you. In all of our talks, I don't remember the ministry being one of your dreams."

"You remember I was all about the money? 'Brother gotta get paid,'" Briggs folded his arms and cocked his head to the side in hip-hop fashion imitating the old him. He then gave a self-depreciating grin. "Yes, God had a plan even if I didn't know about it. I went through some things, and God showed up and showed me mercy. Being brought up in the Word helped me to return to it for my protection. Now, I'm all about saving souls for Christ. What about you?"

"I know you remember me dropping out of school my junior year. I just couldn't pull it together," Esther leaned against her car door self-consciously with her arms and legs crossed.

"I remember," Briggs nodded for her to continue.

"I came home and bummed around for a while. I was so angry with everyone, including God, but especially myself. I was pretty self-serving in those days. It was all about me. What happened with Sheri woke me up."

"Go on," he encouraged, his voice soft and sympathetic.

Esther smiled remembering that they always could talk to each other. "I found out I was becoming my own worst enemy, snapping at everyone, feeling miserable and empty. I woke up one day, and I was sick of myself. So, I decided to change. To fix myself . . ."

Briggs burst out laughing. "Yeah, that sounds like you. Ms. Determined. When did you find out you couldn't fix you?"

Esther smirked. "Not right off the bat. I started with the obvious outside things. I went back to school, changed my hair color, fixed up my apartment, and started getting out again. But I was still dissatisfied. At first all my projects kept me busy, but then I was close to graduating and the emptiness started creeping back in. Yes, I was in church, but the church wasn't in me. Finally, I ended up getting married."

"You're married?" Briggs frowned, then caught himself and straightened his face.

"No, it didn't last. Marriage didn't fix it either. It was an unhappy time in my life. I was so depressed that I sought for answers to my problems in the Bible. Over a period of time, learning the Word changed my thinking, and that changed my life. Things didn't get better overnight, but they did get better," Esther sighed.

"You do have a testimony, don't you, Esther? I always say few of us come to Him because everything is perfect in our lives. We are troubled, in pain, and then we find out He is the answer." He paused not wanting to give a mini sermon. "Hey, how's my girl Deborah?"

"I have no idea. When she first left school I didn't even know where she was headed. Later, her mother shared that she had moved to Atlanta. After many attempts on my part to keep in touch, I finally gave up. I sometimes feel like the amputee who lost her limbs." Esther took her right arm and demonstrated by wrapping it around her body. "First, Sheri; right limb gone." She then wrapped her other arm around her. "Then Deborah; left limb gone. We were sisters for so long. Who do I reach out to now?" Esther asked, lost in her aged grief.

Speechless, Briggs stepped forward and touched her arm. He empathized with her journey.

Esther felt a tingle and rubbed her arm when Briggs touched her. She stepped back and fumbled with the car door. "I need to go. Reverend Gregory would like us to meet tomorrow. I'll see you then." Flustered, she slipped on her shades and seat belt.

Esther began backing out when she noticed that Briggs rubbed his chest absently. She fantasized that he felt the tingle too. Her musing caused her to gun the motor and screech out of the lot. She had had too many daydreams lately.

"Leader, you're so diabolical. I can see where you're going with this," lisped the imp. "It's so exciting. I forgot the devastation you brought to those three friends. When you separate, you defeat. I know what you'll do next will be da bomb. Boom!"

"Fool, calm down. This is not your party. You don't know a thing. I'm the orchestrator. You just run with what I give you. I am deeper than any ocean, wider than any sea. I am the be all, to end all. I have plans for these two—lovely plans. Plans of evil and not of good," The Leader boasted as his tail stood up in orgasmic delight.

The imp slinked onto his belly and slithered through the ashes in the blistering heat. He was not wanted; The Leader was content with his party of one.

Chapter Eight

Esther slowed down and hit three on her cell. "Phyllis, I'm in your driveway. Please open up."

Phyllis played her music loud. Esther learned to call ahead and cut out the bother of knocking and not being heard.

The front door swung open, and Phyllis looked chic in a designer sweat suit with her hair hanging in a smooth ponytail. Her skin was flawless, her thick eyebrows arched to perfection. Her large doe eyes were her best feature, and she and Esther shared the same cinnamon skin tone. She worked out daily to maintain her size ten figure.

"Outta my way," Esther cried as she ran past Phyllis down the hallway to the closest bathroom.

"Goodness! Just like when you were a kid. You were always waiting until the last minute. It would have served you right if I had waited to open the door," Phyllis called out to Esther through the bathroom door.

"Whatever," she shouted. "Please, get away from the door. Dang, Phyllis."

Phyllis chuckled and went into her family room. As she turned off her stereo, Esther slinked in. "Girl, I hope you haven't been anywhere else besides my house because you look a hot mess."

"Please don't tell me that, Phyllis. Do I really look bad?" Esther was embarrassed.

"Yes, child, look like you stank. What were you thinking wearing that old droopy jogging suit, and when are you due for a touch-up on your hair?" Phyllis grabbed Esther's hat off her head.

Esther was mortified even more about running into Briggs. "Ummm . . . I did run by the church."

"No, you didn't! Looking like *that?*" Phyllis circled Esther.

Esther stuttered. "I was only supposed to be there for a minute but—"

"You didn't see anybody but Reverend, did you?"

Red crept up Esther's neck. "Uh, I saw Naomi."

"Well, that's okay because Naomi has no fashion sense, and Reverend loves us so much I don't think he notices what we wear."

" . . . And . . ." Esther said, drawing the word out slowly.

" . . . And . . .?" asked Phyllis just as slow.

"The new interim pastor," Esther finished quickly. Her entire face and neck were flushed.

"What?" Phyllis stood back and cataloged her sister. Esther looked back at her with a deadpan expression on her face. Their eyes caught each other's, and they squealed with laughter.

When Phyllis stopped holding her stomach, she wiped her eyes and said, "Girl, hand me that phone. While you prepare to tell me all about it, I'm calling Ki Ki's to get you a hair appointment."

Esther handed the phone to her sister and plopped down on her sofa. She decided right then not to share with Phyllis her and Briggs's past.

Thank God, back in the day, I never told her my business, Esther thought. Sometimes, it was easier to keep things to herself than hear a lecture from her big sister.

Phyllis hung up the phone. "Okay, you have a three o'clock appointment. I might as well ride along, and get Cathy to do my nails. We have an hour. Let's eat, and you can tell me all about our new pastor," Phyllis said as she headed to her kitchen.

During their drive, Esther and Phyllis talked all the way to the salon. Phyllis tried to get the scoop on Mother Reed and Esther's Sunday conversation, but Esther still avoided answering. Mostly, because Phyllis was too nosy. Soon, they arrived and entered the upscale beauty salon and day spa.

Three hours later, Esther admired her hair as she shook it back and forth in the mirror. She had splurged and had golden highlights added to her rich brown hair. Her edges were smooth, and she could see the shimmer from her hair's glossiness reflected in the beautician's mirror.

Phyllis joked, "Well, now I know that the new pastor is fine."

"Excuse me?" Esther said; then she tripped over the foot railing of the salon chair.

Phyllis waved her freshly colored nails at Esther as she paid for her hair and they left the shop. "You do know your clumsiness is a dead giveaway, you're nervous or excited?"

Esther kept looking straight-ahead, hoping Phyllis would be quiet.

"As a matter of fact, I take back my earlier statement. The new pastor must be supa fine. You even had highlights placed in your hair. When's the last time you did that? Girl, how old is this man?"

Esther stopped walking in frustration. "Sis, it was your idea for me to get my hair done."

"No, I said you needed a relaxer, but you chose to have the works. So, is he fine?"

"Bye, Phyllis, I'm going home now. I'll talk to you later," Esther raced to her car.

Phyllis stopped in the middle of the parking lot, and started laughing. "Now I *know* you're tripping. He must be finger-lickin' chicken, good looking. You're all flustered and losing your mind to boot," Phyllis hooted.

"Losing my mind? Girl, please. You're the one who's nuts." Esther opened her car door.

Phyllis swiftly intercepted and placed her hand on top of her sister's, stopping her from leaving. "Because . . . I rode here with you. Remember?" Phyllis sang smugly.

Esther's mouth fell open. "Get in and not one more word, Phyllis. I mean it. You say one thing, and it better be the word *cab*," Esther snarled.

Phyllis got inside, closed the door, folded her arms, and grinned. "I've been trying to get you to up your game for a minute. And it's always, 'No, I'm too busy for all that nonsense.' Now, all of a sudden, you ready to put some—'Ooh, baby, baby' back in your style. Girl, it's about time."

Esther threw up her hand and sliced the air for Phyllis to be quiet.

"I'm just saying, that's all . . ." Phyllis whispered as she smiled and looked out the window.

Chapter Nine

Esther glanced down at her watch and shut down her computer. She then checked her appearance in her compact mirror. Not wanting to be late, she left her office with time to spare. "I'm leaving for a lunch meeting, Simone."

Simone looked up and smiled. "Yes, ma'am. By the way, I love the new hairdo."

"Thanks, me too," Esther grinned and patted her hair.

"Well, you do look good. That deep chocolate suit is banging on you, and the color brings out the golden tones in your skin." Simone continued to catalogue her wardrobe. "The jacket is too cute, the three-quarter sleeves are different. Yes, there's pizzazz in this new look. Someone is a lucky man this lunch hour," Simone said being obvious in her attempt to get into Esther's business.

"Okay, now you're dipping," Esther joked.

Simone was a serial dater, and she thought that was the only way to live. Esther had caught her on more than one occasion listening in on Esther's male phone calls, always hoping to hear some gossip. Simone was always disappointed.

Simone knew that Esther disliked her borderline ghetto fabulous ways. But, Esther knew that Simone had her back, and there was no one more loyal. She was also a good worker. So, she didn't sweat the little things about Simone that irritated her.

"While you're all up in my business, Simone, you probably have your own plans for this evening."

"Oh yes, I do. . . . I'm gon' be all holed up with this good-looking, chocolate fountain of Almond Joy. Yes Ma'am, I plan to sweat my hair out," Simone said while snapping her fingers.

"Okay, Sweetie, that was way too much information. This is still a business, and I'm still your boss. Hold that kind of talk down. I definitely have to get back to praying for you."

Esther headed out of the building, waving at her coworkers along the way. She was looking forward to lunch, and if given the chance, digging into Briggs's post college life.

The restaurant valet opened an anxious Esther's door. She swung her body to get out of the car, stretched out her leg, caught her boot heel in the bottom of her skirt, and literally fell out. Strong male hands caught her before she could land on the pavement.

"Gotcha," Briggs chuckled.

Esther's face burned with embarrassment. "Hello, Briggs. I guess some things never change," she said as she tugged at her skirt to straighten it and pulled down her jacket.

Briggs was a gentleman, and he didn't answer. Esther imagined he remembered how she would always fall, stumble, or bump into something when she was excited or nervous.

Entering the restaurant, she wondered what Briggs was thinking. He had become quiet and contemplative. "So, Briggs, seems you keep catching me at my best," Esther prodded, seeking some direction of his thoughts.

"Anytime I see you it's good." Briggs grasped her by the elbow to guide her into the restaurant.

At the tingle of skin on skin contact, they both went motionless. "Was that an electric shock from the carpet?" Briggs asked.

Esther shrugged and took off into the dim restaurant. Soulful jazz played in the background of the Chop House. The coziness of the surroundings invited patrons to sit down and relax. The hostess greeted them, and Briggs gave her Reverend Gregory's name.

"Your party is waiting for you. It would be my pleasure to show you to your table," the hostess said, her entire demeanor focused on Briggs.

Esther's eyes shot daggers at her. She spoke low, between gritted teeth and stiff lips, hoping the woman heard her. "He's a man of the cloth. Pull your claws in before lightning strikes you, Delilah."

Briggs looked startled and coughed into his hand. Esther turned to him innocently with a question on her face, and Briggs grinned.

The hostess, ignoring Esther, swayed her hips in tune to her own inner rhythm as she led them to their table. Her emerald eyes twinkled like the hills of Ireland they reigned from as they remained focused on Briggs. "The Chop House hopes you have a wonderful lunch. My name is Maura, if you need anything. Please let me know." As she stressed the word *please*, she winked at Briggs, bending cleavage level to hand him his menu. "We do aim to please. Your waiter will be here shortly."

Briggs gave another short cough. "Thank you, Maura. I'm sure we will enjoy it."

Reverend Gregory shook hands with Briggs, and then reached forward and hugged Esther.

The reverend witnessed the hostess's antics and mopped his brow. "I tell you, Briggs, the way you have with women is something else. As a man of God, you must be careful about the attention women will want to give you. Even us older pastors have women who forget we are just men."

"Amen," Esther said. She then turned crimson. *The man is kryptonite, and like Superwoman, a sista getting a little weak.* Esther fanned her face with her menu.

Briggs unfolded and slid his napkin onto his lap. "Sometimes people just need to be noticed to make their day. I was only being cordial, but, Reverend, thanks for looking out for my welfare."

"So . . ." Esther said opening the menu, "how would you like to start off? Would you like to review the church's special projects first?" She felt rebuked for some reason after Reverend Gregory's comments and her slip of the tongue. She wanted to get right down to business.

"I'm in both of your capable hands," Briggs said.

"Esther, why don't we start with the church's community development project?" Reverend Gregory began.

Esther leaned forward with enthusiasm and used her hands to gesture as she spoke. "Around four years ago, a member approached our Daughters of the Vine group concerning furniture for her child's bedroom. She was a young mother and little Ricky had outgrown his crib." Esther paused to catch her breath. Talking about the church's program ignited her passion for helping others. "Our group believes that scripture speaks to us as Christians to do more than pray for our brethren. Jesus asks that we feed the hungry, clothe the naked, and house the homeless." Esther took a deep breath and chuckled. "Sorry, I can get a little carried away."

The waiter approached their table and took their orders.

"Please go on," Briggs said.

Reverend Gregory beamed at Esther. "I'm enjoying the retelling of it!"

"When I went out to Tracy's apartment I was appalled. There were holes in the walls, windows painted shut, and some were broken. Tracy had used plastic to cover them, but the apartment was still full of flies. On top of everything, the neighborhood was unsafe, with vagrants hanging in the hallways and on the street. The front door was flimsy, off alignment, and wouldn't close properly. Tracy had to put a chair underneath the doorknob each night, and she prayed that nobody barged in."

"What about the landlord?" Briggs asked with indignation.

"If you could find him, he made promises that were never kept. Tracy, and most people like her, didn't know how or who to complain to. Poverty is just as much about the lack of resources as money. Tracy only earns minimum wage."

"Family support?"

"We are her family. Her grandmother was a faithful member before her death. Now we stand in the gap. Tracy was the church's inspiration," Reverend Gregory said.

Esther nodded in agreement. "When I returned to church, I couldn't shake the feeling that something more needed to be done. I wondered what good would a new bed for a child do in those conditions. Tracy didn't even have a bed. She was sleeping on a worn-out couch. I wanted to do more than just complain, and so did the other members. We prayed about the situation, and a door opened." Esther looked up and paused as a waiter placed their entrées before them.

"Briggs, will you bless the table?" Reverend Gregory asked.

Briggs said grace, and they began to eat.

"Esther, I know we need to eat, but please continue if you can. I want to hear the rest," Briggs requested.

"No problem, I can do both," Esther said and waved her fork in the air as if to shoo away any doubt that she couldn't. She was in her element and enjoying relaying the chain of events. "We have a wonderful congregation, and some have been materially blessed. We took the problem to them, and one of our newest members came up and said he had many rental properties, and that he wanted to give a duplex to the church. He said it needed a lot of work, but if we did the repairs, it was ours. Well, every plumber, carpenter, electrician, painter, and one or two Indian chiefs stood up and offered their services free of charge."

Reverend Gregory and Briggs laughed.

"You haven't seen anything until you see church folk outdoing each other," Reverend Gregory added.

"You're so right," Esther agreed, "but they have good hearts."

Reverend Gregory hit the table in delight. "Yes, they do. I was so pleased with them. We had a big celebration after the project was finished."

Briggs assessed Esther's animated face. "You really are in your element." He rubbed his chin as he murmured, "So your clumsiness was due to nervousness or excitement? Wonder which one."

Reverend Gregory leaned over. "Say that last part again, Briggs. My hearing isn't what it used to be."

"Sorry, just thinking out loud," Briggs replied.

"Anyway," Esther continued, "we rented the other side out to another church member, and then used the duplex to leverage other properties. Now we have twenty properties, and we have a full-time housing manager. We make the homeless with children and those families living in dilapidated housing our priority."

Pleased, Briggs clasped his hands together. "Love Zion is doing a lot more in the community than I realized. And Tracy?"

"Our first resident," Reverend Gregory boasted. "Many churches today are helping the community. People are busy talking about how much money we take, but few recognize how much is given back." Reverend Gregory slid his chair back and stood, placing his hand on Briggs's shoulder. "Learning all of this will take some time, but it will come. I hate to leave you, but I have another appointment. I've taken care of the bill, so please stay and enjoy the meal. I'm leaving you in capable hands."

"Yes, I see that. I'll see you at your home later?"

"No, meet me at the church around six; we still have other paperwork to get through."

"I'll be there. I'm sure Esther will take care of me until then." Briggs's eyes rested on Esther.

Esther stood and hugged Reverend Gregory. When she sat down, Briggs was staring at her. "What?"

"The Esther I'm seeing today is the Esther I remember from college and more. You always were in the middle of any good fight, but now you've added compassion for others. The church is blessed to have members who commit not only their tithes, but also their time. Esther, you are a gift." Briggs leaned back in appreciation.

Esther blushed at his compliments. She looked down and used her fork to move her food aimlessly around her plate. Then she exhaled, determined that he wouldn't rattle her.

She dabbed her mouth with her napkin. "I didn't do it alone. It was first God, and then those who answered His call that made all of this work."

Briggs rubbed his hands together in anticipation. "I look forward to meeting with all the members."

"You're excited." Esther grinned at his apparent eagerness.

"Well, Dad is pretty well-known, and he cast a big shadow. This is my chance to break out on my own and see what God has in store for me. Seems I've always been someone's something. Coming here like this lets people know me for just me before they know the family I belong to; they've produced pretty big shoes to fill. I want everyone to know me first as their shepherd, a man of God, even if it is a temporary assignment."

"You always were closed mouth," Esther said. "I remember getting angry with you because you never let the girls who drooled over you know that you had a girlfriend. I was always defending my territory." Esther put up her small fists in a mocking fight stance.

Briggs grimaced. "I wasn't interested in those girls. But you were so popular on campus the guys use to call me Mr. Wiley."

Esther's hand flew to cover her mouth. "Oh no."

"Oh yes, it was humiliating, so, now, I try to keep my own identity for as long as possible. I guess my overreaction came from a lifetime of being the son of such a revered man. Everyone wanted to open doors for me because of him. I wanted them to open because of me." Briggs zoned out, caught in past memories.

"I never knew that." Feelings of empathy for him washed over her.

Briggs shrugged his shoulder. "It isn't something you tell your girlfriend."

Esther's gaze explored Briggs's. "So, you feel that your time has come?"

"Yes, no matter what, this time I rise or fall on my relationship with God; not the people's around me relationship with man."

Esther's smile built slow, and then was wide and bright. "I have faith you'll do just fine." She evaluated him for a moment in silence. "I remember a few things about you from the old days too. Like, your determination to succeed, your willingness to listen, and your sense of integrity in dealing with people. You're assisting God, He's not assisting you. Let Him lead; you just follow."

"Well, all right, Ms. Thang, teach the children." Briggs raised both his hands in a praise salute.

Esther snickered. "A little over the top?"

"Just a touch," he said pinching his fingers together.

"Sorry."

"Apology accepted." He was enjoying her. He shook his head in amusement. "I can't wait to get started. Girl, you've got me motivated."

Esther scooted her chair back preparing to pick up her napkin that slid under the table. At the same time, Briggs jumped up to pull her chair out, believing that she was rising to leave.

His hand covered hers in the confusion, and she marveled at their connection. His voice was full of wonder. "I can't believe you're here. I never imagined I would see you again."

Wisdom led Esther to ease her hand away. She observed there was no wedding band. However, ten years is a long time and people change. He had. He was now a pastor. Esther decided to deal with the elephant in the room. "We didn't part on the best of terms, did we?"

Briggs moved closer by sitting in Reverend Gregory's vacated seat, his cologne merged with her perfume, and created an exotic light scent. "All the more reason to be friends now. This is a new town, and my first assignment as the head pastor."

Esther inhaled their combined scent. "I'd like that. I'm a little rusty in male-female friendships, but it'll come back."

Briggs gave a jubilant laugh. "I'm the one who'll need help. You know you're a handful."

Esther's face tightened. "As a friend, let me warn you to stop making weight references."

Briggs froze at her wintry response. "Whew! Girl, that was cold. I have not been making comments about your weight. I'm a grown man, not a boy. If I wanted to say something, I would say it. You're beautiful, and that's all I see when I look at you. I thought you knew me better than that. I think you owe me another apology."

Esther knew her cheeks were crimson again. "I'm sorry, Briggs. Guess I'm carrying a little baggage."

"Want to talk about it?" he asked, his ministerial calling kicking in.

"Not really. Let's just say my ex-husband was not a nice man and leave it at that."

"Come on, now, we're old friends. We used to talk about anything and everything."

Esther grunted. "Evidently not, since I'm just learning about the identity issues you carried in college. Although I do remember how much you wanted others to be okay with you."

"Touché, but, in my defense, I was raised in a glass bowl. We're older and better now. Let an old friend help," Briggs coaxed.

Esther bit her lower lip. "He left me feeling pretty shell-shocked about how others see me and how I see myself."

"Thanks for sharing that. I hope as your pastor and your friend, I can help you accept the restoration that you deserve. I won't push for more right now, but I'd be honored if you would think about us meeting and discussing this some more in the church office. So . . . tell me more about Love Zion's business holdings."

"Right away, sir," she said as she saluted him and continued their meeting.

Later that night, Esther massaged cold cream into her face as she sat in front of her vanity. It had been a good day. She was curious though. It was the second conversation she had with Briggs, and except for some pretty vague comments, she hadn't a clue to what he had been doing with his life outside of ministry in the last several years. They either talked about her personal business or the church business; but she knew it was time she found out about his personal business. She was feeling some stirrings of old magic, and she was minding what her mama always told her, "You better look before you leap, or you might end up on a big stinking trash heap."

"Lord knows, I've shifted through enough garbage in my life," Esther declared as she used a tissue to wipe the cold cream off of her face.

Chapter Ten

Briggs tapped the phone off in frustration. Monica had hung up on him again. Annoyed, he placed his hands over his face and prayed that this move would improve their life together. He would do anything at this point to turn things around. The constant arguing was draining.

He'd had a good first day, calling his wife and sharing with her should have been its highlight, but it wasn't. She was still upset about having to stay in Reverend Gregory's home. He told her it didn't make sense to rent when the Gregorys' home would sit empty in their absence. But she was not hearing it, and from experience, he knew it was easier to let her have her way. He sat on the bed, his body and soul bone tired. His marriage kept him before the throne of God.

The house was quiet, the Gregorys asleep. Briggs thought about meeting Esther again after all these years. She was beautiful and full of life. If the tingling was an omen, they still had chemistry. He smiled as several warm memories washed over him. He chuckled aloud as he got ready for bed; some of Esther's escapades were legendary. Briggs crawled beneath the covers, the sheets cool against his skin, his head sunk into the pillow, and he fell into an exhausted sleep. As he slumbered his cell phone vibrated on the nightstand.

The following morning, Naomi, Reverend Gregory's secretary, frowned at the phone as she placed it on its hook. "It's too early to be messing with me," she said out loud. It was nine in the morning, and that was the third call for Pastor Stokes from some woman named Monica.

"No home training, that's what it is; no home training at all," she mumbled as the door opened, and Reverend Gregory and Briggs entered the office, laughing.

" . . . and then she said, 'That's what I'm trying to do.'"

Both Reverend Gregory and Briggs laughed again at the punch line to Reverend Gregory's joke.

"I'm glad y'all having a good morning 'cause somebody's working my nerves already," Naomi complained to both men.

Reverend Gregory leafed through his messages in his in-box. "Now, Naomi, we have talked about having a Christian attitude every day, not just on Sunday."

"Yes, Reverend, I know, but it has been mighty hard with all these evil people around." Naomi pinched her narrow nose under her sliding glasses.

"That's when we most need Jesus, Naomi." Reverend Gregory motioned to Briggs to enter his office.

"Right, right. I sho' hope they meet Him," she said turning her attention to Briggs. "Pastor Stokes, before you go, a woman name Monica has called you three times this morning, and she wants you to call her right away."

"Why don't you go on in and use my office, Briggs," Reverend Gregory suggested.

Briggs opened the door, but before he could close it, he heard Reverend Gregory say, "Naomi, Monica is Pastor Stokes's wife."

Briggs paused to hear her response. "Well, why in the world didn't she say so? She just kept badgering me, asking me if I knew where he was. My goodness," Naomi exclaimed as she turned her exasperated glare toward the reverend's closing door.

Briggs walked into Reverend Gregory's office and picked up the phone and dialed. He took a deep breath and greeted his wife when she answered. "Hi, sweetheart, you were trying to reach me?"

"Where did you go last night?" Monica fussed.

"Nowhere. After we talked, I went to bed."

"I called you right back, and no one answered. Where were you?" she badgered.

"Oh, right . . . my phone was on vibrate from earlier meetings. That's why I didn't hear the phone ring," Briggs said, remaining calm during her inquisition.

"Yeah, and where were you this morning? And why isn't your cell on now?"

Briggs held fast to his rising temper. "Monica, I had a breakfast meeting. I cut the phone off during the meeting and forgot to cut it back on. Was there something you needed to tell me?"

"We need at least eighteen hundred square feet of living space," she said, still harping on their previous conversations of having her own home in Detroit.

"Monica, I'll do what I can, but I won't promise. I'll have to rent what we can afford."

"It's always money with you. Ask the church to subsidize it. After all, we're doing them a favor coming to bail them out. Stand up, for goodness' sake," she commanded.

Briggs blew heavily into the air. "Monica, I'm on Reverend Gregory's phone. I'll call you back later."

Monica continued her tirade. "Briggs, no excuses this time."

Briggs knew there was no way he was asking the church for more than they had already generously agreed to pay him. Monica wanted her own way at any cost. They couldn't afford half the things they owned. They definitely couldn't afford two homes, not even for a year. After five years of marriage he wanted a family. If they kept living like they were it would never happen.

"I'm going to need you on this one, God," Briggs prayed.

Minutes passed and Reverend Gregory knocked before entering his office. He folded his arms and watched Briggs pace back and forth in front of his desk.

"Rough time?" Reverend Gregory asked.

"Sort of. You know Monica has her own ideas, and sometimes it's hard to get her to see the other side."

Reverend Gregory perched at the end of his desk. "Do you guys talk about these things?"

"More like she talks, I listen."

"Doesn't sound like a good way to live. Maybe it's time to try something new. Like sitting down and learning how to communicate with each other."

Briggs paused before Reverend Gregory. "You must think we're a piece of work. I may have marital problems, but I hope you know that I am a good pastor."

"Briggs, everyone faces problems in their lives. It's how we handle them that count. Son, it's not enough to be a good pastor, you must be a godly pastor. That means all of your cares must be laid before the Father, and let Him direct your path."

"Physician heal thyself? Or better yet, physician, stop trying to heal thyself?"

"Exactly. A man who can heal himself doesn't need God. But those of us who know, we know that He is the way, the truth, and the life. So . . . how about I give you the name of a trusted friend and therapist who can help both of you get all God wants His children to have out of their marriages?"

Briggs rubbed his chin and nodded in agreement. "I've tried to get her to go before, but she was always afraid we would run into someone we knew, and then people would gossip. Maybe being away from home she won't have that fear."

"That's right, son. But, you can't fix it if you're in two different places. Here's a little wisdom from someone battle scarred, you must make time for your family in ministry. Too many pastors and member's children are in prison, pregnant, or on drugs. It's not because they are bad parents, but this life will take you over if you don't put boundaries around it." Reverend Gregory clasped Briggs's shoulder. "Now, think on what we talked about and let's get back to work."

Briggs bent his head in compliance and opened his notepad. "So, the deacon board was receptive. What's next on the agenda?"

Reverend Gregory pulled out his cell and checked his appointment calendar and notes. "The church mothers can be a little stuck in their ways. We need to approach them next. We'll start with Mother Reed; she's the sweetest and a strong pillar of the church. God uses her mightily. We'll visit her later on today."

"I'm sure everything will be fine," Briggs said, leaning back in his chair, confident. The church mothers at his home church loved him.

Reverend Gregory shook his head at the arrogance of youth. He decided to share with Briggs what he was getting in the Spirit. "Briggs, I promised I would allow you to do things your own way. But I feel the beginning of danger brewing. The shadows are gathering, and nothing is as it seems. Be vigilant in your prayers; sharpen your spirit of discernment. Soon there will be a heavy rain," Reverend Gregory paused. "It will storm, and it looks like hurricane quality."

"He suspects, he suspects," Imp One screeched into the ragtag group of underlings.

Imp Two crawled to Imp One's feet. "It does not matter, sir. Your plot cannot be stopped. You have covered every angle. This decaying carcass is strong in pride and ignorance. There is so much he does not know. Soon, the old one will depart, and The Leader's mission can then be fulfilled."

"You better be right, Imp Two. If wrong, we all burn," Imp One threatened.

Imp Two crept away, wishing he knew how to pray.

Chapter Eleven

Mother Reed hung up the phone and moseyed her way—she never rushed—to the kitchen where she had a cream cheese pound cake baking in the oven. Her lilting voice floated in the air as she hummed about the goodness of Jesus. Slipping her hands into mittens, she took the cake out of the oven. The golden brown cake was perfect, and she smiled in satisfaction. She untied her apron strings and laid the apron over the back of the chair. Shuffling down the hallway, she stopped and looked at her reflection in the mirror. Today she was feeling well, and it showed in the clarity of her eyes and the smoothness of her face. There were no tense frown lines on her brow, and for that, she was grateful.

"Nobody should have to be old and sick," she mused out loud when her phone rang.

It was Esther. After a few minutes of conversation, Mother Reed cut to some real talk. "Esther, I'm glad to know you're still speaking to Mother. After our last conversation, I thought you might be a little peeved with me."

"Oh, I know that you have my best interest at heart, and you gave me some things to look at about myself. I appreciate growth, even when it hurts."

Mother Reed gripped the phone receiver tight before her arthritis caused her to drop it. "Now that's a sign of maturity. Honey, you gon' be just fine. So what can an old lady do you out of this afternoon?"

"How about a little company?"

Mother Reed smiled. "Well, now, I'm right popular today. Reverend is coming by. How 'bout tomorrow?"

"Tomorrow it is. I'll come by after work."

"Sounds good. I'll see you then. I'll even save you a piece of my famous pound cake." Mother Reed knew that would make Esther drool. She loved her some pound cake.

"Did you say pound cake? I'll *definitely* see you tomorrow."

Mother Reed shuffled toward her living room when her doorbell rang.

"Coming," she called out.

When she opened the door, Reverend Gregory entered. "Mother Reed, you are looking mighty good this afternoon."

"Now, Reverend, you trying to charm an old lady?" She looked at Briggs. "Is this handsome young man our temporary pastor?" she beckoned them into her living room.

Briggs offered his hand. "I'm glad to meet you. May I call you Mother Reed?"

"I'd be mad if you didn't. Please, sit down. Tell me a little about yourself." Mother Reed's anointing was so strong that she sensed the greater purpose of his visit before he spoke.

Briggs's body rocked forward. "Well, I was born and reared in Nashville, Tennessee. My parents raised me to love the Lord and to serve Him. I was called to the ministry after college, but like others, it was difficult for me to accept it. I was twenty-four years old when I embraced and surrendered my life to Him."

Mother Reed's smile was appreciative. "I like the fact that you didn't tell me who your daddy was, being the big-time preacher that he is. God bless the child who has his own relationship and knows his purpose. So, how can I help y'all?"

Reverend Gregory spoke in plain terms. "Mother, you know that I love my congregation, but I also know them. We can be a staid bunch when we want to, slow to change and to let others in. I'm hoping you meeting Pastor Stokes today will help him later on."

"I'm glad you didn't try to mince words. So you want my stamp of approval, do you?" Mother Reed cackled with glee.

Reverend Gregory nodded in agreement. "That's about the size of it."

Mother Reed examined Briggs, and he, in turn, considered her. She nodded her head as though she had made a decision, and then rose to her feet. "Let's all go get us a little taste of cake and punch, while I study on this some more."

They followed Mother Reed into her large, airy kitchen. She gestured for them to sit as she uncovered the cake and began to cut and lay slices on the small china plates. Reverend Gregory poured punch into the crystal goblets on the table.

As Mother Reed sat down, she spoke. "I don't like my drink in plastic. I like to have a crystal glass to pretty up the picture. There's enough ugliness in the world today. You gentlemen are looking awful nice, sitting here in my little ol' kitchen. Tell you what, Reverend, leave this young man with me for a couple of hours so we can get acquainted."

Reverend Gregory appeared to like the idea. "That sounds fair. What do you think, Briggs?"

Briggs chewed and swallowed his cake. "I would be honored to stay here and get to know Mother Reed." In obvious enjoyment, he gobbled up the rest of his cake.

"Well, that's settled then. Mother Reed, this is mighty good cake. You know how to make my mouth water, and some of your baking usually does it," Reverend Gregory got up to leave and transferred his cake slice onto a paper napkin.

Both Mother Reed and Briggs walked the reverend to the door. Once alone, they returned to the kitchen.

"You ate that pretty quick. Have another slice," Mother Reed sipped on her punch and looked at him over the rim of her glass. "Well, now, son, anytime you feel like telling me about the lump in the middle of your heart, Mother will be glad to listen."

Briggs looked up shocked and stared at her in silence. She patiently waited. She was used to God using her in strange ways, and she had learned to stay out of His business and just be obedient. She pulled herself up from the table and placed her glass and plate in the sink. Briggs joined her, filled the other side of the double sink with dishwashing liquid, and ran water into the sink. As it filled and bubbles grew, he told his story.

"So where do I begin?" he asked, shutting off the water, and rolling up his sleeves.

"At the beginning," she said. She handed him a dish-cloth to wash the dishes. Then she sat behind him, giving him the space to tell his tale.

"All right. In my senior year of college, I lost my way for a while. I graduated, but it was tough going. I had a major disappointment and felt rejected because of it. Like the prodigal son, I lived a riotous life. I now realize that my behavior was a direct result of me trying to dull the pain. I was promiscuous, and as a result I . . ." Briggs hesitated in his story.

"I'm not judging you, son, I'm just listening," Mother Reed prompted.

"I got someone pregnant." He turned around, waiting to see Mother Reed's reaction.

Mother Reed's countenance held no judgment, and her compassion flowed over him.

Briggs placed the clean plate on the dish rack. "I wasn't stupid. I knew better, but at twenty-three years of age, I thought I was invincible. Nothing bad could happen to me."

"And . . ." Mother Reed encouraged him to continue.

His shoulders drooped. "I wasn't very supportive when the woman told me. I only thought about how it would effect me. My main concern was how I was going to break it to my parents, especially my father. He had high hopes for me, and I was about to disappoint him."

"So you . . ." She wanted him to tell it all.

"It was all taken out of my hands. When I realized how selfish I was being, I went to talk to her, but it was too late. She had gotten an abortion. You see, when I first met her I was bowled over by her good looks. She was a runway phenomenon, a top model who hit it pretty big during her teens. She was raking in the money and men vied for her attention. I needed that ego boost when we were together and everyone was trying to get with her and envying me."

Mother Reed nodded her head that she was listening.

"When she told me about the abortion, it broke me. I tried to talk to her, but she just grumbled and told me I ruined her life. I really hit bottom after that." Briggs's eyes filled with tears.

Mother Reed was still and prayed that he would have the strength to tell it all. "What God reveals, He means to heal," she encouraged.

Briggs sighed. "I went on a partying binge, ended up losing my job, and couldn't half pay my bills. It was a full year of a downward spiral. One day after partying all Saturday night, I woke up face down in my own vomit. It was not a pretty sight. That's when I heard the radio in the background, my R&B station had changed to gospel during the morning, and a minister was preaching his Sunday sermon. He was expounding on all men falling short of the glory of God, and that we as black men needed to get up and not stay in our fallen state. Our families and community needed us."

"Yes, that's right," she added in agreement.

"So I got up, washed up, and then cleaned up. I didn't answer the call that morning, but it was the beginning."

"So, I ask again about the lump in your heart," Mother Reed urged with kindness.

Briggs looked at this feisty petite powerhouse who was like a dog with a bone. He cleared his throat and continued. "When I realized the damage I'd done, I went back to those I had offended to beg their pardon. The list was long, but I got through it. In my attempt to make amends, I began dating the woman that I had gotten pregnant. She was still a hot commodity, and I misunderstood my euphoria of having her temporarily on my arm with the reality of having her permanently in my life. In trying to make matters better, I muddied the waters. That's the lump you see in my heart."

Briggs didn't feel it was right to tell her that in trying to make amends, he had married the woman without loving her, and that was what Monica had never forgiven. He was doing penance for his unborn child and the child's mother.

"Son, deliverance is close for you. I'm glad you were open enough to speak your heart. It doesn't matter who is around. When God wants to move, He always does it with decency and in order. You're safe here."

Briggs nodded his head and began to cry, sobbing out his misery. Mother Reed lifted her hands in prayer. She waited until he quieted before she said, "Son, look at me. I need to share something with you."

Briggs was embarrassed by his display of emotions, but he had been strong for so long that when he felt his release, the floodgates opened and he couldn't push them back. It had been so difficult for him, his father appeared invincible, and all the men of God around him looked infallible. Where was he to turn with his pain?

"You're suffering the weight of rain," she said simply.

Briggs was an intelligent man, but he didn't understand. "The weight of rain?"

"Yes, ya see, when the storms of life rain down on you, they're heavy. So heavy that we start to think that the weight is all we have to look forward to. When that happens, we make decisions from a place of desperation. In most cases, that causes a bigger mess, and the rain gets heavier."

"How do you get out of it?" he asked, seeking answers.

"You don't. What you do is get under the wing of our Father; there is refuge there. And although the rain keeps coming, you're protected, until He sends the rainbow. And when the weight of the rain has lifted, you get to reign. Don't get inpatient during the wait."

Briggs complained. "But the pain makes me feel weak and ineffective."

"Chile, don't let the devil fool you. Cast that fool right out of ya head. Your pain doesn't make you less than, it means you still feeling, still living with an open heart. But it's time for a change, and you have to be tired of something to change it. Mother is so happy to see you coming out of the old and embracing the new. I don't know you so well in the flesh, but in the spirit, I see it. Listen . . . The revelation of a truth may be a bitter pill to swallow, but the effect of the antibiotics is sure to cure the disease. Don't run away from truth; stay in it, and get healed from the scars of deception and the fear of exposure."

Mother Reed stood and placed her hand on Briggs's shoulder. "You know you can lose your mind waiting for your lie to be discovered. Let truth illuminate the darkness, and let the rays of that light bring life to what was once dead. You will find that your burdens will be light and your yoke easy if you just believe in truth. Truth teaches and frees you. Understand that truth brings along its partner in healing—mercy. Together, they destroy the plans of the enemy, turning the tables, making crooked roads straight. You know what? When truth leads you and is the center stone of your life, you gon' be so awesome that the devil is gon' shout . . ." Mother Reed said as she broke into a two-step in her kitchen. She then danced over and pulled meat out of the refrigerator and items out of the cabinets.

Briggs looked at Mother Reed in astonishment. He now knew that he stayed this afternoon for him, not for her. This wonderful woman already knew a lot about him, and flesh and blood did not reveal it. Would she still want someone in his shape to lead Love Zion's congregation? A man who loved his wife, but was never in love with her?

Consequently, he had erected a lie that they were both caught in. Monica's bitterness was present every day, making sure that he paid for failing to give her the love and kind of life she felt she deserved. She had given up a promising career to be his wife. And she never let him forget it. How could he change things around so that the lie they were both living could become the truth that they both needed? He looked to Mother Reed hoping she had the answers.

"Pastor, don't look at Mother like she walks on water. I'm just me, an instrument God chose to use to help set you free. You do have work to do in your life, but I also feel that a man who has been through something has something to offer. Trials and tribulations make us strong; they are the molding of us. I don't want no man leading me who ain't faced a trial or two in his life."

"Amen, to that," Briggs echoed.

"So I suggest we get to work talking a little bit more about all that you've been holding back. While you do that, I'm going to season and flour these pork chops, heat up this frying pan and get us a little supper. Would you like that?"

"Yes, and I want to thank you for allowing the Lord to use you. Somewhere along the way I stopped talking about the real problems in my life. Oh, not that I appeared perfect. I discussed church issues, things relating to wanting to be a better man of God, but not the real things that were going on in my life. You know, a lot of it was due to shame. If I let people know my life wasn't perfect why would they want me to help them with theirs?"

"Whew, I believe that's the enemy's oldest trick. Keep us in the dark, and we get so used to it that the light hurts our eyes, so we avoid it."

"You know you right. Talk to me now," Briggs quipped and did a two-step of his own.

"Right now, we done made the adversary so mad with just this conversation. I bet his imps are paying a heavy price for failing to keep you in the dark," Mother added with glee.

She placed the pork chops in the frying pan and sat down at the table. "Now, go on, Briggs, let's get it all on the table. Don't leave nothing out 'cause Mother got all night. You know what? Call the reverend and excuse yourself from this evening's meeting. God got work for us tonight."

"All right. This was a long time coming. I need to do this for me and for my ministry." Briggs made his call and returned. "Now, Mother Reed, where was I?"

***

The cold, dank, darkness of the cement was slimy from the writhing bodies squirming to and fro. The only alleviation from the blackness was spurts of flames that sizzled as they hit the cold pavement. Noises of agony and shrieks of pain were moaned out in a constant flow heard echoing throughout the tunnel-like area. During the spurts of flame, splatters of blood could be seen on the walls and floors as sounds of whipping ricocheted off the walls.

"You are nothing, you rotting filthy beasts; imbeciles, all of you. Sent to do a job, yet you fail time and time again. How did this happen? Speak, you dung!" The Leader's long solid form raised itself up over the writhing bodies, and venom dripped from his fangs.

"But, Leader," they hissed, "we have done all you asked us. It's that woman; time and time again, she has thwarted us. When will her illness take over?"

They moaned as one, as the invisible licks continued to flail against their scales.

"Do not question me, imps! Do what you are told," The Leader bellowed. "If you fail him again, you will be moved back into the Lake of Fire."

"We will not fail you, Leader," they chorused. "We will go to the Roger creature. He is malleable."

"Then go and wreck havoc," he commanded as they scurried away into the evening.

Chapter Twelve

Roger stretched and sat up in his small rusted iron bed. His sagging mattress gave as he stood up in the dingy, fetid room. His back was sore from lying in a dip in the mattress, and he bent his long, lanky form forward and touched the tips of his fingers to the floor before he straightened and rubbed his face. He could feel the stubble of the spotty beard under his hand. He had once been a handsome man. Now, alcohol, drugs, and hard living had beaten out paths on his face. He shuffled over to his window and looked out into the night. It was dark, but his neighbors liked it that way. Most, like him, were just getting up. He wandered over to his dresser and counted the loose change and crumpled dollars lying there. Taking a swig of the lukewarm forty-ounce beer, he tried to think of who he could hit up for a few bills to tide him over.

"I hate this place; it stinks in here!" he complained as he fell back on his bed. His drink sloshed against him, his rumpled sheet, and the wall as he growled out his annoyance. In his tantrum, the bed frame clanged against the wall, and his neighbor banged back.

"Mother of God—shut up in there! Some of us work for a living," a voice shouted through the paper-thin walls.

The once beautiful Victorian home had long ago been turned into a rooming house, with each decade seeing each room shrink smaller and smaller. Roger couldn't be choosy. He had to live where he could afford to. He remembered when he lived well and his home was the envy of all his friends.

"Phony fools," he groused as he chugged down what was left of his beer.

His mind took the turn it always did when thinking about the past. Sweat ran down his face as he rolled over and banged the ancient heat register. He then pulled his stained T-shirt from over his head, and threw it on the floor with the rest of his discarded clothing. The little room was always too hot or too cold.

"Esther . . . ," he repeated obsessively. His vision of all the things he could do to her, to make her pay, swam through his head. Every year since the divorce he fell deeper into poverty, and his anger and rage grew.

"You shouldn't have left me, Esther," he groused as he turned the bottle up to his lips, and then swore when he realized the bottle was empty. He tossed it into the corner and stared into empty space. As he lay back with his arms behind his head, his arm serpent tattoo faded in and out, illuminated periodically by the neon cross from the building across the street.

Mindless, he swung his arms, fighting invisible demons. His head exploded in small, tiny shards as he held on and tried not to go over the edge. He could feel small licks of pain swirling all around him, and Esther's name reverberated in his mind. In exhaustion, he soon felt himself letting go as he drifted into total darkness.

The small window continued to shine periodic glimpses of light through the torn shade. As his eyes followed the light, they landed on the old building across the street, with its neon cross and the words "Jesus Saves" flickering brightly below it.

Imp Two stood against the wall clapping in glee. "The thoughts you sent were brilliant. He blames everyone for his problems. I love this guy."

Imp One stood over Roger's bed looking for flaws in his plan. "He is simple, but his drug and alcohol abuse make him unreliable."

"Look at him . . . Even full grown demons would find him ugly." Imp Two climbed onto the bed and lay across from Roger, making faces at him.

Imp One watched irritated with Imp Two's antics. This is who he was assigned to work with, and The Leader expected brilliance! "You are a nitwit. You are a pea brain. You are an imbecile," he hissed.

Imp Two jumped from the bed. "But . . . I thought we were getting along so well. The Leader hates us both. We can be a team; Batman and Robin, the Lone Ranger and Tonto."

Imp One spoke as he slithered through the wall. "Beauty and the Beast. Beast, visit our ace in the hole, Monica. We need her on board. This plan cannot fail."

Imp Two frowned. "I wouldn't be the beast, you would be the beast. I am beautiful."

Imp Two's feelings were hurt, and he slithered out the wall opposite Imp One. He lifted into the air, his anger not derailing his assignment. He was still headed south to Monica, and her ultimate destruction.

Monica stretched and looked at the clock. She sauntered into the bathroom, trailing her see-through, chiffon peignoir behind her. Her milk chocolate skin glowed from its life of pampering, and its supple silkiness was satin to the touch, comparable to the ribbon along a newborn baby's blanket. Her luxurious mane of dark hair flowed like the Congo River in the deepest jungle of Africa, and it dipped and waved, ending midway down her back. She bent forward, shook her hair, and twisted and pinned the tresses atop her head. She was vain about her hair. It was a part of her heritage from her Jamaican Pentecostal great-grandmother. It had never been cut, only trimmed. Once, during a cancer campaign, Briggs had suggested she cut it. She quaked with resentment just thinking about it. "He's such a fool."

As she stepped into the shower, a pale hand closed over her upper arm. "Hey, you sneaking out on me, again?" a cultured Southern voice asked.

"Sugar, it's two in the morning. How does it look me creeping in at all hours of the night?" she reached, pulling shower gel from the shelf.

Randall took it from her and squeezed some onto a sponge. "I care about you. It's late, he's not in town; stay. Please, Monica. You just told me you may be moving out of town for a while. I love you. How am I supposed to handle that?"

He threw down the sponge and grabbed her around her waist. He turned them toward the mirror that was fogged by the shower's hot water. He wiped the mirror clear. Revealed was a couple whose faces touched as their eyes showed passion never before experienced by either of them. Nothing else mattered; not race, their marriages, or their backgrounds. The love they felt they found was all that mattered to them.

"Randall, I told you, I stalled him. I demanded an expensive place to live. Believe me, with his tight pockets that will take a while. In the meantime, you need to handle the problems in your own life. Namely, your wife and children."

She rubbed her hand down the side of his face to minimize her scolding. His was a handsome face, aristocratic in its bearing. He was a man of means, and it showed.

Randall caressed Monica's hand and held it to his lips. His lips trailed over her face and down her neck, where he slowly kissed on her bare shoulder. His hands traveled over her as he pulled her closer. "Enough talk," he growled.

Monica's eyes drifted shut as they backed out of the room and fell onto the king-size bed. The running shower's steam joined the combustible heat the couple made as heinous dark shadows danced in frenzied orchestration against the backdrop of a fading night.

Chapter Thirteen

Briggs was home. His time with Mother Reed was well spent. He was feeling unburdened, his yoke destroyed of past indiscretions. He wanted to talk to Monica, guilt free. He phoned her, but she didn't pick up.

Briggs left her a voice mail. "Hi, baby, it's around ten o'clock. Sorry, I missed you. I just wanted to hear your voice. Call me. I love you, bye."

After his shower, Briggs placed his cell phone next to his pillow and lay down. He knew he had early-morning meetings, but he didn't want to miss Monica's call.

Light streamed through a crack in Briggs's bedroom curtains, his hand fumbled around in an effort to locate the ringing phone. He clutched the cell and flipped it open. "Hello?" he asked groggily.

"Hello, hello," came the resounding answer.

"Monica? What time is it?" he asked as he sat up in his bed and pulled back the cover.

"I don't know. It's early," she said defensively.

"I'm sorry, honey. I looked for you to call me last night, that's all." Briggs struggled to get up.

Monica's voice cracked across the airwaves. "So . . . do you want to talk to me or not? I've been so alone lately that I needed to get out of the house. I went to the movies. Do you mind?"

Briggs didn't like the direction of the conversation. His heart moved to redirect it. "Sweetheart, I want to talk to you. Last night, I had a powerful time with God. All due to one of our Love Zion members. Wait 'til you meet her; she's so anointed."

Monica smacked her lips into the phone. "Her? I'm here alone and you're off spending time with female members of the church? You know in my modeling days I was always the belle of the ball; now I'm just the ball and chain."

"You could never be anyone's ball and chain. Monica, she's eighty years old, and you know me better than that. Come on, honey, let's not fight. There's been too much of that. Did you get my message? I miss you," Briggs said turning on the charm.

Monica huffed. "Since when?"

Briggs turned up the heat. "Every day, sweetheart. Think you can arrange to come up for the weekend? We can do something fun, just the two of us."

Monica resisted being agreeable. "No, Briggs, I can't just leave things here to come there and hold your hand. I'm busy packing and trying to find the right replacements on all the committees I chair."

Briggs was wearing himself out just to have a decent phone conversation. "I understand you're busy. It was just a suggestion, but if we're ever going to turn our marriage around, it will take the two of us to do it."

"Everything is not on your schedule, Briggs. Work on you. Oh yeah, have a blessed day." Monica slammed down the phone.

Briggs scratched the morning new growth on his chin, slammed the pillow with his fist, and flopped back down on the bed. "What did I say?"

***

Monica looked down at the phone. "Blast it!"

She leaned back in the kitchen chair and considered her options. Randall had been insistent last night about bringing her home and meeting her today to pick up her car. In a moment of weakness, she had agreed, and now she worried about someone seeing them together. It was bad enough that she had to walk down to the corner to meet him. She had the added dilemma of how to hide one of the most powerful movers and shakers in Atlanta. And, people still recognized her, even though they had the nerve to walk right up to her and ask her where she'd been—as though she owed the little nobodies an answer. Now, Briggs was changing their dynamics and being nice. It made her feel guilty and nervous.

She needed to remain cautious. After their first couple of meetings in public, Randall had moved them into a lavish suite at the Ritz Carlton. He was a man of style, and she appreciated the way he treated her. She always arrived and left separately. Except for yesterday, their system worked.

She nibbled on her finger. She hadn't prayed since Briggs left. When he wasn't watching her, she did what she wanted to. Monica grimaced. She asked herself the questions: What if God is real? Will I be punished for my sins?

When she first met Briggs, he was all busted up over some little girl who had left him high and dry in college. The boy was fronting like he wasn't all torn up. But his drunken monologues were all about some chick named Esther. They were never about God.

He was fun, wild, and fine as could be though. She knew his background. She knew he was a world renown televangelist's son, and he came from money. His father's television appearances, movies, books, and tapes had made him wealthy. It was only reasonable to think the son inherited what the father had acquired. At the time, she needed him, or someone like him. She was no longer a teenager, and her constant tantrums and diva attitude had worn thin on the modeling circuit, and her contracts were drying up. All she had left when she met Briggs was her make-believe industry buzz. She saw he was feeling all the attention he got when she was on his arm, so she played it to the max. When she told Briggs she was pregnant, she thought he would do the right thing. When he didn't, she got so mad, she'd slashed the tires to his Honda Accord and broke out his windows. Fool never did realize it was her getting revenge.

Two months later he came running to her apartment asking if he could talk to her about their baby. She was so angry that she told him she had gotten an abortion. His dejected face was all she needed to set her in a good mood. If he wasn't marrying her, a little money to keep her and a baby in her preferred lifestyle was just not making it.

Besides, she had never been pregnant in the first place.

Chapter Fourteen

Mother Reed and Esther sat in her kitchen finishing their cake. Esther looked good; her face fresh and glowing, her makeup impeccable, and the pale pink jogging suit was lovely on her, accentuating the positive features in her figure and camouflaging the negative.

Esther smiled in appreciation and said with her mouth half full of cake, "Ummm, so good . . . how've you been?"

"Oh, baby, Mother's been fine."

Esther licked her fingers. "Anywhere you'd like to go today? I don't have to be at church until four o'clock, so we have time."

Mother Reed's smile widened. It was just like Esther to be so attentive. "No, baby, but it would be great if we could sit and play a game of Scrabble."

Esther flicked her hand in the air. "So you can beat me, like I stole something again?"

"Now, don't be a spoilsport. Look over in the buffet cabinet and bring the game here. It's time to teach a young lady some manners."

Esther left the room and was quick to return. As she set up the game, Mother Reed put on her bifocals and rubbed her hands together. She loved keeping her brain agile. "Esther, have you found that special young man yet?"

"No, ma'am. But you'll be glad to know that I finally opened my heart to the possibilities of having someone. I've even done a little daydreaming."

"All God needs is a willing heart. Don't worry, he's coming soon," Mother Reed said as she placed letters on the Scrabble board spelling out her first word. She looked up at Esther through her lowered lids. "You remember I was close to your grandmother?"

"Yes." Esther was searching out her word on the game board.

"Good, God-fearing woman. Me and my Anthony, her and your grandfather, we used to have some good times together." Mother Reed was fond of those memories.

"That's nice," Esther squinted focusing on the game board.

Mother Reed pushed the game board aside for a moment. "When you were little you hated your name. Do you remember that?"

Esther sat back looking skyward. "Yes, it was old-fashioned. I wanted a cute name like the other girls."

"Do you remember what your grandmother told you?" Mother Reed rubbed Esther's hand to make sure she was listening.

Esther's face creased with concentration. "Something about my purpose and how I would have authority over darkness."

Esther's grandmother passed when she was ten years old, and she was so spiritual toward the end that half the time, Esther didn't understand what she was talking about. She remembered that after some people visited, her grandmother shook her fist at the shadows on the walls and rebuked them. Then the house seemed to get real light. She would mumble about people not living right and spirits being left in her house.

"Your grandmama was a wise woman. Ooh, I miss that girl. When your mama was pregnant with you, she wasn't in the church. We called it backsliding then. Your grandmama and I began to pray and fast for her and your daddy to come back to the Lord. Baby, it was during all this praying that your grandmama prophesied your birth and that you would be named Esther."

"I do know the story of Esther in the Bible."

"Did you understand that scripture says Esther won the favor of everyone who saw her? Baby, there is power in favor. This was a woman of faith, courage, loyalty, and obedience. She could have used her favor for her own good, but she used it for the good of her people. She's your namesake; there's a reason you are in social services and a reason you are so active in the ministry."

Esther nodded. "Yeah, most of the time, I love my job."

"That's not why I'm telling you all this, chile," she said, somewhat exasperated.

"I'm listening," Esther said in a rush.

Mother Reed tapped her. "Hear me good, little girl."

Esther felt a sense of anticipation.

A commanding voice floated out of Mother Reed's small frame. "The time is coming when the Esther in you will rise. You have been positioned for such a time as this. You will be raised up as an instrument of God to avert the destruction of the church and its work. Thus said the Lord."

Mother Reed noted Esther's look of uncertainty. She smiled and pulled the board game back. "Let's finish this game, daughter. I know that ya have things to do. I do so 'preciate ya time," Mother Reed knew that when the time came, Esther would remember what she said. She had planted the seed; God would see to the increase. She just wanted to be there to help guide Esther through the crucial moments.

Briggs was reading when he saw a pale flash of pink pass by. He went into the hallway as Esther entered Reverend Gregory's office. He told himself he was headed down there because he needed to remind him of something, not to see Esther. As he entered, the Reverend and Esther were already in conversation.

"So you see, it's going to be important not to miss the deadline on both of these buildings," Esther said.

Reverend Gregory held out a piece of paper. "Our problems are deeper than that; look at this letter."

Esther read over its contents. She looked up flabbergasted and noticed Briggs standing in the doorway. She acknowledged him with a nod before she began a rant against the writers of the letter. "We are in violation of zoning laws? We went through all the proper procedures to get the transition house opened. They can't do this," she exploded.

"They can, and they have. What an awful time for me to be leaving town." Reverend Gregory looked up and waved Briggs over. "Come on in, Briggs. We have a hornet's nest dropping into our laps."

"What's happened?" he asked. Esther handed him the letter to read.

"Can you call the mayor's office and ask for a meeting?" Esther paced agitated by the news.

"I did call him. This is the week of the gang summit and he's out, but they promised to let him know when he checks in that I need to speak with him."

Esther whipped around in the small space. "And you're leaving at the end of next week?"

Reverend Gregory wiped the perspiration off his balding head. "I have to. On top of everything else, the doctors called and we really need to be with Jeanette right now."

Esther stopped and touched the reverend in compassion. "We're praying for her."

"Sir, I won't let you down. Leave this with Esther and me," Briggs said. "I pray that your faith faileth not. God is not going to let the adversary take something as vital as our transition program. Those families need decent housing. It brings them the opportunity for a new life. Whatever force is coming against it, it will fail." Briggs prophesied with fervor.

"Speak life, son, speak life," Reverend Gregory raised his hand in solidarity.

Esther clapped. "Here, here." She applauded Briggs determination to take charge and steer them into clear water. "I sit on boards with people who may help. I'll make some calls. I thought when we held all the open community forums, that we had addressed all of their concerns about that 'element' moving into their neighborhood. This zoning problem is just a way to keep certain people out. I see it every day at work."

"Don't worry," Briggs placed his arm around Esther's shoulder.

Reverend Gregory advised them that he had a busy day ahead. He reminded them that they all needed to do what they could to begin to mitigate the damage that the letter was already doing. He had been fielding phone calls all morning from concerned church members and family members of residents of the homes. It seemed some duty-bound citizen put the word out on the street that the housing program was in trouble.

"Esther, Briggs, I expect you both to work on this night and day and get this thing turned around. I'm counting on you," he said and waved them out the door. Before they could leave, Reverend Gregory was already taking a phone call.

"Let's go down to my office and strategize a plan of attack. Since you know all the key players, you'll be instrumental in helping me to know the best approach to take with each of them," Briggs said to Esther as they left the reverend's office.

Esther moved ahead of Briggs. But before they could reach his office, Reverend Gregory's door swung open and he stepped out, calling both their names. His face had gone pale. "That was Mother Reed's neighbor. Mother was just rushed to the hospital. It looks bad!"

Esther and Briggs exchanged looks of horror and took off running toward the stairs. "I'll meet you there," they heard Reverend Gregory yell as they ran down the church hallway and out into the parking lot.

The Leader stood in the shadows of the ambulance, watching Mother Reed labor for breath. He swayed back and forth on the curve of his elongated body, sending out signals of distraction to the paramedics. As the machine beeped a solid line, he swayed faster, knowing that his mission for the old woman was almost finished.

Mother Reed could feel the presence of the outsider near her. She clutched a small, worn piece of paper in her hand, and began to battle in her spirit against the powers that sought to ensnare her. She would not let them take her without a fight. Her mind was clear, and her purpose was unfinished. She knew what awaited her on the other side and was not afraid to sleep, but it was not time to get weary in well-doing. She began to reach deep into her spirit and call on Jesus.

The Leader felt coldness center on his heated scales, a soft sigh was blown into his inner ear, and he retched at the thought of an angel's breath touching him. Knowing who had entered, he reared forward to protect what he felt was rightfully his. He swung his large head around and raised his pointed tail. Angels three deep lined the small ambulance. They advanced toward him, so he lurched against the panels of the van and passed to the other side. As he stood in the road looking after the vehicle, he continued stealthily toward the hospital. He was not giving up.

Chapter Fifteen

Hearts racing, two anxious people flew through the double doors of the emergency room at Henry Ford Hospital.

Esther's steps faltered. She was back in a hospital. A dark tomb of a cold structure she hadn't entered since Sheri's untimely death. This arctic breathing, concrete torture chamber designed to take loved ones and leave devastation in its wake. It claimed to help the sick, but few people she knew who entered ever left. It was a selfish lover, taking but rarely giving back. First in its iron clutches her beloved grandmother and father, then Sheri, and now it wanted Mother Reed.

She slowed to a halt and watched as Briggs approached the desk and inquired about Mother Reed's condition. Her hands tightly clenched in an effort to control the erratic thumping of her heart.

Briggs turned and was surprised to see Esther still near the entrance. Her face pink flushed and perspiration glistened across her forehead. His long-legged gait disposed of the space between them. He covered both her clenched hands with his.

"You okay?" he asked. "We'll find something out soon. The unit clerk is checking on her now."

"I just need a minute," she said short of breath. "I'm worried about Mother Reed, but I'm also a little squeamish about hospitals."

"Let's pray, and then all other concerns will fade." Briggs escorted Esther over to the waiting area where they could pray in private.

Both failed to notice several Love Zion members as they entered the hospital lobby.

"Sister Wiley, Sister Wiley," Deacon Clement rushed toward them, his toupee slipping forward in his haste.

Esther snatched her hands from Briggs's grasp. She couldn't remember when he had taken hold of her. Briggs frowned at her actions, but remained silent.

Esther faced Deacon Clement. "Deacon Clement . . . You've heard?"

"Yes, yes. We came as soon as we could," He dabbed his handkerchief across his head, secretly straightening his toupee in the process.

Sister Abigail Winters stood next to Deacon Clement. She scrutinized Esther, then Briggs with furrowed eyebrows. Although this was a solemn occasion, Abigail was Love Zion's consummate mudslinging gossip maven.

"We are so very sorry about Mother Reed, dear. We all know how close the two of you were. I mean, are . . ." Abigail snidely remarked as she inched closer to Esther and Briggs.

"Thank you, Sister Abigail. We all love her, and we know that God is able," Esther sniffled with disdain. She wished a hole would open in the floor to consume Abigail and her faithless comments.

Abigail dismissed Esther—there was no love lost there—as she focused her attention on Briggs. "Yes, yes. Is this your young man? He is a handsome one. You've been holding out on us."

Esther's face was flush, and she stammered to answer, but Briggs stepped in.

"Hello, as a matter of fact, I'm Pastor Stokes, your interim pastor. I'm sorry we're meeting at such a grave time, but I'm glad to see the love that is evident between the members of Love Zion." Briggs's gaze was intense as he placed emphasis on the word *love*.

Deacon Clement briskly shook Briggs's hand. "Welcome, son, welcome. I was under the weather when the deacon board met you. We're glad you're here."

Abigail studied Esther and Briggs. Deacon Clement knew by the expression on Abigail's face that something was not to her liking. Esther, having experienced Abigail's rumor mill before, also saw the wheels turning in her devious mind.

Esther was priming for a fight. She couldn't wait for God to deliver Abigail from her messiness. She was about to derail Abigail's mudslinging by explaining why Briggs was holding on to her when her parents arrived. She breathed a sigh of relief because if anybody could handle Abigail, it was her mother.

"Esther, how is Mother Reed?" her mother asked as she anxiously approached.

Esther's father stood close waiting for her answer.

"Mama, we haven't . . ." Esther began to sniffle . . . she had just been with Mother Reed.

Briggs held out his hand to Mr. Wiley. "We haven't heard anything yet. Sir, my name is Briggs Stokes. I'm the new interim pastor for Love Zion."

Mr. Wiley shook his hand. "Good to meet you, young man. Sorry it was today. We love Mother Reed like our own. When things get a little less hectic, we'll have to sit down and get to know each other." His grip was strong like the man.

"Thank you, sir, I'd like that." Briggs took measure of Mr. and Mrs. Wiley—both attractive people. They looked as he had imagined all those years ago.

Mr. Wiley placed a supporting arm around Elizabeth. "And this is my wife, Elizabeth Wiley."

"Mrs. Wiley." Briggs took her hand and bowed his head in acknowledgment of the introduction.

Mrs. Wiley patted his hand and gave him a sincere smile.

Abigail loomed over their introductions. "Oh my goodness, haven't you two met the new pastor, Sister Wiley?" Not giving them time to answer, Abigail continued. "He and Esther looked so close, why . . . we mistook him for her young man."

Esther knew her mother was an old hand at church politics and had a Ph.D. in the shenanigans of Abigail Winters. Abigail was in her usual somber colors, gray or black. Today, she sported a gray polyester pantsuit that sagged on her thin frame. Her cast iron-gray hair was in an old-fashioned French roll, and her pinched mouth was turned downward in its customary fashion. Only her eyes were alive, stone black and piercing with interest.

"Abigail, I'm glad that you are now better informed," Mrs. Wiley said, dismissing her; then she turned to the others. She sensed it was time they joined the real struggle at hand. "I feel that we all need to be praying for Mother Reed. I feel urgency in my spirit that the time is now."

Her urgency reminded everyone why they had gathered as Briggs led them in prayer for the recovery of Mother Reed.

Lights chased across the face of the small monitor screen as it foretold Mother Reed's condition with small steady beeps. The doctor stood in the corner discussing the need for bypass surgery with a cardiologist.

As The Leader stood unnoticed in the background, he fumed at the turn of events in the lobby. He had sent fear in to stir up Esther's memory and to prevent her from focusing on Mother Reed.

The Leader knew that self-absorption had derailed many miracles in the making. But, Briggs's reassurance and Elizabeth's spiritual discernment cast out all fear. As a backup, he rounded up Abigail Winters, one of his best church workers. She was usually able to stir up trouble everywhere she went.

Abigail's unhappy childhood kept her gnawing at the happiness of others. Yet, love overcame bitterness, and even the old hag prayed for Mother Reed. He had forgotten the time Mother Reed had nursed Abigail back to health when no one else cared.

He began to feel faint and sickly. The essence of sweet perfumed prayers was getting to him. He called to his minions and demanded they stay, while he went down into the tunnels so he could be refreshed. They squawked but obeyed as he sent scalding licks of fire against their faces.

He entered the dark, dank earth and slithered back and forth, unsure if he would win this round. He needed a new game plan; he was losing too many battles lately, and the master was not pleased with him. He knew one thing; before he was sent back to the pits, he would destroy everything in his path, including all the fools in the lobby.

The number of people in the hospital waiting area had multiplied in the last hour. Everyone who loved Mother Reed was in attendance and in prayer for her recovery.

Reverend Gregory pushed up from his kneeling position and quieted his members. "Saints, I can feel the peace of the Lord with me now. Mother Reed will be all right. No matter the outcome, she's in God's hands."

"Yes . . . mmmm, in God's hands," Deacon Clement echoed.

"While so many of our church's faithful are gathered here, let me make introductions. Some of you have already met Pastor Stokes. He's a fine, godly young man and will lead you well in my absence," Reverend Gregory held out his arm for Briggs to come forward.

Abigail moved around the crowd whispering small words to small minds.

Briggs smiled and acknowledged everyone. But, Reverend Gregory saw when Abigail passed by, faces changed from welcoming to disapproving.

Reverend Gregory knew his people well, including Sister Abigail. But, there were times when a pastor's intervention caused even more dissension. He looked over at his wife. They had been married so long that First Lady Gregory knew her husband's desires just by looking at him.

"We're all so grateful to the Honorable Bishop Stokes for loaning us his assistant pastor, and son," First Lady Gregory advised everyone.

The room became a buzz of conversation. As intended, those who were ready to snub Briggs stopped when they realized who his father was. Many of them had stood in the back of coliseums among thousands, just to hear his rousing and passionate sermons. His son was to be their interim pastor? Wait until they called their friends. . . .

Briggs saw the faces of those before him change instantly. He was saddened that once again it was his father's name that opened doors, not his own relationship with God. Inside his hurt, he searched for the one face that could sooth his wounded ego—Esther.

Once Abigail's intentions were clear, Esther moved to the background. She was the center of hurtful rumors when she was married to Roger, and she vowed never to have her business in the church community again. Esther learned through that experience that everyone shouting, "Hallelujah!" wasn't heaven bound.

She felt Briggs's hurt, but to go to her friend and ease his pain with a kind word and a soothing touch would only make matters worse. She could only send silent waves of comfort and hope he received them.

Mrs. Wiley walked forward and opened her arms to Briggs. "I want to welcome you again. We, at Love Zion, pride ourselves on our friendliness and kindness. My husband and I are here for you as are the rest of our family."

"Especially Esther," Sister Abigail whispered, though she said it loud enough for most to hear.

"Yes, of course, Esther, Phyllis, and my son-in law, Charles, are all faithful members of Love Zion, and more important, of God's will in our lives. We're at your service."

Abigail frowned at the rebuke she received from Elizabeth's comments. She crossed her arms and clamped her mouth shut at the snickers she heard at her expense.

"Let them laugh," she mumbled. "I saw those two, and something was up, and I aim to be watching them."

Chapter Sixteen

Phyllis's heels clicked through the solemn hall of the hospital. She had been out of touch yesterday, and she received the voice mail that Mother Reed was in the hospital today. She felt bad that she and Charles had both missed being here. She was thankful that the voice mail from Esther relayed Mother Reed's condition. She was out of danger, and she could now have a few visitors. Phyllis was hoping she could be one of them. She wasn't as close to Mother Reed as her sister, but she loved her.

Phyllis entered the room and saw Mother Reed's small frame encased in hospital white.

"Come in, darling. Mother is still here," she heard her raspy voice state.

Phyllis pressed her hands together. "Praise the Lord you are talking, Mother."

Mother Reed teased, "Well, chile, Mother been talking pert near seventy-nine years now."

Phyllis smiled. She knew if Mother's humor was intact, all was well. She pulled her chair up to her bed. "I'm glad it was only a mild heart attack. You rest, I'll just sit here and read you some scriptures. Prayer changes things. I don't want you to tire yourself out trying to talk."

Mother Reed slowly pointed to a book on her table. "Read that to me," she instructed.

Phyllis looked at the book, *Joy* by Victoria Christopher Murray. "Isn't this a romance?"

Mother Reed sighed. "Yes, you have a problem with that?"

"Well, Mother Reed, I'm just a little surprised, that's all. This is fantasy, and I would have never thought that the mother of our church would be engaging in this kind of activity," Phyllis chided, forgetting Mother Reed's condition.

Mother Reed struggled to a semi-sitting position. Phyllis looked horrified. She had overstepped her boundaries.

"Phyllis, you make my backside hurt!" Mother Reed said exasperated. "How in the world did you become such a critical young woman?"

Phyllis was alarmed that Mother Reed was expending too much energy to chastise her. Reprimanded, she grabbed the book and began to read.

Mother Reed decided to let the subject drop. She leaned back and listened to the story, amazed at Phyllis's wonderful voice. It was soothing and expressive. Soon, she drifted off to sleep. Later, when Mother Reed woke, Phyllis was sitting in the same chair reading feverishly.

Mother Reed cleared her throat. "Um, you still here?"

Sheepish, Phyllis held up the book. "It's not what I thought. It's a good story."

"Yes, I like a good story. You can't always be in the Bible, even though it is the best book I know." Mother Reed smoothed out her bedding, her eyes focused on Phyllis.

Phyllis hung her head in shame. "I'm sorry I sounded so self-righteous."

Mother Reed decided to be frank. "Well, I know you have some hurts, and sometimes that causes us to be discontented with everything in our life."

Phyllis glared at Mother Reed like she had no idea what she was talking about.

Mother Reed glared back and pronounced, "No harm in admitting you're not perfect, Phyllis. It will really make ya free."

In a fit of pique, Phyllis stood. "Mother, what are you talking about? Please explain."

"You and Charles both want a child. Sweetie, some nights you cry from the aching." Mother Reed shook her head, weary from their pain.

Phyllis gasped at Mother Reed's observation. Had others seen their gnawing desire? Her need?

"Shall I go on?" Mother Reed asked. Phyllis's permission was needed to go down this road.

Phyllis's eyes watered as her knees weakened and she sat. "Please."

"The abortion didn't cause this. God is not punishing you. He—"

Phyllis bolted from her chair and ran out of the room. She saw some church members walking toward her and headed down the nearest stairwell. She stopped after running down two flights of stairs and collapsed on the landing in uncontrollable sobs. She was so ashamed. How could Mother Reed know her secret?

"I'm sorry. God, I'm so sorry," she cried into the empty stairwell.

Mother Reed cursed her infirmity. There was a time she could have sprinted after Phyllis and finished what she had started.

"This medication has my brain rattled," she whispered, "otherwise, I would have said that a lot better."

The door to her room opened abruptly, and Mother Reed was glad Phyllis came back.

"Look at you, Mother Reed, sitting up and all," Abigail said as she entered with two other church sisters.

Lord, deliver me from evil, Mother Reed thought. She needed to finish what she started with Phyllis, and the enemy had just jumped into her camp. Mother Reed looked over at Abigail and immediately felt tired. She refused to call her sister until she became one. This woman had so many emotional cuts and bruises that she tried the most diligent of saints.

"How are you, Abigail?"

"What's more important is how you are," Abigail said in a syrupy sweet voice.

Mother Reed angled her head to see Abigail's eyes. "Well, the good Lord has seen fit to keep me. So I'm blessed."

"You caused all of us some new gray hair. Why, I bet you almost everyone from church has been through here in the last couple of days. We even got to meet the new, young, handsome, interim pastor. He and Esther were both right here, together, so worried about you," she gushed.

Mother Reed knew Abigail smelled blood, and like a bloodhound, she would sniff the trail 'till it led her to her prey.

She turned to Abigail's companions. "How y'all doing? Y'all all right?"

They answered together, "Yes, ma'am." Janie, the younger of the two blurted, "We're just so glad to see you sitting up and talking, Mother. We thought you was dead for sure."

Abigail gasped at the sister's comment. Mother Reed couldn't help smirking. She knew that Abigail really hated being with the sisters—as everyone called them—because both were about a Coke short of a six-pack, but they were all she had.

"Janie, Essie!" Abigail barked at both women.

They jumped and looked startled by her outburst. "What?" they chorused.

Abigail's answer was interrupted by the duty nurse entering the room. "I'm sorry, ladies, but you all will have to leave now. Mrs. Reed has to have her rest."

Mother Reed did somersaults in her head as she leaned forward so that the nurse could fluff her pillows. "Thank y'all for coming," Mother Reed said merrily.

The demons crowded Mother Reed's door. They had gained entrance through Abigail, but couldn't come any closer. Mother Reed's hedge of protection was in place. They scurried in retreat when the three women left the anointed one's room. They would report that their enemy was yet with them. The Leader would not be happy and someone would pay.

The clock ticked, as the large scaly tail moved back and forth in time to its beat. Minions scurried back and forth, bringing large pails of scalding water and adding it to the strong sulfur mix on the steaming rocks. The Leader inhaled and felt better after purging his senses of the sweet perfume that earlier filled his air. He stared at the clock, an invention to monitor time, necessitated because of the fall of mankind. He frowned at the pile of ashes by his feet and kicked the remains of the messenger who brought him bad news. He had not taken the news well when his imps reported they had failed to sabotage Mother Reed's recovery. Somehow, even her doctors and nurses were not open to their evil thoughts. Abigail had been of no real help. He was hopeful that her obsession with throwing dirt on Briggs and Esther would turn people against them. It didn't matter what was invented; dirt thrown even haphazardly still clung.

Time was running out. If he didn't make a strong move soon, all would be lost. He could feel the spiritual hedge of protection getting stronger, and he knew he needed to hurry. His next steps would be tricky, but he knew that they would work if everyone held true to the fallen nature of man's character. However, he knew from experience, sometimes man surprised even him. Humans were funny that way. Right when you had them pegged; they did something crazy, like . . . getting saved when they weren't in trouble, committing self-sacrifice, or standing for good.

This time he was sure that all would be well in his world. He would simply line everything up, as perfectly as he could, and afterward, sit back and watch the confusion and chaos unfold. In the meantime, he had a gangster rap concert to cover. Lately, some of the stars had actually sought out God and moved over to His camp. See? You couldn't trust humans. You just had to keep throwing confusion in their path and hope for the best. They were changeable creatures, all of them.

Chapter Seventeen

The Spirit of Confusion and Chaos was mad with power. The prince of the air had allowed it full reign. It ran to and fro, seeking those caught in weak and inane moments. It was their lack of faith that fed it. It was now airborne, traveling from house to city. It was hungry to be fed, and the victims never mattered. Today, Esther, Briggs, Monica, and Randall would all feel its teeth.

This was Esther's "shouldn'a got out of bed, 'cause I sho' is weary in this here well-doing kinda day." By her mood it should have been raining; instead, it was a beautiful end of summer, sunshine marathon, and the devil was beating on her, instead of his wife. Love Zion's properties had trouble brewing with the zoning commission, and church folk was stirred up over mess that Abigail had spread like manure in planting season. Her mother's phone was ringing off the hook with insinuations concerning her and Briggs being in a relationship. Mind you, Esther wasn't ruling anything out, but a girl had to be asked before she could get on the floor and dance. She shook her cup and gobbled ice to stay cool, crunching cubes under her forceful chews. Suddenly, her forehead crinkled as she was assaulted with jumbled reflections that landed on one horrific thought. What if Briggs heard the rumors too?

The pen flowed furiously over the paper until the pressure punctured a hole in the yellow-lined notepad. Briggs ripped out the page, balled it up, and threw it toward the waste basket. It landed next to the dozen other balled up papers on the floor. His Sunday message was not getting completed early. From his desk he could see the sun was shining outside, but it was cloudy with a one hundred percent chance of rain in his office. With all the outrageous comments he overheard in passing, he needed Monica to get over herself and come to Detroit yesterday. How could people have him having an affair by just seeing him talk to someone? And what about the one where he was seen coming out of a seedy motel? He wouldn't even entertain defending such garbage.

He knew he should have told everyone a long time ago that he was married, but he had requested Reverend Gregory to keep his personal business private. He had lived in a glass bowl all his life, first as the son, then as the husband. He just wanted people to know him, the man, and the pastor. It might have helped his explanation to everyone that he was never hiding his marriage if he wore his ring. However, it was gaudy with diamonds and gold nuggets protruding from it and the heaviness was uncomfortable when he was working at his desk. Monica wouldn't hear of a more modest style. As a result, it was more off, than on. Since moving here without her constant nagging to put it on, it was definitely more off.

Initially, his idea was that people get to know him without the fawning and adoration that came from being associated with his father and/or Monica. People still came up to him after he preached a sermon and after a brief nicety concerning his message, spent all of their time asking how it felt to be the son or husband of someone so famous. Never mind that Monica hadn't modeled in years. Or, they wanted to know if his father was coming to town soon.

His plan would have been feasible, but Monica was never supposed to take this long to join him. The longer she took, the longer he put off telling people. His pride didn't want to admit his wife was not the dutiful, submissive type. He was more than aware that "pride goeth before a fall," and that he was tittering on the brink of disaster.

Now, in retrospect, it all looked wrong. When he made the decision to withhold his familial connections, he had no idea that Esther lived here, or that they would be working so closely together. Everything was a mess, and without Monica's presence, it would be difficult to clear it all up. It was time she made an appearance.

The Spirit of Confusion reveled in the chaos. In Atlanta, it peeked into the bathroom where it saw Monica soaking. As he ushered in an ill wind, he wondered if she and her lover ever left the bed or bathroom.

Monica soaked in the Jacuzzi, her painted toes bobbing above the waterline. She smiled as Randall rubbed his face back and forth across her satiny skin, inhaling her fragrance. He was a man living his desires.

"Stop, Randall!" she squealed.

"You know that's not what you want," he challenged.

"Boy, I'm not playing with you," she countered as she laughed playfully and kicked him away.

Randall climbed into the water, and they continued their fun until her cell phone rang in the adjoining room. He placed a protective hand around her arm. "Don't answer it."

Monica's eyes narrowed, pinpointing his hand on her arm. "Now you know I can't do that, and you certainly didn't bother to turn yours off earlier."

He squeezed her once and removed his hand. "I'll get it for you," he sighed, jumped out of the water, and jogged into the bedroom. When he returned cell in hand, he had a robe wrapped around him, and the ringing had stopped.

Monica was sitting on the chaise lounge toweling herself dry. She reached for her cell and checked the caller ID. The name under the number read Love Zion. "It's Briggs. A little privacy please while I return this call."

"All right, but don't be long. Besides, you always use speakerphone when you're completing your bath. I could just stand outside the door and listen, but I'm better than that." Randall pulled the door closed as he backed out of the room.

Monica smirked as she tapped out the number. She wasn't fooled. She knew Randall was at the door listening. "Hello, Briggs?"

"Good, you saw I called. How you doing, baby?"

"I'm fine. Was there a particular reason you called?" Monica was cordial but stiff.

"Can't a man miss his beautiful wife?"

Monica glanced at the closed door. "Sure. But, I'm kind of busy right now. I was working with some of the volunteers at Faith Cathedral when you called."

"Oh, really? What do you guys have planned?"

"We're planning a summer fund-raiser to assist incarcerated women in reuniting with their children." The lie flowed out of her mouth, smooth as churned butter.

"Honey, that sounds wonderful. You did let them know that you wouldn't be around to complete the project, didn't you?"

Monica crossed her bare legs, peeved. "Your father has thirty thousand members, Briggs. Someone will finish it. Did you find us the right place to live?"

"Monica, that doesn't matter. What matters is your place is here with me. It's past time for you to come to Detroit. It's been over a month of me learning the day-to-day operations, the members, and the community, and at last, I'll be preaching on Sunday. You should be here."

"Briggs, this is the new millennium. Husbands and wives don't live in each other's pockets anymore. Some two-career marriages actually live on different coasts. They make it work," she said in a matter-of-fact tone.

"Well, we aren't going to be one of those couples. And a two-career household has a two-career income. Is someone now paying you for your volunteer time?"

"Oh no, you didn't. As your wife, I have my own duties to fulfill. I'm doing me, while you're there establishing a name for yourself. Stop stressing. I know! I'll come and visit for a week and meet and greet. Would you like that?" Monica suggested. She kept her eyes on the closed door.

"What I would like doesn't seem to count. So I guess I'll have to take a visit. It's past time to introduce you to everyone. Have you spent any time with my parents?"

"Briggs, when you were here I didn't spend time with them. Your dad is always on the road, and when your mom is not with him, she's too busy to worry about her heathen daughter-in-law," Monica criticized.

Briggs slipped into his well-worn role of the pacifier. "Monica, that's just not true. They have tried to include you in family activities, but you always beg off. They got over our elopement a long time ago. In the future, when we present them with Briggs Jr., they'll become your biggest fans."

"You have me mixed up with someone sweating their approval," Monica spat.

Briggs cleared his throat. "Let's keep the sarcasm to a low roar. The purpose of this call is to make sure you're coming to see me. That's all I'm concerned about right now. When can I expect you?"

"I'll call you. Bye . . ." Monica said.

"I love—" Briggs said just as Monica hung up.

Monica heard rustling at the door and knew Randall had headed back to bed. Her hands gripped the edge of the chaise and her eyes sparked anger and frustration. She completed toweling herself off and rehearsed telling Randall that she was going to Michigan. She was not looking forward to his objections. But she wasn't leaving Briggs for Randall until she saw his divorce decree and a wedding ring with her name inscribed on it.

Too many women skipped the sure thing, and then the pie in the sky didn't come through. She always bet on the winner. Men were fickle; she learned that from her dear old daddy. He broke her heart so many times growing up that she should have had stock in Elmer's glue. Her mother did her best trying to mend the jagged pieces together, but the cracks were still there, and only a patient eye could detect them.

Monica strutted out of the bathroom wrapped in her towel. She approached the bed, ready to use every weapon in her arsenal to placate Randall when she shared her news. He looked up appreciatively as she approached the bed; his eyes telegraphed that the phone call was forgotten. She had his attention. He smiled in anticipation and held his arms open for her warmth.

The Spirit of Confusion and Chaos danced across the Atlanta skyline; it radiated joy in its night lights, and it could hear the effect of its power wash over the city. It didn't do the hell thing; earth and its inhabitants were its responsibilities. Briggs, Esther, Monica, and Randall were all in its path of destruction. It circled around heading north. It was time to return to Detroit and complete its assignment. It had other things it wanted to take care of, like what it had in store for that new young mayor.

Chapter Eighteen

Briggs ended the call with Monica and began talking to himself as he tore through his desk. "Man, sometimes . . . Lord, give me a clean heart." He exhaled and answered his ringing phone.

"Briggs, it's Esther. How are you?" she stammered.

To Briggs's ears, she sounded nervous. "Hey, it's going. How are things checking out with the zoning commission?"

"No news to tell you just yet, but I'm looking into things. All of this is just too suspicious. Sooner or later the dirt will come out. In the meantime, we're going to have to call an emergency meeting of Love Zion's board members."

"I'll have Naomi schedule it. And I'll keep praying on it; in the meantime, you keep me posted on whatever you need me to do." Briggs needed a segue to the conversation he really wanted to have with Esther.

"Okay, sounds like a plan. So, I guess I'll see you later?"

Briggs knew this was his chance. "I do have something else to talk to you about."

"Church business?"

Briggs coughed up his nerve. "No, it's a personal matter."

"Oh?" Esther sounded puzzled.

Briggs hesitated before he spoke. "I'd like to do it in person, if you don't mind."

Esther stammered again. "What's going on?" Her voice escalated. "I thought you said everything was okay. I know, you know, to let church gossip pass you by. Don't let people saying we're in a relationship get to you. Ignore them, it will die down, and in the interim, no one is really hurt. It's not like you're engaged or have a wife."

Briggs's time table just moved up. "Esther, we need to talk today. Can you swing by here? No, better yet, let me meet you."

"Okay, now you're scaring me. What's going on?" Esther sounded rattled.

Briggs's voice was determined. "We'll talk when I see you."

"I'm on my way home. Come by my house. The address is 16555 Edinborough Road. So, I'll see you in a few?"

"Yes, I'll be there shortly," Briggs said.

A short while later, Briggs hung his head as he waited for Esther to answer the door. Letting people get to know him without his father or his trophy wife seemed like an innocent plan. He thought of it as a man needing to test his waters and learn who he was for himself. Now, it seemed underhanded and sinister in nature. He honestly never meant to mislead anyone, especially Esther, someone whom he admired and thought of as a real friend. He wished he could either turn back the hands of time or put this off another week, day, or hour.

The door opened. He was out of time. There she stood, and his heart lurched, but he rejected the feeling. Entering her home he noticed the beautiful décor and how well it all came together. Her home reflected her character . . . warm and inviting.

**

On the eastern side of Esther's home, there was cackling of merriment and imps danced in glee as they looked through her kitchen window. A taller shadow dominated the grassy area.

A large, curled claw shoved the small, scaly, pimpled hunchback imp standing before him.

"You dare to stand in front of me, Imp One? Get behind me quickly and you might live. I want to see this unfold," The Leader demanded.

"My apologies, O Great One," the imp said and slithered swiftly behind his leader. "I move, O Titled One. This is so exciting. It is all coming together."

"Stop drooling, stupid peasant. You are such a troll," The Leader said. "This is my plan, my victory. You have done nothing but cause mishaps and missteps. I should make you leave."

"Oh no, please. Finally, something is going your way. Let me celebrate with you. Let me be your cheerleader. I can do it. I can, I can!"

"By all that is evil, shut up! I had to request Confusion and Chaos because of your impotence. Do you think I need you fawning over me?"

The Leader leaned down and blew a fetid fire over the imp's body. Every place it touched, ash followed, until the imp simply faded into dust. . . . Not even a shimmer of memory left behind.

With his large head tilted skyward, The Leader let out an eerie screech of triumph. He then reclined on his tail in ecstasy.

"Now, I can watch this in Technicolor uninterrupted. Bring on the pain . . ."

Esther motioned Briggs over to sit down on the large, overstuffed couch. She called over her shoulder as she went into her kitchen, "It's warm out, so I made us some lemonade."

"That sounds good," Briggs replied, feeling dryness in his throat that had nothing to do with thirst.

Esther entered with two frosted goblets on a tray, with a small plate of Mother's Reed sliced pound cake she had defrosted yesterday from her freezer.

"Girl, I should have come over to visit you sooner. You know how to treat a guest," Briggs said, trying to lighten the mood.

Esther snorted. "A guest who's being mysterious. No more suspense. Talk to me."

Briggs gestured to her sofa. "Please . . . sit down."

Defiantly, Esther crossed her arms. "I'm not so sure I need to sit down. Maybe I want this news standing."

"Esther," Briggs said exasperated.

"Okay, okay, don't get all huffy." She plopped down and folded her arms.

Briggs hesitated, becoming fascinated with his hands.

"Well . . ." Esther watched Briggs stall.

An anxious Briggs stumbled through his explanation. "You know that I consider you a friend, and that sometimes when we talk, it feels like the years have faded away." He paused because Esther looked terrified. "Esther?"

"Yes?"

"Are you okay?" Briggs asked, his face flooding with compassion. He needed to get this out. He was scaring her.

She stiffened even more. "Yes, go on."

His hands opened in supplication. "I wouldn't hurt you for the world, not in any way, and I never meant to mislead you . . ."

Briggs noticed Esther's body language shift to rigid. He was trying to tell her; it was just stuck in his throat.

Esther reached out and slapped his arm in aggravation. "I'm going to hurt you, man. Just say it."

He blurted, "I'm married."

"What?" In disbelief, she looked around, stretched up on her tiptoes, and peeked over his shoulder.

Baffled, Briggs's eyebrows rose and his eyes darted to see where Esther was looking. "Esther?"

Eyes narrowed into pinpoint lasers, she shook her fist in his face. "Oh no, my saved, sanctified, man of God. I'm looking for *Candid Camera,* funniest home videos, or something 'cause I know I'm being punked."

Briggs slowly swung his head in the negative, swiped his brow with his sleeve, and tried to get through his "shoulda told it long ago" confession. "Yes, I have a wife. Her name is Monica."

Esther slumped into a chair. He could tell this was not the news she expected. "Wife?" she repeated, then swallowed. "Not punked? You're for real?"

Briggs babbled. "She was coming; then she got delayed; then she was sick, and . . . She is coming soon though, for a visit."

Esther stared into space. Briggs didn't know what she was thinking. But, by the look on her face, it wasn't good.

She tried to speak, but instead stood. Her lips tightened, and her hands curled into balls. She was in shock as she shook her hands loose and pointed her finger at Briggs. Her voice stilted, she released her pain. "I once hurt you. Your only crime was you loved me. I was an angry and confused young lady. My mind had twisted our relationship into part of the reason for Sheri's suicide. I felt I wasn't there for her. You took up my time. You needed to share the blame and the punishment."

Briggs listened and frowned. "Esther, that was long ago—"

Esther sliced her hand in the air for Briggs to be quiet. "Now, we meet again. And there are tingles and secret smiles." Esther saw Briggs clench his hands in guilt. "And . . . You're married. Briggs, I feel lied to, but you never said you were free. I'm disappointed, but you never made me any promises. And I am humiliated that this makes the rumor and our association so much worse."

Briggs felt her shame. "Esther, I promise it was not my intention to mislead you or to cause you pain. This is not in retaliation for our past. I admit we still have chemistry, but I wouldn't have acted on it." Briggs's heart seesawed. He could only hope he wouldn't have acted. That his relationship with God would allow him to be the man he claimed to be.

Esther's breathing was erratic. "Briggs, I think you need to go. I'm meeting a friend, and I don't want to be late. I'm sorry about the rumors, but as long as we stay away from each other, they'll fade away."

"Esther, I don't care about the rumors. I'm here because we're friends, and the omission of my marriage was not meant to be malicious. I'm married to Monica, who is a well-known model. I'm the son of a world renown televangelist. This is my first ministry assignment away from my father's shadow. And, for a short while, away from my wife's notoriety. For once, I wanted people to see and get to know me. But she didn't come after a week, then two weeks, and we're now in the fourth week of my arrival, and I'm *still* alone."

Esther stood in stunned disbelief. "You married swimsuit cover, *Sport Illustrated, Vogue, Glamour,* the 'Monica'?"

"Yes." Briggs wanted to share how all that fame never helped them make a home. But there was enough confusion.

Esther waved her hand toward the front door to dismiss him. "I'd really like you to go, Briggs. From what you told me weeks ago, you're carrying a lot of issues from being a preacher's kid. Always expected to be perfect, never allowed to make mistakes, held up for others to emulate. I saw it in college when you were frantic about pleasing your father. I saw similar behavior in Sheri. Please pray about this and talk to someone who can help. I know you'll lead our church well, but Romans 11:29 states, for the gifts and calling of God are without repentance. You don't want to miss God."

Briggs's head snapped back as though Esther had delivered a Mike Tyson blow. "This is why I don't talk about my feelings to people. You get judged. I don't need your judgment, Esther. Just your forgiveness if I hurt you." Briggs stepped away. "I'll leave since you are meeting someone."

Esther remained quiet. She walked with Briggs to the door, opened, and then closed it without speaking.

Dejected, Briggs sat in his car quiet and miserable. It was the second time Esther had asked him to leave her house. He thought older meant wiser.

He was wrong.

Chapter Nineteen

Esther hugged the pillow from her living-room couch. She was trying to conjure up the rest and warmth she usually felt there. Instead, she wanted to throw something. She really didn't have anywhere to go or any friends to meet. She only had acquaintances. She felt convicted, she had lied to Briggs. Her childhood friendships taught her it was painful when people moved on. The last time she let people in, it almost destroyed her spirit.

On edge, she grabbed her car keys. She might not have anyone to meet, but she needed to get out of the house. She decided to take a ride around Belle Island Park to dispel her hurt and ease her conscience. Forgiving Briggs was also on the menu; she still had to work with the man.

She entered her attached garage through her kitchen, her mind in overdrive concerning Briggs and his shocking announcement.

"Lord, I'm going to lose my mind at this rate," she complained, as she clicked the remote door opener and backed out of her garage.

Bam!!!

Startled, Esther looked in her rearview mirror as she slammed on her brakes. She couldn't imagine what she might have hit. "Briggs?" she jumped out and spotted Briggs still in his car. "What in the world?"

He ignored her outburst. "Are you all right?"

"Yes," Esther inspected the back end of her car. She noticed a small dent in her bumper.

"Please add this apology to all the others I've said to you today. I am sorry, but you really should look behind you when you're pulling out." Briggs looked at the front end of his rental and squinted at the damage.

Esther glared at him as though he was from outer space. "Are you *serious?* Why were you still sitting in my driveway?"

"Praying."

"Oh." The wind seeped out of Esther's sails. She had been so disturbed by Briggs's revelation that she didn't even think to pray.

To cover her discomfiture, Esther spouted, "I need your insurance information, and we should call and report this accident to the police."

He pulled out his information. "Yes, that's the right thing to do. Maybe we can go back inside and wait for them to show up?"

"Well, okay, but then I have to go. Someone is waiting for me," Esther frowned at her continued lie. *For sure the gates of hell are opening.*

"Going to meet your mother?"

"No." Esther pulled out her cell and reported the accident as she and Briggs went back into her house. "Briggs, the police are on their way."

"Your sister?" Briggs glowered, fixated on her face.

"Pardon?" Distracted, Esther dug in her purse for her insurance card.

"Going to visit . . . are you meeting your sister?" he asked annoyed.

"No," Esther said sweetly.

Briggs sighed heavily, muttered, and watched as Esther dialed another phone number.

Seeing his discomfort, something naughty made her needle him more. "Hi, change of plans. I'll be a little delayed. I had a small fender bender," Esther spoke into her office voice mail. "No, no, I'm okay. I'll just be a little later. Okay, bye."

Briggs moved closer, straining to hear who was on the other line. Esther, sensing his motives, countered his moves every time he approached her. Aggravated, he sat down.

Curiosity rode Esther until she became short-tempered. She growled, "So, how long have you been married?"

He froze. "So we're just going to dive right in," he murmured under his breath.

She shrugged. "Yes, so please answer."

"We've been married a little over five years and you have really good hearing," Briggs said frustrated.

In silence, they locked eyes; then the silence spiraled into something else. Uncomfortable, Briggs and Esther broke eye contact, speaking over each other. "Maybe we should wait outside. . . . Let's get some air."

Uneasy, they chuckled, looking everywhere, but at each other. They moved outside, hoping the police had arrived.

Briggs ended the awkward silence. "It was never my intention to mislead anyone," he rubbed his hand absently over his chin. "I apologize. My prayer revealed you were right, and I should not have been offended. The actions of a boy shouldn't still reflect in the behavior of the man. Now that I know, it's an area I'll work on."

"That's good, Briggs," Esther whispered as she smoothed her hands down her curvy hips. She blinked but spoke her acceptance of his married state. "You have a beautiful wife. I'm sure we'll love her as our first lady."

Briggs made an offhanded remark. "At thirty-three, I know what I didn't know at twenty-five. I've learned the measuring stick that will have her in your arms for a night is a lot different than the one that would have her there for life." He realized his disclosure and clamped his lips shut.

Esther was heavyhearted with the realization that nothing was simple.

A car door slammed, and a police officer approached them with his ticket book in hand. "So how'd it happen, folks? Someone pulling in or out?" the officer inquired.

"Out," they chorused.

The officer shook his head. "There was a time when people handled their domestic squabbles in private. Since when does a husband and wife settle a little fender bender with outsiders? You look like a lovely couple. Why don't you just pay for the car repairs and call it a day? My parents always said don't let the sun go down on your wrath. Maybe you should just kiss and make up," he advised as he walked around the cars and surveyed the damage.

Briggs immediately interjected. "We're not married."

The police officer looked at the wedding band Briggs made sure was on his finger today and repulsion dawned on his face.

Esther followed the officer's line of vision and stared at the wedding ring on his finger. "Was that always there?"

"No," Briggs said, "I—"

"So you're one of those, huh?" the officer sneered.

"What?" Briggs exclaimed, "You really are jumping to conclusions. I'm a man of—"

"Whatever. Let's get down to business. Please pull out your driver's licenses and proof of insurance . . ."

"Oh, I liked that, Leader. You have such a delicate stroke when you paint people into unbearable corners," the minion lisped.

The Leader looked at his latest imp, a small insipid reptile, and wondered for the millionth time, why he couldn't have full-fledged demons like some of the other legion leaders. Yet, he knew he was up to the task and could even whip this sorry bunch into shape.

"Yeee . . . sss," The Leader hissed. "I thought the police officer with his sanctimonious ways was a real nice touch. New Christians can be so judgmental. You know that he just accepted salvation a week ago. He's on my radar. He had a little problem in the past with adultery. Like I said before, humans are so contrary. What they hate, they do."

"You are so wonderful, so mighty, so—"

"Cease your groveling, insect! You tire me."

"He tires, he tires," his minions chorused as they slivered into the shadows on the walls.

Knowing he had other assignments, The Leader looked down into his book of words spoken carelessly by others. He loved to use these murmurings to kill the life of their dreams and provoke new attacks against them.

"Let's see, there were 8,112 'you make me sick' phrases spoken on Tuesday in the city of Detroit alone," he exclaimed in glee as he sent down coughs, nervous ticks, headaches, and his personal favorite, STDs.

The power of peoples' words was undeniable. When would they learn? He hoped never. Words caused disruptions and negative disruptions ushered in distractions. It was his experience that some people let any little thing keep them from receiving the goodness that "He" had for them. Small distractions were the best. They kept man from "Him" (he hated saying "His" name—it always caused him to convulse). When man stayed away from "Him" too long, they usually ended up coming back to his master. He had found that distractions were his friend. Soon, those who had moved away were back living next door to him. As his tail swayed happily back and forth, he swooned, and sang a little ditty he heard through a miniature human's open window. "Just another day in the neighborhood . . ."

Chapter Twenty

Briggs listened to the phone ring. Irritated, he vented on Monica's voice mail. "Why can't I ever reach you when I need to?" He spat his words like poison-tipped arrows. "Something is very wrong here. Call me."

He punched his fist into his hand. His heavy footfalls trudged in defeat. He was a saved man who was getting tired of lonely nights. His conversation with Esther was uppermost in his mind. He felt like a fraud. He needed a word from God.

Laying across his bed he prayed, "Father, I know you love me. But, I want to be touched, and I hunger for a woman's soft words. I now understand the temptations of my single brethren. Staying strong is hard work. Help me to do right."

Twenty minutes later, Briggs grabbed his cell phone, slid it open, and dialed before he could talk himself out of it. He was like a junkie needing a fix; he couldn't stop himself.

A sleep-filled voice yawned, "Hello."

His greeting was near a whisper. "Hey, did I wake you?"

The phone rustled in his ear. He imagined her rolling over before she spoke. "It's okay."

"I'm sorry," He said hating how they left things.

She stretched, concerned. "Is something wrong?"

"Don't be angry with me." Briggs wanted absolution.

She pushed sleep away. "I'm trying not to be."

"That was honest," he said, surprised.

"Right, I must be sleepier than I thought," she joked softly.

"I have this gnawing hole," he continued.

She smothered her yawn. "A hole?"

"Yes, I thought that since we were being honest, I'd tell it all. Is this a night for telling it all?" Briggs whispered.

She hesitated. "I don't know, Briggs."

He could tell she was struggling, and he was going to tell her to forget it when she said, "Tell me about the hole."

His conscience cautioned him to hang up and have this conversation with the right person. But, he said, "It's large, and I keep packing stuff inside of it, but it just keeps getting larger."

"What kind of stuff?" her tone was soft and compassionate.

Conviction pulled at Briggs to keep his emotional meltdown to himself. "People, places, and things," he kidded.

She cajoled. "Don't get squeamish now, you were doing so great."

The phone was quiet. They had slipped over an invisible line. The sad part of it all was they knew they had nothing to hide behind since Briggs had let her know his situation.

Briggs's conviction won out. He was determined to end the conversation that was becoming too intimate. "I'm sorry I woke you. I'll talk to you later."

She had a smile in her voice. "Yes, you will. We have zoning issues to resolve."

"Have a peaceful sleep," Briggs said, and with tenderness, he closed his phone.

Briggs and Esther both lay back on their beds and closed their eyes. A tear trickled down a mournful cheek—whose cheek didn't matter, when both their voices were crying out in a repentance prayer as the night air cooled.

***

The morning was bright and calm, the air was clear, and the sound and smell of sizzling bacon drifted from the kitchen down the hall. Briggs stretched in his bedroom mirror and stared at the circles under his eyes.

Bad call, he thought. *I never should have let loneliness pick up that phone.*

He bent and slipped on his shoes. It was in the serenity of daylight that he could see the misguided confusion of his night. A new day—brand-new mercies.

"Briggs . . . Briggs," Mrs. Gregory called through his closed bedroom door.

He opened the door. "Yes, ma'am."

"The telephone is for you, dear."

Briggs hadn't heard the house phone ring. He picked up the extension. A loud voice bellowed. "Since when does a man need to be reminded to call and let someone know he's doing all right?"

Joyful, Briggs grinned. "Dad, how're you doing?"

Bishop Stokes's voice thundered. "No, son, the question on the table is, how are *you* doing?"

"Well, Dad, I won't complain." Briggs was used to his live out loud father and waited for his point.

"That's my favorite song, but as an answer, that's not cutting it for me right now. Talk to me," Bishop implored.

Briggs sighed, knowing his father was like a grizzly on the scent of fresh meat. He never gave up, at least not without a fight. *So how much do I tell him?* "Dad, I believe I'm struggling with making the right choices in my life."

"Harrumph. Did I ever share with you my view on choices?"

Briggs thought about it. "About making sure you prayed about them first?"

"Well, yes, but more than that. Son, your choices make choices for you."

"Excuse me?" Briggs disliked appearing ignorant in front of his father, but he was not going to let pride get in the way of him finding out just what he should be doing. His father's reputation was not all hype; he truly was a man who heard from God.

"It's like this. Let's be real in this conversation."

"Yeah, Dad, be real." Briggs went over, closed his door, and sat down.

"Son, once you make a choice, the other choices are made for you. Visualize, if you can, a young girl choosing to be led into fornication by her young man. The feelings are there, the opportunity presents itself, and they go for it. All she chose was to be intimate with her special someone. Am I right?"

Briggs leaned with his elbow on his knee, the phone clutched in his hand. "Yes, you're right."

"Now come with me into the realm of the supernatural. Let's see what happens after she makes that choice."

"I'm still with you," Briggs said, slowly getting the picture.

"Choices start lining up to meet with the choice she made. There is HIV trying to get a spot, unwanted pregnancy is there fighting for its chance, the choice of abandonment is jockeying for a place—because we know once a young man hits it, he sometimes quits it—then there's . . ."

Briggs stood excited. "Man, I get it! That's an amazing analogy. She chose to lie down, but not what happens after she gets up. Those choices are now out of her hands, and her choice begets other choices."

Bishop Stokes caught his son's excitement. "Exactly . . . No one chooses to have an STD. It chose them after they made an unwise decision. Nobody wants to be alone and pregnant at fourteen. Even if they chose the pregnancy, they didn't choose to be left, which happens in most of these cases. See how this thing is going? You make a choice; then your choices make choices for you."

Briggs wanted to get the whole picture. "So what if I choose right?"

"Well, let's see. You choose to be obedient to God and follow His path, even though it's lonely and a struggle . . ."

"Uh-huh," Briggs encouraged his father to go on.

"As God sees you choosing Him, and He has already chosen you—what you loose on earth, is loosed in heaven. And what you bind on earth, gets bound in heaven. So healing is loosed, prosperity is loosed, new fruit is loosed, and son, love is loosed."

Briggs gave a shout. "That's awesome, Dad, and it helped. Thanks."

"Well, I don't know when I didn't need my father's guidance. I stayed before his wisdom right up until he left this earth. Never think that I'm too far away or you are too old to come to Daddy. Do you hear me, son?"

"Yes, and I miss you, Dad. I've been so busy here, but I shouldn't have let so much time go by without calling you and Mom. How is my Georgia Peach?" he asked as he placed his wallet in his pocket from the dresser.

"She's fine. We're still on the road a lot, and she's still the wind beneath my wings. God is my pilot, but she helps carry me in the direction He points. Speaking of wives, I haven't seen yours lately. Is everything good down there with the two of you?"

Briggs paused, startled by his father's question. "When was the last time you were in town, Dad?"

"Um, let's see. You left about four and a half weeks ago?"

Briggs grabbed his car keys. "Yes, sir."

"Let's see, we were in Africa for two weeks, then Haiti a week, so we've been back around a week."

"Monica is not here yet, Dad. She's joining me this weekend." Briggs prayed he was telling the truth and Monica would show up.

"Well, I don't think it's good for married couples to be far apart for too long, but if she's moving there this weekend, then I guess you guys will be okay."

Briggs faltered. "Well, uh, she's coming for the weekend, but not to stay."

"What? Why not, Briggs?" Bishop Stokes choked out.

Briggs cringed at his father's acrid tone. "She wants me to find a place as big as our house, Dad, and I just can't see paying two house notes every month. So she's being stubborn."

Bishop Stokes's agitation escalated. "Son, I didn't raise a fool. You're a young man and she's a young woman. As a man of the cloth, the most sanctimonious churchwoman in the world will throw her panties in your face like you're Rick James if you give off any signs of weakness. And, boy, a man without his woman for this long a time will send up smoke signals Stevie Wonder could read."

"Dad!" Briggs said shocked by his father's candor. Bishop had never been this open with him before.

The bishop was on a roll. "Don't 'Dad' me. Let me school you on something, young blood. I'm an old warrior. Been out on the battlefield a long time. When I first started preaching, I had to go out on the road a lot. I didn't have a home church, but I was invited to speak at a lot of tent meetings, revivals, and church functions. Early in our marriage, your mother started out going with me. Later you were born. You were a little tyke, and your mama didn't want to drag you around with us. There were a lot of days, and weeks, that I wasn't home. Some towns where I went, they didn't even have a spare bed for me. I slept on lumpy family-room couches, and others couldn't do enough for me. I was invited to many homes for a home cooked meal. Some of the church widows, singles, and even married ladies wanted to feed me more than a plate of food. There were times when my body and my soul were tired and they hungered, but I can say that by the grace of God I never cheated on your mother. I can't say that I was never tempted."

"I never knew," Briggs said stunned at this revelation.

"Wasn't for the boy to know, it was for the man to understand."

Briggs had a determined stride as he walked over to the phone base. "I'll do what I can to make godly choices, Dad. You've helped me this morning and not only as my bishop, but as my father."

"Thank you, son, I know your heart, and I'm sure you'll do what's best for everyone concerned. And that includes you. I'll talk to you soon . . . and, son?"

"Yes sir?"

"Call your mama. She misses you."

"Yes, sir. I'll talk to you soon."

Chapter Twenty-one

The nervous shaking of the man's leg accompanied the flicking of the Bic lighter in his dry, calloused hand. Discarded cigarette butts gathered at his feet in a small molten pile. Buses slowed, and then continued on as he failed to get on any of the steel coaches. The sign over his head hung worn and rusted. It read Bus Stop, DDOT (Detroit Department of Transportation). Buses passed as he sat waiting, eyes transfixed on the building directly across the street.

Even the casual eye could take in his slow descent into an invisible class of people. He wore a sweat-stained T-shirt, dingy from multiple washings, with the sleeves ripped off to reveal his personal glory, a coiled serpent tattoo. Below his shirt, wrinkled khaki pants sagged like a delinquent teen's rebellious salute to urban myth and decay. A pathetic visage.

Roger leaned forward and mumbled a curse. He lit another cigarette and looked down into the crumbled pack. He had one left.

"Esther, bring your big tail out here," he slurred as he peered through the cheap generic smoke.

If her steroid-induced cousin Tony hadn't warned him of a fatal beat down, he would have staked out one of her family members' homes. And after the parking lot incident, where his only crime was trying to teach her how to be a real wife, he stayed away from Love Zion at all cost. Those church folk would surely send out an SOS if they saw him lurking around. Plus, he didn't relish a Holy Roller beat down from church security. *Come on, Esther, you owe me.*

So here he was, sitting across from her job. From there he would follow her home. He had a little raggedy car stashed around the corner. His drunken neighbor would never notice it was missing as long as he brought it back by nightfall.

"You can't hide from me forever, Esther," he sang in a slurred voice.

He sat there for hours, moving around the small bus shelter as the morning dragged into late afternoon.

"Are you having a problem, sir?" a voice thundered at Roger.

Roger jumped as he looked over at the Detroit police cruiser sitting slightly to his left. In his preoccupation, he hadn't heard it pull up.

Roger wiped sweat-drenched palms down the sides of his pants as he stood. "No, officer, just waiting for the bus."

The officer left the cruiser idling as he stalked over to Roger. He lifted and placed his large black boot on the bench next to him. "Well, according to one of the neighbors, you've let every bus pass you by for the last three hours."

Roger spluttered. "Uh, see . . . first, I was trying to decide if I should catch it, 'cause my girlfriend lives around the corner, and I was going to go back and get with her. We had this argument—"

"What's her address?" the officer demanded.

Roger went still. "Huh?"

"Her address? What's your girlfriend's address?" the officer repeated, tapping his foot in time to his question. The bench shook with the force of the taps.

"She just moved in about a week ago. It's the brick two-family flat."

"Nice save, but that describes the whole street," he smirked. The officer looked up as a rumbling sound approached behind him. "Here's your bus now," he said.

Roger convulsed. "No, that's not the bus I was going to take. I catch the—"

"You're missing my point. So let me make it plain. You are making the good citizens of this neighborhood nervous. So, make like Spike Lee and get on the bus!" the officer ordered as he stretched out his brown muscled arm and halted the bus.

Roger grimaced as he shoved his hand in his pocket and fingered his last crumpled dollar bill as a few loose coins jingled next to it.

He got on the bus and slid money into the fare box; then he flopped down onto the seat. He planned to get off at the next stop and walk back.

"Hey, hold up," the officer hollered at the bus driver.

The bus doors swung open with a hissing sound as the officer ran up the bus steps.

"Don't get off this bus until you are well out of this neighborhood. If I see you back this way, I'll cite you for vagrancy. You got that?" he asked and took off his sunglasses and gave Roger a hard glare.

Roger slumped back in the seat. "Yeah, everybody got that," he replied as all the passengers looked back and forth between him and Detroit's finest.

"Then my job here is done. You folks have a good day," the officer said as he slipped his sunglasses back on and tipped the brim of his hat to the crowd in general.

"Doggone cops always tryin' to be in a grown man's bizness. You shoulda dropped that punk, son," a surly youth slurred to Roger.

Roger pulled a greasy baseball cap out of his back pocket and pulled it on his head, down past his hooded eyes. He then fell back into his seat determined to sleep.

He figured he needed the rest because later on today he would have to walk all the way back to get the car he had stashed around the corner.

The officer waited and watched as the bus rolled out of sight. Lawton Redding loved his job. He was raised on the streets of Detroit, and the ebb and flow of everyday urban life pumped in his veins. His commander always said he had a sixth sense about people. Lawton knew it was no sixth sense, but a discerning spirit operating. It was this gift, coupled with his belief and love of Jesus Christ, that kept him protected. There were times when his intuition told him that he stopped more crimes than his natural senses recognized.

"That's a bad one," he whispered out loud as his eyes followed the bus. He surveyed all of his surroundings and caught sight of a fine-looking sister striding out of the building across the street. She was like he liked them—thick and delicious. His trained eye said a size fourteen or sixteen. The sway of her hips called out to him with a siren's allure.

As she looked up, he caught her eyes and smiled. She looked back with surprise and shyness. He shook his head to himself and remembered his last girlfriend who never believed he really cared for her. Her insecurities eventually took their toll, and he took his leave.

It had been a year since he had been in a relationship, and he promised himself he would pray before he engaged himself again. This sister was fine, but her eyes said she didn't know her worth. This time he was passing her, and all her potential drama, by.

Lawton leaned down, swung into his squad car, and slowly pulled off. As he looked in his rearview mirror, the sister who had just been in his thoughts stumbled down the steps and fell. He could hear her exclamation of pain through his open car window.

He backed up, got out of his car, and jogged over to her. She was sitting upright on the ground holding her bleeding knee.

"You okay? Let me look at that for you," he said.

"Ouch, my knee. Guess I wasn't looking where I was stepping." Esther's earlier embarrassment faded as the pain intensified.

"Can you bend it?"

"I don't know. It hurts," Esther covered and protected her knee from inspection.

"I know it hurts. I'm trying to see how badly it's injured. Please try to bend it." Lawton worked to get Esther to remove her hands.

Esther pushed his hands away. "Stop, I see the blue uniform. Where's the white one?"

Lawton rocked back on his heels. "Excuse me?"

"I said it hurts! Therefore, I'm not trying to bend it back and forth. Right now, I'm trying to sit here and catch my breath. Go play doctor somewhere else," Esther said, exasperated with the effort it took to converse.

"Whoa, you're a little feisty when you're in pain, aren't cha?" he said reassessing his first impression. "Can I help you up now?"

"No, no. Just leave me. I'll get up in a minute. You run along now," Esther said sweetly using her fingers to imitate walking away.

"Excuse me? Run along? You want to pat me on my head now?"

"See, you are a clever boy," Esther retorted, then looked convicted.

Lawton sat on the concrete steps in silence.

"Look, this ground is hard, and my knee is throbbing. Okay, I may need help getting up. Please . . ." Esther said in a small low voice.

Lawton spoke without moving. "Pardon?"

"Please help me up, Officer Redding, right?"

He stepped back and scanned her up and down. "Do we know each other?" He bent over and in one swoop, brought her to her feet. Esther grunted in pain. "Hold on to me. I think we should go to the emergency room and get this checked out."

Esther nodded as they headed to his squad car. "A couple of weeks back, right up the street, you gave me a warning for a rolling stop." She paused near the door of his cruiser. "Hey, thanks for giving me a break then, and help now. Uh-uh, don't seat me in the back."

Lawton had opened the door to the back of the squad car. "I'm glad I was able to help. And, sorry, all civilians must ride in the back."

Esther tapped him to stop. "Stop flexing your cop muscles. I'm not riding in the back of your car like a common criminal. Okay, here's what we can do. You help me to my car, and I promise to go to my doctor's office."

Lawton slid Esther to an upright semistanding position. "You're tripping. What's the big deal?"

Esther leaned on him for support. "Number one, as a black female, I'm not going to the back of anything, especially not a squad car. Jesus ain't in that, and neither am I." Esther shoved the car door closed with her hip.

"You're funny," Lawton laughed as he helped Esther to her car. He lifted her and placed her in the driver's seat.

"Dog, man, you got muscles," Esther spoke before thinking, then chagrined, she moaned, "Sorry, must be the pain talking."

"I like its conversation," Lawton said, and then realizing Esther was probably embarrassed, he changed the subject. "Nice car. I do remember you."

"Not exactly flattering, you remembering my car but not me. No matter, maybe, I'll let you ride in the backseat of it sometime." Esther grinned in a cheeky manner.

"You're both very distinctive." Before standing up, Lawton gently fastened her seat belt, tapped her nose affectionately, then shut her door and hummed as he walked away.

A beginning can be so special that you know, God took a moment and fashioned it as an answer to your prayers. In the hospital's emergency room, Esther felt His hand at work.

Now, hours later, Lawton fluffed the pillows behind Esther on her living-room couch. "Are you sure you don't want me to help you into your bedroom?"

"Not in this life," Esther simpered, sweet as honey.

"I'll keep hope alive," Lawton answered playfully in a Jessie Jackson monotone.

A simple tumble down two stairs, and what could have been agony and pain became her personal gain. Lawton had followed her to the emergency room and stayed with her until a doctor examined, treated, and released her, which all went faster with a uniform police officer by her side. He called and arranged for a fellow officer to pick up his squad car and gallantly drove her home. Now, here, he sat, playing nursemaid to a woman he hadn't even known yesterday, nor remembered from weeks before.

"Impressive," Esther purred.

"What's impressive?"

"Not what, who." She said it so low, Lawton swayed forward to hear her better.

"Okay, I'll bite. Who's impressive?"

Esther regarded Lawton in admiration. "You are. You've done so much for me, a total stranger."

"You don't have to keep thanking me. I'm just glad it was only sprained and not fractured. By the way, we don't have to remain strangers. I would really like to be your friend."

Esther considered Lawton with interest in her eyes.

He met her gaze head-on. "What do you think?"

"Well, I love the way you handled yourself today. I also like a man who can take a joke and who has a good sense of humor. How can I say this?" Esther reached for diplomacy.

Lawton's hand was over his heart. "Don't hurt me now."

"I need to pray about it," Esther said in a decisive manner.

Lawton's smile widened. "I like that. I like that a lot. You're a woman after my own heart."

Esther checked out Lawton's clean-shaven face, his trimmed mustache, and his clear, penetrating hazel eyes. His eyes spoke of honesty, compassion, and something she had seen before: male appreciation.

Esther felt comfortable sharing her views. "Good. And just so we're clear, I'm looking for a man who loves the Lord with all his heart, so he'll know how to handle mine."

Lawton rubbed his hands together in appreciation. "Watch out, girl, you're about to make me fall in love. Falling in like is enough for one day. . . . Don't you think?"

"Yes, and with that, I'm going to ask that you give me my pain pill now. I think I need to get some rest," Esther pointed to her medication.

"Are you telling me to go home?"

"No, like they used to say back in the day, 'You don't have to go home, but you sure got to leave up outta here.'"

Lawton stood to leave. "Hey, I remember that saying."

"You're telling your age," she smiled.

"Well, I guess I did." Chuckling, Lawton became reflective. "Before I go, do you mind if I say a prayer for you?"

Esther gave a blissful sigh. "That would be lovely." She bowed her head as he touched her shoulder and prayed.

Afterward, she watched Lawton palm her business card complete with her number scribbled across the back. He made sure everything was secure and quietly walked outside and waited for his ride.

In wonder, Esther slid down and nestled into downy-laced six hundred-thread count sheets. She then kicked her sheets off with her good leg, pumped her fists in the air, and cheered, "Go God!"

"Stupid, stupid, stupid! Who was assigned to the Roger situation?" The Leader howled.

"Me," a sniveling voice whimpered.

Swoosh! The fire singed the ground where the imp had once stood. For the third time that year he had been killed, only to end up back in the furnace. The ground floor of hell was everyone's worse nightmare. It was the hottest, therefore, nicknamed the furnace. Every time he returned there, it was harder to work his way back up and out. He was getting tired of the climb and cursed The Leader.

"Cretins!"

"We're so bad, so bad, so bad," the imps said in mindless chatter.

"Leave!" The Leader blasted.

The dark shadows scattered across the wall, sounding like a thousand mice, then silence.

Chapter Twenty-two

Briggs's phone call with his father left him humbled. He had the lesson now. His choices made choices for him. His choice to omit the truth led to the rumors, and his now confusing relationship with Esther. Truth was now at point, and he needed to make a change. Briggs picked up his phone.

"Hello, sweetheart," he said with determined gusto.

"I assume you know you're talking to your wife?"

"Yeah, babe . . . and I'm missing you, lady. I tried to call you last night," he crooned while placing his feet up on the ottoman.

"Sorry, my cell died, and I lost its charger. Did you need anything?"

Briggs continued his sweet-talk campaign. "First, disregard, my voice mail. I was venting out of loneliness. Second, I just wanted to hear your voice and tell you how happy I am about having you here for the weekend. I plan to get us a suite at the Renaissance Center."

"Oh, nice. Anything special I should pack?"

"Well, you know I like you best in nothing at all . . ."

"Now, Pastor Stokes, I do believe y'all gon' make me blush," Monica said in an exaggerated Southern drawl.

Briggs sat forward mimicking her drawl. "Well, you do make my heart skip a beat, Ms. Monica." Briggs then added in a seductive whisper, "Especially when you're a bad girl."

Monica's voice was teary. "You have my eyes watering, Briggs, I will not cry. It has been so long since you and I talked like this. I forgot that once this was a natural thing for us, this intimacy."

Briggs spoke his thoughts out loud. "I remember when all we did was talk, flirt, and make love. Where did those days go?" The phone was filled with awkward silence. "Monica, we can get this right. This move will allow us a new beginning. Please text me your flight number and time of arrival." Briggs's voice held resolve.

"Okay." Monica hesitated, "and, Briggs?"

"Yes?"

She made a kissing sound through the phone. "Pleasant dreams."

Briggs planned to woo his wife back into his empty arms. He angled his head at the mirror, a specter of Esther floated past, and he closed his eyes against the sadness that reigned where joy should have. He had made his choice.

Two days later, planes lifted off, and people bustled by rushing to their destinations. Monica sat in the airport restaurant with Randall. Airports were always busy on Fridays, so they role-played business acquaintances waiting on their flight. She sipped her drink and observed his brooding facial expression through her extended lashes.

"Please stop," Monica snapped.

Randall forgot their roles and took her hand. His earnest gaze into her eyes exposed his agony. "I've never been in sync with any other person like I am with you. Come back to me," he pleaded.

Monica marveled when tears formed in the corners of his eyes. Her eyes glistened in symbiotic response; they were connected. Briggs was far away, Randall was here and now. "I can't do this," Monica whispered with droplets of tears spilling down her cheek.

"No—don't say that. I'm sorry I spoke out of turn. We can work anything out. Go see your husband," Randall said in a rush, his cheeks ruddy from panic.

Monica lost her composure and grabbed Randall's arm. "No, I can't go. Briggs is so far away, and I'm not talking about miles. I don't want to leave, and I'm selfish enough not to."

Randall covered her hand, then pulled out his phone. "Here, call him . . . now."

"No. He's expecting me, and if I call, he'll just needle me until I get on the plane. It's better for him to think I missed my flight." She pushed the phone away.

Randall rubbed his cheek. "I never want to feel like I've felt since you told me you were leaving." His chest expanded with news. "Monica, I'm asking my wife for a divorce."

"Hallelujah!" Monica shouted as she bolted from her seat and ran around the table to Randall. She grabbed him by the face and kissed him full on the lips. No more hiding.

Randall stood before her with the most lopsided wide grin on his face that she had ever seen. "Can we go home now?" he asked.

"Yes, darling, we can go home. Together," Monica said.

She took a step toward the outward ramp and stumbled. Startled, she glanced up, and hanging from the ceiling a sign read "CAUTION—PLEASE WATCH YOUR STEP." She read the large bold words and shivered as though something horrible awaited her. She shook off the ominous feeling and strutted out of the airport with Randall striding behind her. They were golden people. What could possibly go wrong?

***

Briggs sat at home in an empty house. Monica hadn't been on the plane, and she wasn't answering his fifty attempts to reach her. This was classic Monica. He knew in his heart she was fine; it was his marriage that was in trouble. He was glad he didn't spring for the suite.

The Gregorys had overnight plans elsewhere and had gladly given them the house. Briggs passed the dining room, a beautiful table setting gleamed against lights turned down low, and candles illuminated a soft glow against the silken walls. In all the time he had lived here, the Gregorys had never used the room.

He continued into the kitchen where a sumptuous spread was laid out before him. Apple and almond-crusted tenderloin, asparagus with cream sauce, garlic new red potatoes, and black-eyed peas with shrimp salad. The dessert was his favorite, chocolate turtle cheesecake. A note card was propped up for him to read. The food was still warm and there was a greeting for Monica.

Bless her heart, Briggs thought, thinking of Mrs. Gregory.

The message light was lit on the home phone. He checked and found Monica was the third message on the list.

"Briggs? This is Monica. I don't feel so well. I was at the terminal, and I felt faint. My head feels clammy, and my hands are sweaty. I don't want to meet people for the first time ill. Please send my apologies. I'm going home, and then to bed. I'm shutting my phone off until this awful migraine passes. Please send my suitcases back. I just felt too bad to pull them off. Bye, sweetie . . . ooh . . . ." *Beep.*

Briggs looked at the phone as though it had offended him. *"And the Academy Award goes to . . ."* Who did Monica think she was kidding—migraines, clammy hands, night sweats?

Briggs was angrier than he could remember. This was the woman he had pledged his life to love, and as of late, it had been a struggle, but he had remained faithful to her. And *this* was his reward? Why was he fighting this? Choices? She had just made hers.

Chapter Twenty-three

Briggs punched in Esther's number. "Hey, what are you doing?"

A groggy Esther growled, "Sleeping."

"At eight o'clock?"

"Yeah, I had a little accident yesterday, and I'm still recuperating."

Briggs was concerned. "Why didn't you call? What happened?"

"Calm down, I fell on my knee, and it's a little swollen. I'm fine, just a little sore."

"I'm coming over. What can I bring you?" Briggs said on a mission.

"Nothing, I don't feel like getting up and pulling myself together so you stay home, okay?" Esther's breath heavy with exertion.

"Have you eaten?" Briggs ignored her plea.

"Briggs . . ." Esther whined.

"Have you eaten?"

"You're stubborn. No, I haven't eaten, but I will. Please let me get back to sleep. Bye, Briggs," Esther said with authority.

Briggs begin packing food from the stove into plastic containers. "All right, Esther, see you."

In a darkened room, Esther scooted to the end of her bed and pulled herself up. She couldn't believe the

number of times she was being disturbed today. First
Briggs called, and now someone was ringing her doorbell.
She slipped into her robe and hobbled to the front door.
Through her peephole she couldn't believe who stood on
the other side. Heart racing, she opened the door wide
enough to peek out.

"Lawton! What are you doing here?" Esther smoothed
her hand over her tousled hair and pulled her robe closer.
She was no sleeping beauty, it was Friday, and her ratty
underwear whispered Tuesday. She couldn't feel more
dumpy.

"I'm checking on you," he said. "May I come in?"

"Well, uh . . . I'm not really feeling up to company."
Esther patted her hair and rubbed at imaginary sleep
lines around her face. Roger once told her she woke up
with railroad track lines across her face. An unattractive
trait.

Lawton quizzically took in her frantic face rubbing.
"You good? Does your medication make you itch?" He
watched Esther smooth her hands down her robe and
shake her head no. He then inched the door open and
edged into the room. "Good, glad you're okay. And,
I'm not company. You can be obstinate, and I figured
that same personality trait would keep you from calling
anyone for help. So I came to offer my assistance. Have
you eaten?"

"Why is everyone concerned with my eating habits?
There is such a thing as pizza delivery." Esther clutched
her robe.

"Why are you strangling your robe? Is it being bad?"

Esther rolled her eyes. "Okay, since it looks like I'm not
getting rid of you, I'm going to put some clothes on and
run a comb through my hair." She motioned for Lawton
to come all the way inside.

He glided past, moving toward her kitchen. "That's not necessary. I've got a sister, and I learned a long time ago, y'alls rolling out of bed look? It don't meet up with cute until half past makeup and a quarter to your flat iron. So, go lie back down and let this Good Samaritan take care of you."

"Uh-huh," Esther ignored him and hobbled to the bathroom to fix herself up.

"You don't have to be Superwoman for me," Lawton called out to her humming.

Lawton went into Esther's kitchen and rummaged around, making sure she had what he needed. He then ran out to his car, opened the trunk, and leaned in to pull out two grocery bags. As he straightened, a car pulled up, just as a green bell pepper rolled out of his bag. He leaned further into his trunk to retrieve the pepper when a voice echoed and pierced through his grumbling.

"How you doing, brother? Need any help?"

Lawton turned and a polished man of comparable age in a conservative suit stood before him. He slammed his trunk and sized up the stranger. He also had two bags in his hands. Only this brother's bags sent heavenly cooked aromas wafting into the air.

Lawton pointed to his bags. "No, I'm good. But if I wasn't rescuing a damsel in distress, I might need to bum-rush you for whatever smells good in your bags."

Both men grinned and saw kindred spirits in each other's makeup. They nodded at each other as they continued on their way.

Briggs stopped and looked over at the man to his right, "You following me?" he said jokingly and continued walking.

"Nah, I'm headed straight up this walkway."

Briggs stopped. "So am I."

Lawton frowned. "Esther?"

"Yes, Esther," Briggs nodded.

Lawton dipped his head toward the bags. "That's her dinner?"

"Well, I thought so."

Lawton looked down at his uncooked dinner, plans of chicken and rice flying out the window. "She know you coming?"

Briggs jiggled his car keys in his hands. "No, she told me specifically not to come."

"Spirited . . ." Lawton liked what he heard.

"You know that's right."

Lawton sized up his competition again and couldn't believe God sent him into what looked like a brewing fiasco. "Listen," he said, "I didn't know I was honing in on anyone's relationship. My mistake."

Briggs shook his head. "No mistake, man. I'm just a friend and nothing more. Actually, I'm married. So you see, this was just a friendship meal. Nope . . . nothing going on with us. We're just—"

"I got it . . . friends," Lawton interrupted with a smirk.

Briggs looked sideways at Lawton but held out his hand. "Briggs Stokes, nice to meet a friend of Esther's."

Lawton shook his hand. "A new friend, but a friend nevertheless. Good to meet you."

A car horn blew and Briggs looked up and waved at one of Love Zion's members driving up the street. He smiled that he was recognized and turned to continue his conversation.

"Going in?" Briggs asked.

Lawton's face tightened in concentration. "Well, I showed up unannounced, and if, as you say, Esther doesn't want company, I should probably go. Anyway, I don't want to intrude."

"Nah, I have a feeling you're exactly what she needs right now. As a matter of fact, take this food. Let it be a blessing to both of you this evening." Briggs handed him the food.

A smile dawned on Lawton's face. "You sure?"

"Positive," Briggs said with fervor. "Look, why don't we just pretend I was never here and you kids go on with your evening?"

"Thanks, Dad!" Lawton said sarcastically as he got a handle on all four bags.

Briggs gave a sheepish shrug. "Sorry. You know what I mean."

Lawton's tense lines were smooth, and he nodded pleasantly. "Yeah, and this is really decent of you. Thanks. I won't turn you down. I know how important it is to plant a seed in season. So, I won't block yours."

"Hey now, a man of the Spirit. Now, I know I need to get out of here and let you and Esther have your evening." Briggs looked up at Esther's door with a resigned expression. "I think I'll enjoy an evening of prayer." He stepped backward, got into his car, and drove off.

Lawton trotted back into the house before the food got any colder. He was placing the food on the table when Esther hobbled into the kitchen and sat. She looked at the food and broke into a wide smile.

"Sir, you definitely know the way to a woman's heart. This looks delicious. Nobody I know makes black-eyed peas with shrimp salad better than the first lady of our church, Sister Gregory. But by the looks of things, somebody is giving her a run for her money." Esther spooned food onto her plate with gusto.

Lawton hesitated but wanted to be honest. "To tell the truth, I don't know who made the dinner."

Esther stopped serving herself midspoonful and replaced her spoon in the bowl. "Chile, I can't eat when I don't know who prepared it."

Lawton grinned and shook his head. "That's not true. You eat at restaurants, don't you?"

"Well, yes, but . . ." Esther frowned. "Hmmph, you got me with basic common sense."

"See? Anyway, a friend of yours dropped it by, so I'm sure it's safe."

"Who?" Esther said puzzled.

Lawton observed Esther for her reaction. "An Armani suit-wearing brother said you're friends. Name is Riggs?"

Esther smiled and corrected him. "Briggs?"

"So you do know him, huh?" Lawton relaxed when she showed no signs of anything out of order.

Esther stood and hobbled to serve him a glass of ice tea, and then herself. She sat down with her head bowed to bless the food. When she raised her head she found Lawton staring. "You okay?"

Lawton was lost in thought. "You have a servant's heart," he said in awe. "That's truly a gift from God. The ability to be humble in service to others."

Esther blushed, gave a small smile, and kept eating. She glanced over at Lawton. "You're staring."

He nodded. "You're nice to stare at."

Esther laid down her fork. "You're making me uncomfortable."

"Then, I'll stop," Lawton said and began to eat his food.

"No doubt about it," Esther proclaimed, "This black-eyed pea salad is the work of Sister Gregory. Um, um, um . . ." she moaned.

Lawton burst out laughing, reached across the table, and startled Esther by taking her hand. "Don't look like a deer in the headlights. I'm just feeling all is right in my world, and I wanted to share a little of that affection with you, okay?"

"Okay," Esther said with satisfaction and picked up her fork and continued her splendid meal.

***

"Are there no real men left in the world? What kind of wimps settle their differences with a handshake? His wife stands him up, the one he longs for has found someone else, and he goes home like a gentle soul. Where is his thugged-out anger?" The Leader whined.

His mentor stood four inches over The Leader's height. He lifted his long gargantuan tail over his shoulder and delicately brushed it across his brow. He peered over at The Leader and sighed deeply. "Stop," he rattled with authority.

"Yes, Most High Leader."

"I believe you are whining. However, I must be wrong, because leaders do not whine. We are decisive, bold, and strategic. In addition, our attributes include being treacherous, deceitful, and diabolical," The Most High Leader said with imperial flourish. He then jeered as his tail snapped back in rigid attention. "But we never, ever, ever, whine! Therefore, I didn't hear you sniveling over a little setback!"

"Oh no, I am planning Briggs's ruination as we speak. I spoke without thinking, Most High. Briggs is a done deal. It's just my helpers; they are so incompetent."

"Then send them down to the furnace and get new help. New souls are promised every day. Be about our master's business. No more excuses."

"Yeeesss," hissed The Leader as he turned to leave.

"By the way," Most High said to The Leader's back.

The Leader stood stock-still and rotated his large head in deliberate increments until he faced Most High. He waited, impatient for his esteemed mentor to expound.

"Never fail me again. Tsk! You are proving to be a big disappointment. I will not mentor a failure."

The Leader slithered out. He was headed to the war room, to review tried-and-true strategies that worked in the past. At the stone entrance, he placed his claw on the engraved scripted marble. The sizzle of his burnt skin could be heard as the wall moved to reveal tombs that were as old as time. Only those who held the status of leader or higher could access this room. He began at the beginning of the list, starting with the fall of Adam—the ruin of mankind, and moved with craftiness down the rows of ash-crusted volumes. His large clawed finger stopped, and his huge fanged teeth grinned at his luck. He hurried and opened the tomb, relishing the sulfuric dust that rose from its pages. With mischievous glee, he laid the book open and crafted his next move.

Chapter Twenty-four

Wireless cell phones all across the Motor city were flying with scandalous news like brand-new Cadillacs off the assembly line. Each caller had heard how Abigail's empty tittle-tattle was validated by one of Esther's neighbors. She swore she saw with her own eyes, Pastor Stokes going into Esther's home on Friday night carrying groceries. And when she honked her horn, he brazenly waved. Since she was such a reliable source, everything else Abigail insinuated became true, and soon, every meeting Briggs and Esther had was a torrid affair of the heart. Each time the tale was told, it worsened. As the weekend unfolded, imps danced, sat on shoulders, and spoke into uncovered ears and hearts.

The Eggbeaters, one slice of unbuttered toast, and the snippet of parsley looked forlorn on the fine china plate. Mother Reed pushed the food with her fork. "Phyllis, I appreciate you coming over here on a Saturday morning, but, I don't care how nice this plate is. This here food ain't enough to fill up a pea and looks just as tasteless. I might as well be eating paper."

"I did do the best I could," Phyllis said.

Mother Reed softened her tone. "Chile, Mother is trying to get her taste buds to follow her mind and get in line with this new 'heart smart' diet."

Phyllis put her hands on her hips. "I know it's a change, but we want to have you with us. A mild heart attack is a warning sign, so this is what we have to do." Phyllis started moving pots into the sink.

"Well, baby, I guess I deserve that." She watched Phyllis's busy work.

"Ma'am?" Phyllis said wiping the stove with her dish-rag.

"You didn't say that any better than what I said to you in the hospital," Mother Reed said contrite. "Don't act like you don't know what I'm talking about either. Don't have time for that kinda foolishness."

"No, ma'am. It was hard for me to come here today. I felt exposed by your insight. But I love you. So here I am," Phyllis hit the dishrag against her thigh.

Mother Reed puffed her distress. "I'm sorry if I hurt you. I was under the weather and spoke out of turn."

Phyllis nodded her acceptance. "I'm sorry I ran away. Just surprised me, that's all."

"Surprised me too. Li'l gal, you can move."

Mother Reed and Phyllis looked at each other and laughed.

"We a pair, ain't we?" Mother chortled.

Phyllis hooted. "Yes, we are."

"So . . . you holding on?" Mother Reed asked with more laughter.

Phyllis cracked up laughing at the reference Mother Reed made to the rendition of the song, "We'll Understand It Better By and By." She then wiped her eyes and said, "Honestly? I was upset. Okay, the truth: I was angry, then depressed. But I received a call from Esther last night. She fell and hurt her knee Thursday. I wanted to run to her rescue, but she said no. I hung up and started praying; then I could feel in my spirit that God wanted to rescue me."

Mother Reed slapped her knee. "That's right. He sent His Son so we could all be rescued. I can't promise you He'll give you a child, but I can promise you Romans 8:28 that says, everything works together for the good of those who love the Lord and are called according to His purpose. Just ride His wave, chile. Just ride."

"Amen to that," Phyllis answered. "Now, Mother, I'll leave here and go to Esther's to fix her lunch. She should be moving around better tomorrow. But before I go, I believe it's time to eat your breakfast."

"Um. . . um . . . um . . . you know this here meal is doggone awful." Mother Reed's hand clenched her fork. "Phyllis, my phone has been ringing with some slap dap foolishness. Yesterday, my window was open, and dis little boy on the corner tol' his friend he was gon' 'blow it up.' Now, if this here thang don't get right, I'm gon' blow it up at the church house tomorrow. I will snatch the 'hell' right out of Abigail Winters."

Phyllis covered her mouth in an effort to stifle her burst of laughter. Arching her brow in response, Mother Reed daintily forked more fake eggs through her pursed lips, daintily dabbing them with her napkin.

In 1992, Abigail Winters caused a Love Zion controversy over Virginia Johnson, a thirteen-year-old girl in her Sunday School class. It was later learned that she felt it was her Christian duty to report the child's weight gain and bloated stomach as an incestuous pregnancy. She had watched the exchange of loving looks and touches from father to daughter. When she heard the father assuring his daughter that her condition would be taken care of soon, she knew she had to act. Unfortunately, what Abigail assumed was an abortion appointment turned out to be a date with a hot water bottle and some *Midol*. It turned out the teary-eyed Virginia Johnson was a late bloomer experiencing her first menstrual cycle accompanied by cramps. The Love Zion fallout was monumental.

Abigail could take the whispering behind her back and even the slap across her face from Virginia Johnson's grandmother. But the hardest thing for her to bear was the fact that she misunderstood the truth of these things.

She was only eight years old when her father first came into her room at night. He pleaded with her to be a nice little girl, rubbing her young body and crooning her name softly into her ears. Then in the brightness of the day, he ignored her as though she was the lamp on the table he could turn on or off at will. She learned to hate the sound of her name coming from a man's lips.

It was those nights Abigail Winters cried for a mother who had run off two years before. When she left, taking Abigail's younger sister with her, she learned her first lesson about love—people leave you when you most need them, so don't need them. This mantra caused a bitter root to form, and evil its harvest.

Abigail never had a boyfriend, never wanted one. After her daddy, she hated three things: musk cologne, unshaven whiskers, and men. However, she had a score to settle with the Wileys, so they were all open game. It was Elizabeth Wiley who stopped the rumor concerning Virginia Johnson, and in the process, made Abigail a pariah in her own church.

Once again, Abigail had been busy. She sniggered, remembering how Esther used to bring her husband to Love Zion at the outset of their marriage. He was so easy. A word here and there about his successful wife and how awful it was that Esther was overheard talking about having to take care of everything. On the pretense of helping him, she even got Roger a job at her neighbor's garage. She spoon-fed that fool misinformation, and he fed it to Roger. Whoever said men didn't gossip was a liar. The night he grabbed Esther in the church parking lot, it was she who stepped out and called her neighbor to tell him Esther's whereabouts. She knew what would happen. After all, she was the one who planted the seed that Esther was in church too much in the first place.

Chapter Twenty-five

It was Sunday morning, and the whispers of several clusters of church folk could be heard as the small group passed. As the Wiley family and Mother Reed entered the sanctuary, most of the people who were dawdling in the hall crowded in behind them. The tight-knit group found their seats and ignored any harsh glances and whispers surrounding them. They focused on God and as the praise and worship band tuned their instruments, they tuned into Him.

At ten o' clock on the nose, the praise and worship team entered, and in no time, they were destroying the works of the enemy. For many, the shackles of doubt were falling off, and shame was being lifted from burdened shoulders because the anointing was breaking yokes. The congregation held their hands in the air and swayed from side to side, caught up in the mesmerizing voices that sung about the joys of serving Jesus.

Briggs's previous evening was tortuous. He had to explain to the Gregorys that Monica had not shown due to illness. Mrs. Gregory looked skeptical, and Briggs didn't blame her. She mentioned before turning in that she was glad that the food didn't go to waste and, instead, went to Esther and her date.

He never reached Monica, and exhausted with defeat, he went into worship mode and played his favorite music until he could feel the atmosphere in his bedroom shift.

Now he sat behind the pulpit, silently praying and giving praise that the praise and worship team was setting the atmosphere for God's Word to fall on receptive ears. Earlier, the atmosphere had been cold and heavy. But God was moving, and the people were getting free. Briggs approached the pulpit. "He's worthy, saints! Come on and give Him some praise. He woke you up this morning in your right mind and set you on the path of righteousness. My beloved, nobody can do you like Jesus."

The church musicians began a rousing drum and guitar melody of the song "Can't Nobody Do You like Jesus." Briggs sang into the microphone attached to his suit lapel as he danced across the platform; every previous hurt, pain, and rejection melted away under the healing power of his love for God.

"Beloved, I come before you today . . . humbled and in a place of peace surpassing all my understanding. If you don't have love, you don't have peace. Some of you got up this morning, and you forgot the reason you were headed to Love Zion. You thought you came to check out the fashions. Uh-huh. You thought it was about that juicy rumor going around. Uh-huh! But God knows. He changed the venue on the menu. Are you disappointed? The reason why is because you missed your appointment with God. He's here. Where are you? He's moving through the church, touching those who want to be touched. Don't you want to be touched?"

The church got quiet as Briggs mopped his face. He could hear their souls saying, *Who is this young man to tell us why we came to church? How dare he!*

"Oh, I'm stepping on a few toes now. I'm ruffling some feathers, but that's all right! I'd rather have y'all mad at me, than Jesus. Y'all can't do to me what He can do for me." Many of the saints were standing to their feet as Briggs brought the Word. Reverend Gregory was his amen corner. And, somebody in the back started beating their tambourine. "Here you are—fearfully and wonderfully made, yet, you're living below the benefits of your calling. Who would take a dream job and tell their new boss, 'That's okay; I don't need any benefits. I'm fine.' Someone not quite right! Turn to your neighbor and say, 'Get right!' Now, turn to the neighbor on the other side and tell 'em, 'Don't get scared—Pastor's taking us somewhere.'"

The congregation was hyped, and they repeated after Briggs. Those who were lukewarm had gotten off the fence and heard the trumpeting of the angel's message; God is in the house!

Briggs could see Esther was enthralled. The Holy Spirit even let him hear her tell her sister in a whisper, "He can preach." The faces of her family sitting next to her had the same look of pleasure.

Briggs ran across the sanctuary in joy. He was so thankful. "What's wrong with me, you might ask. What benefits? Well, today, we want to talk about the benefit of peace. I'm talking about the peace you can have when your life is upside down. The benefit God wants to give us is when your checks are bouncing all over town, your car just broke down, and you don't know where your wife is! Help me, Holy Ghost! It's a supernatural peace. Stand with me for the reading of God's Word. Turn to Philippians chapter four and let's read versus six through eight. God wants to teach us to be anxious for nothing."

Love Zion stood and opened their Bibles. Briggs read the passage that had gotten him through the night. The more he prayed, the more God poured His love down on him. Today, his cup was running over and everything that was in him poured forth to the people.

Once again, God was moving supernaturally, and Briggs could hear and see into the sanctuary as though people had microphones attached to their hearts and lapels. *What was God doing?*

Mother Reed opened her Bible to the yellow high-lighted passage, and she laid her open palm over the words. Her countenance announced she was delighted by them. Briggs saw that this was familiar scripture for her and had stood her in good stead when God called her husband, Anthony, home. He was glad to know that peace surrounded her, even on the days when she prayed for a son she had not seen since his infancy. Briggs's heart was full.

"You may be seated. Let us pray . . ."

Mother Reed openly nudged Esther. She placed her palm faceup. Esther took her hand, and they prayed together.

Briggs completed his prayer. "When you're anxious, that's a form of fear. When people are fearful, they get dangerous. It takes them into territory like unforgive-ness. You sit in your dark house talking about a dark time in your life, speaking to people who have moved on, 'I'm mad at you because you caused me sleepless nights, hurt, and pain.' People! They have moved on! Unforgiveness causes the peace that was reigning to flee. If we want to have supernatural peace, we have to forgive supernatu-rally. I'm talking about stupid forgiveness. Forgiveness that makes you keep giving good for others' evil. It's not easy. You pray, and then pray some more . . ."

Briggs continued to preach the Word, and the people received. Many undecided hearts changed, and many decided hearts strengthened. Briggs could preach, and God was at work.

God still had His Superantenna on Briggs, and he could see that Abigail was stunned at the power of God operating in him. As he opened the altar for prayer, she was one of the first to come up.

***

After service, Reverend Gregory, First Lady Gregory, and Briggs stood in the church receiving line. Briggs was still shaken by his experience with God. Member after member expressed their pleasure in the day's message, and that although they were sad Reverend Gregory was leaving, he was leaving them in good hands. The Wiley family and Mother Reed finally made it to the first family.

"That was good meat, son, in season," Mother Reed said as she took Briggs's hand. "Can't preach it unless you've walked through it."

Briggs smiled. "I knew you would understand."

Mother Reed nodded her head and moved on to hug the Gregorys.

Esther approached Briggs and grinned widely. "You did a wonderful job. If I wasn't sure before, I'm sure now. You were called to the ministry. The message was moving, and it definitely broke some things for me. I'll study all you gave us the rest of the week."

Phyllis hip bumped Esther to move over. "My little sister is right; your words were a blessing. Forgiveness, even of one's self, is so important."

Briggs put his hand on top of Phyllis's and said, "Thank you for those kind words, but God brought the message, and I'm just His vessel. Glad to finally meet you. I see that good looks are a Wiley family trait."

"He speaks the truth," Charles said as he shook Briggs's hand. "Charles Davis, and the stunning woman you were talking to is my wife, Phyllis. I know you are new to the area, and I'd be glad to have you join me and some of the fellows for some basketball. In fact, I'd be glad to show you around the city if you're up for some male bonding."

"Thanks, I haven't had time for anything like that since I've been here. My jump shot could use some dusting off," Briggs pantomimed the move. "Please call the church office so we can set something up."

Hickman and Elizabeth Wiley brought up the rear of the line. Mr. Wiley said, "A sermon like that needs to settle on a stomach full of good old-fashioned food. Please join the Gregorys at our house for Sunday dinner."

Mrs. Wiley enticed him with vivid dinner details. "It will be good mouth-smacking, down-home cooking, and lots of it. We won't take no for an answer."

"Then I guess you have an additional guest for dinner. It really would be my pleasure." Briggs searched Esther's face over her mother's shoulder to see her reaction.

Esther smiled in acknowledgment of Briggs's silent query. Her smile transmitted yes, she had forgiven him for their earlier misunderstanding concerning his marriage. He was welcome to her parents' home.

Esther stayed back as the others walked off. "It seems I owe you a great meal after yesterday. Thank you for dropping dinner by. It was delicious. Our first lady can really burn." Esther stared over his shoulder looking around. "I don't want to be rude, but Monica couldn't make it?"

Briggs looked uncomfortable. "She's under the weather and will have to reschedule her trip. I better go and close up my office. I'll see you in a few."

Esther nodded and watched Briggs hurry away. She had a thoughtful look on her face as she walked out of the church.

Chapter Twenty-six

The Wiley dinner was a hit. The smell of fried chicken, beef brisket, mashed potatoes, collard greens, and corn bread still permeated the air.

After dinner, everyone moved to the heart of the home, their family room. The burnished hardwood flooring gleamed with pride, and the striped wallpaper boasted mounted porcelain plates illustrating scenes from early African American life. The overstuffed olive-green couches, striped olive-green and lavender chairs, and the wide-screen television invited, "Come on in and sit a spell."

"So how are you getting along in Detroit? We treating you well?" Charles asked as he got up and gave Briggs the universal brother handshake.

"Man, I've been so busy I really haven't seen the city."

"That may be a good thing," Phyllis said. "Just kidding. I love my city."

Briggs made his way to an overstuffed chair when he noticed Wiley family portraits lined across the cherry wood fireplace mantle. Esther's high school graduation picture glowed like a pot of gold compared to the others that surrounded it. And like a miner in the California gold rushes of old, he was getting feverish being near it. Looking at her back then sent memories sweeping through him like currents from a raging river: smells, sounds, lips. He frowned. If he couldn't control his thoughts he needed to leave.

"That dinner was the best I've had, Mrs. Wiley," Briggs said, determined to turn his attention elsewhere.

"Don't make me smack you, Briggs," Mrs. Gregory threatened playfully.

Briggs blushed at his error. "Oh, right! The only equal to this meal is when Mrs. Gregory cooks dinner. You're both superb cooks."

Mother Reed joined in. "So, what you saying about the meal *I* fixed you?"

Briggs turned redder and stammered, "*All* the home cooked meals I've eaten since I've been here are exceptional."

Everyone laughed and teased him about his new skill in diplomacy.

Phyllis tapped her fork on her dessert plate to change the subject. "Pastor Stokes, I found your topic of forgiveness an important one. Often, people won't let their past mistakes go. We live in an Internet society where your business is on front street every minute of the day. People are so punitive. No wonder society is depressed and lonely."

Briggs was passionate in his answer. "Many spend time in a desolate place, trying to search for what's missing. In many cases, being depressed and lonely leads us into making more mistakes, because we're trying to appease our appetites with empty calories like alcohol, drugs, sex, gossiping, and bitterness. What we need is a spiritual eraser to remove the mistake so we can begin again."

Mother Reed clapped her hands. "Say that . . ." She pointed at Briggs. "We were given the eraser long ago, son. Jesus supplied it with His blood. We have to stop being people pleasers and vow to please God. You know what the hardest thing was when I learned to walk in God's obedience?"

Elizabeth Wiley encouraged, "Tell us, Mother."

"Blocking out what seemed like God. Yeah, that was hard. Remember back in the Garden of Eden?" Mother Reed clasped her hands and rocked.

"What happened in the garden, Mother?" Reverend Gregory egged her on.

"Well, that old serpent sounded right, he walked right. Surely, he couldn't be wrong, right?" Mother Reed chortled in glee. "Took two saints and all of mankind straight into sin, listening to what seemed right. Adam had the Word of it by God Himself. Yet, they faltered. How many of us falter doing what seems like the right thang?"

Reverend Gregory nodded. "I've been trapped and made that mistake myself. I still have to be watchful that I'm following the will of God and not the will of my congregation. Sometimes the pressure to give in is so great, I just fall to my knees and seek His face."

Phyllis added, "But how many men fall on their faces? Not many. I've seen enough of these religious television shows to know something is wrong. How come you can only get a blessing if you in the one hundred-dollar line? What I get for my two dollars?"

Mr. Wiley interrupted. "See, y'all done started something . . . now . . . here we go."

Everyone began to talk and throw their opinions across the room. Dessert was served and forks and spoons clicked against bone china. Over the loud din Briggs and Esther sought each other and smiled.

As the evening set, people gathered in clusters talking. Briggs and Charles had hit it off and exchanged phone numbers. Over by the entertainment center, they had a lively discussion on sports and the stock market.

Mother Reed had a knowing look on her face when she called out in a loud voice, "Elizabeth, just because I'm down here quiet 'bout it don't mean I'm over that meal you gave me. I know I was sick, and you believe you helping, but, chile, I needs to have something to look forward to. I don't believe in speaking darkness; otherwise, I'd tell you something 'bout this tasteless gelatin dessert. You'd best know that."

"Yes, Mother, I know. I'm sorry, but I love you enough to be okay with you being mad at me. It's not as bad as you think. You just have to get used to it," Elizabeth said.

"Oh, I ain't mad at you. I'm gon' save my wrath for the enemy. Get ready, y'all, 'cause he trying to come to a party he ain't been invited to." Mother Reed shook her aging fist.

"There you go being all mysterious. I ain't scared, bring it on!" Phyllis laughed. "This cheesecake is wonderful, Mama. Real tasty, um yum, real good."

"We ain't friends no more, Phyllis," Mother Reed said giving her a mock glare.

The crowd howled with laughter as everyone enjoyed themselves into the evening.

The Leader sat outside and peered through the window. He looked down at his imps lined across the outside wall and cursed the Wileys' daily prayer life. He hated being on the outside looking in. "Imp One!"

"Yes, my leader," the imp answered as it scurried to his leader's side.

"You did read the plans?"

"Yes, O Mighty One. Brilliant, just brilliant," it lisped.

The Leader started to scream at the sycophant's empty flattery, when he remembered Most High's previous annoyance with him, so, he was calm when he said, "Then what happened at the church?"

"I can explain it all. Everything was set; the old gossip was moving through the congregation filling all the right ears. Ears that we knew would twist and turn new

lies into slanderous mudslinging. It was so good, the sanctuary was heavy with the stink of it."

"How do you know?"

"We were able to get in once the maliciousness started. You should have seen them, Leader. This one ran to this one, and then this one approached that one. Only a handful turned and walked away, shaking their heads. The majority of those so-called Christians got right down in the dirt and played."

"Watch what you say, you've been warned before. We don't call out that name in any form here. Then what happened?"

"The pastors and the praise and worship team weren't in the room; they were somewhere closeted off, praying. When they came in and the praise and worship team started singing, I could see the fabric of our influence begin to tear. Then the smaller imps began to call out in agony and disappear from the room."

The Leader spoke in a soft voice mindful of Most High's lecture, "Continue."

Imp One began to relax in his storytelling. "Then our assignment, the Briggs human, got up and began to speak. His voice filled the sanctuary and soon a perfumed ambiance saturated the air. Bit by bit, my subordinates shrieked out their distress, and then vanished. I hung in there, O Great One; there was fire singeing my scales, and painful sores materializing on my upper torso, but I stayed. All of a sudden, one minute I was standing inside the sanctuary, and the next minute, I had joined my legion writhing on the outside."

"Imp One?"

"Yessss . . . Leader," he lisped.

"You're fired!" The Leader said as a ball of fire previously known as Imp One exploded in front of him. "No pun intended," he smirked while bringing his tail up to

circle his shoulders in an intimate caress. He needed the comfort of self-love. Already he could feel a demon-size headache coming on.

After loving on himself, The Leader then turned to the shaking throng of miscreants, "Imp Two!"

Imp Two was hesitant, but all of the other imps reshuffled around him, leaving him open for display. He finally wobbled before The Leader, ever mindful of the ashes strewn at his feet. "Yes?" he squeaked.

"You have been promoted. You'll now answer to your new level, Imp One. Familiarize yourself with the plan . . ."

Later, The Leader lay warming himself before a raging furnace. He had studied everyone involved. He knew his plan was a good one. Soon, he would be able to destroy them all.

Chapter Twenty-seven

Esther sat at her desk frustrated by the government bureaucracy that was stifling her at every turn. This zoning problem was becoming an albatross around her neck. She'd reach someone, only to be told to call someone else, and then so on. She noted her lunch hour was over, blew a silky strand of hair out of her face, and closed church business.

The buzz of the phone interrupted her musing. "Yes?" she answered as she hit her intercom.

"A tall, fine, upstanding citizen is here to see you, Ms. Esther. 'Bout time too," Simone giggled.

"I can do without the descriptive narrative, Simone. Does the gentleman have a name?"

"Now you know, you know who this hunk is," whispered Simone, "however . . . your game, your rules."

Esther sputtered as she heard Simone say to her visitor, "Sir, may I have your name?"

"Lawton," he answered with a smile in his voice as he flashed his law enforcement identification.

Simone repeated into the intercom. "His name is Lawton. As in . . . the law—he can lock me up anytime. You know—law, as in let his justice be served. As in book me and hook me, Dano, as in—"

"I get it, Simone. Please ask Lawton to have a seat; I'll be right with him."

Esther turned the intercom off. She rambled to an empty room as she cleared her desk. "I will have a long talk with her about professional decorum. She is back on my prayer list. That child need Jesus."

Esther peeked out the door and saw Simone leaning toward Lawton in a too familiar way.

"Can I get you anything, anything at all while you wait?" She then whispered, "Me?"

Lawton hid a grin at Simone's blatant invitation. He appeared to be used to this type of attention and to be unmoved by her boldness. "No, thank you. I'll just sit over here."

Esther stepped back with a satisfied grin and opened the closet door in her office; she peered into the long oval glass and fluffed out her hair. She was impressed he didn't flirt back. She rummaged in her purse, pulled out a lipstick and gloss, and touched up her lips. She then spritzed perfume in the air and walked through it, after which she opened her office window and tried to fan out the residue. After putting lotion on her hands, she was ready.

The door to Esther's office opened and a calm and collected vision walked out of the door, summoning Lawton. He strode toward Esther without hesitation. Esther kept her eyes trained on this fine specimen of God's handiwork. At his approach, she backed into her office, and lay back against her door so he could pass by her and enter. Before she closed the door she stole a peek at Simone. She smiled at her reaction and her statement.

Simone remained seated with her mouth open. "Dang, you work it, girl. Still waters do run deep."

Esther motioned for Lawton to have a seat. Instead, he kept coming forward. Her early finesse began to dissolve as he invaded her personal space. "You smell really good."

Esther stuttered. "Um, th-th-anks."

"You look really good," Lawton said emphasizing the word, *good.*

"Oh, well, yes, thank you," Esther stumbled backward.

"And . . . you look . . . uncomfortable," Lawton said with a Cheshire grin.

"Well, you're all up in my personal space," Esther replied with false bravado.

Lawton folded his arms. "You did summon me."

Esther shook her head in the negative. "No, I just invited you in."

"Felt like a summons," Lawton said, rubbing his chin.

Esther tapped her foot. She was now on the defensive. "No, I was being polite, and, by the way, I didn't invite you to visit me today. You came here on your own."

"Man doesn't live by bread alone," Lawton advanced toward her.

Esther pushed out her hand for him to stop. "Lawton?"

"Yes?" he asked with a sneaky grin on his face.

"You're about to aggravate me," Esther said in a sing-song voice.

Lawton gave a full belly laugh. "Then I'll stop."

Esther sighed in relief. "Good. I don't know why you like to do that. Now please have a seat."

Lawton sat. He looked around the office and liked the small personal touches he saw reflecting Esther's warm personality. He folded his arms and came to the reason for his visit. "Would you have dinner with me tonight?"

"This is kinda short notice." Esther looked down at her calendar.

Lawton exhaled. "Look, I'm a straightforward person, and I'm not into playing a lot of games. I'm hungry, and it crossed my mind earlier, you might be hungry—if so, maybe we could get something to eat together."

Esther paused. "I am hungry. You're in for a big bill," she warned.

Lawton stood. "Baby, you just let me worry about the bill. How about six?"

"Make it five-thirty and we got a date. I told you, I'm hungry," Esther snapped saucily.

Lawton laughed and opened the door. "I'll pick you up at your house."

"Good enough," Esther replied, "Oh, Lawton?"

"Yes?"

"Thanks," she said with a splash of impishness and sass.

Lawton grabbed his heart. "Lord, hav' mercy!" he exclaimed as he exited the door.

Esther bit her lip with a secret smile as she watched Lawton leave. Her eye feast was interrupted by someone blocking her vision as they moved down the hallway—fast. It looked like John, her housing manager. She wondered if he had been waiting to see her. If so, why did he leave in such a hurry? Esther wondered at Simone's irritated face as her eyes followed John's retreat.

She waited on her to say something about John. Instead, Simone nodded after Lawton. "Girlfriend got skills," she said in admiration.

Esther's eyes stretched wide in disbelief. "Simone, come in my office please."

"Uh-oh . . ."

Roger sat in the bus depot in front of Esther's building. He frowned as he saw the same police officer from the previous week skip down the front steps. He cursed his displeasure. "What the heck is he doing here, again?"

He pulled his hood over his head and scooted down the worn bench in the opposite direction. Quickly, he picked up a discarded newspaper and peered over it as he ambled down the street. As he camouflaged his exit his chest felt on fire. The burning was becoming unbearable, and he had not slept. When he did sleep, his dreams were of Esther cringing in fear from him, begging him to take her back. In his warmest visions he never showed her mercy. Instead, he watched the blood drain slowly from her face. Roger thrust the visions away from him. He had to make it home before the landlord did his weekly evening rounds. The deadbolt lock he stole had done the trick and had kept the landlord out. The problem was he had to get inside before he ran into the old geezer. He still didn't have his rent. He did have a plan. Soon, Esther would take care of his cash flow issues.

Hours later, night descended. Outside, a short distance away from the stench of Roger's apartment, garbage trucks could be heard removing the refuse of wasted lives on a street that was a way station for the lost and tormented. As Roger turned in his slumber, his dreams were those of lust, greed, and revenge. Flies flew around his unshaven face, and his roughened hand swatted them away. His snores batted out loud rumblings from the awakening sounds of morning and were interspersed with an incoherent mumbling of his obsession. "Esther."

"Well, Imp One, you seem to be lining things up quite nicely," The Leader reviewed Imp One's latest log entries.

"Yessss . . . Leader; I am using finesse to destroy them all. I feel it is a much-better move to yank happiness away then to never know it. Let Esther feel joy, and then steal it—that's my plan. It worked so well when she wanted to be Cinderella. And, then again, when she fell in love with Briggs. She faltered for years after each event. Let history repeat itself," Imp One bowed in humble regard.

The Leader stood on his tail. "And I like that. You may leave me now, but continue to stay on top of things. I grow tired of training new help."

Imp One scurried out of The Leader's sight without answering. He hated The Leader, hated his assignment, and even more, he hated this place. There were times when he had glimpses of others lives and the peace called to him. But the feeling was fleeting. He remembered once trying to rub against the silkiness of perfumed hair as a faint voice sang of love, but there was a hedge of protection and he could not connect. In the past, he would concentrate on the song and try to make out the words, but he could only make out, "For the # tells me so." No matter how hard he concentrated, the middle word was always garbled, and then he would feel hot, searing fire across his face and chest. Over time, he had learned to let the thoughts and memories go. Somehow, he felt he was better off without them.

Chapter Twenty-eight

Briggs met with Reverend Gregory at noon and received all the keys to the church building. Keys meant power; they also meant accountability. It was official, Briggs was in charge. The problem with being in charge of the church was that he felt out of control in his life. He heard another minister call it leading while bleeding. He felt the supernatural movement of God on Sunday was His way of letting him know he was called.

Briggs pulled the car over and pulled out his phone. As he tapped numbers, he hoped his day would take a turn for the better.

"Hello?" a strong male voice answered.

"What's happening, man? This is Briggs; I was hoping you were free to maybe show me some Motor City sites today or even pick up a game of basketball. Afterward, we can catch something to eat."

"Sounds like a plan," Charles responded.

"Why don't I swing by there in about an hour?" Briggs maneuvered the car into traffic.

Across town, Lawton opened the door for Esther to enter the restaurant. The place resembled a cathedral with its high beamed ceilings and stained glass windows. It was close to her home, had good food, and was popular. Her five-thirty suggestion allowed them to beat the crowd.

"Thank you, kind sir," Esther flirted.

Lawton grinned in approval at Esther's lighthearted mood. "You're welcome."

A hostess escorted them to their table, and when the waiter came, they helped each other choose their meals. The pair continued their upbeat conversation, soon turning their chatter to family members and family stories.

Lawton's laugh was hearty as the waiter placed his plate of crab cakes in front of him.

Esther howled as Lawton shared more stories about his family. "Please tell me more. Your grandmother sounds like a lot of fun. A straight shooter, but fun."

"Okay, let's see now . . . how about instead, I let you get to know her husband, my grandpa Larry? Here's an old story the family tells. Grandpa went to meet my uncle Langston's ship when he came home from the navy. Oh, they were so proud of him. But it was Grandpa who was the proudest. So, here comes Unc' off the ship, and he and Grandpa hug and laugh like they crazy. When they let go and turn to leave, Grandpa notices that Unc' is walking, leaning sideways, like he's about to fall off the path." Lawton sipped his water. "Grandpa asks, 'Boy, why you walking like that?' Unc' says, ''Cause, I been on that there ship tossing and turning in the ocean for three years, Daddy. So, I don' learned to adjust.'" Lawton paused, and then brought the joke home. "Grandpa replied, 'Adjust? Boy, I been married to your mama for pert near thirty-five years, don' had twelve children wit' the woman. You don't see me walking like this.'" Lawton lifted from his chair and pantomimed a pumping motion with his body.

Esther sputtered out her drink laughing hard. She was wiping her eyes, when she said, "You betta stay saved, boy!"

"Grandpa Larry was a pastor," Lawton said with an earnest look on his face.

She looked surprised, and then they both fell out laughing again. Esther hadn't dated much so she didn't have a lot to compare it to. But, she was having an amazing time with Lawton.

Later, he was paying the check when she made a decision. "Would you like to come over for coffee or tea?"

"Is that anything like being invited up to see your etchings?" he teased.

Esther grabbed her purse and hit him with it lightly. "Now, you *know* I mean just coffee, tea, but none of me."

He guided her toward the exit. "Man, and here I am needing a caffeine fix."

"Well, you're welcome to stop at Starbuck's."

He bent over holding his stomach as he cracked up. While his head was down a pair of expensive wing tips stepped into his line of vision.

Esther was flustered to see Briggs and her brother-in-law, Charles, entering the restaurant. "Oh, my goodness, how're you guys doing?"

Charles hugged her. "My favorite little sister. Girl, you guys were laughing so loud, I want to know what all the ruckus is about."

"Shush, you can't talk about loud. Let me introduce you. Lawton, this is my brother-in-law, Charles, and my friend and pastor, Briggs Stokes. Hello, Briggs."

Lawton greeted both men. "Charles, it's good to meet you. Briggs and I have already had the privilege of meeting."

"And here you are again." Briggs gave him the "what's up" head nod.

Lawton returned a stiff smile. Esther felt the tension between the two men. In the awkwardness of the moment, she concentrated on arranging her pashmina scarf.

Charles turned to Lawton. "Good to meet you. We'll let you get back to your date . . . uh, I mean . . . yeah, bye."

Lawton shook his hand, amused at his discomfort. "Great meeting you too, Charles."

He then nodded his head toward Briggs. "The food here is the best I've ever eaten, or maybe it's just the company. In any case, enjoy your meal."

Briggs and Charles smiled in answer and walked by.

Esther placed her hand on her hip and arched her eyebrow. "Is this going to spoil our evening?"

Lawton took her hand off her hip and placed it on his arm. "No, I wouldn't let anything spoil tonight. I'm having a great time."

"Me too," although, the truth was, she was straining to concentrate on the rest of her date and ignore her curiosity that Briggs's wife was still absent. *And now he's hanging out with Charles?*

"I'm glad the restaurant is so close to your house." Lawton relaxed and beamed at her.

"What house? I thought you wanted to go to Starbuck's?" Esther tossed out as she walked off into the night.

As a customer opened the restaurant door, the sound of Lawton's loud, happy laughter could be heard inside of the restaurant where Briggs and Charles waited for a table.

Esther and Lawton sat on her couch sipping coffee. Soft lighting illuminated the atmosphere, creating a warm and inviting glow. It allowed her to sneak glances at Lawton on the sly.

In return, he scrutinized her in blatant appreciation. When she rose to refill his cup, he stomped his foot three times on the floor as he observed her hynotpic sway to a hidden rhythm all her own. "Girl, you are putting a hurting on a brother. Uh, uh, uh."

Esther's grin widened and with a mischievous gleam she stopped, curtsied, and twirled.

He laughed in obvious pleasure, "And you're entertaining too." She made a silly face, and his laughter dwindled. His demeanor transformed to one of wonder. "I have had a wonderful time tonight. You are so beautiful, girl; inside and out. You are a good thing."

Flustered, Esther fanned the napkins forgetting to hand him one. "Um, you sure have a way of speaking your mind."

He gave her a smoldering look. "It saves time and misunderstandings. What I wanted to ask is, if you don't mind, I would like to pursue you."

"Pursue me?" Her hands twisted the napkins, shredding them.

He was gentle as he removed the napkins out of her hands. "Yes, pursue you, woo you, and then, God willing, keep you."

Her cheeks flooded with color. "Lord, Jesus. You can't be serious—after one date?"

Lawton pulled Esther into his arms. "I don't believe in starting something we can't finish. So you think about it. I'll be in contact." He hugged her in a tender caress and released her. He then headed toward her front door. "By the way, my father knew he was going to marry my mother the first time he saw her. That was *before* their first date. And my grandfather who had twelve children? Well, he started the trend." Lawton winked at Esther. "I'll see myself out."

Esther remained seated on the couch for the next half hour, too dazed to move.

At the restaurant, it took over forty-five minutes for Briggs and Charles to get a table. Crowded for a weeknight, they talked sports until they were seated.

Charles looked at Briggs over his menu. "You know you got it bad, right?"

Briggs didn't pretend to misunderstand him. "I do not have it bad, but if I did have it bad, I don't have the right to have it bad. I'm married, Charles," Briggs scanned his menu, wary of the conversation's direction. "The fried catfish sounds good." He couldn't help adding, "She looked good, didn't she?"

"See? You couldn't keep your eyes off of her at dinner on Sunday or tonight. And I know you're just getting to know me. And you're a pastor, and you can tell me to mind my own business. But I love that girl as if she was my own flesh and blood. I mean no disrespect, but you have an itch, son. And you need to go get your wife to scratch it."

Briggs sat quiet for so long that Charles felt bad he had butted in where he wasn't wanted. After all, they had just met, and maybe it didn't matter that they had connected so well. What he really wanted to know was where Briggs's wife was while he was here in Detroit.

Charles had not intended to offend. "Man, I'm sorry. I was out of line. I . . ."

Briggs shook his head for Charles to let it go. "First, it's not like me to talk to strangers. I'm a very private person. Mother Reed had me spilling all of my business to her. I understood that. It was a move of God. I do feel a spiritual connection with you, and a brother's bond . . . although you shoot hoops like a girl," Briggs said and laughed.

Charles scowled. "You wish. I was easy on you, being a pastor and all."

Briggs smiled, and then he blew heavily and sat back. He closed, then opened his eyes. "Okay, maybe talking it out man to man versus man to spiritual father will give me another perspective. My wife, Monica, is in Atlanta avoiding me. It's a game she's played before. Monica likes to play games. She hated the idea of me coming here and getting a temporary church."

Charles sat in contemplation. "Man, that's deep. I appreciate your openness, and I will respect your confidence. I haven't been in your situation, but I can't imagine not fixing this face to face. You should go home, Briggs."

Briggs pulled a plane ticket out of his pocket and laid it on the table. "Already on it. I guess my pride was prohibiting me from doing it before. I've run behind her for so long, I just got tired. I have prayed about it, and I feel God is telling me that I'll find answers when I get there."

"Why don't we pray in agreement right here and now, that you stay in God's will concerning your marriage?" Charles said, giving him the dap handshake.

They bowed their heads and prayed in silence.

Briggs's eyes glistened. "I tell you, Charles, first Mother Reed, and now you. Whew . . . what's in the water here in Detroit? I've never talked so much about my personal life or felt lighter because of it."

"We care," Charles said. "I don't make new friends without due consideration; I'm a deliberate man. As a structural engineer, I'm methodical. But, there has to be somebody you can be yourself around. As a pastor, the pedestal is so high up, it can get pretty lonely. I got you, my brother. And I believe that whatever you find waiting for you in Atlanta, God will be in control."

"Amen. Man, I'm so glad we hooked up," Briggs told Charles as the waitress approached for their order. "You should be happy too. Because, next time, I'll teach you how to make that jump shot."

Chapter Twenty-nine

Esther was startled by the midnight ringing of her phone. She was cautious when she answered. "Yes?"

"Ms. Esther, this is Simone. I'm sorry for calling you so late, but I've been struggling all night with telling you something. And I just have to do it now. I've chickened out too many times before. Please don't be mad at me."

Esther's sigh was loud at hearing Simone's dramatic plea. "Go on, Simone. It must be important to you to wake me up at this hour. What do you need? You want to take more time off?" Simone had taken two leaves of absence in the past.

"No. See, you try to look out for somebody and they try to act like they doing you a favor . . ."

"Simone—please, what is it? It's too late for this nonsense." Esther was irritated and sleepy.

Simone said in a frantic rush, "They got it in for you."

"Who is they?"

"John and his people. I swear I didn't know they were stealing money, but they were . . ."

Stunned, Esther moved from the bed to her vanity chair. "What money are you talking about?"

"The housing grant money. It started with John overcharging the agency for work that he had his bootlegged friends perform. The money then got split between them. Somehow, some real lowlifes got wind of the scheme and decided to take it even further and add substandard merchandise to the table. Everybody's been getting paid."

"But, Max, in housing quality control, is supposed to sign off that the work is up to standard. And I checked the vendor bids myself. We picked only those who met the requirements and had the best bids."

"Max's wife left him, and he's paying child support, alimony, and has a new young girlfriend. He signs off; they kick back. The scam is in from the beginning. They use dummy businesses and put in sky-high bids, so that their bids look good."

"But the Request For Proposals went out in the classi-fieds and other correspondence," Esther felt weak in her stomach at the scandal that this would cause.

Simone became even more agitated. "Stop trying to look for a way this couldn't have happened. It happened. The Requests For Proposals never saw the light of day. The copies you see in the grant file are from years ago. The dates have all been doctored. I'm telling you, I have done my homework. It's bad—real bad."

"And you're just letting me know? Simone, I trusted you."

Simone began to whimper as though she was in phys-ical pain. "But I only found out something was wrong a few days ago and confirmed it today. John was in the office earlier, and I knew my suspensions were justified when he kept trying to see the new bid folder. When you opened the door, he took off down the hall. I was going to bring up my concerns, but you were so busy chastising me about my office decorum that the moment passed."

"Are you for real? This is fraud—something way bigger than your hurt feelings," Esther shrieked, biting her nails, a habit she had stopped in her teens. "How did you figure it out?"

Simone, her voice etched with pride, said, "Well, ever since you moved everything dealing with housing to our offices, all related paperwork crosses my desk. For example, I collect the vendor bids on projects, put them in priority order by job, and then place them in your box for your review." Simone finally paused to breathe.

"Go on," Esther encouraged.

"When I was placing the latest faxes in your bin, I noticed that at the top of the page, several had the same fax numbers. I thought that, in error, I had made duplicate copies. But I cross-referenced them, and they were different companies' bids. I then pulled out all the bids from the last six months, and no matter the name of the company, the same three fax numbers were used, time and time again," Simone ended in triumph.

Esther's eyebrow was raised as she said, "Uh-huh, now that explains some of what you know, but not all of it. Spit it all out. No sense in hiding any of it."

"I'm trying to, but this ain't easy telling. Anyway, earlier, John was at my desk while you had Lawton in your office, and I talked to him about it. He told me he would check into it, and that I needn't worry you."

Esther sighed heavily. "I'm still waiting for you to tell me how you found out the rest."

"Uumm . . . me and John have been kicking it romantically, and I overheard him tonight on the phone in the bathroom. He thought I was asleep," Simone said in a rush.

"You and John? Didn't you call him a dog?" Esther asked incredulous.

"See . . . and I was right! I should have followed my first instinct," Simone moaned. "Now, I realize he approached me only after you restructured the bidding process to go through you."

Esther started pulling paper out of her drawer and writing notes. "Sorry about that, Simone, but you deserve and can do better. What else?"

Simone hated admitting this part. "I didn't think it would do any harm in letting him see the bids as they came in. He still couldn't approve anything."

"No, just underbid any legitimate bidder," Esther fumed.

"I hate to tell you this, but it goes even deeper. You know how sometimes you go on about your church and their community projects? That made John take notice of the renovations you guys did on those houses, and his new crew bought up the surrounding properties for cents on a dollar. They are going to use what you've accomplished as a model, and then get people to buy from them, and they'll use cheap material and cheap labor to dupe people out of hundreds of thousands of dollars. In two years, those people will have plumbing, electrical, and all sorts of other problems. And once they can't keep up with the cost to maintain those shoddy buildings, the neighborhood will go down again."

"But we worked so hard to turn that neighborhood around," Esther lamented.

"Yes, and you did such a good job that they want to take it over. I'm so sorry. Ms. Esther, am I fired? I need my job," Simone wailed.

Esther was firm in her response. "Simone, do not, I repeat, do *not* tell *anyone* any of this. I'm going to do everything I can to get both of us out of this mess."

"Thank you, Ms. Esther," she cried. "Thank you. You gave me a chance when you hired me six years ago, and I've never forgotten it. I promised I would always look out for you. I'm sorry, girl. Whatever you need, just let me know. I know I let you down. But, please let me be present when you fire John's butt."

Esther was seething in a cold rage. "Simone, good night."

In the waning night, Esther was frantic. She looked at her notes and tried to think of a strategy to make things right. After three hours, she realized she couldn't. At the end, all she could do was pray.

Chapter Thirty

Esther sat in her office and stretched her arms over her head and wished for more hours in a day. She was whipped. Between Simone's late-night bombshell and Lawton's missile, she hadn't slept at all. She asked herself how she could save the church, the agency, and herself from the machinations of evil. And then she wondered about the true heart of this deep brother who claims he's seen what God has for him, and it's her. She had to wonder, right now, what could he really do for her?

The beeping of the office intercom signaled an incoming call from Simone.

"Yes, Simone?"

"Lawton is on line one. You all right?"

"Put him through, please," Esther said in a monotone voice, ignoring her question. She knew none of this was Simone's fault, but dang if she felt like talking to her about it. She was glad Simone told her, and she would protect her privacy from the backlash as much as possible, but that was as much grace as she could muster today.

Lawton's strong voice was calm and soothing. "Hey, sweetheart, I told you I'd be in touch. I'm just checking on you. I want you to know that giving you time to think doesn't mean I'm going to punish myself by not seeing or talking to you."

"I appreciate the candor, but I'm not the best company right now," Esther said. Then an inner nudge prompted her to share. She didn't think she could do this alone.

"Maybe I can help. I'd like to be there for you. Whatever it is must have come up after I left you yesterday evening. Am I right?" Lawton said in investigative mode.

"Yes, Dear Watson. How'd you figure that out?"

"Because I might have left you stunned, but you weren't afraid. I hear fear and worry in your voice."

Esther wanted—no, needed—someone to confide in. She decided to take the risk and trust Lawton with the entire story. *I pray this is the right thing to do.*

Thirty minutes later, Lawton whistled when she was through with her tale. "Wow, that's quite a story. Let me make some discreet inquiries with the fraud unit here. In the meantime, sit tight until I call you back. And, baby . . ."

"Yes?" Esther said, hope infused in her response.

"You did the right thing in confiding in me."

Esther decided to believe that, for once, she could get in the passenger seat and let someone else drive her safely home. It had been a long time since she had believed in happily ever after.

The morning stretched into late afternoon as Esther watched the clock and her phone. She was anxious to hear back from Lawton.

She bemoaned. "Come on, man, call." She smiled when her phone rang.

"Ms. Wiley, this is Richard Parker, of the zoning commission, returning your call."

"Thank you so much. I was calling on the matter of the residential housing program Love Zion Fellowship Church sponsors for families who need assistance. We've received word that the commission wants to rezone the neighborhood and make our families move out. I'm sure, there has been some miscommunication."

"No. I remember the matter coming before the commission and several area residents complaining about the type of people who are moving into your properties."

"I cannot understand why, Mr. Parker. The church is very conscientious in the screening of applicants and helps them budget and save so that they can move out and purchase their own home. So far, four families have moved out and purchased homes in nearby neighborhoods. Not only is the program good for them, but it is also good for the community. Houses once boarded up are now restored and filled with people who are hardworking homeowners. They cherish having their own places. Detroit's once thriving neighborhoods are dying. We're reviving them. How can you close us down?"

Mr. Parker wavered. "Well . . ."

Esther pushed ahead. "Mr. Parker, can I ask you something?"

"Yes, at this point, I think it would be futile to try to stop you," he said with humor.

"Is there any particular person or entity pushing this move?" *Besides the devil.*

"Now, Ms. Wiley, some zoning business is private."

Esther huffed. "Yes, but most is a matter of public record. I thought you might help me forego having to look the information up. It would be a shame if it came to light that people had their own agendas for the neighborhood."

"Lawton said you were feisty!" Mr. Parker said with a chuckle in his voice.

"Lawton? Lawton Redding?" Esther said, astonished.

"Yeah, Lawton and I go way back. We're frat brothers. Frat so nice they had to name us twice."

"Oh, I see . . . anyway . . ." Esther dragged out the word *anyway* almost as an insult.

"Cold, girl, you cold."

Esther now knew he was on her side. "My information?"

"Okay, there is a small group of investors who have taken note of the growing possibilities in the neighborhood. You were right when you said your church cleaned it up. You did such a good job that all those old stately but dilapidated homes are about to be bought by this group. Ever heard of gentrification?"

"Yes, but it sounds to me like plain greedification. And if you know what's going on, why don't you stop it?" Esther asked. Lawton's frat brother or not, she had no intention of tipping her hand and letting anyone else know just how much she knew.

"It's already too far gone. Whoever in your group picked those properties, they knew what they were doing. Those are the choicest lots, and that's what the new and improved urban dweller is looking for. The money stakes are high."

"Noooo," Esther said, upset at this newest information.

"My sentiments exactly. Let me leave you with some advice. First, you never spoke to me; second, I have, before me, a list of three people who may feel like you do about big business pushing out the working poor, and they have enough power to do something about it; and three, Lawton's a good man. Hold on to him. I'll e-mail you the names from my home e-mail."

Esther gave him her e-mail address and smiled as she hung up. She looked at her watch and dialed Lawton's cell. "Hey, you, I just heard from Richard Parker. You do good work."

"Oh, I'm just getting started. I wasn't sure what Richard could do for you, but I remembered who he worked for and thought it was worth a shot. How are you, sweetheart?"

"I'm a little less stressed, but he'll e-mail me the names of some people who might be persuaded to help."

"Good. I also talked to our fraud unit, and if you come down tomorrow, they've agreed to talk to you. So many people getting scammed these days they almost said no, but a brother gotta little pull. How are you handling work?" Lawton's voice carried genuine concern.

"I know it's not her fault, but I'm not talking to Simone. And if John hadn't called in sick today, I'm not sure what I would say to him. I figure by tomorrow, I can fake the like."

"Just think of it as your own private acting lesson. You can't let them know what you know, or they'll get rid of the evidence." In a Mr. T voice he said, "Sit tight, girl. We gon' bust these fools."

"You are my A team. My hero," Esther gushed.

"I'm auditioning for becoming your man. Esther, I will always put forth my best effort to take care of you, if you let me," Lawton said sincerely.

"Now, you have me over here blushing. You should stop all that daytime flirting."

"Then maybe we ought to do some nighttime courting. The ball is in your court, and it is your serve."

"Bye, Lawton," Esther wondered what any of her next moves would be.

"Bye," Lawton said softly. "A man can always hope."

Chapter Thirty-one

It was Sunday, and Esther's previous week had been grueling. Her visit with the fraud unit went well, and after she gave them all of the evidence she and Simone had gathered, they were impressed. They were working with the prosecutor's office and the federal government to gather all the charges because federal Housing Urban Development grant funds were being stolen. Her nerves were frayed some days, just pretending that everything was business as usual, but they had sworn her to silence, so mum was the word.

Esther spent several days catching up with the three contacts Richard Parker had given her. She understood that even when the police caught the thieves in action, the community would still need to be convinced that her tenants were not a threat. She was excited because all but one had sat on community boards with her. Finally, she had meetings scheduled, and she could report back to Briggs. She had been so busy that she hadn't had time to think about him or Lawton. She hadn't even called her mother for her twice-a-week check-in.

She looked in the mirror and adjusted her hat. She was going to church old school today. The deep golden color of the fabric and the chocolate band complemented her gold and brown suit. She pulled the veil across her face, and then adjusted her brown satin gloves. Her chocolate Giuseppe Zanotti pumps clicked as she strutted across her marble tile foyer on the way out the door. She was invigorated by all she had accomplished. At least now she had a plan. She couldn't wait to get to church.

Esther watched as the parishioners dwindled at the altar. Briggs had blessed the people with God's Word and had finished praying for them. The congregation seemed to be taking to him. As she sat thinking, he gave the benediction.

She had been concerned when, weeks ago, rumors flew back and forth concerning her and Briggs, but God was merciful, and they had died down. Now that Reverend Gregory was gone, the members looked as though they were going to take the high road and help, not hinder, the transition.

Esther hid a yawn behind her hand. Her earlier pep had left her. The past week's endeavors and her long days and nights of preparation were exhausting her. She promised herself a long hot bath and early night. Working in a time bomb atmosphere and keeping up with her church duties was difficult.

Esther greeted her family and friends as she made her way to shake Briggs's hand. "Powerful message . . . you really blessed us today, Pastor Stokes."

"I'm humbled by your kind words. It's all Him," Briggs was modest and wearing his position well.

Esther stifled a yawn with her hand. "Excuse me. Yes, He's worthy. I need a little of your time to update you on my progress with the zoning commission. After everyone leaves, do you have about thirty minutes or so?"

Briggs was happy to make time. This issue had been on his mind. "Absolutely. I want to know what's happening, and how I can help. I'll meet you in my office." Briggs placed his hand on Esther's shoulder in dismissal, turning toward the next person waiting behind her in line.

Esther stood smiling at her dismissal. She could tell that Briggs was embracing his new position. He appeared to be a natural, and he was still young. She wondered what his future would bring.

She turned and noticed Abigail watching their interchange, and she had a knowing smirk on her face. Esther was determined not to be intimidated, so she walked in her direction on her way out. She was just about to sail past her, when Abigail's words froze her in her tracks.

"You may not know it, but you two create quite a picture standing together. I could see sparks of chemistry between you. And, my dear, I believe, where there's smoke, there's fire, and it's the duty of a good citizen like me to sound the alarm," she said with a threatening glow in her eyes.

It was obvious that Abigail just played church. Esther walked out of the building without responding. Thinking of Abigail's threat, she decided to drive around to the back exit, closer to the church offices. There she used her key to enter the building. There was no one at the front desk, so she went into Briggs's office to wait.

The leather wingback chair was large and inviting. Esther kicked off her pumps, laid her hat on the desk, and before she knew it, her head was nodding.

"Asleep on the job?" Briggs asked as he hustled into the room and noticed Esther's shoes scattered haphazardly under her stocking'd feet and her eyes closed.

"Hey," Her voice slurred with sleep. She used her foot to scout around for an errant shoe. "Must be the hours I'm keeping. It's been a hectic week."

He motioned her to sit back. "Go ahead and relax. We can take a few moments to unwind before talking," he took off his clerical robe and stepped to the mirror to put on his suit jacket.

He stood in the full-length mirror and adjusted his tie. His charcoal suit hung well on his athletic body, and his black alligator shoes shined. In many ways, he was an old-fashioned man, mirrored in his father's image.

After adjusting his tie, Briggs turned to Esther. "Now you know inquiring minds want to know. How was your date?"

Esther gave a secret smile. "It was good."

"Good, good? Or so-so good?" Briggs asked as he sat behind his desk.

Esther's smile was no longer secretive. "Good, good."

Briggs grimaced at her reply.

"Briggs?" Esther's smile turned downward.

"Yes?" he said, concerned with her sudden mood swing.

"Where is your wife?"

Briggs tented his hands on the desk. "It's a complicated story."

Esther decided not to pry further. "If you need a friend . . ."

He shook his head no. "Thanks, but it's the life I created with my choices. My wife and I see some things differently. I never wanted to make a big splash. I've always been happy if God chose that I would just make a ripple." He sighed. "Anyway, I plan to go home and straighten everything out."

For Esther, the last few words of conversation told her more about the state of his marriage than all their other conversations put together.

Briggs sat up tall. "I apologize, and replaying this conversation in my head, maybe I've revealed too much. Please forgive an old friend for dumping my baggage on you."

Esther waved away his apology. "No, I asked. And I pray it'll all work out for you. Why don't we go over the zoning commission information now?"

Briggs pulled open his iPad. "That's a good idea."

***

Abigail listened as the ebb and flow of male and female voices drifted out of the pastor's office. "I knew it. They at it, right in Reverend Gregory's office. For shame, for shame . . ." she whispered. Then Abigail looked up as Deacon Clement came around the corner.

Deacon Clement strode over to her. "Good afternoon, Sister Abigail. You waiting to see Pastor Stokes?"

Abigail pointed her head toward the closed door. "I was, but then I saw Esther Wiley slip in there right before I got here. Been in there awhile too." She cozied up to the deacon as though he was her coconspirator. "I wonder why she acted like she was leaving the church, and instead, pulled behind the building and came in from this end. Oh well, it's not my affair. Oops, slip of the tongue. I mean, my business."

Deacon Clement stepped back as though Abigail was contagious. "Sister Abigail, as far as I know, Pastor is a happily married man. Why don't we knock on the door and let them know you're waiting?"

Abigail's face lit up in delight. "A *married* man, you say?"

"Yes, sister, married. And, as a member of the deacon board, I know this is true, because I read his full background report. The man is married. So, please, let this be," he pleaded.

"Oh my!" she snickered. "Never you mind, now. No need to bother them, they seem . . . well . . . busy. I got things I need to attend to," she said as her peripheral vision zeroed in on one of the choir members at the end of the hall.

"You have a marvelous day in Christ, Deacon Clement. Oh, yes, and your hair is crooked again. Yoo-hoo, Sister Muriel, may I have a word?" Abigail said as her spindly legs mimicked a fifty-yard dash.

Self-conscious, Deacon Clement looked around and straightened his toupee. He shook his head in amazement. He knew that Abigail intended to sling mud before she even left the church. Sister Muriel was just the first of many who would have their ear bent with her malicious gossip. Yes, phones would be ringing in church folk's cars all up and down the highway. He doubted she would wait for them to get home. Since the invention of the cell phone, Abigail had wrecked more lives than car accidents from the merging lane of the I-75 freeway.

"Lord, help us all," he sighed as he patted his hair making sure it was in place before he strode away.

Chapter Thirty-two

Esther lay back in the warm sudsy water with her eyes closed. "Hmm, so nice," she purred as she listened to soft jazz floating through the air.

She had called Lawton earlier, and they had a wonderful conversation. She let him know that she was interested in seeing where their relationship could take them. Initially, she felt he was moving too fast. They had only known each other a little over a month. But he had stepped up and made her problems his own. She let him know she couldn't wait until she saw him again.

After her bath, Esther dressed for bed but decided to wind down with a little TV. She sat on her couch and grabbed her remote to see what was on cable when her doorbell rang. She pulled her robe closed and went to the door and looked through the peephole.

Lawton?

When she opened the door he scooped her into his arms. "A man can only wait so long," he stated as he kissed her lips with passion.

"Man, you're a mess!" Esther laughed, and then her eyes glazed over when he cut her off with another soul-stirring kiss. She stopped laughing and enjoyed the kiss.

Lawton's gaze was intense. "Our phone call this evening just wasn't enough. I wanted to look into your eyes, kiss those tantalizing lips, and assure you that you are safe with me."

She touched his face. "Thank you. Let's believe the best in each other. This will be a relationship that begins and remains in integrity. I'm tired of lies, omissions, and whatever else people use to do what they want to do."

He nodded in agreement. "Yes, let's do this right. Our Father in Heaven knows, I've done and had wrong. Now, you get a good night's sleep, knowing I've got your back. I'm going to treat you the way I treat God, giving Him all of me."

Esther walked Lawton to the door where they hugged. He stood outside while she locked everything up, and then called out good night.

She staggered as she walked into her room, feeling drunk with pleasure. She knew tonight she would have sweet dreams. Then her shoulders tensed at the abrupt ringing of her telephone and the intrusion of the outside world. "Hello?" she answered a little grumpy.

"Now, Mama didn't raise you to answer the phone nasty, sweetheart."

"Sorry, Mama, what's going on?" Esther said, contrite.

"Nothing much, just calling. How was your dinner?"

Esther wondered why the niceties. Her mother wanted something, but she'd play along. "Same old, same old. I was just about to lie down."

"Oh, well, then I'm going to talk to you later. By the way . . ."

Uh-oh, here's the real reason for her call. "Ma'am?"

"Where did you go after church? I looked for you, but your car was gone."

Esther had no idea where this was headed. "I probably had left for home."

Elizabeth Wiley sought details. "Straight home?"

Esther tried to review her evening, but all she saw was Lawton's handsome visage. "Well . . . yes, no, wait . . ."

"What?" her mother asked, eager for her breakthrough.

Esther said in triumph. "I stopped at the corner store and picked up some soda pop."

"Oh, okay. Talk to you later," her mother sounded rattled.

Esther could tell her mother hadn't gotten the answer she sought. "Mama, what's the third degree about?"

"Sweetie, you're imagining things. I was being curious, nothing more."

Esther exhaled a breath she didn't know she was holding. "So you say. Bye, Mama."

"Bye, darling. Daddy says he loves you."

After hanging up the phone, Esther settled down for a pleasant night's sleep.

The Wiley household was suffering the fallout of Abigail's earlier dirty work. The industrious Sister Muriel had evidently helped spread the word.

"Don't be dragging me into your schemes, Elizabeth," Hickman growled, tickling her backside.

Elizabeth smacked his hands away. "How can you play around at a time like this? I told you what Sister Melissa said Sister Jackie told her."

"And I told you not to listen to it. Here you are, calling up our child and secretly grilling her. If you wanted to know if she was in Pastor's office doing the do, you should have come right out and asked her," he said, putting his hands back on her backside.

"Hickman, you know I don't believe that. I just wanted to find out what got misconstrued. But that child has been through so much, I couldn't ask. You know, ever since the last time the good God-fearing folk of Love Zion blasted her business, Esther hasn't done well being the subject of gossip. I'm afraid if she hears this, she'll shut down again," Elizabeth groaned, frustrated. "And, Hickman? Move your hands."

Hickman took his hands off of her backside and rubbed her back to calm her down. "Yeah, after that Roger business, people acted as though they didn't have anything else to talk about. I even heard some of the men running their mouths. Course, me and Jesus had a little talk with 'em. Still makes me angry just thinking about it. Now, we got this business with her and Pastor Stokes. The first time we heard it, it was right before he spoke his first sermon."

"Yes, but he preached so good, everyone put the mess behind them. But now . . ." She was beside herself with the constant drama.

"But—nothing! We have to have faith, woman. Our daughter has grown a lot in the last several years. She can handle more than you think," Hickman said with strong assurance.

Elizabeth became weepy. "I just have this awful feeling. The enemy is busy, Hickman. I feel it deep in my spirit."

He wiped her tears and hugged her. "Our best defense is His Word. Let's go back in our prayer closet and pray." The two headed toward the back room that was set up as their home sanctuary.

Elizabeth said to her husband of thirty-eight years, "Babe, remind me to talk to Mother Reed before the night is over."

"I will. It's good in times like these to have wise counsel. Now, let's get ready to clear our minds and hearts of any doubts. God is able," Hickman said with conviction.

"Yes, He is . . ." Elizabeth echoed.

They bent to pray when their doorbell rang. Hickman looked at Elizabeth, and she shook her head and shrugged her shoulder. They were coming out of their room when the front door flew open.

Phyllis came barreling into their home. Charles flying behind her.

Hickman rubbed his eyes. "I'm almost afraid to ask. What's wrong, Phyllis?"

Charles slapped Hickman on the shoulder in greeting. "Dad, I don't even know what's wrong. She gets off the phone in an outrage, and then pulls me out of the house. She knows I have to be at work in the morning."

Phyllis narrowed her eyes and yelled, "People, they're so wrong. No-good gossipmongers. I've got a good mind to start calling and cussing out a whole lot of people, starting with Abigail Winters."

Charles looked at his in-laws. "What's she done now?"

Phyllis's foot shook in agitation. Her mother and father sat down and watched the fireworks. Phyllis could wear anyone out.

Phyllis seethed. "According to our cousin Tamela, who is best friends with Sister Essie's niece, Esther is having an affair with Pastor Stokes. To make matters even more disgusting, they're supposedly doing it *in the church office*. Oh yeah, and Esther's been chasing him since he moved here."

"I take it Sister Winters is behind the gossip?" Charles asked. He sat down next to her, cool and calm.

Phyllis ranted. "I know it's her, that old biddy." She paused and stared at her husband. "Charles, why aren't you acting outraged?"

He crossed his leg. "Because I'm not surprised somebody picked up on the sparks flying back and forth between Briggs and Esther."

Phyllis, Hickman, and Elizabeth all exclaimed at once, "What?"

Phyllis began to sputter. "What sparks? Charles, you've been holding out on me. I thought she had met someone else. Didn't you see her out eating with someone? Ooh wee. Esther will have two men trying to court her." Phyllis's hand danced in the air. "*That's* what I'm talking about." She rubbed her hands together, shifting from anger to giddiness in record speed.

"Hold on now, Phyllis. Briggs is married," Charles interrupted before Phyllis made Briggs a bigamist, ordered the cake, and had the reception hall booked.

Hickman and Elizabeth looked at each other, sat back down, and waited.

"What?" she grabbed at Charles. "Since when? You knew this and didn't share it with anyone? Where is First Lady Stokes?"

Charles answered in weariness, "I'm not answering questions, Phyllis. If Briggs wanted everyone to know his business, he would tell them, and he hasn't. He trusted me, and I'm not breaking his trust. As it is, I'll have to tell him about you knowing this much."

"No, you *didn't* just throw shade on me," she fumed.

Charles smiled; Phyllis and slang were not a good mix.

He grabbed her around her waist and squeezed. "You still my boo?"

"Your boo? Boy, please! Let me go. Mama we got to figure this thing out. They don't know who they messing with. The Wileys will ride on some people," Phyllis raged as she walked away, forgetting all about being upset with Charles and her past feelings of depression. She loved a good fight.

"That's my baby . . ." Charles said as he looked at the Wileys. "I better call and give Briggs a heads-up," he chuckled.

Hickman watched Phyllis getting herself something to drink in his kitchen at ten o'clock at night. "Sweetheart, you want to put your daughter and her husband out or shall I?"

"You do it, honey." Elizabeth said as she turned away. "I'm going to bed. That child just wore me out."

"I must say, Imp One, I'm impressed with your work thus far. And don't worry about the old one. She's my

assignment. *Soon her heart will give out. I'm working on it,"* The Leader slurred.

"Thank you, Master. It is my intention to serve."

"Four houses and counting that are in an uproar. When the dust finally settles, the whole church will be effected. I can see it now: Those on her side, those on the naysayers' side, those who choose to remain neutral— too scared to take a side. Oh, the chaos will be wonderful to view. The icing on the cake is a pastor too weak to come to terms with a crumbling marriage."

Imp One jumped in, secure now that The Leader was pleased. *"He tries to hide. His pride won't let him come clean with the people. So, it gets worse, and worse. Meanwhile, his self-esteem gets lower and lower. The best thing of all . . . His Holiness's work will be left undone."*

"I warned you, do not speak the name!" The Leader hissed. *"Do-not-speak-that-name!"*

"Sorry, sorry," Imp One whimpered. *"Tell me how to make it better, Master."*

"Kneel before me," The Leader demanded.

Imp One fell to his knees. *"I am kneeling, Master."*

"Let me rest my hooves on your head." Imp one promptly lay down and The Leader reclined with his feet on Imp One's head. The Leader removed his hooves and said, *"Hmmm, that was only mildly satisfying. I know—since you're already down there, shine my hooves with your spittle."*

Imp One felt bile rise up in his throat as he began to do his master's bidding.

Chapter Thirty-three

Esther flicked the fringed hem of her red dress around her legs as she danced the Salsa with Lawton. Her hair gleamed in the light, and her platinum earrings twinkled in the darkened room. They were swaying and stepping side to side when Lawton did a calypso body shake, partnered with a rhythm and blues Chicago step that had every head in the place turn his way. Esther was having a great time. She had heard about Christian clubs but had never been to one. Lawton and his friends frequented this place and vouched for it being the real deal.

Lawton reveled in Esther's bright smile. "Having a good time?"

She grinned and did some fancy footwork around him.

He laughed. "Oh, it's like that, is it?" as he strutted around her to the calypso beat.

Esther didn't want to speak right now or he would know just how winded she was. She hadn't danced outside her living room in years. It was so freeing, she felt young again.

The song ended, and Lawton bowed at the waist, took her hand, and guided her back to the table. They came back to catcalls and whistles, as his friends razzed both of them.

Lawton's ex-partner Kevin Green was impressed. "You guys were awesome. Lawton, you've met your match."

Kevin's fiancée, Tanya, attended Love Zion although Esther had not previously interacted with her. "Esther, you have to show me that hip move. Girl, you've been holding out on a sista."

Lawrence, the new rookie police officer they had taken under their wing, was awestruck by their talent. "Hey, you guys should enter the rumba contest next month."

"You should learn some of those moves, Shug," Lawrence's wife, Cassandra suggested.

Esther laughed out loud in amusement. They liked her, she liked them, and this night was magical.

Lawton held her hand on the table and said, "So, what do you think? Want to sign up for the contest? Come on, it should be fun."

"Oh no, I don't know how to rumba. I barely kept up with you out there," Esther protested.

"Are you kidding? Girl, you're a natural," said Melrose, the wife of Lawton's current partner on the police force, Glen. "You make me want to take lessons. After you two went out there, we all stayed put."

"Yea," added Glen. "We knew ol' boy could throw down, but beg my pardon, you *stunned* us."

Lawton butted in, "Okay, everybody. Leave my lady alone. If she decides to dance, I'll let you know. In the meantime, can somebody pass the wing platter and pitcher of lemonade? I need to get my grub on."

Esther tapped him, and then stole a wing off his plate. He pushed his plate over so that they could share. They sat shoulder to shoulder as conversation flowed around them well into the night.

For the next two weeks, Lawton continued to introduce Esther to fellow officers, friends, their wives and girlfriends. It was a great balance against the craziness of her days spent in clandestine meetings working on the plan to correct the mess John and his cohorts had made of things. She liked everyone, and they all had a good time laughing and joking around. She was glad to see that Lawton's closest friends were Christians like him.

Things were going so well between them that she planned to invite him to Sunday dinner at her mother's so he could meet the family. It was a big step considering the last man they met was Roger. She already felt that she could trust Lawton. He was mature and knew where he was going. They shared common interests and goals. If he had some hidden agenda, her family would smoke it out. They had promised to never sit back again while her life was going up in flames.

The pearl-colored Escalade smoothly ate up miles while Esther tried covering her laughter behind a fake cough. The leather steering wheel's surface was slick with sweat, while Lawton's rigid posture screamed uptight officer of the law.

"They're going to like you," she reassured him, working to ease his mind about dinner with her family. ". . . unless, of course, you do something really stupid."

Old neighborhood haunts indicated they were close to her parents' middle-class home. She needed the man to relax before he had a coronary. "Babe, you'll be fine . . . just don't make any sudden moves." She laughed in pure glee. This was fun. She had no idea he was such an easy mark.

"Ha, ha, ha, stop torturing me or I'm going to return the favor when I take you home to meet my mother. Dad's been gone for a few years now, so her children are her life. So be nice or I'm gon' tell my mama."

Raucous laughter met melodious chuckles, while luxury tires glided to a silent stop in her parents' driveway. Under the cover of the car's darkness she squeezed his hands to reassure him that all was well.

The black version of June Cleaver, sans pearls, came out on the porch to usher them into the house. Esther was mortified. Her mother behaved as though she had never brought a man home before. And even though it had been a long time, she didn't want Lawton to know it. So the escort inside was over the top.

Norman Rockwell painted this picture, the patriarch standing tall and imposing, the mother in her apron starched and white, her elderly Aunt Gert with granny glasses propped at the tip of her nose, all swathed in soft lighting, casting a warm radiance. Lawton had to be impressed. Heck, she was. Aunt Gert stepped forward running her arm through Lawton's. Aged hands firmly pressed firm young muscles, followed with whistles of appreciation. A sheepish grin spread across Lawton's face as Aunt Gert went into the cougar role Esther promised she would pull. "Now, this c'here is what I call a man. Tall, good looking, and employed. You do have a job, don't you, baby?" Aunt Gert snooped.

"Yes, I'm a police officer. You must be Aunt Gert," he said, escorting the elderly woman down the hall.

She peered over at Esther. "Baby girl telling tales on me, has she?" she flicked her hand in dismissal. "Pay her no nevermind. These folk today going around calling older women cougars. Well, I'm an old mountain lion, baby. But since you already taken, we just gon' be good friends. How about that?"

Lawton tightened Aunt Gert's hand on his arm. "You try to get rid of me after this."

Hickman harrumphed several times. "Gert, you hogging the man to yourself? Let him breathe." He stretched his hand out for a handshake. "Welcome, son. Come on out of this hallway and sit. Women won't even let a man get in the house good."

Esther shook her head and walked behind Lawton and Aunt Gert. Aunt Gert put her hand back and Esther took it as they all walked through the wide entrance into the family room.

Everyone started talking at once, and Esther winked at Lawton as he smiled at the wonderful clamor of welcoming noise.

Later, as Esther and Lawton sat in her kitchen having coffee, they reviewed their progress.

"Looks like so far we're batting all home runs," Lawton mused. "My friends like you. Your family loves me. And if you don't do me right, Aunt Gert may be the one who'll help me heal my broken heart."

"Don't play. When I was younger, I wanted to be just like her when I grew up. She scandalized the family by having a nude painting of herself hanging in her bedroom. But she made sure her long silky hair covered all the appropriate places," Esther tittered, somewhat embarrassed now.

"Get outta here," Lawton said in disbelief.

"Yep. Daddy would say she needed Jesus, and Aunt Gert would just shake her head and say she already knew Him. We really do pray for her, but she was hurt by church folk antics and she won't join what she calls 'organized religion.'"

"What do you mean, 'church folk'? We both go to church."

"Club folk, work folk, neighborhood folk, church folk. People doing business as usual. The only difference is the place. I'm a Christian in love with my church and my God. Church folk be killing people softly."

"That's real talk. Together, you and I will keep Aunt Gert lifted. It was fun. I'm sorry your sister and brother-in-law couldn't make it. Mom's next. Mama is kind of protective, but you'll hold your own." On the sly, he snuck a glance to catch her reaction.

Esther swallowed. "I ain't scared of your mama."

"Just checking. I better get going." He paused searching her face. They hadn't discussed the elephant in the room.

"You know you've done a great job cooperating with all the authorities and keeping the fraud investigation quiet. Although the church is involved you haven't shared anything with anyone outside of your boss and the investigating team. That had to be hard. All day we've ignored what a big day tomorrow is. Are you ready for this?"

Small beads of sweat popped across her forehead. "I'm nervous. The plan for me to set up John is an important part of getting the whole house of cards to fall. But I've never tried to set someone up before. You'll be with me, right?"

Lawton came around the table and pulled Esther out of her chair. He planted a small kiss on her cheek. "There's not a chance that I will let anything happen to you. I'll be close by the entire time." Enveloped in his arms, she relaxed.

She blinked, her smile tremulous. "It's been a lovely evening, Lawton. Thank you for being patient with my crazy family."

"Aunt Gert might steal me," he joked, his eyes glued to her lips. "Being a saved man, and you being a saved woman means I need to leave before repentance is needed. No more kisses tonight; they're becoming a little too addictive," he explained, keeping a small distance between them.

Esther pushed Lawton out the door in a lighthearted way. "Yeah, keep your distance, you're irresistible." She could hear his chuckle as he stepped off the porch.

She needed some quiet time. In spite of Lawton's reassurances, tomorrow could be a rough day. The sweat pouring from her pores guaranteed it.

Chapter Thirty-four

Arms stretched up as instructed, Esther and Simone were fitted with listening devices. Simone's flirtatious tittering and cutesy wiggle captivated the handsome fraud unit officer's attention. Undeterred from his duty, his eyes twinkled as he taped the small microphone under Simone's sweater. Esther rolled her eyes at the spectacle, her nose scrunched at Lawton in disapproval.

To soothe Esther's frayed nerves, Lawton spoke in a soft, confident voice. "It's going to be all right. Everyone here is a professional. We have gone over this enough to be confident that you will do fine. Remember—no heroics—all you have to do is get him to admit the truth."

The fair-skinned officer in charge had curly, auburn hair, and his ocean-blue eyes were compassionate and sincere. In a gravelly voice, abused by years of unfiltered smoking, he assured Esther, "Miss Wiley, we wouldn't put you in any danger. If we can bait and catch the employees involved, the bigger fish will fry. The best-case scenario is they'll turn on each other for a plea bargain. And when they do, they become the property of the City of Detroit."

Esther frowned. She had butterflies in her stomach, and she was fighting rock icy fear. She could taste her dread. It was metallic and brought memories of the well water at her overnight Girl Scout camp. Last week with an *S* on her chest, Superwoman was going to bring down the bad guys and save the day. Today, she didn't want to bring home the bacon or fry it. She wanted to be in her flannel pajamas with the cover over her head awaiting a phone call that it was all over. She wanted to be able to do like Esther of biblical times and ask everyone involved to fast and pray. But her promise to keep everything a secret stopped her from reaching out to her church. Her one light in darkness was Lawton's ability to pray. He was a man who knew his Word and knew it was his weapon. He had become her idea prayer partner. However, this morning was a new clear day, and she was only human.

Last night she tossed and turned, tormented by thoughts that John would turn violent. The plan sounded easy when law enforcement pitched it to her executive director, Mr. Woodson. As her boss, he was responsible for what went on in the agency. When the fraud unit cleared him of involvement in any of the nefarious activities, they went to him with the illegal and unethical operation that had been going on right under his nose. After getting over the shock and threatening to fire Esther for not telling him first, Mr. Woodson became gung ho to get in on the act and pursue all parties with righteous vengeance. Hence, her current dilemma. Microphone in place, her body mimicked the Harlem shake.

Irritated, Mr. Woodson clapped his hands at Esther and her out of control shaking. "Enough, Ms. Wiley, calm down. If you're not going to do it for this agency, do it for your church that you're always running to. They're in just about the same boat we're in. Doing this helps everybody."

"Do not clap your hands at her," Lawton chastised. "She's not a pet poodle."

Esther grinned in spite of herself. He was becoming her knight in shining armor, even in the small things. "Let's just do this."

Simone hugged her, "I'll call John to your office. If I can get him to talk first, you won't have to."

Mr. Blue Eyes—nicknamed by Simone—shook his head in the negative. "You will do as we asked—nothing more. You don't want to tip him off. Just act natural."

Simone tossed her weave over her shoulder and sashayed out the door, mumbling.

Mr. Blue Eyes called after her, "I can hear all that."

Simone retorted, "And I know this."

Lawton touched Esther's shoulder. "We'll be close by. You only have to say the code sentence, 'I'm not having a good day' and we'll be here."

Distracted, Esther nodded. She sat behind her desk, fidgeting and waited. Twenty minutes passed. Finally her buzzer sounded.

Esther wiped sweat-drenched hands down her black pants. "Yes, Simone?"

"John's here to see you."

Esther inhaled and exhaled deeply. "Send him in."

John's entrance was forceful and intimidating to even an unobservant eye. "You asked, or should I say, demanded, to see me?"

Looming over her desk, he appeared to be larger than life. Esther could feel a tension headache grip her. "Yes, I did." She cleared her throat and motioned to an open folder. "Tell me, when you were handling the bids, did you find any irregularities in the vendors' paperwork?"

John leaned forward without looking at the papers. "No, and that's why I wanted to keep doing it." He then smacked the papers on her desk. "You don't know what you're looking at."

Esther stood, her hands braced on the desk. "Let's not start this conversation with insults." Anger chased away her previous fear. "I understand the paperwork. I understood it so well that in my review something seemed off.

It led me to compare last year's bids to my most recent public bids. The incoming bids look totally different." She again motioned for him to review the paperwork in the file.

John backed away from Esther's desk. "I'm not sure what you are alluding to."

Esther pressed her advantage. "You say I don't understand. I say, I understand better than you think. Where's the confusion?"

John's face turned red, his chest rose, and then deflated in rapid succession. "Lady . . ." he gritted out between clenched teeth, "if you have something to say, speak your mind."

Esther maneuvered and made sure the desk was between them. She picked up and held out the folder of bids. "Why are you so defensive, John? I asked if you could tell the difference between the bids you accepted and the ones coming in now."

John snatched the folder and flipped it open. His eyes scurried over the pages, and he then threw the folder on the desk. In the blink of an eye, he was around the desk in her face. "You don't want to play with me." His saliva splayed her face. "You would be wise to back off."

Esther's desk phone buzzed. She hit the intercom function. "Yes, Simone?"

Simone's voice cracked as she asked, "Do you want me to hold your calls, Ms. Esther? You have the State on line one."

Esther was not going to fold now. She refused to do this again, and John hadn't admitted one thing. "Yes, Simone. Thanks for checking before you *interrupted*, but John and I will finish in here before I take any calls. Let anyone who needs to know that I'll get back to them."

John was livid. "Don't answer the phone again. You wanted to play bad, well *bad* is here."

Esther slid backward. "I'm not following you."

John gripped her arm. "Oh, you follow too well. Who knew you could take your eyes off your church long enough to see what was really going on here. It doesn't matter. I no longer need this little job. I quit." He released her and turned to walk out the door.

Esther saw the whole plan falling apart. She had failed. In panic, she grasped at straws. "Yeah, you run, John. And hope your puppet master doesn't get mad that you made a move on your own."

John whipped around and rushed back to her. "Who you calling a puppet? I make my own decisions."

Esther goaded him further. "You know when I hired you, I thought twice because you didn't have a degree. Sometimes when you're not smart, you can easily be manipulated. Is that what happened, John? Did they trick you?"

John snatched both Esther's arms in a tight grip and shook her as he spoke, each sentence punctuated by a hard back-and-forth jerk of Esther's body. "You don't know what you're talking about. *Nobody* pulls my strings. I brought this plan to them. And I included your precious church and it's neighborhoods in the bundle."

Esther struggled to get free, but his grip was ironclad and she was dizzy and nauseated from his manhandling. His tirade escalated. "How to fake the bid process was all me. For the last year and a half, all we've done is make money." Abruptly, he pushed her away from him, and she fell limp against her desk. "You've never given me the credit I deserve," he taunted. "As a result, I'm more than ready to make it on my own. You can't prove a thing. You signed off on every job I put in front of you. Maybe *you're* the stupid one. You can keep this job and shove it up your—"

The door burst open and Lawton, accompanied by the Detroit Police and Federal Fraud unit, streamed through. Lawton headed directly to Esther while everyone else surrounded John. He quickly checked her for injuries. Seeing her drawn face and how she held her head and neck, he spun in anger toward John.

Touching her neck with one hand and pulling Lawton back with the other, Esther motioned for Lawton to hold off. She pushed through the men surrounding John, standing nose to nose, tears of fury gushing down her cheeks. "You know what? I gave you a chance when others felt you were too young and too arrogant to be a manager. But you couldn't find it in your flawed character to be grateful. You ignorant, backward thief! You once said to me you were a paper chaser. Well, here's some wisdom for you: Christians in the Kingdom don't chase paper, paper chases us. Get a clue." Esther saw she had returned the favor when errant saliva flew into his face. She then growled, "And don't you *ever* put your nasty hands on me again."

Lawton's eyes widened at the fact that his hunch was right. John had touched her. He lurched forward, but abruptly pulled back and nodded to the men to give John his Miranda rights so they could take him away. Officer Blue Eyes touched the tip of his hat and nodded in respect as he acknowledged Lawton's restraint and maturity.

Shocked, John turned aggressive when they snapped the handcuffs on. "Esther, you better watch your back. This isn't over."

Before Lawton could react, Simone raced up to John and with savage strength, punched him. Officer Blue Eyes grabbed her around her waist and swung her away. "Hey, cut that out." His voice was filled with mirth at the dynamo he held in his arms. "How can I take you to dinner from jail?"

John kicked out as he struggled with the police. Simone ground her teeth, angered at his threats to Esther. "Shut up, fool. Ain't nobody scared of you. Where you headed, you need to be concentrating on not dropping the soap. Don't nobody use me, trick. I'm straight-up Gratiot Avenue. You shoulda asked somebody. Tell my cousin Gator, cell block H, I said holla."

Mr. Woodson moved Simone away from the door as they dragged John through it. Simone yanked her arm away from him and scowled as she went through the door and back to her desk.

Esther pumped her fist in the air in victory. "Yes!" she roared, and then grabbed Lawton into a tight hug. She could breathe now. "We have enough, right, Lawton? The paperwork and his admittance to being the mastermind?" Esther hugged him once more with all her pent-up emotions.

"I like, hug me tighter," Lawton said, squeezing her back. "In a matter of hours that chump will roll over on his accomplices. And Love Zion's properties should be safe from those crooks. I almost came in here a couple of times. We had Simone call in here, but you held it down. Girl, you're something else. And when you broke down for the brother the scripture, money cometh—now that was classic."

Esther couldn't hide her relief. "Yeah, it was close a couple of times. Then I got angry. It helped me forget my fear and tune into his crimes. This has been a successful day. Right before you showed up, I had a seven o'clock phone conference with the people Richard e-mailed me. They all plan to vote down closing our program residences. They even suggested I put Love Zion's residential plan in writing for other struggling impoverished neighborhoods."

"When God has a plan, man can't destroy it," Lawton added as he rubbed the stress out of her shoulders. "I have to sit in on the debriefing and do some paperwork at the office before this is all wrapped up. Are we on for a late dinner tonight?"

Esther looked disappointed. "Oh, sweetie, I can't. I have to go talk to my pastor about all of this."

Lawton frowned. "The Briggs guy?" He stepped away from her and began to gather his equipment to leave.

Esther made quote marks in the air while she spoke. "His name is Pastor Stokes, not that *Briggs guy*." She rolled her eyes as he continued to move around the room. "I wouldn't disrespect your man of God. Please don't disrespect mine."

She was glad when that statement made Lawton stop and turn around. She now had his full attention. "I've noticed whenever his name is mentioned, you get irritated. Honey, he's my pastor. That's all. Now, I can see you tomorrow night. How about I cook?"

"That sounds fine, baby." He appeared embarrassed that she had picked up on his insecurities involving Briggs.

"See you then," Esther smiled.

As Lawton left, Mr. Woodson entered the room. He strode over to Esther's desk in a jovial mood. "Good job, Ms. Wiley. I'm impressed. At first, I thought you were blowing it. I almost ran in here. But your fella said to wait, let you play it out. You did well. This will please the board; our catching and fixing this. Shows we stay on top of things. I'm not half-finished punishing John and anyone else we find out was involved. Prosecution alone is not good enough. I want their retirement, vacation pay—shoot, and I want the company T-shirt back. Then we'll sue for the rest of the missing funds. Legal is already on this. By the way, Simone is safe, thanks to you. You'll need to watch her, though, because she'll only get this one pass."

Esther murmured her appreciation for Mr. Woodson's comments and agreed to keep an eye on Simone. However, as he left, her focus was on his remarks concerning Lawton. His having faith in her abilities meant everything. He was turning out to be her unexpected blessing.

Chapter Thirty-five

The dull-gray desk's cigarette burns, dents, and gashes spoke to Detroit's underclass's frustration and angst at being voiceless. Too many stories of pain were etched in each mark with very few fairy-tale endings. It all depressed Lawton. He wasn't a desk jockey, but he had experience where some poor souls had hit, kicked, and poured out their sorrow—on the desk—at being robbed of their hard earned cash or worse, a loved one's life. Today's report would be a good one, and he wanted to get it done. He wanted to get back out on the street for the rest of his shift.

He pecked out his report when his phone rang. It was Tanya, his friend Kevin's fiancée. "What's up, girl? You planning something with Kevin?"

"Hey. I know you appreciate straight talk, so I'm going to get straight to the point." She took a shallow breath and rushed on. "Even though Kevin told me it was none of our business, I felt you should know—"

Lawton hated gossip so he interrupted her spill. "If Kevin thinks you should keep it to yourself, do that."

Tanya wasn't listening to Lawton or hanging up without sharing. "Oh no, after seeing you and Esther all hugged up when we hung out, I was not feeling the rumor about her and Pastor Stokes getting busy. As a faithful Love Zion member, I was tryin'a take the high road on all this messiness. But, this latest news? Imagine them going at it in the church office. Honey, the angels is crying over this one. In the church? Really! They say Naomi, the church secretary, fell out when she walked into her office after service and heard the sounds coming from Pastor Stokes's closed office door. How a lady that old ran out of the church as fast as they say, is beyond me. Lawton, she coulda keeled over in the parking lot from the shock or exertion. Poor baby was scandalized."

Stunned, Lawton stared blankly at his computer.

"Hello, hello . . . You there?"

"Which was it? Did she fall out? Or run? A body can't do both." He could hear Tanya sputtering.

"Listen, girl, next time, listen to Kevin. And don't pass this lie on to anyone else. Good . . . bye."

Fussing under his breath and ending the call, he was drawn immediately into another. The mobile radio on his belt went off, and he was ordered to hit the streets. The one hundred fifty-fourth homicide in Detroit had just occurred. He kicked his desk, marking it again, grabbed his hat, and marched out of the office. The petty drama Tanya tried to bring was nonsense. What he faced daily was real.

Lawton peered over at his partner, Glen, who was staring out the squad car window. "You mighty quiet over there. What's up with that? I know you looking for a suspect, but come on, man."

Glen looked embarrassed. "I was tryin'a mind my own business. But since you pulling me in . . . did Kevin's girl, Tanya, call you?"

Lawton gripped the steering wheel. "I'm going to say this one time. Esther's not like that, okay, dude?"

"That's what I told Kevin, but he gets caught up in drama. He even watches those reality shows. Everyone knows they're scripted," Glen said, now self-conscious.

Lawton watched a gold Sebring round the corner without braking. "Hey, what's the description of the one dude we're looking for? Was it tatts all down his arms driving a gold car?" Lawton saw the driver's arm resting outside of the car's window as he turned the corner. In a wifebeater, the driver's arm was tatted from his shoulder to his wrist.

"Yeah, that him up ahead?" Glen asked as he braced for a chase.

"Affirmative," Lawton hit his siren and pursued. "Call it in."

Lawton could tell exactly when the suspect decided to make a break for it. The gold Sebring's speed accelerated. He pushed his pedal down and stayed right there with him as Glen called out their location. Lawton's mind blurred his present situation with his earlier news. He saw Briggs bringing food to Esther's house. The scene skipped to Esther swinging her body to the cha-cha. Then a closed door and sounds of pleasure floated through the wood. Lawton pushed the pedal harder, the car in front pushing his speedometer to ninety to stay ahead. Lawton saw Esther lean forward to kiss him, his face waxing into Briggs's. He was now pushing his speedometer to ninety too.

Glen's voice was urgent. "We're approaching the Livernois and Davison intersection. All units to the vicinity. We are pursuing a gold 2005 Chrysler Sebring. License plate: Young—" Glen's voice was muffled by a screeching of tires and a loud metallic tearing sound. There was static, and then the line went dead. Both only saw a red haze as smoke and feeble groans curled into the air.

Esther was at work when she received a phone call from Mother Reed who commanded her to come to her home.

It was so uncharacteristic of Mother that Esther put her pile of work away and left the office. Now, she drove down Livernois Avenue and slowed as traffic came to a standstill. She could see and hear an ambulance weaving past her through traffic, and police directing people away from the scene of a four-car accident.

Esther groaned. She looked behind her, and she wasn't in a situation where she could turn around. She accepted her fate and rubbernecked like the other drivers. She could see a squad car was included in the pileup.

"Thank you, Jesus, Lawton's still doing his paperwork from earlier today," Esther whispered.

Esther eased the car forward as the police officer directed them around the scene. She looked over and thought she saw a dazed Glen being pulled from the wreck. *Naw, that can't be.* Her hand shook uncontrollably as she then saw two firemen pry the car door back, as two paramedics lifted out another body. This body was the same length and bulk as Lawton. Immediately, Esther swung her car to the side of the road and jumped out.

"Hey, lady, you can't do that! Keep it moving," the officer barked at her as she approached and ran around him. He looked furious when he couldn't leave his post to pursue her.

After Esther dodged him, she couldn't get to the ambulance in time. They had loaded the body and were driving off. She turned, searching for the man she thought was Glen. She saw him being loaded into another ambulance. She overheard him speaking to another officer who was taking notes. "It was like he was crazed . . ."

"Was that Lawton?" Esther screamed. "My God . . . was it Lawton?"

Glen nodded in affirmation. "Henry Ford Hospital, hurry."

Esther ran back to her car. She hit Mother Reed's phone number on her cell as she peeled past the wreckage. "Mother? You won't believe what happened. I was on my way to see you, and I came on my friend Lawton in a car accident. It looks bad. I'm on my way to the hospital," Esther stated, tears falling, frantic.

"That's good, baby. You go ahead and call me later. I'll be praying for him," Mother Reed said simply.

Esther ended the call and concentrated on her driving. Her hands were trembling, and she felt faint. *Come on, heart . . . beat.* Esther's hand patted her heart as she steered on to the freeway. "Satan, you can't have him. I'm just getting the chance to love him."

Chapter Thirty-six

"Briggs? This is Charles. Man, you got problems, and your problems are directly connected to my beautiful sister-in-law," Charles blurted into his cell phone.

Briggs was working on his sermon for Sunday. He didn't know what had his friend so rattled, but he knew it couldn't be good. "You need to slow down, Charles, and tell me what's going on. What problems?"

"A pretty ugly rumor is going around the church that you and Esther were caught having sex in your office."

"What!" Briggs jumped up.

Charles continued the bad news. "Yeah, man. That's the gist of it, but adding to that tidbit, they all know you're married. Brother, your stuff is imploding all around you. And I know you had your reasons, but folk just ain't gon' care."

Briggs huffed. "Esther doesn't deserve her name dragged through the mud. Oh . . . man. Somebody needs Jesus or a beat down bad. Sorry, man." Briggs breathed in and out. "God is in control. You said you would have my back, and you're a man of your word. I can't believe nobody else brought this to my attention. I thought I was reaching my flock, but it looks like we all have a long way to go." Briggs heaved a sigh. "What's Esther saying about all this?"

"I don't think she knows. She's had some bad experiences with rumors in the church, and everyone keeps dancing around telling her. Last time she didn't handle it well."

"Charles, this is the last thing she needs right now. She's still trying to get this whole zoning issue wrapped up. I need to go. I'll talk to you later."

Charles had given him the heads-up. He was finished. "Hang in there, Briggs. I'll be praying for y'all."

Briggs knew he needed to call Esther, but he needed to figure out how he could put a positive spin on the whole mess. The zoning board, rumors, and he was scheduled to go out of town tomorrow to confront Monica. He bowed his head to pray when the phone rang.

"Hello, Briggs?"

Briggs was surprised. "Reverend Gregory?"

"Yes. Son, I hear the weather is a little rough at Love Zion right now."

Briggs swallowed and tried to think of something optimistic to say. "It's a storm I can handle. I've learned through some hard times to tread water."

Reverend Gregory answered him with the authority of one who commanded the waters. "Stop treading, Briggs. That means as coheir to the throne, you have the authority to speak to the elements. So speak. Get your personal life in order. I personally felt the chemistry between you and Esther, and it was an initial worry for me. But I knew God had sent you, so I knew that everything would work out."

"We're innocent of any wrongdoing, Reverend," Briggs said, humbled.

"Innocent in deed, but maybe not in thought. I don't want to spend a lot of time debating that issue. As your mentor, I'm telling you that the prayer closet is open. Through His power, get your house in order."

"Reverend, I know . . . Reverend? Reverend?" Briggs stared in astonishment at the phone. Reverend Gregory had hung up on him.

Briggs stormed out of his office. He wondered what it was about storm analogies for Reverend Gregory and

Mother Reed. Was it an older folk thing? God was merciful, and he didn't encounter anyone as he headed for the sanctuary. He needed to take everything to God in prayer.

Monica and Randall luxuriated in the opulence of the penthouse apartment. Leftover champagne, and half-eaten chocolate-covered strawberries lay amid rose petals strewn on the oversized satin lounger. They lay in bed feeding each other succulent peaches. The juice flowed down Monica's chin, and Randall wiped his finger across her chin with tenderness. They then kissed again.

After Randall asked for his divorce, they spent a blissful week in bed and only emerged to dine at the most fabulous restaurants in Atlanta. Monica was so sure of Randall that she no longer cared when she ran into one of Briggs's fraternity brothers. She was finally with the man she loved. They were in a world of their own. To her, the fallout from discovery no longer mattered.

Both were startled by the heavy knock on the door.

"I'll get it." Randall pulled on his robe.

"No, darling, for once you stay and let me serve you." Monica's face shined with happiness.

He beamed, and lay back with his arms behind his head, while she jumped up and walked to the door tying her robe. Peering through the peephole she couldn't see anyone, she turned to Randall twisting the door knob. "I don't see—"

A small whirlwind of a woman came barging into the room. Her angular pale face was almost translucent in the morning light, but her eyes were flaming sparks of midnight blue. She was a miniature duplicate of Randall.

"Randall, get-out-of-that-bed-right-now!" the pint-sized woman's voice of steel dripped with centuries of mint juleps sipped beneath magnolia trees, under Southern skies.

"Mother?" Randall cried in disbelief as he pulled his robe around him.

Her face was filled with loathing at the sight before her. "You have shamed all of your family. You have wreaked destruction on our lineage and our future generations. Get up, put your clothes on, and go home to your wife and children."

Monica wanted Randall's mother to know that they were more than a one-night stand. "Ma'am, I know it looks bad, but truly we're in love . . ."

The eyes that had focused solely on Randall now turned their wrath to Monica. The hatred that leaped from her pupils was so vivid that Monica could feel a physical blow to her body. "Young woman, listen to me very well. I won't repeat myself, and I won't lower myself to talk to you after this moment. The men in our family lineage have toiled with the likes of you since the first one was taken in chains off the slave ships. The women in our family have endured, and we have prospered *despite* this blight. Never has one of our own deemed it necessary to leave his home for one of you. It has *never* happened before, and it will *not* happen now."

Randall tried to shield her from his mother's wrath. Monica was getting to see in action the woman Randall had called a true dowager of her time.

As Randall started to put his arm around Monica, his mother turned to him.

"Do *not* touch her in my presence. Do not shame yourself more before me. A divorce, Randall? A divorce? Did you not think Meredith would call me? And here you are playing house in the same room as your father before you. In one of our buildings. I almost killed the private detective when he informed me. Finish dressing, and I will meet you downstairs in the car." She dismissed her only son and turned to Monica. "I have spoken to the manager of our building, and you have until Monday to vacate. This is a check for twenty-five thousand dollars, which I think is more than enough to compensate you. There are no common children involved; therefore, it is our usual payment for services rendered. Take it. I won't ask you to leave town, because we really don't care where you go. Perhaps you can convince the young pastor to take you back."

The petite commando glided through the door with a bearing so regal even Monica had to admire her carriage through salty tears. She followed behind watching the older woman enter the elevator. When the elevator door closed, Randall took her in his arms.

She fell into him, sobbing. "She was awful, Randall. How could you let her talk to me like that?"

Randall kissed her tears. "Darling, darling . . . my interference would have only riled her more. Listen, sweetheart, I'll have to go and meet her in her car or she'll send some very unseemly men up here to get me. Mother is a bit of a control freak, but don't worry, I love you, and I'll find a way for us to be together." Randall pulled on his pants, then grabbed his wallet and keys. His open robe flapped around him.

"I'll wait here for you, my love. We're stronger than this." Monica threw her arms around his neck for a passionate kiss.

After Monica flung herself across the bed and began to weep, Randall rushed from the room to meet his mother's demand. Monica tossed and turned through her sleep and was awakened during the night by a messenger at her door. He held a letter for her, and she signed for it. She opened the letter and read. When she was done reading, she hollered out in pain and crumpled to the floor.

> *My Dearest Monica,*
> *It's not that I don't love you, because I do. But I can't be cut off from everything I know. How could we live? Even if I get my children to come around—a forty million-dollar inheritance is a lot to lose. And Mother has promised I will lose it all. Please understand.*
> *Love, Randall*

Monica stood at the airport sobbing into her handkerchief. This had been the worst week of her life. She needed Briggs. She couldn't believe Randall would fold like he did. She knew one thing. He had underestimated his wife. Randall's mother's ambush was carved on Monica's heart by the cold hard nails of a true Confederate woman of the South.

She stood in line to give her ticket to the agent. Earlier, the luxury building manager advised her that she had to vacate the room before noon. *So much for a week to vacate.* She would miss the opulence, the in-room gourmet meals, and most of all Randall. She had tried to phone him, but every number she had was disconnected or she was told he was unavailable. No manner of crying or pleading changed the answers she was given. Her only chance now was to fly to Detroit and salvage her marriage.

Two hours later, Monica had gotten off the airplane at the Detroit Metropolitan Airport. With her address book in hand, she hailed a cab and instructed the cabdriver to take her to her new home. She had spent the flight rehearsing what she would say when she saw Briggs. She knew that she would have to make it good and that it would take every bit of acting skills she had to persuade him to believe her lies. Since he had history believing her before, she was confident that he would again.

Briggs sat in his car in the church parking lot, and the words of his prayer and God's answers resonated throughout his being. He wasn't really happy about his instructions, but he knew that God's Word was irrefutable. It wasn't going to be easy; his flesh was going in an entirely different direction. And his heart? It was beating in time with his flesh, his soul giving it instructions that weren't holy or in accordance with the will of God.

He had to face things. He had been hiding behind righteous words, but dwelling in unrighteous thoughts and feelings. Choices had been made, and now he had to live with them. There was one person who deserved an honest conversation with him. It was time he called her.

Chapter Thirty-seven

Esther could feel the vibration of the cell against her thigh as she sat in the waiting room at Henry Ford Hospital. She touched Lawton's mother's hand and motioned to her cell phone that she had an incoming call.

Esther's phone went silent as she moved away. She hit the callback feature on her phone. "Hello? Did someone just call me?" she said in a strained voice.

"Esther? It's Briggs. You don't sound well." He worried that she was upset from all the gossip.

"Yes, my friend Lawton was in a horrible car accident today. I'm at Henry Ford Hospital, and it doesn't look good. Can you pray for him, Briggs? Can you pray real hard?" Esther fought through a sniffle.

"I'm really sorry to hear that. Yes, I'll pray for him, and I'll send up my prayers for you and his family's strength. You shouldn't be alone. Who's there with you?"

"I'm sitting with his family and some of his fellow officers. I'll be okay. I'm so worried about him. What if he doesn't make it? I never told him how important he was becoming to me. I'm so scared," Esther whispered.

"Hold on. As your friend and pastor, I'm on my way."

After weeks of trying, Roger found where Esther lived by following her home. Now he was back. He crept outside the brick colonial looking for a way in. He tried to remember Esther's habits, but alcohol and weed muddled his mind.

The black wool mask he was wearing was hot and made it hard on his peripheral vision. However, he was keeping it on. In case he was seen, he didn't want anyone to recognize him. He searched for an entrance and decided he'd take his chances breaking the basement windowpane, when he noticed a cracked window into Esther's bathroom. Memories assaulted him as he remembered—his then wife—opening the window to let the steam out every morning before she curled her hair. He lifted the window up and climbed in, crashing against her toilet paper holder and taking it down as he fell. When his scrutiny stopped on the holder, he remembered Phyllis's smug face holding the toilet paper holder years ago when Esther moved out. Furious, he longed for a chance to close Phyllis's smug mouth too. He ripped off his mask. Somewhere in the house he could now hear oldies R&B playing low. The house smelled good; fresh and clean. It wasn't the sweet incense-thick scent he associated with their home, and this angered him. He was pissed off. Nothing from him in her life was left.

Roger explored Esther's house and was surprised to find an expensive bottle of champagne in her buffet. The Esther he knew didn't drink. He rifled through her photo album, and just like he thought, she had erased him from her life. Roger found his way back to Esther's bedroom and sat on her bed; a raggedy .22 pistol rested on his lap. He was nervous and swigged his champagne bottle of liquid courage. Small beads of perspiration rolled down his neck. He had one hundred and seventy-three dollars in his pocket. That was the amount he found in Esther's emergency cash, stored in a fake orange juice carton in her refrigerator. He wasn't fencing anything big, but some of her jewelry might tide him over during the cold Chicago nights he would soon endure.

When Esther arrived, he planned to take the cash Esther had in her purse, her ATM card, and then trash her place.

He figured her ATM pin was still her grandmother's birthday. Roger planned for it to look like a random robbery. If he could get his old mojo back, he may even take her for a little ride on his own personal roller coaster. He frowned as he remembered saying that to his last girlfriend and her laughing in his face and calling it the kiddie ride. All women were mean-spirited and cruel. He never met one he could love forever, including his mama. He shuddered and thought of the earlier newscast, Esther would be Detroit's one hundred and fifty-fifth homicide of the year.

Roger took another swig, shrugged it off, and laughed in deranged glee. All Esther needed to do was come home. She was late.

"Wonderful work, Imp One, you are turning out to be very inventive. Maybe you will make it to full demon status," The Leader growled with satisfaction as he looked at the turmoil unfolding below.

Imp One looked with a furrowed brow, puzzled at the new events occurring. He sneaked a look at the plans he had written with so much care and detail. There was no car accident for Lawton Redding included. Lawton was supposed to get angry and barge into Esther's house after she got off of work and Roger had offed her. He would be charged with murder for storming in her house in heated anger.

Briggs would be left in scandal and shame, standing alone, trying to convince people that he and Esther never had an affair. His public shame would rub off on his father's reputation, soiling him too.

The ripple effect would continue when the image of the Wileys, as an upstanding Christian family, was ruined. Best of all, by the time Reverend Gregory returned, Love Zion would be in disarray and most of the real

Christians would have moved on, leaving church folk like Abigail Winters in charge.

Imp One stood frozen to his spot. He dared not mention to The Leader that there was a small glitch in the plans. If he had to turn to ashes, later was just as good as now.

Chapter Thirty-eight

Briggs entered the swinging doors of the hospital while the Wiley family was pulling into the parking lot. He had called Charles, and, as usual, the whole family responded. Mr. and Mrs. Wiley even brought her elderly aunt Gert who was visiting.

Esther looked up and gave Briggs a tentative smile as she hugged him. She then guided him to Lawton's mother. "Mrs. Redding, this is my pastor and good friend, Briggs Stokes."

"Oh, a pastor! Thank you so much for coming. We need your prayers. This reminds me of the time Lawton's father passed. I just can't take it. I just can't . . ." Mrs. Redding cried, grabbing and squeezing Briggs's hand.

He gently squeezed her hand in return. "I'm here for you and your family, Mrs. Redding. Let's pray together. I believe that God's plans are not always known to us, but He is sovereign and able."

"Yes, yes," Mrs. Redding mumbled as Briggs led her away.

Esther stared after Briggs. *What a good man, just not my man.* She heard a commotion at the entry hall as the Wiley clan walked in.

Her father spoke for all of them. "Esther, when one of us is hurting, we're all hurting. How is your young man?"

Esther approached her father and lay her head on his shoulder. "I don't know, Daddy. They haven't come out and said anything in over two hours. Everyone is on edge."

Hickman placed his arm around her shoulder. "Well, introduce us to his family so we can pray. Corporate prayer is powerful."

"Yes, sir. Briggs was about to do just that." Esther led the group over to Briggs, Mrs. Redding, and the other Redding family members, including his sister, Angela. They were joined by two police officer friends who were still there from earlier. A news reporter sat in the corner interchanging typing in a tablet and speaking into his cell phone. All waited for news.

After prayer, Esther sat with her father in a corner of the waiting room where she had moved to be alone. "I believe I could love him, Daddy," Esther stated in a low voice.

"Now he seemed to be a good person when we all met. But . . . love? Already?"

"See, that's exactly how I feel too. It's just too soon. It's only been a little over a month."

"Yes, time is a consideration in these matters. What else bothers you?" Hickman searched her face for clues as to the real matter at heart.

Esther looked over at Briggs standing with the Redding family. "Well, in a kind of weird way, there was someone else—or, maybe the idea of him."

"Yes, go on," her father said with a grimace on his face.

"Then—" Esther was interrupted by the doctor entering the room.

"Redding family?"

"Yes?" they all answered in unison.

"Mr. Redding is out of surgery and things look stable. The next twenty-four hours will tell us more. He had internal bleeding from blunt trauma; possibly the steering wheel. He has a concussion and some swelling of the brain. He has a broken leg and several lacerations. We stopped the internal bleeding and now we want to monitor him closely. In cases like this, blood clots can occur. The brain swelling should decrease, but he'll remain in ICU where he can get around-the-clock care. If all goes well we should be able to move him to a regular room in the next forty-eight hours."

"Doctor, when can we see him?" Mrs. Redding asked, clutching her daughter's hand.

"He's in post-op, but I'll have a nurse come and get you when it's time. Although his body took a severe beating in the crash, he was in excellent condition. Please don't let his appearance and the tubes alarm you. We really are very optimistic concerning his case."

"Thank you. Thank you," Mrs. Redding sobbed.

She turned to her daughter, and they hugged. Esther stood with a smile of relief on her face as Mrs. Redding pulled her into an embrace. A news reporter stepped up to speak to Mrs. Redding on Lawton's condition, and Esther excused herself.

Mrs. Wiley put her arm around Esther. "Your dad and I are going to get going. I'm so happy Lawton is holding his own. I won't suggest you leave, but please call us when you get home."

Phyllis stood next to Esther. "Girlfriend, when he comes to, you might want to look a little more presentable. How about Charles and I go and get you a change of clothes and a little necessity bag to take care of yourself?"

Esther laughed for the first time in several hours. "Phyllis, only you, girl, thanks. I'll take you up on that."

"Come on, Charles, duty calls," Phyllis said over her shoulder as she marched out of the room with purpose.

"That's my baby, always in charge. Esther, we'll see you a little later." Charles followed his wife out and saluted Briggs good-bye.

Aunt Gert wrapped her crochet shawl around her small shoulders. "I betta catch my ride home. Your mama walked outta here like she forgot me. I'ma hurt her."

She then, gentle in her touch, grabbed Esther's chin. "Things don't always turn out the way we plan. Yet, God is working it out on our behalf. Don't look at me like that. Just because I don't go to church doesn't mean I lack faith. I love the Lord, and I know He loves you. Change is a good thing, honey, and it is inevitable. Embrace it and let go of everything you thought was what you wanted."

Esther held her aunt close; she didn't have a clue about all the cryptic words, but she knew her aunt always spoke truth. She would sort it all out later. Right now, she needed to sit by herself for a little while and give thanks.

Esther turned toward the corner chair when she heard her name whispered.

"Sorry, you seemed deep in thought. I see everyone's gone. Do you have a few minutes?" Briggs asked.

In Esther's preoccupation she thought Briggs had left. "Hey, thank you for coming and for calling my family. When everything happened I only had time to call Mother Reed. Would it be okay if we spoke tomorrow?"

"I know that you've been through a lot, but I really need to speak with you now." Briggs's voice expressed urgency.

Esther was a little taken aback. "Okay, if it's that important to you." She motioned him away from everyone.

They sat in the corner of the empty waiting room.

Briggs didn't hesitate to get to the point. "Esther, there are rumors going around about us in the church."

Esther was lost. "What? Why?"

"Who knows what goes on in the minds and imaginations of misled, wounded people. I wanted to tell you myself, and I also wanted to talk about truth with you."

"Truth?"

Briggs clasped his hands as though in prayer. "Yeah, truth unvarnished by how I would love to spin it in my favor. Look, when I sat in meditation this morning, God showed me a personal video clip of what has transpired since I moved here. Like Abraham coaching Sarah before entering Egypt, it began with a lie. You see, Abraham didn't want to deal with the famine in his country, so he designed a lie to get out of it. I didn't tell you I was married to Monica because, in my heart of hearts, I didn't want there to be a Monica. My thoughts have been impure, and my actions have reflected that. You were my first love, the one who left me and broke my heart in the process. Instead of letting God heal my heart, I thought I healed it myself. I have been less than honest with you, Monica, myself, and God. So I'm here to apologize."

Esther was speechless. She had to admit to herself that everything he said was true. She had played her own fantasies out in her head and heart even after she found out he was married. Aunt Gert's words fell open in her heart. "It's time to let go, isn't it, Briggs?"

"Yes, it is," Briggs said with sadness and regret.

"Will you fix things with your wife? Have you spoken to her?"

Briggs was standing on a new foundation. "No. My marriage has been in a famine season, but that's my problem, not yours. It's time we left each other's personal lives behind. Whatever happens between Monica and me will be between us. You and I still have to face the gossips, but I believe God will turn all of that around. He is merciful."

Esther understood Briggs's discretion. "You're right. And I'm not worried about the rumors. I have worried about the thoughts and deeds of other people for so long that I have missed blessings meant for me. Right now, I have a wonderful friend fighting for his life, and I need to direct my energies to helping him heal. By the way, the zoning problem is handled. I'll send you an e-mail report. Good-bye, Briggs. The next time I see you in church, you'll be Pastor Stokes." She got up to hug him, but then sat down with her arms at her side.

Briggs dipped his head in agreement. "And you'll be Sister Esther."

Both looked at each other, letting go and finally—moving on.

"I have a plane to catch to Atlanta." Briggs strode out of the room, and for all real purposes, Esther's life.

Chapter Thirty-nine

Phyllis and Charles sat in the driveway of Esther's home while Phyllis dug through her purse for Esther's spare key.

Charles observed his wife, her soft profile reminding him of his love for her. He reached across the seat and placed his arm around her shoulder, pulling her close.

"Charles, not now," Phyllis gasped, but closed her arms around her husband and kissed him ardently.

The two sat in the car, necking like teenagers. Ever since Phyllis had begun to cope with her depression, she felt like she had been given a second chance at everything. Getting geared up to fight for her sister made her remember that she was worth fighting for too. Knowing the truth that God was not mad at her and had accepted her repentance long ago was her blessing and her road map to healing. She knew she needed more help, and she was now willing to get it. She had called a Christian counseling center and had already scheduled her first appointment.

Charles came around and opened Phyllis's car door. He hugged her up under his left arm and bumped his hip to hers on the way up the walkway. They were acting silly, and both loved it. Charles took the key from his wife's hand and unlocked the door.

"Oooh, so manly," Phyllis teased as she squeezed his left bicep. Charles shook his finger at her friskiness. "Don't start anything in your sister's house, woman. I promise when we get out of here, it's on," he stated as he pushed the door open.

Phyllis moved to the alarm control panel, but it was off. She shook her head absently at Esther's forgetfulness in the mornings. Esther was known for always rushing out of the house. "Charles, Esther left her stereo on. She better quit bugging me about going green and she's leaving her appliances on. She didn't even set the alarm. This my jam, though."

Phyllis snapped her fingers, turned up the stereo, and old school R&B floated throughout the air as Charles headed toward the kitchen to get a soda. Phyllis went down the hallway to Esther's bedroom. As she turned the doorknob, she thought she heard something. She froze when Charles came up behind her silent like a ninja.

"Want a soda?" he whispered.

Phyllis slapped his arm, "Man, you scared me. Why are you whispering?"

Charles looked sheepish. "I don't know. Why are you?"

Phyllis made note they were still whispering. Things felt off. "Guess I feel a little spooked for some reason. Let's get her stuff and go," Phyllis said as she opened the door.

In slow, three-dimensional Technicolor horror, Charles held out the hand holding a bottle of soda and bowed in a gallant motion for Phyllis to go first as a loud pop filled the air and the soda bottle burst.

Phyllis screamed, and Charles roared as he threw Phyllis down to the ground, crawled over her through the door, and made for the masked man holding the gun.

Roger tried to aim the gun for a second time and fire, but the hammer jammed. He threw the gun at Charles and made for the window.

Charles tackled Roger and punched him. "Stay down, Phyllis, don't you move," Charles struggled with the masked man.

Roger squirmed his arm loose, and threw a roundhouse and connected with Charles's chin. Charles fell back and leaped up with more force. Roger wasn't as physically fit as Charles, but he had been out in the streets of Detroit surviving. When Charles grabbed him again, he elbowed him. Then he crawled toward the window when Charles grabbed him by the shoulder pulling him back. Roger bit Charles's hand viciously and kicked him in the stomach. Charles doubled over in pain.

Roger noticed the gun, and then looked over at Phyllis facedown in the hallway. She was crouched on the floor, her arms covering her head. The discarded gun lay a few feet away. All Roger could think was payback time.

Charles was lifting up when he saw Roger's intent. He went berserk, leaping on top of Roger and punching him repeatedly. Punches to Roger's back, to his side, a blow to his head—over and over. Grabbing Roger in a headlock, he then snatched the mask that was already askew and pulled it off.

"You?" Charles snarled.

Roger struggled to get free, but Charles kept him in the headlock, twisting his body into submission.

Phyllis rose, her face colorless in terror. "Oh, sweet Jesus. Charles." She struggled to find her composure, her hand shaking as she pulled out her cell phone. She breathed heavily. "I'll call the police," she said, her whole countenance traumatized. She keyed 911 into her cell. "Hello? We've caught an intruder. Yes, yes, my husband is holding him. 16555 Edinborough Road." After the call, she slumped down, whimpering in stunned disbelief.

"Hear that, punk? The police are on their way." Charles observed Phyllis's breakdown and took a cleansing breath. "Hold on, baby, hold on," Charles said through stiff, swollen lips. Incensed, he pressed down harder on Roger, unshed tears gleaming in his eyes.

***

Briggs strode into the house and stopped in shock; Monica sat motionless on the couch. "Monica?"

Monica's sulk was tremulous. "I've been here since late afternoon, Briggs, waiting for you." Briggs's stare at Monica was blank. She gave a slight gulp and redirected her approach. "I came as soon as I could, sweetie. When I was sick, it gave me time to think about everything that was happening. You know, leaving my friends and all, coming to a new place. Yet, you were all I kept thinking about, and I realized wherever you are is home."

He clapped his hands together. "Brava! Brava! What a performance."

"That's mean, Briggs," Monica countered with a pout of her full lips.

Briggs crossed his arms in defiance. "You finally used the key I mailed you to come here, full of manipulation and falsehood. You're unbelievable. Do I look stupid to you? Did you ever see me on the little special yellow school bus with my name tag on upside down? I'm a pastor, but I'm also a man, and you are trying my patience." He marched down the hall to his room.

"Where are you going? Briggs?" Panicky, she scrambled behind him.

"I'm going to bed. When the truth hits you and you care to share it, let me know." Briggs shut the bedroom door in Monica's face.

Chapter Forty

Antiseptic fumes comingled with hushed whispers in the ICU waiting room. Many of those who had waited for news of Lawton's progress had gone home. They had to, Mrs. Redding had insisted, but Esther refused. Mrs. Redding and other family members went in, leaving Esther outside, but stalwart. She curled up in the lobby-room chair, waiting, hoping that Mrs. Redding allowed her at least a moment with him.

She squirmed in the chair. She could feel Mrs. Redding observing her. Holding her breath she prayed she'd be allowed inside to touch and see for herself that Lawton was going to make it. He mentioned earlier in the week his conversation with his mother concerning their budding relationship and his desire for them to meet. Surely she wouldn't begrudge Esther a visit.

"Esther?" Mrs. Redding took her hand pulling her from her pity monologue.

"Yes, ma'am." Esther held on to the hand engulfed in hers. "How is he?"

"He came to, briefly, and then fell back asleep. He has a long road of recovery ahead, but I'm hopeful. Would you like to see him?"

"Yes, I promise not to disturb him. And if it's all right with you, I'd like to stay. Your son is very precious to me."

Mrs. Redding hesitated in her answer, and then came to a decision. "Sure, honey, and we can take turns sitting with him. Go on now."

Esther tiptoed into the ICU room. "Oh, sweetie," she sighed. He looked ashen and weak lying in the darkened room, machines beeping, and his IV hanging above his bed, looming like a prophecy of doom. Esther lightly touched his neck, the only area not bandaged or plugged with tubing.

The nurse was writing down something in his chart as she gave an encouraging smile and quietly left the room. *Father, you know I don't like hospitals.*

He lay battered and helpless, nothing like her knight from earlier today. *How come you can only slay my dragons?* It hadn't been twenty-four hours, and everything had changed. She pulled her chair up and laid her head near his on the pillow; then she closed her eyes, inhaled, and prayed.

Later, Esther sat in the ICU waiting room and wondered where her sister was with her change of clothes. She was starting to feel a little grimy, and she wanted to be fresh when it came her turn to sit with Lawton again. She didn't like meeting Lawton's mother, Mrs. Redding, like this, but they were becoming fast buddies. In the quiet of the night, they were learning each other's hearts.

Esther yawned and pulled the soft, plush throw Lawton's sister had left her, over her shoulder. The ottoman in front of the sofa supported her legs, and she was not uncomfortable.

"Esther . . ." her father stormed through the ICU lobby's swinging doors.

Casting off the throw, Esther scooted forward. "Daddy?"

Hickman Wiley squatted down, placing Esther's overnight bag next to her.

Esther kissed his cheek. "Where's Phyllis?"

"Baby, there was an incident at your house—"

"Oh, Lord. Every time I enter a hospital nothing good happens." Esther stood and paced.

"Everything is all right, now. Charles and Phyllis walked into your home and your ex was waiting. Simple boy meant to rob you. So in a way . . . a good thing did happen. Instead of you, he met Charles's fists." He hadn't intended to downplay the situation, but this had been an emotional day for everyone. Erring on the side of less, rather than more, was needed.

Esther froze. "And they're really okay?"

"Yes, they couldn't come because they're completing a police report. Tomorrow as the home owner, you can go down and press charges. Stay here and take care of your young man. Everything is under control." Hickman hugged her. "You okay?"

"I'm good, Daddy," Esther said. "Thanks for the bag."

He scrutinized her face, satisfied she was handling the news; then he hugged her again and left.

Esther then phoned Phyllis. "Esther, you not over there tripping, are you?"

"Not now. Your bossiness lets me know you're good."

"Girl, my baby took Roger out. Remind me to tell you later how awful your taste in men used to be." Phyllis sounded upbeat on the phone.

"All I can say in my defense is that you should never let the spirit of lack pick your mate. I've learned my lesson. I'm in abundance now." Esther sat back down and put her feet up.

"Yes, you have, and how is Mr. Abundance doing? Any news?"

"Not really. His body is pretty banged up, and the doctors feel total rest is needed. His mother and I are taking turns sitting with him. It's her turn. Phyllis, I need to put my eyes on you and Charles. I'll be by to see you first thing in the morning."

Phyllis negated Esther's need to come. "We're both fine. Go do you."

"I am so sorry."

"Girl, now that it's all over, I actually feel sorry for Roger. We're going to put all of this behind us; Charles and I are safe. Now, see about your man, because I've got to see about mine. To tell the truth Charles going caveman kinda turned a girl on."

"TMI, sis, TMI. I love you," Esther said. "Give my love to Charles. He's the man."

"I will."

Phyllis closed her cell and looped her arm through Charles's before she spoke. "Don't think you're getting out of that earlier promise."

He cupped her face and kissed her with his swollen lips ever so softly. "I won't. Although I'll need a rain check until these ribs heal. There is no way I am ever going to forget that kind of promise. I love you." He shuddered. "If anything had happened, I would have gone into heaven or hell after you."

"Don't say that, Charles." Phyllis gently placed her hand over his mouth. "You know I love you too, but there'll be no following each other into heaven or hell; well—hell, anyway. Let's go home, baby," she ended with a loving promise in her eyes.

Charles paused and asked. "Do you think we should have told Esther we were in emergency at another hospital?"

"No. Esther is pretty strong but a lot has been going on. I know the rumors have been ugly, and then there was something going on, at her job, she wouldn't share with me. Then Lawton's accident, and now this? We can share it tomorrow." Phyllis looked down at her watch. It was one o'clock in the morning. She sighed. "Today, honey, we'll share it all later today."

***

Imp One paced back and forth. "All my hard work down the drain, and The Leader coming to see me. Not good, not good," he moaned, fretting.

"I told The Leader that it would not be good to use that Roger human," Imp One screeched. "The same thing that made him weak for us also made him too weak to carry out a simple plan. How hard could it be? Take her, get the money, and then my underling hits the arm that carried the gun and bang, bang, no more Esther. No Esther, no Briggs in the pulpit, and then the Wiley family falls apart. My ultimate gift, no more Mother Reed, because if she lost Esther, she would surely have a heart attack and die."

The large, lumpy head of Imp One hung low, his shoulders hunched over in grief. "I dislike using humans, especially the flawed ones. The liquor and drugs fog their mind. Roger couldn't even hear us tell him who was really at the door. I will let him rot in jail. No intervention with any of the lawyers or judges on our payroll. He is to rot!!!"

"We understand no intervention, no help, rot, rot, rot . . ." the imps and sprites chorused.

Imp One lifted his head in defiance. "We were once turned into pigs and run off a cliff, but they are the pigs, the lot of them! By all that is evil in this world, I need a plan. This one must be foolproof, the masterpiece. I cannot and will not be sent to the bottom tier; there is no air there. Even the ash is settled nine hundred feet deep. Nothing moves, nothing!"

The imps and sprites sat with ears accustomed to Imp One's words. They were all selfish creatures and none cared what happened to him; they just didn't want to share his fate.

They began to howl in a nervous frenzy as they chanted, "Plan, plan, plan."

Imp One bent over a large area of ash, and with his tail, started to sketch out the only thing he could think to do to bring everyone in the Wiley clan down.

Chapter Forty-one

Briggs looked at his alarm clock for the tenth time that night. Its large digital numbers read five-twenty. He thought back to his conversation with Esther and knew that if his soul would let him, he could break every vow he ever made with God. She had always been the one he wanted, but they had lost the right to be with each other. They both let go today, and all he wanted was a chance to grieve in private for what might have been. The problem in the next room, he would brave tomorrow. For what was left of his night, he would use to really let go.

The door crept open, and Monica slipped into his semi-darkened room. Her peach-colored negligee was barely a wisp of colored cloth. Briggs breathed, "Man, not now."

Monica drifted over to his bed and sat down so close that Briggs could smell her desperation. Her thoughts were so strong; Briggs felt he could hear them. *He's been here a long time, and if I know him, and I know him, he has been as faithful as a puppy. He has to be feeling that familiar itch that only I can scratch.*

"I couldn't sleep. I was wondering if you were having problems sleeping too." Monica's husky low voice swirled into the silence.

Briggs saw her eyes fastened to his naked chest. "Monica, what will this solve? We have so many problems to overcome, and I believe that through God, we can overcome them. Let's not muddy the waters."

Monica stiffened, Briggs waited. This is where she would usually storm out. Instead of leaving, Monica asked, "Muddy the waters? Briggs, we would be clearing things up."

Briggs took her hand.

Yes, her face screamed. She was transparent to Briggs.

He placed her hand back in her lap. "Not until you and I get marriage counseling and you take a series of STD tests."

Monica leaped up. "What!"

"Please, Monica. Stop the drama. Did you actually think it would be that easy? That you would sashay yourself in here, and it would all be forgotten? Girl, I'm saved, not stupid. You know I couldn't even speak about the thought of your cheating. Or allow myself to dwell there. But make no mistake about the fact that I am not an ignorant man. I've counseled too many trusting spouses with HIV to not use wisdom about this."

Monica stood with so much fury on her face that she couldn't speak. She spun around and stomped out of the room.

Briggs could hear the sound of glass hitting the walls and prayed she wasn't breaking all the first lady's imported, expensive Lladró knickknacks.

It was Tuesday morning, and Briggs leaned against his office window at Love Zion church and daydreamed. It was a wonderful fall day in Detroit. The sun was shining bright, and the sky was clear of smokestack pollution, but none of that registered for Briggs. He had awakened to the smell of cinnamon rolls, sausage, and Blue Mountain coffee. Monica was doing a Donna Reed routine, and he didn't know what to say to this new side to her. Whatever happened in Atlanta must have been a doozy. Monica's usual routine was to tell him to hit Starbucks on his way to work. He wasn't complaining about the food, just the intent behind the gesture. On his way out the door, she told him she would be cleaning the house and washing his clothes. Monica then stole a smooch to his cheek and smiled serene that she would see him for dinner. Briggs blinked in confusion and scratched his head. If Monica wanted him to die of a heart attack for his life insurance, she almost had her wish because he couldn't take any more shocks in a twenty-four-hour period.

Briggs shook it off and sat at his desk to study his Sunday sermon. This was his most difficult message. He wanted to preach against the people from the pulpit, but the God in him said no. He wanted to call out the hypocrites and liars, but couldn't because his conscience was not clear. He had not acted, but he had lusted in his heart. He breathed heavily. This is why you shouldn't sin. At the end of day, it didn't allow you to throw any stones. And Briggs wanted to pitch a rock or two.

Last night, after Monica left him alone, Briggs called out to God in frustration, anger, and then acceptance. Yes, he had given Esther the "we're Christians and we must do the right thing" speech. However, there was still this imp telling him he didn't have to let go. It said, surely, he could have the dream of his youth. When he admitted to himself his role in his own pain, he got out of his bed, kneeled in a posture of submission, and repented. No lip service, no fake platitudes, just real tears of letting go. His shift brought the understanding that his sermon was needed to heal hearts, not tear them apart.

The phone rang, and as Briggs looked at the caller ID, he picked it up. "Hello, Mother Reed. It's good to hear from you. How are things? Are you feeling all right?"

"I remember when a body had to answer the phone to find out who was on the other end," she said, chuckling.

"Other than that, I'm blessed. This newfangled diet every-one is making sure I keep to be boring me to tears. Takes all the spice out of enjoying a good meal, but Mother is being obedient." There was a calculated pregnant pause before she went on. "I was wondering if you had spoken to Charles."

"No, ma'am. Naomi told me about the incident when I came in this morning, and I tried to call, but his cell went to voice mail."

"I know this thing hit him harder than he's sharing," Mother Reed explained. "That devil don't mean any of us any good. We gon' need to hear a powerful message this Sunday, something that will slay the dragon in his steps. We need to steal his thunder, kill them nasty rumors good-bye, and destroy his designs against our church."

Briggs could feel a spiritual split in the road. He'd tried to check on Charles. Should he call Esther? It would make sense as her pastor, but with his new resolve, he felt they both needed time and space.

Mother Reed interrupted his musing. "You there, son?"

Briggs refocused. "Yes, I was just thinking. I'm seeking God's counsel more than ever on this week's sermon. I'm praying for a word that will unite us. I'm disappointed in some of our members, but I'm going to love them even when it seems like they don't deserve it. I call it loving the unlovable and hugging the unhuggable."

"God's done the same for you. If we waited to deserve love, we would all be alone. But God decreed that it wasn't good for man to live by himself. You keep calling to speak to Charles, okay? He's acting like ain't nothing happened."

Briggs remembered the truth he had recently learned. "We have a need to be strong, even when bending will assure our position in strength; otherwise, we might just break. He needs an in-time Word to propel his way through this season. The good news is God is already on the job."

Mother Reed shouted her amen, and then settled down to finish talking. "Phyllis is a good wife, and she's growing in maturity. But sometimes wisdom has to come from someone who has walked the same path, so the person going through doesn't make the same mistakes they made."

"Mother Reed, that's a nice way to say, 'Don't let the boy mess it up by being silent like you did.' I hear you," Briggs stated without shame.

"Humph, what you learn the lesson for if it wasn't to help others bypass it?" Mother Reed asked. "Anyhow, what's going on with you and your wife? Ain't it past time she made an appearance? If she did, this other foolishness could filter on out."

Briggs was saddened people actually brought the lies to Mother Reed. "You've heard that nonsense?"

"Uh-huh, I've heard it. Don't know how much non-sense it is. Don't get me wrong, both of you have a special place in my heart. You snuck in where Esther has been lodged since her birthing. I've been praying for that child for years. See . . . I know her spirit; she's not one to covet nothing her neighbor owns, so I know that she didn't intentionally do nothing wrong. But, honey, that's why we have to be prayerful about guarding our hearts. It can run away with us, and the enemy just waiting for a chance to catch us in some mess. And that is what all this talk is—a mess!"

Briggs sat and wondered if he should even try to defend himself when he had already been found guilty as charged. It had taken him a full night of prayer to come to the conclusion that Jesus had paid the price for his shortcomings and to lay in guilt and shame would be to let the enemy win this round. For Briggs, that wasn't happening. He had cried for what could have been. Now it was important to fight for what was promised.

Briggs confirmed his new standing. "I'm good, Mother. As a matter of fact, I was going to call you for that very reason. My wife, Monica, is here."

"My goodness! You've just let me go on and on and haven't given me your good news. No wonder we haven't heard from you. You over there courting. Now, Mama gon' go in this c'here kitchen and pull out y'all favorite food. What she like, Briggs? I'm gon' make y'all an old-fashioned country feast. So get ready to come on over Saturday." Mother Reed was excited to be cooking what she considered real food again.

Briggs tried to catch her enthusiasm, but this was Mother Reed. "We have some problems to get through, Mother."

Mother snorted. "So, you fasting all week?"

Briggs knew he was caught short. "No, ma'am."

"Humph, besides the point that you probably ought to be, there's nothing stopping you from eating. So I 'spect to see you two Saturday. All right?"

"All right, I love you, Mother. You keep me straight," Briggs said, smiling.

"God always sends a ram in the bush, Briggs, always."

Briggs felt Mother Reed's last statement was mysterious. But growing up with elders visiting his home and making cryptic remarks, he was used to deep revelations. He was sure he would understand it later.

They hung up, each in their own world. Mother Reed was happy about cooking something with seasoning and butter. Briggs was making note to call Charles. Trying to figure out how he would tackle the problems between him and his wife was a steep mountain he would hike up later.

After a full day at the church, Briggs ended the call he was on with his mother. He was pulling into the gas station and he didn't talk and pump gas. A young man was filling his tank while his music blared loud through his window. When the gangsta rap fouled the air with cursing, he decided to speak up. "What's up, young brother? You think you can give us a break on the sounds?"

The young man's hardened stare pierced Briggs's heart. *When did we lose these children?* he wondered.

"Man, I don't know you. Back up off of me," he barked, pulling his sagging pants up.

Briggs rounded the car. "Well, now, that can be remedied. I'm Pastor Stokes. I'd like to invite you to Love Zion Fellowship this Sunday, or even on Thursday evening. That's our youth night. We serve some great pizza."

"You serve pizza? Oh, goody, I'll run right over," he said sarcastically before he stopped with a look of recognition on his face.

"Hey, did you say, Stokes. Love Zion? Oh, snap. You that pastor that be getting it on in the church office?" the young man said, laughing. "Yea, I'll show up at your church, and you can introduce me to them saved little honeys. Shoot, you the mack daddy. Wait 'till I tell my grandma I'm coming to her church this Sunday."

Briggs's mouth stood wide open as he watched the young man get in his car and screech off. The music's foul lyrics lingered in the air.

Chapter Forty-two

An agitated Briggs walked into a house that smelled delicious. He sniffed the air in appreciation. Monica hadn't cooked liked this since—well—never. He paused before entering the kitchen, wondering what approach was best. He and Monica needed to talk, and then talk some more. He heard humming and looked up to see a vision of Monica he didn't know existed. She was clean faced, sans makeup, with worn blue jeans molding her slender hips. Her plain blouse hugged her in all the right places, but was not low cut. Her only jewelry, her wedding ring and the two carat diamond earrings he bought her on their second anniversary. No bling, no skintight jiggling.

Monica smiled. "Good, you're here. You couldn't have arrived at a better time. I think your mother's lemongrass chicken came out perfect. And I just took the rosemary potatoes out of the oven. And if you think I'm playing, wait until you taste the asparagus. I grilled it just the way you like it. Go wash up, and we can sit down."

Briggs would have loved to give Monica the silent treatment. But, lemongrass chicken? He could taste the lemon and lime rolling across his palate. Indeed, God directs our path. We just need to be observant and take the right road. Briggs chose the road of obedience.

"I'll be right back. It smells delicious." Briggs hurried to the bathroom.

He returned to the kitchen and was surprised by the simple, but charming place settings.

"I hope you don't mind sitting in here. I thought it would be cozier than the dining room." Monica continued to place food on the table.

Briggs rubbed his hands together and started filling his plate. "This looks great." He placed his full plate in front of him and stretched out his hand to Monica to bless the food. "Father, bless the food for the nourishment of our bodies. Bless the hands that cooked it, and the means to provide it. Allow our dinner conversation to be of one accord. Amen."

Monica grinned at the first satisfied moan out of Briggs's mouth. "Good?"

"So good, I believe seconds will be in order." He took a few more bites, and then wiped his mouth with his cloth napkin. "You know, we have major problems a good meal won't cure."

"I know that, but I thought if you saw I was trying, that maybe you would believe we could get past our issues." Briggs studied her as tears welled in her eyes making them glisten and her appearance vulnerable.

Briggs took another bite and asked the deciding question. "Can you tell me the truth? And allow me to tell mine?"

"What if the truth hurts? What if you can't take my truth?" Monica asked, fearful of his answer.

Briggs laid down his fork and patted his mouth dry. "I can't make any promises. I've met a wonderful woman. Her name is Mother Reed, and she invited us to dinner on Saturday." Briggs paused before continuing. "I shared some things from my past with her, and it was the most painful and exhilarating experience. Afterward, I felt free. Maybe with God as our guide we can re-create that atmosphere of acceptance here, tonight."

Monica nodded her head in agreement, and they both silently decided to finish their meal in peace.

Their meal completed, Monica cleared the table, and Briggs went into the family room. He put on a worship CD and walked through the room praying. The room was so peaceful; he could tell Reverend Gregory must have spent some quality prayer time in it.

Monica stood at the door, tears spilling down her cheeks, her face draining of color. "I can't do this, Briggs, I can't. Maybe next week," she sobbed.

Before she could turn to leave, Briggs grasped her hand and guided her into the room. "Yes, you can. We have to, or we're destined to fail even further."

"You start then, Briggs," Monica said through her sniffles.

Briggs rubbed at the tight feeling in his chest. "I don't know if you remember when we first met, there was a young lady named Esther I used to talk about."

Monica snorted. "You mean you used to sing about, dream about, drink about . . . *that* Esther?"

Briggs considered that this was easier said than accomplished. "Okay, let's lay some ground rules. When we are telling it all, no one gets to interrupt, because it's hard enough to tell it the first time. No one gets to make snide remarks, even when their feelings are hurt." Briggs looked over at Monica's dried tears and heated eyes at the mention of Esther's name. He noted her small fists balling up in anger. "And no one gets physical."

"Yeah, well, you remember all these rules when it's your turn to listen." Monica folded her arms with an evil glare. "Continue, Briggs. I'll be quiet."

Briggs cleared his throat. "Esther lives in Detroit." He heard Monica's snort and paused. "And, no, I didn't know that when I took this assignment."

Monica nailed him with a piercing glare.

Briggs stumbled to clear up his statement. "Okay, let me rephrase that. Yes, I knew she lived here, but I didn't know she was a member of Love Zion. Detroit's a big place, and it's been ten years."

Monica gasped when Briggs stated Esther attended Love Zion. She stood, and then sat back down, rigid and unmoving.

Beginning to perspire, Briggs hurried to finish. "I felt a strong attraction for her when we met again." Monica clapped her hands and rubbed them together in angst at his admittance. He held up his hand and continued. "An attraction I did not act on."

Frowning, Monica folded her arms and waited, but Briggs appeared done. "My turn?"

Briggs nodded, and Monica unfurled her arms. "I had an attraction too." She exhaled, her voice becoming brittle. "I, however, did act on it. I've . . . had an affair."

Briggs grabbed the couch pillow and pounded it against his knee. He strode to the door, and then returned. He gulped, but no words were formed. Finally, he sat and gritted his teeth. A teardrop slid down his face and rested in the cleft in his chin.

Monica moaned and wept freely. "I . . . don't . . . want to hurt . . . anymore. Forgive . . . me please," she hollered.

Compassionate for anyone hurting, Briggs gathered her in his arms. He held on until the tightness in his chest eased and resolve replaced it. Monica sobbed out her pain, her fears, and her insecurities that she was never good enough for him, his parents, or the church.

Together, they slumped to the floor. Briggs revealed his own insecurities and his need to be seen as his own man. He shared his feelings of rejection, abandonment, and embarrassment when she refused to take her rightful place and join him in Detroit. He admitted to Monica his shortcomings behind the malicious rumors, and how he now saw the part he played in them.

They listened, they accused, the rules were broken, and more of Mrs. Gregory's Lladró was smashed.

Chapter Forty-three

Concealing his true state of mind, Charles periodically bobbed his head to the music playing through the stereo earphones on his head.

He was startled when Phyllis appeared before him mouthing that the telephone was for him as she passed him the cordless.

Slow to respond, Charles pulled his earphones off. "Hello, Charles speaking."

"Hey, man, this is Briggs. I wanted to call and see if you had some time to hang out today."

"I don't need any hand holding, Pastor Stokes. I got this," Charles barked.

"It's not Pastor Stokes calling, it's Briggs. And, now I know you've gotten all my voice mails the last three days. How about if I let you hold my hand? Earlier this week, when I got home, Monica was at the house."

Charles mellowed his tone. "Nah, man, you're kidding. What did she say?"

"Initially, she said a lot of mumbo jumbo about trying to find herself and missing me. It took all I had not to strangle her. Then it got real."

Charles whistled. "Hey, we should hang out for a while. Why don't you come by the house? Phyllis has a hair appointment every Friday, man. She'll be gone around four hours."

Briggs snickered. "That's all? Listen, Monica used to leave the house and be gone all day."

"Yeah, hair, nails, eyebrows, on and on. I must admit my baby looks good when she gets home. Although, truth be told, that sleeping pretty thing really ain't that pretty. But when a woman looks good, she acts good, if you know what I'm talking about," Charles stated jokingly.

"I hear you," Briggs said wishing he had the same testimony.

Esther rode up in the hospital elevator clipping her plastic visitor badge to her cashmere sweater. It had been three grueling days of sitting vigil over Lawton as he fell in and out of consciousness. Not mentally or emotionally ready to go home, she'd been staying in her old room at her parents'. She was learning it was true, home is where the heart is.

Leaving the elevator, she waved to the hospital staff, stopped at Lawton's door, and peeped in. She was excited to see that he was alone. *Yippee, got my baby to myself.*

"Who's there?" Lawton asked shakily as he tried to sit up.

"Lawton!" Esther said, happy and surprised to see he was lucid and talking. She pumped antibacterial wash on her hands and rushed to his bedside.

"That's me; at least, I think it's me."

"Sweetie, it's you. All that big head can't be anyone else," Esther teased as she bent over his bed and stroked his face.

"How are you going to make fun of a man on his sickbed?" Lawton croaked.

"You're such a perfect specimen, kidding you is easy," she joked adjusting his pillow.

Lawton was quiet and had failed to make eye contact with Esther.

"Lawton?" Esther asked, unsure of his reaction to her presence.

Lawton turned and looked directly at her. "Hey."

"How do you really feel?" she asked, concerned that he was in pain.

"Fine," Lawton answered, turning away from her.

"Is there something wrong? No, scratch that. Lawton, what's wrong with you?" Esther was bewildered. She had waited three days for him to wake up. Too many times she had played nice. She was never playing the fool again. "If you don't want me here, please say so." Esther couldn't believe she was getting the cold shoulder.

Lawton turned and asked sullenly, "Isn't there somewhere else you'd rather be?"

"For heaven's sake, where else would I need or want to be?" she said, exasperated.

"Church maybe," Lawton said sarcastic as he grimaced in pain.

Esther was at a loss as to why such a usually sweet-tempered man was acting so rude. *It's obvious he's hurting. I'll just ignore it.* "Baby, you had me so worried."

Lawton pointed at the wires connecting him to the monitors. "These make me look worse than I feel."

Esther was relieved that Lawton's distance was due to him not wanting to look weak. She decided to share so he would understand that they could be vulnerable with each other. "Poor, sweetie, I know how it feels to be vulnerable. Can you believe that yesterday, my parents told me about a horrible rumor that was going on about me and Pastor Stokes at Love Zion? People are so wrong sometimes." She shook her head.

Lawton tried to sit up. "What rumor?"

"That Briggs and I are having an a-a-affair. If it wasn't for your accident, I might have been more upset by the lie, but knowing you were here fighting your own battle made mine seem so insignificant."

Lawton's grimace eased at Esther's simple explanation. Loathed to let her know the damaging thoughts he had harbored and mentally kicking himself for doubting her, he sought the means to move forward. "Don't let these wires scare you. You can move a little closer. Mom told me you've been here every day. Did I tell you how much you mean to me?" Now his demeanor was warm and inviting.

Esther gave him a relieved smile. "Well, you were acting a little strange when I first came in the room, but you seem to be acting like yourself now. I guess you were just in pain."

"In more ways than one," he mumbled. "Can I have a little kiss? It would be the perfect medicine," he implored with an impish twinkle in his eye.

Esther leaned over and placed a tender kiss on Lawton's forehead. Her heart blossomed, and she felt a feeling of contentment just being able to talk to him. Today's progress was miraculous. "So tell me, Mr. Serve and Protect, what have you heard from the doctors this morning?"

"That today, I've turned a corner. I'm surprised they haven't barged in here already. I seem to remember them in and out all night and hearing Mama pleading for them to let me rest."

Esther laughed. "I was here too. But, your mother, well . . ."

Lawton peeked at her. "You were? Well, about my dear mama. I told her that I had asked you to be my wife, and that when we married, we wanted her to come and live with us."

Esther stood up sputtering. "But, Lawton . . . I haven't even said I would marry—live with us? Do you have any idea—?"

Lawton held his side and grimaced a shaky laugh. "Ooh, that hurts, stop, stop! Your face was so comical.

Do I look like a mama's boy? Babe, we would drive her crazy!"

Esther laughed in relief. "I don't know, after meeting your mama." When she saw the offended look on his face, Esther tweaked his nose in a gentle way. "I think you better take it easy. Your ribs are bruised and laughing that hard could throw something out of whack."

Lawton settled back into his pillow. "Out of whack, Nurse Esther?"

"Oh, please . . ." Esther stated as the door swung open and the nurse entered.

The nurse was brisk and professional. "Sorry, ma'am. The doctor will be here shortly. So if you don't mind . . ."

Esther moved to leave. "I'll be right outside, and I'll come back in when they say it's okay."

"Okay, sweetheart." Lawton frowned when the nurse pricked him with the needle.

The door swung closed behind Esther, and Nurse Williams then stuck a thermometer in Lawton's mouth. He wanted her to finish so Esther could come back in. He hadn't shared that Sergeant Ford had visited him right before she came in and stated his car chase and subsequent accident was under police investigation. It seemed his partner, Glen, claimed he was reckless.

Chapter Forty-four

Charles and Briggs sat nodding their heads in time to the music.

"I hear that old dude didn't stand a chance," Briggs said about Charles's fight.

Charles brushed the incident off, even with Phyllis, preferring to perform like the hero who took it all in stride. But he couldn't pull off the act for himself, and he'd had some sleepless nights since it all went down. His heart froze just thinking about what could have happened.

In restrained motion, Charles balled his fist and tapped it against his thigh. "Argh! I was scared. Man, I could've lost that fight," Charles winced. "The bullet could've hit Phyllis or me. Instead, I played conquering hero."

Briggs stood and clasped Charles's shoulders. Both men felt the other's strength. Briggs understood his feelings. "When I prayed for you in the spirit, I felt that you weren't at peace. As men, we try so hard to carry it all."

Charles wiped moisture from his face and used the remote to shut the stereo off. "You're right. I needed to admit that something could have gone wrong. I feel lighter just saying the truth of it. Thanks for listening. Oh yea, and . . . thanks for not trying to fill me with tired clichés."

Laughter slipped from Briggs's pressed lips. "So it's too late for me to tell you that a 'hero ain't nothing but a sandwich'?"

Charles joined in his mirth, and the residue of pent-up tension floated away. He then went to the bar refrigerator and retrieved and tossed Briggs a bottle of water. "So much for my issues. Spill the beans on Monica."

"I really don't know what to say. We had the first authentic conversation in our marriage the other night. The truth was powerful. Now we have to learn to heal from it." Briggs started chuckling. "I'm going to owe the Gregorys a grip. Monica has broken almost all Mrs. Gregory's knickknacks."

Charles smiled but refused to stray from the subject. "Does your struggle have anything to do with Esther?"

"No. At one time Esther was the focus of some of my not-so-right day-and-night fantasies. Shoot—I'm a man, trying to be worthy of wearing the mantle of a saint. We are now just friends in passing; even close friendship would be dangerous. The temptation to do wrong would be too strong."

Charles took a swig of his water. "I don't want to pour salt on open wounds, but I think Lawton will really be good for her."

Briggs waved his comment away. "Naw, man. So do I. Maybe in another life . . ."

Charles rolled his cold water bottle in his hands. "We only got this one, bro. And this may not make me very popular in your eyes, but has whatever Monica been doing while away from you any different or worse than where your heart has been these last months?"

"I want to storm out of here, but the Holy Spirit in me says I have to at least consider what you're saying." Briggs weighed Charles's words before he spoke. "It seems we both haven't been happy for a long time."

Charles continued. "I'm not as eloquent with my speech or as learned in my word as you, but I don't remember being unhappy as a perquisite for getting out of a marriage. Oh, I know that many do, but I feel that our God calls us as Christians to a higher calling. You have to at least try to make it work God's way."

"Don't hurt a brother too bad, Elder Davis. I left my wallet out in the car, but if you hold on, I'll be right back with your offering," Briggs halfheartedly joked. He felt sideswiped by Charles's comments, especially when he had come to enlighten, not be enlightened.

Charles rubbed his cheek thinking. "Hey, must be the Holy Spirit 'cause even I don't know where that came from. I just know that you're a man who happens to love and follow God in spite of all your human foibles and scars. Don't let your hurt feelings make a decision that all of you will have to live with. I would hate for you to do anything that would cause you to falter in your walk."

Briggs's sigh filled the room. "Yeah, well, I have a lot of battles to fight this week; I'll just add this one to them."

Charles hesitated, then shrugged his shoulder. "Those rumors are no joke. Every time my phone rings, the lie gets bigger and uglier. And I have to tell somebody to quit calling my house with trash and that none of that nonsense is true."

"I hear you. I was trying to ignore them, but when I went to the gas station yesterday, some young man tried to give me play as a mack daddy preacher. Now you know I'm not trying to be down like that."

Charles shook his head as he tried to hold back his laughter. "A mack daddy? Where do these young men get their mentalities from? 'Thugs 'R' Us?' I want to take every one of them home, give them some pants that fit, take the gold out of their mouths when their mamas, daddies, or the state paid good money for straight white teeth, and spare not the rod."

Briggs spoke with fervor. "We have to love them into submission. The hip-hop generation has stolen from us the best and the brightest, and it wasn't anything but a plan of the enemy. He took their low self-esteem and put them in low-sagging pants. Now their sagging spirits match their oppressive future. The enemy has played to the beat of their soul, and now they're just beat down."

"Amen, brother! Now I need to give *you* the offering. I feel you. I heard Cornel West say that they were so busy being peacocks who look good but who can't fly that they forgot they were born to be eagles that soar. Maybe you can help do something about that. Start something right here."

"Now I can see how that would be a plan; thanks for volunteering to help me."

"I didn't volunteer . . ."

"Oh yes, you did." Briggs waved his hand in the air. "Sing it with me, 'I believe that children are our future . . .'"

"Oh, you real funny, but this appears to be another conversation, for another time. Now, what about the fight you have against these rumors? Whatever you have planned, I'm in. For a nonviolent man, I'm beginning to become good at this fight thing."

"Well, here's what I was thinking . . ."

Esther's visit with Lawton was so encouraging that she decided to pack her bags and return home. If he could face the road ahead of him, she could handle returning to her home. She couldn't believe they were investigating Lawton's car chase and crash. However, God was not slack about His promises, and she had faith that all would be well. Thursday, she had left Lawton prone and in a state of semiconsciousness. Today he was functioning beyond expectations. God was good.

She wasn't ready to sleep in her old bedroom, so Esther was settling into her guest room for the night when her phone rang.

"Hey, sis. You good?" Phyllis asked.

"Yes, I went to the hospital earlier, and Lawton's progress is so reassuring. He was up talking and joking." Esther became teary. "Life can change in an instant. I've made a lot of mistakes in my life, Phyllis."

"We all have. That's why every day He provides us with brand-new mercies. We just can't keep making the same mistakes over and over. We need to seek Him and live according to His Word. But we get lost, and lonely, and then something happens to snap us back on the right road before we begin to live a lifestyle of rebellion. Charles and I had that kind of 'snapback moment' with the Roger incident."

"I'm so thankful you guys are okay. I'm glad Dad and Mom told me what really happened. I can handle more than you know, Phyllis," Esther said, needing Phyllis to see her as an adult.

Phyllis blustered. "I know what you can handle, Esther."

Esther pushed back. "No, you knew what the child could handle. You have to learn me as an adult, Phyllis. You still see me running around, falling, and coming to you with the boo-boo on my knee."

Phyllis argued. "And I'm still right here. You're a church girl, Esther, what is there to know? Those stupid rumormongers should know you as well as I do."

Esther pushed harder to get Phyllis to hear her. "Phyllis, would it surprise you to know that there was smoke near that fire?"

"What are you saying, Esther? You and Briggs had a thing?" Phyllis said in a cold, hard voice.

Esther cried at her sister's coldness. "Not a real thing . . . but I have needs and wants, and my salvation doesn't always keep them at bay. You snuggle with Charles and forget that a lot of us are sleeping alone. I'm not going into everything with you, but Briggs brought a hunger out I didn't know was lurking."

Phyllis's soft response was calmer. "Look, I'm sorry, and I won't judge you. I have some skeletons in my own closet. Let's promise each other that we'll establish a real level of intimacy and not just support for each other. And, I promise, little sister, I'll work on knowing the adult you."

Esther grinned. "I'd like that. Let's cross our hearts on it."

Laughter filled the phone. "Your heart's on the other side of your chest, nutcase."

Esther looked in the mirror, and sure enough, her hand was on the wrong side of her chest. "How do you know I crossed the wrong side, Phyllis?"

"Because you've been doing it since you were a toddler. Never could get it right."

Chagrined, Esther chuckled. "Well, maybe some things from my childhood haven't changed. Good night, Phyllis."

"Night."

Esther was assaulted with her childhood memories. She went to her closet, digging through boxes, and pulled out her picture album. On the front of the album, a seven-year-old Esther sat in a princess dress, wearing a tiara and holding a jeweled scepter. Her dad painted an old chair gold and put cardboard turrets on the back of it. She sat confident on her throne.

Inside the album on the first page was an eight-by-ten photo of three knobby kneed youngsters with their arms around each other smiling into the camera. Their hair was all over their heads, wind blown from bike rides and grass rolling. Their clothes rumpled and in disarray with two jump ropes lying on the ground before them.

Remembering treasured times, she smiled and touched first Sheri's, and then Deborah's face reverently. Clutching the album, she lay down and stretched out over her pillow. She stared at the young faces on the picture, and for the first time, noted a shadow in the background of the photo-graph. Esther peeled back the plastic, took out the picture, and held it in front of the light. She rubbed her eyes, shook her head, and placed the picture gently back in the album.

Tomorrow, I'll call about new reading glasses. I swear that looked like a serpent against the background of the photo. Lord, I'm really sleepy.

Chapter Forty-five

It was Saturday, and Monica and Briggs were on their way to Mother Reed's. After Tuesday's emotional breakdown, they continued talking throughout the week. A house does not make a home, and Briggs would not share his bed. Monica hoped that this evening would turn all that around. She missed the lure of a rock-hard body, and she needed to keep thoughts of Randall at bay.

She had chosen a demure outfit and had promised herself to only speak when spoken to. She meant to put her best foot forward. In the past, her mouth had gotten her in trouble with some of the older women at church. She wouldn't make that mistake today.

Briggs continued to fill her in as he drove. "Mother Reed is not only the mother of the church, but she has become a surrogate mother to me. You know how busy my parents are, and in the short time I have been here, Mother Reed has become very dear to me."

"I understand, Briggs, and I promise to get along with her. I'm really looking forward to this." Monica looked at Briggs for his approval.

In an accusing tone, Briggs said, "You've never wanted to meet or spend time with the church elders before."

Monica turned. "But I'm different now. And when you finally say you forgive me, it will be worth it to you. You'll see."

Briggs pulled up in front of Mother Reed's large brick home. "This is a very nice house, Briggs," Monica said, surprised.

"Yes, Mother Reed's husband provided for her well, and she believes in living a modest lifestyle." Briggs parked.

Mother Reed watched Briggs park from her living-room window. She came out on the porch, hands on her hips. "Well, bring the child in out of the evening air. She's such a pretty little thing," Mother Reed exclaimed as she hugged Monica and drew back from the coldness of her spirit.

"Come in, come in," she hugged Briggs and led them into the living room.

Briggs was puzzled. "I haven't sat in this room since I first met you. It would be fine for us to sit in your kitchen."

Mother Reed continued into the room. "Chile, Monica looks so pretty I would hate for her to get her clothes all full of kitchen smells or spills. We'll just rest c'here a might before we head to the dining-room table."

Briggs's puzzlement grew. "The dining-room table? Mother, you shouldn't have gone to all this trouble. You don't even use your dining room. We'd be fine in the kitchen. Right, Monica?"

"Absolutely, please don't go to any bother," Monica said, eager to please.

Mother Reed smiled, but failed to change their eating arrangements. "I'll be right back. Let me check on something in the kitchen." She went into the kitchen and shuffled around the stove mumbling all the way, "All right, then, Lord. I don' seen enough. My thoughts are not Your thoughts, Your ways are not my ways. But you must really gon' pull somethin' off on this c'here situation. That child's heart is cold as ice. She ain't sitting in my kitchen, tainting the air with her unclean thoughts. Um, um, um."

She returned to the living-room. "Well, children, let's eat before it gets cold," she announced as she took food into the dining-room. When she reentered the kitchen, she passed the table with place settings for three. She grabbed more food, turned, and bumped into Briggs, who entered behind her to help with the heavier serving bowls. He eyed the place settings and went back into the dining-room, where a duplicate dining-room table was set.

Mother Reed felt bad. Briggs had saw her duplicity, but it couldn't be helped. When she was a young girl, her grandmother always fed who she considered family in the kitchen, and she would feed those who were thought of as company in the dining-room. She always said that her kitchen was too intimate, and the heart of her home, and not everybody could sit in it. And family wasn't defined by blood; she had a roguish cousin who was never allowed to sit at their grandma's kitchen table.

She could tell by Briggs's response to the seating arrangements and his sluggish movements he understood what her actions meant. Monica was company.

So far, it had been a quiet Saturday night for Esther. Her head was bent over a book in the cold, sterile room. When she arrived at the hospital, Lawton lay sleeping and per his protective mother, she shouldn't disturb him.

"Good book?" a raspy voice asked.

Esther looked over at the man who, with every glance, seemed to telegraph her tomorrows. "Not as good as talking to you. I've been passing the time waiting for this real good-looking brother to wake up."

"If I could paint, right now, I would sit up in this bed, and use the colors of the rainbow to describe my feelings for you." Lawton stared at Esther, and then burst out laughing. "Dang, girl, you got me waxing poetic and all that. Don't you go telling people I'm whipped, especially not my mama."

"Oh, baby, I'm *especially* gon' tell your mama," she laughed with him.

"See, you're not playing fair. You've met my mama. That's a formidable woman. When Dad died, she didn't miss a beat. Maybe that's why I love an independent woman; I'm looking for my mama."

"Honey, I do not want to be your mother."

Lawton held his hand to his head. "Feel my temperature. I think I just caught a sudden fever."

Esther placed her hand on his forehead. He caught her hand and laid it across his chest.

The room was quiet as they enjoyed each other's company. They could hear activity in the hallway as an orderly dropped what sounded like numerous metal trays. This could have disturbed the mood, but it was too thick with the knowledge they both had stumbled on to something solid and good.

Lawton looked at Esther and said under his breath. "I wonder if you understand that you're in my future." He then sighed. "I'm wanting out of here."

Esther understood his mood, because suddenly, she wanted him out of there too. "What does the doctor say?"

Lawton grunted. "Who? The one who fears my mother? She's threatened to sue everyone in here if I am not 100 percent perfect when I leave here."

Esther put down the book in her hands and crossed her legs. She swung her hair back from her face and leaned into Lawton. "Then she better call the lawyer. You weren't 100 percent perfect when you came in," Esther said, laughing.

"Now a man should not be abused when he's lying helpless in a hospital bed. Woman, do you have no shame?" Lawton pretended to be insulted.

"No shame at all. I'm becoming quite transparent, and I believe that's a good thing. But if I were the doctor, I would tread light around your mama too. The woman does not play." Esther shivered.

Lawton noticed her actions. "Is she being difficult? You've been looking a little strained these last few days. Talk to me, sweetheart."

"It isn't your mother. There's been a little drama lately," Esther said in a hesitant voice.

"What kind of drama?" Lawton used the bed's remote to tilt the bed forward.

Esther decided to share all. "The day of your accident, unbeknownst to me, my ex-husband, Roger, broke into my house. He lay in wait for me, but I was here. As a favor, Phyllis and Charles went to my house to pack a small bag for me." Esther pointed her finger at Lawton. "I had no intentions of leaving you until you were out of danger."

His jaw rigid, Lawton nodded for her to continue. "Roger shot at them. It's my understanding that if not for a bottle of Vernors Ginger Ale, my sister would be dead. Charles overpowered Roger in a fistfight, and now Roger is in jail."

Lawton's gaze was brooding. She waited for the outburst; she knew she should have told him more about her past with Roger.

"Come here." Lawton held out his arms, and Esther cautiously joined him on the bed. She made every effort not to disturb any tubing and wires and to keep most of her weight on her leg that was on the floor. It was awkward but effective.

Lawton fingered her hair and kissed her brow. Emotional, he groaned, "It's times like these that I am so sure of my feelings for you. When you were speaking, all I wanted was to hold and protect you from Roger and all the other predators of the world."

Esther wanted him to know it hadn't always been bad. "He wasn't always a predator."

"Tell me about him," Lawton encouraged as his fingers rubbed her arm.

"When we first met, there was a vulnerability about him. He told me all the time how good I was for him, and how much he needed me, and I guess I needed that. I had let someone down before by not being there for them, and I felt that I could make that up through Roger. Sort of like balancing the cosmos, you know?" Esther hoped he understood her youthful mind-set.

Lawton only asked, "And did you?"

"No, the more I did, the more he resented me. Soon the yelling turned into hitting, and I ended the marriage." Esther spoke without rancor. She had made peace with that part of her past.

"He abused you?" Lawton rumbled so low Esther almost didn't hear him.

She bowed her head. "It's hard to admit, even now. Yes, he did abuse me—emotionally, mentally, and in the final days, physically. Everything he was doing to my soul, he finally tried to take out on my body. But in some ways, I think I abused him too. My eyes never lit up when he came into a room. I never longed to hear his voice or to see his smile. I couldn't love who I pitied, and knowing someone will never love you is painful."

Lawton shook his head at her generosity of spirit. "You sound like you feel sorry for him."

"No, I just forgive him. He tried to make my life a living hell, but the gates did not prevail. The contrary spirit in him failed to overcome the godly spirit in me."

Lawton motioned for Esther to move back over to her chair, "A man who findeth a wife, findeth a good thing. You are my good thing, and before it's all said and done, I'm going to marry you, Esther Wiley."

Esther smiled, content to be in this room, with this man. She couldn't say she was even surprised by his declaration. Their connection was just that special. "Say that to me again. When you can declare your love by getting down on one knee, then you may just have yourself a bride."

Lawton grinned, and then began to push the bell for the nurse.

Esther was alarmed. "What are you doing? Are you in pain?"

The door flew open, and a nurse rushed in. "Are you all right, Mr. Redding?"

Lawton's smile was blinding. "I've never been better. I just need to see the doctor right away, and a physical therapist. I've got two goals: to get out of here, and to be able to get down on one knee."

Esther cracked up as the nurse looked disgruntled at her time wasted and marched off. She looked at Lawton lovingly and decided to share with him all about her childhood as a member of the tenacious three and how their separation shaped her.

As Lawton settled down and closed his eyes, a small gasp escaped Esther's mouth. Should she share with Lawton her past with Briggs? She had a deep suspicion that answer was no.

Chapter Forty-six

Sunday morning was overcast, the sun hid behind polluted laden clouds. It was as if the sun didn't want to start the day either. Briggs commiserated with it. The dinner at Mother Reed's house went downhill from the moment he realized she was only being polite to Monica. Monica was clueless and thought she had won Mother Reed over. The entire ride home was filled with how she would do the same with the rest of the congregation.

Arriving home, Monica was pumped, twirling, and cha-chaing around the house. She snapped her fingers in triumphant glee. "I have a plan to shut up all the noise at the church. I got you, babe. Listen . . ." Monica outlined her strategy as Briggs pondered her scheme.

"You know, I hate to say this, but your plan will work better than the one I thought up."

"Of course . . . men aren't as good at this type of thing as us women." Monica then continued her dance, undressing on the way back to his bedroom.

Briggs held up his hands. "Hold up there, Gypsy Rose Lee. Grab up those clothes and cha-cha on back to the guest room."

"Really? You gon' put a halt to this?" Monica swept her hands down her camisole, G-string-clad body.

Briggs shook his head, strolled past her, and locked his bedroom door. He peeled off his socks to doors slamming, brushed his teeth, and cringed at the foul language, and before his head hit the pillow, the breaking started. He fell asleep counting the number of items he would need to replace before the Gregorys came home.

The morning had been tense, and Briggs was no longer sure if Monica was up to her own plan. He looked at her as they entered the church. She was dressed to the nines and looked beautiful in her burnt-orange designer suit and matching hat. Her Stuart Weitzman rust and tan pumps showcased a catwalk across the checkered tile. He marveled that someone who looked so good could be so tainted. He admonished himself. If he couldn't bring forgiveness into his own home, how could he ask it of others?

Dear Father, I pray this works. You said to be as wise as a serpent and as harmless as a dove. And I'm trying. I know that I allowed all this to get out of hand. But if You will just give me mercy, Lord, I promise, I'll be a better Christian and leader. Please, Father, for everyone's sake. Amen.

Briggs and Monica walked into his private office to prepare for service as other members entered through the front entrance of Love Zion Church.

Esther strolled with her mother into the church vestibule, updating her on Lawton's progress. Phyllis trailed behind, speaking low to Charles. "Does this feel like déjà vu to you?" Phyllis asked.

Charles took his wife's hand and kept up with the others. "Being a part of the Wiley family has never been dull. I seem to remember us coming in here once or twice to do battle. Guess what?"

"What?" Phyllis asked.

"God always won." Charles held her hand. He noted the stares of people, and the muttering that accompanied

their promenade down the hallway heading to the sanctuary. He had always admired his in-laws, and today they
were doing him proud. No rushing for cover, but they
sauntered, heads high, as though they were attending an
afternoon stroll through a flowered park. He grinned at
Phyllis.

"You look good, baby. Strut your stuff," he whispered.

Phyllis put even more emphasis on the swing in her
hips as she tilted her head up in the air.

Charles admired the view. "Awww, sookie, sookie,
now."

Phyllis pointed when she sighted a purple plumed hat.
"There's Mother Reed, and it looks like she's waiting for
us."

Mother Reed stood staring at the family her heart had
adopted when her good friend, Esther's grandmother,
befriended her all those years ago. Together, they had
buried Esther's grandfather, and finally, Mother Reed
was left to bury her. They were closer than sisters, and
these were her children who were being messed with. She
and her God wouldn't stand for it too much longer. She
had heard the sniggers and snippets of, "I'm just telling
you, so you can pray for them," or, "Now, honey, I ain't
the one to gossip, but did you hear about . . ." Mother
Reed held her arms open, and Esther stepped into them.

"I'm sorry, I haven't seen you. There's just been so
much going on. But you're too important to me to be
placed on a back burner. Forgive me?" Esther bent over
to lay her head on Mother Reed's shoulder.

Mother Reed smiled at the gentleness of Esther's touch,
and her memories flitted back to when Esther had first laid
her head on her shoulder when she was a little freckled-faced
girl. As the years passed and their positions switched, Esther
still showed reverence by pretending that Mother Reed was
physically the same robust woman she once was.

Mother Reed patted Esther's hand. "I know your heart, child. I know your heart. What I don't know is this new young man of yours. I'm gon' make a lovely supper and hav' you both over as soon as he's up and about. You just let me know."

"Yes, ma'am, but it's going to be awhile. Lawton's pushing it, but healing has its own time table. He's now in the trauma wing, and then he'll be moved to rehabilitation." Esther nodded when her parents walked up.

Elizabeth put her arm through her husband's and spoke to everyone. "We're all here together, strong, invincible because of the God we serve. Head up, Esther."

Hickman winked at his youngest daughter and led the way into the sanctuary. Everyone paused when they saw a vision of loveliness in burnt orange sitting on the dais next to Briggs. Hickman recovered first and continued into the sanctuary. Amid whispers and staring they slid into the pew.

Comments circled around them, "Well, he left her high and dry, didn't he?" "Who's the woman in orange?" "Is that his wife?" "She's gorgeous. Poor Esther."

Esther's answering thoughts were malicious. *I got a man, thank you very much.*

Phyllis directed her glare in a 180-degree sweep, making sure they received her full venomous wrath. She touched her sister in support.

Abigail Winters slowed at the Wiley pew and bowed her head to Esther as though in mourning. Esther gave her a hostile glare and tuned everyone out. She didn't come to church for this. She needed a word.

Briggs approached the podium. "Good morning, Love Zion," he said in a loud, jovial voice. There was a hush, and then a very weak response from the congregation.

Briggs smiled confidently. "Now, I know y'all don't want my wife to think that Love Zion's members are not pleased to have her here." There were several gasps and an explosion of murmurs as he started again, "So . . . good morning, Love Zion."

"Good morning, Pastor," a resounding echo retorted.

Briggs shouldered on. "This lovely lady, who was delayed in coming to be with us, is now here, and as you can see, in full effect!"

Several members laughed, and some men in the congregation returned, "Amen to that."

"I'll let her speak to you in her own words. Let's receive her by saying, 'Thank God for Sister Monica.'" Briggs turned and gestured for Monica to join him.

The church responded and waited in anticipation as Monica stood at the podium.

"My brethren, I am so glad to join you and have heard so much about all of you from my husband and dear friends. I have heard about the generosity of saints like Mother Reed and Deacon Clement. However, I would be remiss in not thanking one person in particular. I want to publicly thank a good friend to all, and especially me, Esther Wiley, for assisting Briggs in becoming acclimated to his new job. It's good to have God's people in your corner. Am I right, church?"

"Amen," they chorused back.

"Yes, I want to thank you all. It is the pure heart that gets the job done. Oh, before I forget, I also wanted to thank Sister Abigail Winters. It is my understanding that she was very instrumental in keeping our members in ministry. She stirred things up and kept people in constant communication with each other. We need someone who encourages us to stay at the foot of His throne."

The church snickered and looked over at Abigail who clutched her purse to her bosom as she rocked in agitation.

Briggs stood next to Monica and hugged her as he led her to her seat and motioned for the choir to begin ministering. Eyes downcast, he combed the congregation, connecting, and then disconnecting just as quickly, with Esther.

Monica leaned toward Briggs, her church fan hiding her words. "Well? Am I once again in your good graces?"

Briggs turned to her and stated between a fake grin, "I didn't ask you to lie. You laid it on pretty thick about Esther being your friend."

"I didn't say she just was my friend. I said she was a friend to all. By the way, Sister Winters will not be a problem anymore. Someone like her could never get the best of someone like me. Baby, we're going places."

Briggs sighed, "Evidently."

Briggs's sermon had the entire congregation fighting to get a place at the altar. He had pulled them from the valley, and raised them to the mountaintop. There wasn't a person there that wasn't shouting to the heavens and asking for God's mercy. The healing at Love Zion had begun.

Many of the members stood talking, waiting in the receiving line to welcome their new first lady. Monica dazzled many with her polished manners and haunting beauty. Some went through the line with the gossip residue from before the anointed service still on them as they waited to see if any sparks would fly when Esther got to their new first lady.

Esther moved forward, examining Monica for a physical flaw in her appearance. It didn't sit well with her that she couldn't locate one. Physical perfection was overrated. "First Lady Monica, so glad to see you again." Esther loudly alluded to Monica's earlier announcement.

Monica ground her back teeth in annoyance, and noisily responded, "Is that you, Esther? Girl, you've put on some weight since the last time I saw you. You're kinda chunky there, girl. My bad that I haven't been to see you." She coyly tittered behind her hand. "You know how it is when you haven't seen your husband."

Phyllis bumped Esther from behind, egging her on. "No, I'm sorry I don't. When you have a man like Briggs, it would be foolish to ever leave him alone for too long. Shoot, some big, ol' bad blast from his past might just snatch him up," Esther growled.

Monica's fingernails dug into her palms. "Honey, you need to remember Lot's wife. Looking back cost her."

Esther gasped that Monica had pulled out the Word of God on her. Phyllis bumped her hard, but Esther disengaged and gave a stiff smile as she nodded; checkmate.

Briggs's eyes got large, and he looked to make sure that no one could hear the sparring words exchanged after the women's initial greeting. The harsher the words, the lower they spoke. Both were gritting teeth and spitting nails.

"Esther, you and Monica must do this again some other time," Briggs said meaningfully, looking over her shoulder at the line snaking the hallway.

Monica's smile was electric when she took Briggs's arm. "Well, Esther, you heard from the man, himself. You've been dismissed."

Esther went total hood in her response. "Oh, you don't want this. Child, please." Then she swished away.

The still air had a supernatural aura. Only the most attuned could hear the symphony of rattles.

Chapter Forty-seven

Esther's boots glided across the worn tile, her coat hanging open as she clipped the visitor's pass to her lapel. It had been a month since Monica had set the record straight at church, and their ridiculous showdown afterward. She'd endured her mother's scolding of her behavior and Mother Reed's silent disappointment. It was a good thing they were the ones standing behind her in line. Esther couldn't understand what came over her, but she just couldn't seem to shut up. She wanted to say, like Geraldine, on the old *Flip Wilson Show*, "The devil made me do it." But she knew that her Bible-studying mother might have hit her with some old-time wisdom. The devil ain't powerful, God is.

The upside of Monica's arrival? The rumors had died a sudden death. The downside? Monica had arrived. She managed to be everywhere at church where Esther was, lording her position over everyone. In the best of circumstances, Esther admitted it would be hard-pressed to like her. But, for real? This girl was a trip and a half.

Esther grunted, "Looking forward is the key; just keep moving forward." Her concentration needed to be on Lawton. She made it to the hospital every day, and when he was moved to the rehabilitation wing, she came at least four times a week. Her honey got bored lying around.

Their only dark cloud was waiting for Roger's trial to end and Lawton's clearance from the car crash investigation. Esther checked her watch and hurried down the hospital rehabilitation wing's corridor. Lawton's progress remained impressive. No longer in a wheelchair, his walker was put away two days ago. Getting the hang of using his cane had him hoping his doctor would release him soon.

Esther reached Lawton's room, but the hospital bed was empty and the room dark. *That's odd; rehab is usually over by this time of day.*

She settled down in a chair when music floated through the curtain from the next bed.

The curtain crawled open, revealing an empty space where the bed used to stand, and in its place was a linen-covered table for two with candles burning in soft luminosity. Lawton held his body tightly to minimize his discomfort, and then limped on his cane toward the set table and motioned Esther over.

Esther rushed to help him sit. "What have you done, crazy man?"

After sitting and taking a breath, he eased from the chair and sank in slow motion to his knee, using his cane as a brace. "I was cleared of all charges today, so I'm gainfully employed. The camera showed—yes—I was in a high-speed chase, but the other driver slammed on his brakes causing the accident." Caressing her hand he kissed it. "The hospital is not the best setting, but I'm on bended knee, and if it means anything to you, I'll stay here the rest of my life honoring you, as I honor God. There will never be a minute of any day when I won't love you, and in my last moment on earth, you will be in my thoughts as I go to meet our Father."

Teary eyed, Esther sank to her knees and faced him. "And I will marry you and cleave to you. I will submit to you and make you a home where you will be my love. I've had wrong, so I know that you are my right." She leaned forward kissing him sweetly, giving him a seductive smile, then wiggling her bare hand. "I'd like an engagement period of a year, oneness classes, and you need to put a ring on it . . . uh, baby . . . my knees are killing me."

Lawton gave a full belly laugh, pulled himself up, and then sat and assisted Esther. "Sweetheart, I'm already ahead of you. We have an appointment with the jeweler two weeks from today. The doctor told me that's the day I'm out of here. Everything else you mentioned is on the agenda too. A year is fine, because at the end of the year, I get you."

There was tenderness in their kiss as they shared a perfect moment in an imperfect setting.

Lawton was happily sitting in the kitchen of Mother Reed's home, exclaiming over her cooking. He had been released from the hospital for a week and was now making his way to resume some of his activities. On medical leave from the police force, he hoped they would at least let him have desk duty next month.

"These field peas are excellent, Mother Reed. I love down-home cooking, and I've been told by several of the Wileys that no one does it better than you. They were right."

Mother Reed smiled in appreciation of the way Lawton ate up her cooking. It did her heart good that others enjoyed it.

He sipped his water. "You might wonder why I asked to meet with you without Esther being here."

"I'm happy to have you, but a body wondered."

"I know you are an important part of Esther's life. I've gotten to know her family from their visits to my hospital room and while I was in rehabilitation. I appreciate that you had us over for dinner earlier this week. But I'd like to know you for myself, to truly feel a part of Esther's entire family."

"You sure you want to do that? Hav' you met Gert?" Mother Reed joked.

"Yes, ma'am, even Aunt Gert!" They both laughed.

To emphasize her words, she tapped on the table. "Life is a series of seasons; beginnings and endings. All we can ever do is live each to its fullest, giving honor to every minute. As you and Esther go forward, you need to know that she's special, she's favored."

Lawton went to interrupt, but Mother Reed held up her hand for silence. "I know you love her, but I'm talking 'bout who she is. That's much more than who you see."

Lawton listened, not wanting to miss any of her wisdom.

"When she was just a spark of the fire she was meant to be, she knew she was a princess, a Cinderella. But the enemy came to put her flame out early. Too many of our children's potential has been stolen before they can fulfill their purpose. I remember Elizabeth calling her mama in tears, 'bout that baby's pain. Who could turn a Cinderella contest into a hellish experience but the devil? Prejudice is an evil thang. And too many of us have had to endure that hurt. It can make a person question if they as bad as people say they are. Am I really ugly, stupid, dirty? Chile, the enemy been throwing punches at Esther as long as I can remember. She has lost people and things."

Lawton couldn't help but interrupt, "Mother Reed, Esther acts secure, mature, and confident."

"Yes, but at a cost. We all pay it, sometime. When you learn to grow from the pain, you make the trip forward in spite of your limitations and the stubbing of your toes in the dark. You've heard of growing pains, ain't cha'?"

"Yes, ma'am, I have."

"There's a group of praying women who call themselves Women of Zion. They say 'Embrace the pain, refuse to go insane.' I understand the message. Life can be hard, but if we learn to say, 'I trust you, Lord,' ooh wee, we can put the enemy on the run. So . . . what I want to know is, are you ready to allow Esther to be all she can be in God, support her in the rough times, and cheer her on in the good times? Can you be joyful when you see God using her to free others? It's her calling."

Lawton contemplated all he'd heard. He thought about being fortunate enough to have such wise counsel, and he understood how Esther valued this woman so highly. It was one of those times in life where he wanted to say something profound, to be deep, but he knew enough to settle for truth from the heart. "When I was a little boy, I loved the unique, and I dreamed of great treasure. I was always excited about fortuitous pleasures. Esther—"

"Boy, you ain't gotta give a speech, and if you don't mind my asking, what in the Himalayas is fortuious, fortuis . . . uh, that word you just used."

Lawton chuckled. "I apologize. I meant to keep my words simple because what's on my heart is plain. The word means unexpected, and that's what I felt the first time I saw Esther. I felt she was my unexpected treasure. When I came to know her, I believed she was the answer to my prayers to God, and my blessing for a lifestyle of obedience and holiness."

Mother Reed pushed up from the table and walked over to the cabinet. "Baby, you said that so good, you don' made me pull out the moistest cream cheese pound cake you ever tasted."

"What if I had answered wrong?"

"Oh, Mama don't do people wrong. I had a little store-bought cake in the icebox for you." She giggled as she sliced him a large piece of cake.

"In that case, can a brother take an extra piece to go?"

"Honey, you can take the whole cake. This is you and my baby's season, and I'm gon' honor it."

Lawton smiled deciding against questioning her further. He felt he had passed a test, and he didn't want to end up taking another exam anytime soon.

Chapter Forty-eight

The key in the deadbolt lock turned with ease as Briggs entered the darkened house. He wished that the key to fix his life would work as smoothly. A low watt light glowed in a back room beaconing him closer. He could smell Monica's perfume wafting through his nostrils. The exotic scent was reminiscent of past evenings of volatile heated exchanges; sometimes anger, sometimes passion. He was pleased with the way Monica handled the church rumor mill and how she had become active at church. She was making a place for herself. However, he still insisted they sleep in separate rooms.

As God's man, Briggs had forgiven her, but he was still working on the forgetting part. He had learned long ago that the measure of a man was gauged by the amount of self-control he exhibited. Although it had been too long since he had the pleasure of his marriage bed, too much had occurred to just fall back into past toxic patterns. He hardened himself against his flesh weakening.

Stiletto heels clicking on hardwood floors signaled he was no longer alone with his thoughts. "Briggs, honey, why are you standing here in the dark?"

Briggs pulled his tie loose as he laid his briefcase on the coffee table. He stared silently at Monica and struggled to remain unmoved by the alluring picture she made. Her silhouette was a sensual banquet to his senses. Ultrasheer in texture, her lavender gown flowed over her nudity like a second skin. She was all soft and sparkling from iridescent lotion. But what put the hammer to his beating heart were her feet encased in the most decadent spiked heels he had ever seen. The height was making her legs longer and shapelier than he remembered.

"I'm so glad you're home. Wait 'til I tell you about my day. You'll be so proud of me. It started with a call to Naomi, and after discussing my desire to help you adjust more, your secretary was kind enough to fax over the church membership roster. She highlighted the women at church who I should get to know better. As first lady, I felt it was important to get started building your power base," Monica continued to move toward Briggs in a sexually predatory sway.

"Power base?" Briggs shrugged out of his jacket.

"Yes, power base. Please, don't get all holier than thou on me. I simply mean that for you to get anything done here, you will have to have people behind you, and as your wife, I plan to assist you in making that happen."

Briggs was thoughtful, while loosening his tie. "You have been a great help at the church. I still can't help wondering what's in this for you."

"Making you happy." Monica wrapped her arms around herself and stepped back, her head slanted, so that Briggs could look into her eyes. "If I could take back the affair, I would. I'm sorry for all the times I caused you grief, for always putting my needs before yours. I've tried to show you these last weeks that I can be better."

Briggs fingered his bottom lip in wonder. "Wow, what else could you possibly say to top all of this?" he asked, while he examined her face for signs of deception.

Monica stepped into his personal space and seemed to suck the air out of the room. She trailed her finger down his chest and pulled his already-loosened tie off his neck. "Briggs, it's been more than a month, and I have a present for you." She handed him a gold foiled box.

Puzzled, he opened it. Inside was a folded piece of paper. He read her sexually transmitted diseases medical report: HIV—negative, Herpes—negative, and on and on it went—all negative.

"And the feelings that kept you in Atlanta, is that negative now too?" Briggs needed to know.

Monica kissed his jaw and purred, "Yes, and on that, I'm positive. Would you like to talk about it?"

"No, talk time is over. What I want is for this marriage to heal, and we can do that together. Marvin Gaye might have had an inkling to what kind of healing I'm needing in his song, but don't tell my father, the very honorable Bishop Stokes," his voice filled with laughter.

A soft sigh escaped Monica's lips. "I was so worried, Briggs. Thank you. You've never stayed angry with me this long. I promise no more chances will be needed. I'm going to make you so proud."

Briggs sobered as he thought about his past and his need to move on. He had learned so much in this city about himself, his needs, and his shortcomings. He was flawed, but God's son. He didn't need to defend his connections but should celebrate every step toward fulfilling his purpose. Could God give you the ability to love fiercely—twice? He put his arms around Monica and inhaled loudly as he took the first step in healing his marriage. "You smell wonderful, and you look beyond beautiful."

"Well, husband, what are you waiting for?" She snuggled into his body.

Briggs captured her in an all-or-nothing kiss. He then picked her up, her shoes falling off as she wrapped her legs around his waist. He glided backward, carrying her down the hallway. As the bedroom door swung shut behind them, her soft sigh of satisfaction reverberated in the otherwise silent house.

Chapter Forty-nine

Fall ended and the holidays found her and Lawton meshing their families and lives. Now it was January, and the wind howled past the church's beveled windows. The Bible said, "for everything there is a season."

Esther and Lawton faced each other in ornate king and queen chairs. They were beginning a session of their marriage oneness counseling at his church. It was their third class, and both were determined to make their marriage a success. Lawton's pastor had announced that this class would be a lesson in transparency and vulnerability to build trust. Esther thought it would be a walk-through like the other two classes.

Pastor Adams reached over and placed their hands together. "Lawton, can you look at Esther and tell her if there is anything that bothers you in the relationship?"

Lawton squeezed Esther's hand. "Nothing to report, sir. I love Esther."

"Lawton, if we are going to move forward, honesty is key. I know you love Esther, but please answer the question."

Esther shifted uncomfortably in what she suddenly felt was the hot seat. Her hands were slipping out of Lawton's due to their mingled perspiration. "Go on, honey," Esther's stomach rolled.

Lawton's facial expression was one of thoughtful concentration. Esther could tell it was his "thinking hard" look.

"Well, when I first saw Esther, she drew my interest." Lawton pressed her hands between his larger ones. "When Esther noticed my interest, she became self-conscious. I was going to walk away, but she stumbled and fell, and in my attempt to rescue her, I knew she was the one. But I still see glimpses of that uncertainty in her from time to time. I don't want her to act like she knows, but I want her to know her worth."

"Oh my," Esther attempted pulling away from Lawton to no avail.

Pastor Adams nodded for Lawton to continue.

He stroked Esther's cheek. "I love you so much. You are God's greatest creation, because He fashioned you for me. Knowing your worth allows you to value mine."

Esther bit her bottom lip and allowed tears to wash down her chin. "I don't know why I'm like this. I don't want to be. It just seems like the times in my life that are the most important, I mess up."

"Tell us what you mean, Esther."

Esther had a faraway look in her eyes. "When I was seven I wanted a physical symbol that I was special. My daddy always called me princess, so Cinderella seemed to be a logical choice. But, even though my foot fit the shoe, I was turned away. My skin color made me unworthy." Esther's smile wobbled, her head dropped. "Never did get over something that stupid. Later, in college, my best friend committed suicide, and my other best friend who found her responded by rejecting me and leaving town, leaving no forwarding address. My life was falling like dominos."

"How'd you handle so much pain?" Pastor Adams asked. Lawton's pressing hand encouraged her to answer.

Sniffling, she pressed back. "I made so many mistakes as a result of my experiences, trying to fix myself when God only wanted me to rest in Him. My marriage was so broken . . . oh . . . oh . . . I need healing—" she wept.

Lawton slipped from his chair holding her as she sobbed.

Pastor Adams smiled. "Daughter, it is well. You are on your way to a greater intimacy with God, Lawton, and yourself. You shall shine. I want to see you by yourself for some sessions. Is that okay with you?"

Esther nodded as she wiped her eyes and gave a self-deprecating chuckle. "Yes, I think we better finish the job."

Lawton hugged her, and then his pastor. "This was so good. Thank you."

Pastor Adams clasped Lawton's shoulder. "Son, we're only half done. Now it's your turn."

Lawton gulped as they all sat back down.

Monday afternoon, Esther sat at her desk working at a fevered pitch to lay out her latest project. She thought about the activities of the last several months. Roger's court trial resulted in his conviction on several counts. He currently was the guest of the state of Michigan's prison system.

She was a multitasker, and as she signed personal leave requests, she continued her mental backtrack of the last two months. While Monica may have brought up the rear, Esther had pulled off getting the zoning board to back off by putting the right people in the know. She had no idea she knew people who could green-light a project or kill it with their yea or nay.

Mother Reed was right; she'd been positioned for favor. People she'd done favors for rewarded her by backing her protests against the zoning board's restrictions. She beamed, acknowledging her hard work in the past helped today. Just goes to show that God loves a cheerful giver, and giving of your time and talent was as important as your money.

She now attended Lawton's church on alternating Sundays. Yes, the rumors had died, but she felt more comfortable with Lawton's pastor. Reverend Gregory had phoned and promised to return to perform her marriage ceremony. Surprisingly, she wasn't having any issues with Monica. She just felt that her place was with Lawton at his church. She still didn't like Monica, but she didn't have to.

Esther tenderly touched the framed picture of her and Lawton resting on her desk. "Well, sweetheart, it's time to earn this paycheck." She turned her chair in the opposite direction, humming as she pulled up her computer screen and put on her glasses.

New seasons meant changes for everyone; it was good to embrace them.

The click clacking of purposeful steps echoed down the silent hall. Under a time limit Esther wanted to drop off the last of her Love Zion committee paperwork to Naomi. The empty hallway in the administrative wing made her believe her delay at the office might have made her miss out. She approached the door to knock, when it suddenly swung open and Naomi stepped out, closing the door behind her.

Esther smiled in relief, "Oh, good. Hi, Naomi, I have the last of all my committee's paperwork to turn in. I'm so glad I caught you before you left."

Naomi gave Esther a furrowed frown. "Oh, you missed me." She pointed behind her. "My desk is in there, and I'm out here. I'm gone for the day. You know I don't stay beyond 6 p.m. I got children to feed."

"Your cats?"

"That's what I said, Esther. You need to remember these things. If you really want to be rude, Pastor's inside getting ready to leave. You can try to catch him, but it really would be—"

"I know . . . rude," Esther said to Naomi's back as she fled down the hall.

Esther debated going through a door that was mutually closed months before. The papers in her hands were important, and she wanted to minimize her interaction with Monica who seemed to be taking over everything at the church. She knocked and opened the door to Naomi's office area. In response to her knock. Briggs entered the room shrugging into his jacket.

"Esther? It's good to see you." He went over to hug her, and then halted midstep clearing his throat. "How can I help you? Naomi already left for the day."

"Yes, I ran into her, and she let me know in no uncertain terms she was already gone."

Briggs laughed and crossed his arms in fondness. "You gotta love her." He noticed the files in her hands, and pointed. "Are those files for us?"

She held out the files and handed them over. "Well," she sighed and looked around the office remembering how much at home this once felt, "it's been an honor to serve Love Zion, and I wish you—"

Briggs pulled her in and hugged her until she hugged him back. They stood there, both needing this last opportunity. Slow and silent they let go. It had all been said.

Esther headed out the door, this time feeling like the last piece of the puzzle had fallen into place. No one was in crisis, angry, or distraught. They both understood life took you where you least expected it.

And, that wasn't necessarily bad, despite the tear that clung to her cheek.

"No no no," hissed The Leader as he watched Esther leave Love Zion. Everything was going wrong.

"*Imp One, come here!*"

*Imp One, nervous and shaky, flew to his boss's call.
"Yes, O Great One. How may I serve you?"*

"*Visit Roger in prison. Have him write a letter, manipulate it where he causes Esther to believe she has failed
him. Oh, and stir up Lawton's jealousy of Briggs for the
next several months. Esther still hasn't had that Briggs
conversation with him. I believe we can still do something
with jealousy; it's such an ugly human emotion. Then go
to Briggs and whisper words of love for Esther to him.
Have him believe he cannot live without her and have
him disrupt the wedding. And, when Briggs and Esther
feel they can now be together, I want Monica to announce
she's pregnant. Let's keep a link between her and Briggs.
Do you have all of that?" he yelled.*

"*Oh yes, Great One," Imp One stated as he headed to
the prison yard. Did he say, have Esther get pregnant,
have Briggs love Monica? Oh dear, oh dear, the imp
thought as he struggled to remember his assignments.
The thought of demon ashes blowing through his sub-
conscious had shattered his concentration.*

Chapter Fifty

Mother Reed straightened her wig as she finished her prayer for Roger. She had prayed it crooked. She wanted that young man saved and free. Just because he was physically in prison didn't mean he had to be bound up in his spirit. He was brought to their family for a reason, and Mother Reed believed that God was not finished with him. *How could He be, if He kept bringing him into her spirit?*

In a stark prison yard, miles away, Roger sat and listened to the prophet speak to the assembled eleven men. For the motley crew, the prison yard had become a sanctuary, and the ground they walked on, holy.

Prophet's voice reverberated through the inmates perched on worn wooden bleachers. "I say that as Paul prayed and the prison doors opened, so shall they open for you. Your minds, in the seat of your souls, shall be free. Brother Roger, please step forward."

Roger sprinted forward when he was called.

"Please, brother, roll up your sleeve," Prophet told him.

Roger, who was embarrassed by his past, was reluctant, but did as he was told. Where a serpent's inked picture was once prevalent, his arm was now mangled burned flesh.

"Roger, explain to our three newest disciples how you hurt your arm. Don't be ashamed; that's a trick of the enemy. God loves you. Let your testimony free someone else," Prophet said with compassion.

Roger stood ramrod straight as he gave his testimony. "I was an abuser of drugs, alcohol, sex, and most of all, people. I had a wonderful wife, but the enemy continually pointed out what he labeled as flaws to me. She was too fat, too self-righteous, too educated, too much of a daddy's girl, too much in church. I believed the enemy and mistreated her. I let her pay for all the bills and all the hurt in my life. I wasn't accountable, she was."

Roger breathed deeply. "One drunken night, I used her money to get a serpent's tattoo on my arm. That night began the end of us, and my life spiraled completely out of control. She finally had the good sense to leave me and even gave me the house she had paid for when she left. I'm in here for breaking into her new house because I wanted to kill her. I met Prophet after being jumped my second month in here. I'm not anybody's punk, so I was plotting my revenge on how I was going to get each one of these cats back. Prophet approached me, and my life hasn't been the same."

He looked around the group. "First, I hung out with all you guys because there is protection in numbers, but then I started to see the real me and in my remorse, I grabbed some rubbing alcohol I stole out of the infirmary, threw it on the serpent, and threw a match behind it."

One of the men spoke up. "Man, what was that supposed to do?"

"I thought I'd burn the enemy out of my life. But the enemy didn't want me to have Jesus, so he was willing to manipulate my mind and tell me I wasn't worth saving. Some guard ran into my cell and put the fire out. I spent four days in the hospital, and when I came out, I vowed that this serpent would never have me again. I don't let him speak to me anymore without me calling on Jesus and telling the enemy to get behind me."

All the men stood up and shouted. Some had tears in their eyes because of their own personal abyss that they had endured and survived. The world might not have known it, but they were free indeed.

Imp One stared in dismay at the gathering. Who was in charge of this prison? They were failing terribly. He released a loud screech, and the demon in charge came forward. "What is happening here? Why are there saints assembling in this place? This is our territory!" Imp One raged.

"Those few puny men—they're weak. They have all been abused—physically, mentally, sexually, and emotionally all their lives. When they came here it was just more of the same. The one they call Prophet was treated worst of all. He was on the verge of suicide the night he cried out to a mother who had abandoned him as a child. But somehow, a flickering light came into the room, and he began to moan and to ask for forgiveness for his numerous sins, especially the one concerning killing his own father. Ever since, he's been reaching out to other lost souls. There is no need to worry; they are few. A remnant, at best."

"Fool!!!" Imp One roared, as he spun away to see what damage he could do.

Roger was in his cell writing. He didn't know why, but a strong urge came over him to write Esther. As he wrote, old feelings of pain, rejection, and anger flowed from his poisoned pen.

He barely acknowledged the sound at his cell door. "Who are you writing, brother?" Prophet asked.

"Esther."

Prophet frowned and came into the cell. "I'm being led to share something with you, brother. Did I ever tell you that I finally found my mother?"

Roger slowed his breathing and placed his pen on the small metal table. "No, Prophet, you didn't. How? You've been in here a long time."

"Yes, I have. Going on thirty years. I'm fifty-four. Should've been in here before then. I wallowed in filth, and anger. When I was seventeen, I believed I killed my father. It's a pain I lived with, so I didn't cry about being in here for a robbery and rape I didn't commit."

Roger was silent, hearing these details for the first time.

Prophet continued his tale. "My daddy was a mean-spirited man, beat me like I stole something daily. Told me I was so worthless, even my mama didn't want me. It was years before I found out from a relative that my mother didn't abandon me, but that she suffered similar abuse from him before he kicked her out of our house for a new woman. It turned out the woman only wanted my daddy for his money. He always was a shrewd businessman. Anyway, even this woman couldn't stand the harshness of living with such an evil man, and finally she left, taking him for a lot of money in the process. After that, his rages got worse. One night, the beating was so bad, I knew that if I didn't kill him, he was gonna kill me. So I fought back, and after landing some good punches, I threw him down a flight of stairs. I ran into the night and never returned. I later saw on the news that his death was ruled an accident, and I was left with a house, money, and anger at the world."

Roger whispered, "Then what happened?"

"I tried to find my mother, but all of my father's relatives pleaded ignorance. So, in my bitterness, I began to do drugs, but you can't shut down pain. It comes back. I couldn't drink, dope up, sex up, or strike out enough to stop it. Seven is the number of completion, and seven years after I came into the money, I met my fate. Some girl I had been playing with set me up for a fall. I didn't know she was underage, not that the person I was then would have cared. I've been sitting here ever since. She sued me in civil court after she had me thrown into prison for raping her, even left some of her jewelry in my bedroom so they would add burglary to the charge. She was awarded two hundred fifty thousand dollars. Even after that payoff, I'm still a rich man. My father had a million-dollar insurance policy that I've never touched. Her corrupted lawyers didn't even know about it because I never claimed the blood money. I did the paperwork ten years after I got in here. It has been gaining interest for the last twenty years."

Prophet stroked his goatee. "God had a plan. When I got here, I was so bitter, I spent my first five years racking up more time. I'm finally up for parole this year, and I'm going to look up my mother and do some good in the world. My investigators tell me she is still living. We had a scare a few months ago, right before you came here, and I went into a season of fasting and praying for her. I feel in my spirit that she's getting better now."

"Have you contacted her since you found out?"

"No, I don't want to talk to my mother for the first time through prison bars. I know that the one who the saints call Mother Reed would forgive me, but that's not God's plan. I want to hold her in my arms and tell her I love her and that we can be mother and son at last."

"Did you say Mother Reed? My ex-wife used to go to church with a Mother Reed. She was very close to the family."

Prophet exclaimed, "The investigator tells me that my mother's surrogate family is named Wiley."

"Man, that's my ex-wife's maiden name. The Mother Reed I know is your mother. Prophet, she is a powerful woman of God. I can see the connection."

Prophet cried tears of joy. "God doesn't miss a beat. Listen to the end of my story. I found out a year ago that my father didn't die from the fall I caused. His second wife came back to the house with her lover for more money after I ran that night. When my father refused, they killed him. Her ex-lover revealed it last year after he found out he was dying of cancer. He wanted absolution from a priest. The priest convinced him to turn himself in." Prophet shouted with joy. "And, you're here, and you know my mother to boot . . . He's Alpha and Omega!"

Roger just sat in wonder. All his illogical anger was gone as Prophet finished with his plans for the future. "I'm hoping that when I leave, you will help lead the prayer group. They'll need a man who, though tempted, will not falter. That's why I wanted you to remember the burn on your arm today. The enemy can try, but it's our job to make him fail."

Roger was solemn, reflecting on the responsibility he was being given.

Prophet stood. "Man, finish your letter, and then come and find me. I want you to tell me all you can remember about my mama."

Roger smiled. He was excited for Prophet. He looked at his letter to Esther and tore it up. He picked up his pen to rewrite it. He now had something he could do for someone else after being a taker for so long.

He chuckled to himself. *I might have tried this giving thing a long time ago if I had known it felt this good.*

Esther opened her front door and leaned out to get the mail. It was cold outside, and the weatherman predicted snow. She had some after-holiday shopping to do, but she wanted to wait until later in the day. She was curious about the envelope with all the special stamps on it. You rarely saw letters anymore. She hesitated when she saw the letter's return address was a prison. Why was Roger reaching out to her? Her life was so good right now, she didn't want to feel bad and that was Roger's usual gift to her—making her feel bad. She threw the letter on the table, walked away, stopped, and went back for it. If she didn't open it, she knew that she would always wonder what he had written. She threw caution to the wind and ripped it open.

> *Dear Esther,*
>
> *I pray this letter finds you well. I want to say I'm sorry for all the pain I've caused. It was never about you, but my own failings. I am responsible for me being here, no one else. Strangely, I'm at peace, and God has showed me that freedom is beyond these bars. Freedom is spiritual. When I first thought about writing this letter, I was focused on getting you to forgive me. In the old days, I would have manipulated you and made you feel guilty. But this God thing has me trying to figure me out, so I can stop making the same mistakes. Some days, I'm exhausted just examining the minefields of my past. You know I never talked about my family and there were reasons for that. I still won't go into details, just know that I never experienced love, not even with you. What were we thinking when we married? Maybe we thought if we could hold on to someone, we would somehow feel better. I hear you've found the real thing, and you're getting married—be happy.*

Here's the part of my letter where you and I get to help the people we love. I have a mentor who is known by the name of Prophet; his real name is Joshua Huntley. This man is Mother Reed's son. He is a true man of God and has helped many of us in here find our way. He is for the Kingdom. He will be out soon, and I was hoping you would help me make his homecoming a blessed event . . .

Sincerely,
Roger

Esther hiccupped her tears as they fell on an already sodden letter. She couldn't lie and say she didn't regret her time with Roger, because she did. If she had to do it all over again, she would have skipped ever knowing him. But at least now, she could say this chapter in her life was closed. When he went to prison, she kept waiting for the other shoe to fall. She had thought he was out of her life before. Is he really gone this time? she wondered. She could only hope.

Moving into the kitchen, she filled a glass of water from the faucet, sipped, and breathed deep to minimize her heaves. She dried her tears with the kitchen towel, and clutching the news to her chest, thought about what this would mean to Mother Reed. They all knew she had a son, but it was rare for Mother Reed to mention him. Whenever someone tried to get more information, she just got a faraway look in her eye and asked you to leave it alone. Esther would write this Joshua, known as Prophet. She needed to make sure that he was not up to something. But if he could turn someone like Roger around, he must be the real thing.

Esther wondered if she could pull off a grand wedding and surprise celebration at the same time. Lawton had enticed Esther to move the wedding date up two months. Instead of a yearlong wait, they were tying the knot ten months after his proposal. They wanted to stay holy, and it was getting pretty hard to hold out. Their marriage oneness classes had taught them a lot about each other. They were still in attendance, but barring some deep secret, even Lawton's pastor was convinced that they were ready. At any rate, with a little help, she would figure it all out.

Today was a day to celebrate. Esther's time in her counseling sessions pointed out her residual pain from childhood. Who would believe that denying her the role of Cinderella would open up a lifetime of unworthiness? She found out her later young adult self-absorption was her attempt to deny her inner pain and to feel special. Her trying to atone for Sheri's death by being everything to everyone was the last piece of her pain puzzle. It was a toxic circle.

Thanks to Pastor Adams and counseling, she was facing her pain and reconciling with her own imperfection. This gift for Mother Reed would be the pinnacle of her wedding celebration.

Chapter Fifty-one

Monica set a plate of steaming spaghetti in front of Briggs. She poured sweet tea in his frosted glass and stood with her hand on her hip. "You need anything else, sweetheart?"

Briggs shook his head and marveled at the change in Monica over the last months. *Lord, don't let me wake up if I'm dreaming.*

She cleared her throat. "I was wondering if you thought it would be a good idea to start a teen girls group at the church. The program for the young men has taken off so well that I think we should consider branching out."

Briggs questioned her. "Who would run it? I'm already busy with the new young men's program, and I'm hesitant to add more to my schedule right now. We did promise to make more time for each other, and I don't want to go back on my word."

"What would you think about me running it?" Monica touched Briggs's shoulder. "Hear me out, please. My childhood was pretty rocky and as a result, I made some mistakes because I didn't have a Mother Reed in my life. I've been watching these young girls in church, and while the young men's pants may sag, these girls' leggings are too tight, and their blouses too low."

Briggs chuckled. He was delighted that Monica was really sincere in wanting to do something for someone else.

"Don't laugh at me, Briggs," Monica sulked.

"You've got it all wrong. I'm pleased that you came up with this all on your own. I don't ever remember you wanting to be involved in church like this." *Except when you were faking it,* he thought. Briggs shook off the past and vowed to keep moving forward.

Monica clapped her hands. "Good. Guess who I'm putting on the committee?"

"I can't imagine. Enlighten me," Briggs said as he continued to eat his food.

Monica announced. "Ta, ta, ta, da . . . Sister Abigail Winters."

Briggs's fork paused midair. "You're kidding, right?"

"Nope. One thing I learned in the modeling business, keep your friends close, and your enemies closer. I promised she would no longer be a loose cannon at church, and I meant it. And, just to show you, I'm keeping all my promises; I did as you asked and scheduled us for counseling sessions. I'm ready, now." She placed her arms around Briggs's neck and snuggled into its crook. "Besides, we have to keep my baby's daddy happy."

Briggs threw down his fork and pushed his plate away. "Yes!!!" He grasped Monica around the waist, and she squealed as he placed her over his shoulder and headed down the hallway. He pushed the half-open door to their bedroom in and slammed it behind them, the food long forgotten.

With the northerly wind whipping around the city, the temperature in the Stokes's bedroom was Caribbean hot.

Lawton and Esther cuddled on the Wileys' love seat. It had been a great dinner, and afterward, the family lounged in shared contentment.

Mrs. Wiley called over to Esther. "Did you remember to ask Tamela to let her youngest be the flower girl?"

"Yes, Mama, she was excited, but still ghetto."

Her mother grinned. "What did she say?"

Esther paused, looking around to make sure she had everyone's attention. "She wanted to know if I was buying the dress, because I know she still hadn't been able to find a job yet. So she can't be helping nobody else be happy right now."

Elizabeth bubbled up in laughter along with everyone else. "Girl, that child is so wrong. I hope you set her straight."

"I sure did; when we finished, not only am I buying the dress, but I'm buying her shoes and having her hair done as well," Esther stated with a straight face.

"Honey, those are your daddy's people," Elizabeth said, laughing out loud, joining her daughter's amusement.

Hickman Wiley winked at his wife and had a belly laugh.

Esther quieted, threading her fingers through Lawton's. "It would have been nice if I could have found Deborah and had her as a bridesmaid." She looked faraway. "We always promised to be in each other's weddings."

"I like the idea of a simple wedding, since it's your second one. Just Phyllis will be fine, honey, you'll see. If Deborah's family hadn't moved away, we might have had a chance of finding her. We just have to always remember Deborah in our prayers."

As Lawton rubbed Esther's hand gently between his more brawny pair, Mother Reed smiled. She could honestly say, she didn't see any of this coming. But, like she told Briggs months before—God always had a ram in the bush. After a turbulent year, they were going into a season of calm winds and golden skies.

"Share the good news, Mother," Mr. Wiley said. "Your smile brightens this day."

"It is well," she stated.

"Thank you, Jesus. It is well," Phyllis cried out, intending to share their great news with everyone tonight. She and Charles had finally decided to adopt.

Each person seconded Mother Reed's statement with joy and thanksgiving. It was important to be grateful in the good times and thank Him from whom all blessings flow.

Esther kissed Lawton's cheek and whispered into his ear, "It is very well."

They grinned and burrowed even closer. They knew whatever the season, they would embrace them together.

The Leader sat with his head in his claws. He would have to face the Mentor, and it would not be a good meeting. He had fired everyone who worked for him, and he would soon join them in the fiery dungeon. Many of his plans had failed, but he knew that some weeds planted would eventually flourish. Maybe then he would be allowed to prosper once again. He knew the history of man, and if they took their eyes off He who is Holy, he and those like him would be ready. All he needed was time . . .

Book Club Questions

1. At the beginning of the book, Briggs and Esther's affection was very physical. This affection was leading toward sexual intimacy. Should Christians engage in "playing around"?

2. Esther's desire to be Cinderella was thwarted by prejudice. As a result, she felt shame and guilt. Have you ever experienced a situation that was done to you, but left feeling you, were at fault? How did you handle it?

3. Satan had a plan to attack Esther and Briggs in their youth. Why do you think he destroyed Esther's relationship with her two best friends? Has anything ever come between you and a childhood best friend?

4. Mother Reed was a strong mentor and spiritual guide for those around her. Her health emergency caused an uproar in the church. Why do you think so many members panicked at the possibility of her death? Do you have a spiritual mentor?

5. Briggs and Monica's marriage were based on a lie. Can a couple overcome a lie of this magnitude and have a successful marriage? What does the Bible say concerning this?

6. Monica's character in the book began as selfish and controlling. She later said she was committed to the work it would take to change. Do you believe

Monica's change was real? Should Briggs believe that she can remain a good wife?

7. Lawton came into the picture after Esther's feelings were hurt by Briggs. Do you believe that Lawton and Esther moved too fast? Can their relationship last?

8. Several characters in the book at some point did the difficult work of self-examination. Is this something you think everyone should consider doing? How often?

9. Roger was a character that professed Christ and accepted salvation in prison. Do you believe that people in prison who get saved stay committed when they are released? Why or why not?

10. Briggs and Esther had an emotional affair. Is this adultery? Why?

11. Did you want Briggs to leave Monica and have a relationship with Esther? How does that line up biblically?

Stay tuned for the second book in the

Heaven over Hell trilogy

Tell The Truth and Shame the Devil . . .

Love Zion church was enjoying a time of togetherness and favor. But, the devil wasn't giving up, and now the angels are showing up to engage in battle. In the midst of it all, did Esther get her happily ever after? And what about Briggs and Monica? Was she really pregnant this time? And more important, is Briggs the father? Have Esther and Briggs closed the book on their past? One thing is for sure, all of Esther's past is not behind her. Deborah's back and she knows the secret Sheri took to her grave. Will Esther be able to forgive her childhood friends? So many questions . . . *Tell The Truth and Shame the Devil* provides the answers.

The second book in the Heaven over Hell trilogy is due to be released in 2015.

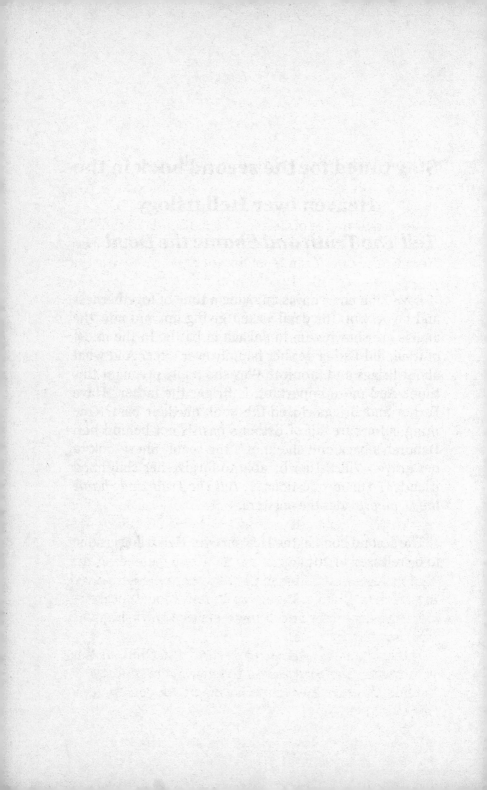

About the Author

At the mature age of sixteen, Colette (Ford) Harrell had a severe case of chicken pox. Not even wanting her best friend to see her Frankenstein appearance, and being bored out of her mind (no smartphones, Xboxes, cable, or Netflix in those days), the two friends decided to write a soap opera. Every morning, Colette would place her written pages in the family mailbox, and then she would retrieve her best friend's pages in return. This was the beginning of her love for telling a good story in written form, and she has taken pen to paper ever since. By the way, the *Mod Squad* script they later sent to Hollywood was never picked up . . . but Colette's dream to one day write a novel was birthed.

Colette is a wife, mother, author, poet, songwriter, and playwright. Holding a master's degree, she is a director of social services. No, she's not Superwoman—red is not her best color, but she believes God has a plan for every life. She is cofounder of COJACK Productions, a Christian entertainment company and is an active member of her church, Kingdom Christian Center, where she is involved in several ministries. She is also a motivational speaker—teaching customer and human service workshops on state and national levels.

A Detroit native, she currently resides in Ohio, writing with humor and compassion to engage and minister to the human heart. Her motto is: *Whatever you do, do it "for love alone."*

About The Author

The Devil Made Me Do It is her debut novel. It looks at our choices and shows us the natural and supernatural consequences behind them. You get a close-up, Technicolor view of the devil's intent to destroy us in any way possible. She wrote the book to answer the question: What would happen if you knew what *really* went on behind the scenes of your life? Would you make different decisions? Or, would you continue along the path of destruction, claiming at every turn that "the devil made you do it"? In this delectable read, romance, suspense, humor, and the paranormal supernatural all come together, and some lives will *never* be the same.

UC HIS GLORY BOOK CLUB!

www.uchisglorybookclub.net

UC His Glory Book Club is the spirit-inspired brain-child of Joylynn Jossel, Author and Acquisitions Editor of Urban Christian, and Kendra Norman-Bellamy, Author for Urban Christian. This is an online book club that hosts authors of Urban Christian. We welcome as members all men and women who have a passion for reading Christian-based fiction.

UC His GLory Book Club pledges our commitment to provide support, positive feedback, encouragement, and a forum whereby members can openly discuss and review the literary works of Urban Christian authors.

There is no membership fee associated with UC His Glory Book Club; however, we do ask that you support the authors through purchasing, encouraging, providing book reviews, and of course, your prayers. We also ask that you respect our beliefs and follow the guidelines of the book club. We hope to receive your valuable input, opinions, and reviews that build up, rather than tear down our authors.

What We Believe:

—We believe that Jesus is the Christ, Son of the Living God.

—We believe the Bible is the true, living Word of God.

—We believe all Urban Christian authors should use their God-given writing abilities to honor God and share the message of the written word God has given to each of them uniquely.

—We believe in supporting Urban Christian authors in their literary endeavors by reading, purchasing and sharing their titles with our online community.

—We believe that in everything we do in our literary arena should be done in a manner that will lead to God being glorified and honored.

We look forward to the online fellowship with you.

Please visit us often at *www.uchisglorybookclub.net*.

Many Blessing to You!

Shelia E. Lipsey,
President, UC His Glory Book Club